PRAISE FOR *THE WEEKENDERS*

'A novel of real ambition and verve, *The Weekenders* ranges from wartime Italy to sixties Glasgow to explore the past's dark hold upon the present. Harrowing and compelling in equal measure, this is David F. Ross at the top of his game' Liam McIlvanney

'A masterpiece from one of Glasgow's finest authors.
The Weekenders is epic in scale but told through the deeply personal accounts of its luckless, damaged characters. Excruciating vulnerability meets the harsh daily realities of sixties Glasgow and the brutal machismo of its poisonous, smoke-filled institutions. Told with a wit as sharp as any razor, David F. Ross's style has been honed to perfection' Callum McSorley

'David has a seemingly natural gift for pungently memorable phrasing and dialogue that feels you're listening in rather than reading' Damian Barr

'This fiction is furious. David F. Ross goes deep and dark in an attempt to understand the criminal mind [and] writes with a righteous anger as he examines the evil that men do'
Alistair Braidwood, Scots Whay Hae

'Stark, uncompromising and gritty, David F. Ross takes us to a dark place that is no easy weekend away' Douglas Skelton

'With believable characters and wickedly mordant dialogue, David F. Ross continues to carve out his own space in Scottish literary fiction ... A gripping tale of secrets and excess, and a stylish, mesmerising thriller, boldly delivered in Ross's signature style'
George Paterson

'The writing is as exquisite, descriptive and visual as ever, and I was drawn deep into the story by a desire to see justice done for the many victims in this case. It takes real skill to make something so absorbing from a cast of characters who are, largely, just vile. Definitely recommended. Fans of the author will love it'
Jen Med's Book Reviews

'Simply a brilliant debut novel' John Niven

'A masterclass in transatlantic intertwining storytelling from one of Scotland's finest writers' *Razur Cuts*

'Ross's fifth novel is his most mature and his most accomplished to date' *Ayrshire Magazine*

'It's great when a book surprises you. This is a story with a punch, clouded by memory and regret' The Bookbag

'Powerful and punchy, with well-placed, darker-than-dark humour' LoveReading

'As warm and authentic as Roddy Doyle at his very best' Nick Quantrill

'A solid gold hit of a book!' Colin McCredie

'Just brilliant' Bobby Bluebell

'Somehow, Ross interweaves two tales into a tragic, hilarious, harrowing and fascinating novel that demonstrates more than most of his readers would expect from a firmly Scottish-based author' Stephen Watt

'It's incredibly difficult to describe how this book made me feel, the range of emotions I went through and how much it made me ponder life in general as well as the impact seemingly rather meaningless events or decisions might have on the rest of your life' From Belgium with Book Love

'A rawness and sensitivity that is so visceral ... another extraordinary novel from David F. Ross' Random Things through My Letterbox

tHE WEEKENDERS

ABOUT THE AUTHOR

David F. Ross was born in Glasgow in 1964. His debut novel, *The Last Days of Disco,* was long-listed for the Authors' Club Best First Novel Award, and received exceptional critical acclaim, as did the other two books in the Disco Days Trilogy – *The Rise & Fall of the Miraculous Vespas* and *The Man Who Loved Islands*.

There's Only One Danny Garvey topped several Best of the Year lists and was shortlisted for the Saltire Scottish Fiction Book of the Year 2021, and was followed in 2022 by the highly acclaimed *Dashboard Elvis Is Dead*.

He is a regular contributor to *Nutmeg Magazine* and in 2020 he wrote the screenplay for the film *Miraculous*, based on his novel.

Follow David on X/Twitter @dfr10, Bluesky @dfr10.bsky.social, facebook.com/david.ross, Instagram @davidfross10 and his website: davidfross.co.uk.

Other books by David F. Ross, available from Orenda Books

The Disco Days Trilogy:
The Last Days of Disco
The Rise & Fall of the Miraculous Vespas
The Man Who Loved Islands

Welcome to the Heady Heights
There's Only One Danny Garvey
Dashboard Elvis Is Dead

THE WEEKENDERS

DAVID F. ROSS

ORENDA
BOOKS

Orenda Books
16 Carson Road
West Dulwich
London SE21 8HU
www.orendabooks.co.uk

First published in the United Kingdom by Orenda Books, 2025
Copyright © David F. Ross, 2025

A catalogue record for this book is available from the British Library.

ISBN 978-1-916788-30-5
eISBN 978-1-916788-31-2

Typeset in Garamond by typesetter.org.uk

Printed and bound by Clays Ltd, Elcograf S.p.A

*For sales and distribution, please contact info@orendabooks.co.uk or visit
www.orendabooks.co.uk.*

For John Byrne and Paul Auster

Raskine House sits high up on an open moor. Even on clear days, the building can be clouded by a mysterious haar that appears to rise from its grounds rather than drift in from a cold eastern sea. The fog – and the dull, prolonged grinding sounds that often accompany it – has been claimed by witnesses to be evidence of the structure breathing. But it's just smoke. Smoke wafting here and about. Smoke clinging to the stonework from the numerous fires that have failed to destroy the shell. A smoke concealing dark secrets.

In its three-hundred-year history, Raskine House has been a home, or given shelter, to a tobacco lord, a slave trader, a member of the Russian royal family, a fire-and-brimstone preacher and his followers, a Nazi fugitive, a Hollywood movie star, a porn baron, a recalcitrant rock star, recuperating war veterans, a gaggle of mental patients, and, of course, Big Jamesie Campbell ... most famously the cynosure of a sinful socialite set known as 'the Weekenders'.

This building, and the ancillary structures around it, with their rigidly symmetrical geometry, are a man-made triumph; in them the rugged, natural beauty of God's creation is tamed. But Raskine House is also a living organism. The sweat of dishonest toil has seeped into its porous fabric. And when least expected, it re-emerges like an airborne toxin, influencing and controlling the behaviour of subsequent generations.

I know this to be true.

'Hell is empty, and all the devils are here'
—William Shakespeare, *The Tempest*

part 01

MINTO

EPISODE ONE:
Long Agos and Worlds Apart (1966)

Stevie 'Minto' Milloy starts a new job – Gerry Keegan lays down the law – Stevie shadows Jock Meikle.

11th July

Jock Meikle and Stevie Milloy walk along the Saltmarket, Meikle hirpling, Stevie ambling to equalise his pace.

Meikle's Ford Anglia is an unpredictable shock. A wing mirror missing. Cardboard decomposing over a rear window. Filthy layers of brown tape holding rusting bodywork together. Unlike the polished appearance of its owner, it looks like its next journey might well be its last.

'Where are we goin', Jock?'

'Cranstonhill.'

'Somethin' happenin'?'

'Must be.'

'Ye got some contacts in there?'

'Aye.'

Jock Meikle is an enigma.

Dressed in the all-black. Yul Brynner in *The Magnificent Seven*. A woollen scarf wraps his neck. He sleeps with the scarf on, according to Gerry Keegan, the *Daily Star*'s news editor: 'Cunt calls it a cravat. Must have the fucken combination tae a bank vault inked oan his neck,' he says.

Sat amongst the pasty-faced skin-flakers with bulbous, red drinkers' noses that comprise the *Daily Star* press office, Meikle's face is like a sandy-coloured leather satchel. And his glowing white teeth look out of place alongside the broken piano keys of his colleagues. He has the lustrous greying hair of Cary Grant, rather than the uncontrolled wispy Bobby Charlton strands of his fellow scribes. Jock Meikle either has continental blood coursing through him, or he spends the Glasgow Fair somewhere more exotic than Rothesay.

Jock Meikle is a man of few spoken words, but is renowned for the verbosity of his written ones. His colleagues' articles are full of padding and repetition, struggling to hit the count. But a fifteen-hundred-word target piece from Meikle will regularly file at twice that length. His work is widely admired for its uniqueness. And for its humanity. But his bosses at the *Star* consider him a dinosaur. A nightmare to edit. A pain in the arse.

The newspaper's owner is driving the publication towards a populist market. Shorter sentences. Shorter words. More pictures, especially of young women. More gossip. Less reliance on substantiation. Meikle is a man out of time. Despite his assured facade, Meikle's days at the *Star* are numbered. Meikle is a crime correspondent. He is a functioning alcoholic. These facts are related. Jock Meikle has witnessed evidence of the worst atrocities perpetrated upon one human by another.

Stevie Milloy is the mondain embodiment of young manhood freed from the stuffed-shirt austerity of a post-war childhood. Blonde, shoulder-length hair, swept back. Continental sallow skin. Sandy-coloured suede jacket. A navy turtleneck. Tight white trousers. Tighter than they were when Denice bought them. Black ankle boots. Like Milan's San Siro was his previous place of employment and not Maryhill.

Stevie is new to the Fourth Estate. He has been hired to write sports reports. Football, mainly. Stevie's background is expected to gain him access. He was a professional footballer, capped twice for Scotland, then kneecapped once, and permanently, by Geordie McCracken, Scotland's captain. Even a lexicomane like Meikle couldn't assemble the words to properly articulate the depth of

Stevie's hatred for Geordie McCracken. That pain runs far deeper than the chronic ache from nerve and tissue damage he suffers.

For some reason it has been decided that it's Meikle's wing under which Stevie is to be taken. Stevie suspects that he is being groomed to take over from the older man. It has only been a week, but Stevie's football columns are being noticed upstairs. Gerry Keegan has grudgingly passed on favourable notes from Editorial. Meikle is unimpressed.

The Glasgow weather is predictable. Overcast with rain expected. A typical Scottish summer. They're only in the car five minutes and the rain starts. Five later and it's lashing the front windscreen like the hoses from a car wash. Stevie turns the radio's dial. He leans in. Like a bank robber working a safe combination. He deftly finds Radio Caroline on the medium wave.

'Aw, here we go!' he says. Then laughs as Ray Davies describes him as a 'dedicated follower of fashion'.

'Christ, turn that racket off,' snaps Jock. 'We're on a job here.'

They drive the rest of the short distance soundtracked only by the incessant percussion of the pelting water.

'Whit's on then?' Stevie asks. He drums fingers to an imaginary tune.

'Find oot when we get there.'

'Did ye get a tip?'

'Aye.'

Jock pulls the car into the kerb at Blythswood Square. It's still early. The weather has turned again. A rainbow appears through sunshine that makes the wet roads blinding. Only the most determined – or desperate – prostitutes are touting.

'Aw'right, son,' says one as they get out of the car. She looks old. Weather-beaten.

'He's wi' me, Mags,' says Jock.

'That yer laddie, then?'

'Naw,' says Jock.

'Looks like ye.'

'Ye jokin'?' says Stevie.

'Is he still a virgin?'

'Fuck knows. Probably, wearin' that getup.'

Mags and Stevie laugh. Jock retains the stone face.

'Ah'm Stevie. Ah work wi' this aul' duffer. Just started.'

'Nice tae meet ye, son,' says Mags. 'Come back an' see me, sometime. Withoot him, tho'.'

'Aye, mibbe,' says Stevie.

'Ye can stick yer willy in me for ten bob,' says Mags. 'It's another five shillings if it's in the bum.'

'Ah'll bear that in mind,' says Stevie.

Mags cackles.

'C'mon you, we're late,' says Jock. 'Mags, love, keep an eye on the motor for us, will ye?'

Stevie shimmies past pavement puddles like they were static defenders. Meikle straight-lines through them, down towards the cop shop.

'Ye know aw the hoors about here, or just that yin?' says Stevie.

'Best sources in Glesga,' Jock replies.

'That right?'

'Punters urnae very discrete when their knobs are gettin' sooked. They lassies know how tae listen, know what ah mean?'

'Aye. Ah suppose.'

It takes ten minutes to walk down Argyle Street, making Stevie wonder why they didn't park closer to the station. He doesn't ask though. Meikle probably wouldn't answer anyway.

Cranstonhill Police Station is, like many of its civic kin, an imposing hulk. Heavy mass. Dirty-brown brick. Coated in industrial smog. Minimum fenestration. Impenetrable. It is a building suggesting that pain will be regularly administered within. That no amount of screaming would alert anyone passing by outside. In the grime of a full-height glass panel at the main entrance, a finger has written slogans no-one bothers to clean:

SODJERS 0 – 1 TOOGLE TONGS, YA BASS!

BRADY IS INNOCENT

And a game of hangman, completed to reveal:

F U C K / *T H E* / *P I G S*

They go in.

The building imposes its weight on those entering, but it's not a deliberate design concept. Dense concrete and oppressively low ceilings suck the air from the interior.

Nods and winks from the coppers. Jock's a regular.

'Just watch. An' listen. Nae speakin', right?' Jock tells Stevie.

'Righto, bossman,' he replies.

A young copper breaks formality. He reaches across the front desk to Stevie, nervy, sweaty hand outstretched. 'Saw yer goal against Wales at Hampden. Whit a shot!'

The face is familiar, but from where? Who knows.

'Thanks, man,' says Stevie, shaking the hand. Noticing the funny grip. Another one of the brotherhood.

'Can ah get yer autograph?'

Stevie senses Jock's disapproval.

'Mibbe when we're done, eh?' says Stevie.

Jock shakes his head. He is clearly not enjoying this babysitting detail.

The young copper ushers them down painted concrete steps with chipped edges. Into the bowels. A room at the end of a dark, featureless corridor is their destination. Loud chatter draws them towards it.

The noisy room is too small for the day's purpose. Not for the claustrophobic. Hastily arranged, Stevie thinks. Hard surfaces everywhere. Nothing to absorb the loud, echoing voices.

Glasgow Corporation green paint flakes from the walls. Wires hang down from parts of an exposed ceiling. A foot of thick cigarette smoke tries to escape through the gaps. A wooden ladder is propped against a wall. A heavy radiator lilts off its brackets. All the warmth of a subterranean garage in Iceland.

They find seats in a row in the middle right of the briefing room. Metal chairs rattle and squeak around them as more fat arses land on the thin ply.

Two tables at the front. Covered by a white cloth with a circular brown stain. They're set to look like one long table, but are betrayed by their different heights. Four seats line up behind. Currently unoccupied. On the tables, a jug of water. Four glasses; only two from the same set.

A framed picture of a pretty girl propped up to one side. She is the reason everyone is here. The girl is smiling. Sparkling blue eyes looking through round-rimmed glasses, not directly at the camera but beyond it and to the left. She has an unusual hair colouring; a deep reddish brown, like the leaves that drop in late October.

Stevie is momentarily shaken by the picture because it looks a little like Denice from before they were married. That was a long time ago.

He tunes in to the general hubbub:

'Get tae fuck! Nicklaus didnae win it ... Doug Sanders threw it away.'

'Wilson's aff his heid diggin' a tunnel under the Channel. Fucken World War Three made a lot easier, that's aw ah can say.'

'Ye see that dozy bastart fae Tayport, him that's just went a year withoot eatin'? "Ah've forgotten whit food tastes like," he says. Dinnae be gettin' ony ideas, ah says tae the wife.'

'You'se runnin' wi' the World Cup oan the front page?'

No-one is talking about the girl in the picture. Whatever this is, it is news to all of them.

Stevie turns. He clocks the pallid faces of the pressmen. The glances at him on their way to becoming stares. Most will know him from a different context. Might assume it is not him. Just someone like him. He has been out of circulation for a while. One of them winks. He thinks he can hear their thoughts:

Whitever happened tae Stevie Milloy?

Whit a player he wis.

Could trap a baw drapped fae the moon, so he could.
Whit would he be doin' here?

He feels suddenly awkward. Like his gauche attire disrespects the young girl in the picture frame. He is the *Star*'s new sports correspondent. He isn't sure why he is here. Why he has been partnered with the paper's serious-crime reporter. Stevie wonders if his presence is a punishment for Jock – for something he has done. Other explanations currently evade him.

A door in the corner opens. Quiet descends.

Four men file in. Three in uniform. Two cops; senior ones judging by the peaks and epaulettes. The third is in God's squad. White dog-collar against mournful black. He holds a large, worn, black leather Bible. Grips it to his chest like it's armour plating.

The last man; young, sweating, struggling with a battered briefcase full to bursting and probably older than him. A lawyer, Stevie presumes. Fresh from law school, if not still in training.

The four sit in the order they entered. The trainee lawyer drops the briefcase on the table. The picture frame topples over. It falls to the tiled floor and the glass smashes. Another indignity for the young girl.

The lawyer rushes round to the front of the table. Says 'sorry' several times, perhaps to the girl. Picks up the frame. Puts it back on the table. The main break cuts through the girl's face. As he sits, he nudges the table, causing the picture to fall again. Face down.

'Just leave it, eh?' says the pastor. Quiet, but annoyed.

The senior copper sitting far right opens proceedings: 'Good morning, everybody, I'm Acting Chief Superintendent Edward Montrose.'

Formal. Posh. Educated.

'The body of a young woman was found yesterday evening on remote moorland near Gabroc Hill. The body has been identified as that of Miss Janina Žukauskas. She was nineteen years old and newly resided in the staff quarters at Campbell House, the Sovereign Grace Mission.'

Stevie glances at Jock Meikle. Staring ahead. Listening. Taking notes without looking down.

Stevie opens his notebook, takes out a bookie's pencil. Makes notes of his own. Underlines some of them. That's what real reporters would do.

Edward Montrose.

The talking cop clears his throat.

The other one is breathing heavy.

Minister's head dips.

'We are unable to divulge the full details of Miss Žukauskas's death, but we can reveal that she was the victim of an especially brutal attack. Miss Žukauskas was from Kaunas in Lithuania. She had only been in Scotland since the beginning of this month, in our country on a young person's international care exchange programme.'

The top copper stops for a drink.

Beads of sweat on the forehead of the other one.

He looks familiar.

'Our inquiries are ongoing, but we are appealing to any member of the public who was in the vicinity of either Springhill Road or Ralston Road, Barrhead, on Thursday the seventh of July, or Friday the eighth of July to come forward. We want to speak to anyone who might have seen Miss Žukauskas get into a car on either of those evenings. The car in question is a brown Vauxhall Viva.'

Stevie side-eyes Meikle's notebook. He reads:

Murder. Renfrewshire. Why Glasgow City investigation?

Stevie scribbles more notes.

The minister's fingers touch the photo frame.

It is still face down.

Wee lawyer's looking at his watch.

Wants to be somewhere else.

Brown car!!!

Renfrewshire v Glasgow City.

'Pastor McTavish is now going to say a few words about Miss Žukauskas. Michael?'

'Em, yes. Thank you, Edward...'

Flashbulbs.

McTavish makes it more interesting news.

First names.

They know each other.

'Janina – Miss Žukauskas – was a lovely girl. She was, em, hard workin'. Polite. Always had a smile oan her face. Everybody at the Sovereign Grace is absolutely devastated by her death.'

Death, he said. Not murder.

'Janina was headin' into town on Thursday. She was goin' to ... she wis meetin' a friend. She didn't come back tae the mission on Thursday night.'

He's working-class.

He's trying to sound posh.

The slang's slipping through.

He cannot stop himself.

'Someone might've seen her – or somebody lookin' like her – oan Friday, the next night, in the streets that Ed ... Chief Superintendent Montrose mentioned.'

'Right, thank you, Pastor McTavish.'

The top copper stepping in quickly.

Shutting God's man down.

The pastor takes a big drink.

Looks anxious.

'Okay, gentlemen. That's it for this morning. There will be another press briefing when Forensics have digested the post-mortem results.'

Montrose spots a hand up at the back. 'Yes, Mr...'

'Dave Porter, *Glasgow Herald*. Can ah ask if Miss...' he reads this from his notes. 'Zook-*Kow*-Shaw's relatives have been informed?'

'Miss Žukauskas was an orphan. She had no known relatives. The Sovereign Grace Mission looks after young people with no families – orphans – as I expect you're aware.'

'Boaby Deans, *Evenin' Times* – where wis the girl workin'
before she wis seen in Barrhead? Sovereign Grace Mission's awa'
ower in the East End.'

No response.

Looks around the table.

Straight question, no?

'Janina was workin' on the Southside. Doin' some domestic
cleanin' work,' says the pastor.

'Whereabouts?' asks Deans. Stevie doesn't think the question
is a tough one. But it challenges the panel.

'Different places,' says the pastor.

God's man shuffling in his seat.

'For example?'

The pastor searches for guidance from his colleagues.

'Raskine House,' says the other copper. His face immediately
regrets it.

The top copper and the pastor stare.

Something is being hidden here.

'Yes, thanks, Inspector McCracken. Janina was helping out
with some weekend work. Cleaning shifts at Raskine House.'

MCCRACKEN!

No. Surely not, Stevie thinks. Could he be a relative of...?

FUCK.

Stevie notices Meikle sitting forward at this point too. Scrib-
bling furiously on his own notepad. Stevie remains intent on
reading the body language at the top table.

'Okay, that's enough.' Montrose stands.

McCracken and McTavish follow him. The lawyer takes a
sheaf of paper from the briefcase. It is the girl's photograph for
distribution. The press pack remain seated, however. Only one
stands.

'Scuse' me! Stevie Milloy, fae the *Star*...'

Jock Meikle tugs at his trouser leg. 'Hey, whit did ah tell ye?'
he whispers.

All movement in the room stops. Paused for the ex-footballer's interruption.

'Seems a bit odd for Cranstonhill tae be the station leading this. Is there no' one ower in the Southside closer tae the murder scene?'

There's a dismissive snigger from the top table.

'Trying to tell us how to do our job, son?' says Montrose.

'Me? Naw, not at all.'

'Cos I was wondering something similar: seems a bit odd for an ex-fitba player to be asking questions at a murder-investigation press briefing.'

Touché.

Stevie ignores the dig. And his colleague's under-his-breath appeals for him to sit down.

'How do ye know about the brown Vauxhall?' Stevie is asking the question of all on the top table. But only looking at Inspector McCracken.

'Our enquiries are ongoing, son.'

'But what led them tae such a specific colour ae car?'

Once again, a fair question, and if asked by a seasoned crime reporter, maybe it would have been addressed. But you had to earn the right to ask such questions in these briefings.

'Ah mean, every motor's black,' Stevie continues. 'Round here, anyway.'

'Is he with you, Jock?' asks Montrose. Meaning: *Do not bring him back.*

Meikle meekly nods. The inevitability of a call made to Eddie Pink. Resigned to the private bollocking that is coming. And raging that an interest he has in aspects of this case won't now remain surreptitious.

Stevie Milloy stands outside, waiting for Jock Meikle. It has been twenty minutes. He is wishing he hadn't given up the fags.

'Mr Milloy?' A voice over his shoulder.

He turns. It's the young copper who shook his hand earlier.

'That's me, aye,' says Stevie. The *Mr* is disconcerting. They must be a similar age.

'Ye probably dinnae remember me,' the young copper says.

'Sorry, pal, ah don't.'

'My da wis a massive fan. Thistle season-ticket holder.'

'Aw aye,' says Stevie. Still none the wiser.

'Game against Hibs at Firhill … sixty-three. Ye hit a thunderbolt. Just missed the top corner…'

It's starting to come back.

'Hit ma da's wee invalidity motor an' smashed the windscreen.'

Fuck…

'Aw, aye … of course. Look, ah'm really sorry about—'

'Naw, naw. Ah wisnae meanin',…' The young copper holds out spread hands like a pleading keeper. 'Ah just wanted tae say thanks, oan behalf ae the family. Ye came ower at full-time an' gave him yer shirt, remember? He wis so bloody chuffed wi' it.'

'Aw, right. Jeez, that wis the least ah could dae. It's nae problem, mate. Tell yer da ah wis askin' for him. How is he, any road?'

'Ach, he passed away last year. Hudnae been well for years. But that day wis one ae the best ae his life, he'd tell everybody.'

'Christ, man. Ah'm really sorry.'

'Don't be. Watchin' you play gave him real joy, Mr Milloy…'

'Stevie, please.'

'We buried him in that shirt. He loved it that much.'

'Well, ah suppose that makes it worth the week's wages it cost me for gie'in it away.'

The young copper nods.

'So, ye stationed here then?' asks Stevie.

'Naw. Ah'm ower in A division. Turnbull Street. Just a driver for the top brass th'day, y'know?'

'Aye. Understood.'

'Listen, if there's ever anythin' ah can dae for ye, just let me know. Speedin' tickets needin' ripped up … ah'm yer man.'

Stevie smiles. 'Ah might haud ye tae that, PC...?'

'Dryburgh. Dennis Dryburgh. Ma da wis Walter Dryburgh.'

'Cheers, Dennis.'

'Aw the best, Stevie.'

The rain starts again; that fine, smirry drizzle that sneaks up on you. Assaults you softly. Before you know it, you are completely soaked. He wanders around the back. Into the sheltered rear lane where the prisoner vans go. He reaches inside his jacket. A wee nip from the hip flask.

A metal door opens across the cobbles. Pastor McTavish comes out. Finger-pointing and aggressive. He is being restrained by a younger man.

Stevie leans back. Out of sight.

The target of the pastor's anger remains inside. His handler turns.

It's Geordie McCracken.

The Scotland captain. The leg-breaking, career-ending, filthy wife-shagging cunt. Too much of a coincidence that he's here when there's an Inspector McCracken inside.

Stevie slips back up the lane to the front of the station, just as Jock Meikle comes through the front door.

'Hey, Milloy!' Jock is furious. 'Whit did ah fucken tell ye, eh? Keep yer mouth shut if ye're wi' me. Don't ever – *ever* – let these cunts know whit ye're thinkin'. Ears. That's aw ye need in this business. Ye got that, ya bloody amateur?'

'Whit d'ye know about that Inspector McCracken?' Stevie glances back down the lane.

'Are you no' listenin' tae me, son? Ah've just had ma baws booted 'cos ae you!'

'That other fella from the *Times* – Deans, wis it? – he asked a question.'

'He's time-served. You're a fucken novice sports reporter. You dinnae ask a question in a murder briefin'.'

'Well, naebody else wis askin' it.'

'They tell ye whit they want ye tae know. That's it! You ... *ah* have tae dae the rest. That's whit fucken journalism is, son.' Jock's beetroot face. Exertion and anger combining. 'An' even then, oor gaffers only print whatever angle suits them. If they want somethin' coverin' up or somebody protected, then that's what we have tae write,' he spits. 'Or else we dinnae fucken write at aw. *That's* yer lesson for th'day.'

'So, whit the fuck wis ah even doin' there then, eh?' Stevie's turn to be annoyed.

'Fuck'd if ah know,' says Jock. 'Nothin' makes any sense tae me anymore.'

+

Someone in the crowd shouts, 'Hey, Minto, your wife's a midden!' And he hears it.

Forty-three thousand, two hundred and sixty-one people inside this stadium. Still, he hears it. It's all he can hear. Rattling around inside his skull since before the first whistle. Thrown in his direction as he emerged out of the tunnel. The game begins. Soundtracked by that incessant howl and growl of opposing supporters; cresting and dipping, chanting and yelling:

'We are the people.'

'You're gonnae get your fucken head kicked in.'

'Follow, Follow, we will follow Rangers...'

Yet all he can hear clearly above the sing-song clamour and the hellish hubbub is that one voice:

'Hey, Minto, your wife's a filthy midden!'

It has been raining constantly for weeks. The Ibrox pitch is heavy. Caked thick with mud in the penalty boxes. Surface water on the flanks. Not one for the tanner ba' players like him. This is the natural habitat of industrial centre-backs with a screw loose. They use the conditions as an excuse to launch into brutal tackles.

'Couldnae stop the slide, ref.'

Somebody might get a bad yin.

'Every cunt's so maukit you can't tell one team from the other.'

'Game should've been called off.'

'Pools panel should be sitting.'

Two mediocre teams. Knocking in the goals regularly enough. But conceding more at the other end most weeks. A score-draw prediction most likely. But that's on paper, and this game's not being played on paper. It's being played on a pitch that looks like the aftermath of the Somme.

'This is fucken ridiculous. Ba' keeps stickin' in the mud.'

Torrential rain in the faces.

'Som'dy's gonnae get their legs done, ref!'

'Shut yer yappin', Milloy, or you're goin' in the book!'

That's not right. The ref can't be saying that.

'Ref?'

'Fuck you, Minto, ya ballet dancin' cunt, ye!' Geordie McCracken. Needling him the whole match. Elbows right in the ribs. Rabbit-punching at the corners. Spitting. Pulling hair. This cunt's the Scotland captain tae. Butter widnae fucken melt, eh?

There it is again. That voice:

'Hey, Minto, your wife's a filthy midden!'

His head's not in the right place. His head takes McCracken's boot. His head's swimming. Double vision. Ball's up the other end. Him and McCracken, together on the halfway line while everyone's looking back at the Thistle penalty box.

'Haw, Minto, ah fucked yer dirty wife tae. Passed her roon the whole team. Me an' the boys. Rode the hoor rotten, so we did.'

Ignore him.

'Her fanny was like the Clyde tunnel when we'd done wi her.'

Jesus Christ, ref, send this bampot off!

'She's a fucken spunk bucket, son.'

Make him stop! This isnae fitba.

The ball's out of play. He turns. His head clears enough for the punch to connect. Right hook to the jaw. It barely registers. McCracken's a tree. McCracken laughs it off.

'*Ref!*' *A feeble sound, he's making. He's like a clipe, clipin' to the teacher.*

Pointless. Tiny Wharton is one of them. A fucking Mason. Everybody says so. Rangers' twelfth man.

'*Ref!*'

Wharton laughs.

'*Nae baw through the legs th'day, then, ya wee prick?*' *says McCracken.*

Wharton winks at McCracken.

The ref points at him, and then says, 'But he's right, yer wife is a filthy midden!'

'*Fuck sake, gaffer, did you hear that?*'

His mud-caked hands are out, pleading. Appealing to the away dug-out. His manager points. Cups hands. Yells back. But he can't hear. All he can hear is...

Wife.

Filthy.

Midden.

Fanny.

Fucked.

Her.

He doesn't see the ball. Launched up. Lost in the clouds and the sleet and this never-fucking-ending rain. It drops out of the sky. A sodden leather bomb, twice the weight it should be. It lands at his feet. He kicks out with a right boot. But the ball's stuck in the mud. His left foot is planted. His good foot.

Minto Milloy could open a tin ae beans with that left foot.

McCracken scythes in.

'*Couldnae stop the slide, ref.*'

And then the crack.

That awful hideous sound of bone breaking.

It's always the crack that wakes him.

The sofa soaked. Forehead sodden. He looks down. Pulls back

the blanket. Expecting to see it again. The mucky socks rolled down. The boot twisting awkwardly. Facing away at an unfeasible angle. As if it can't bear to look either.

But he sees what he always sees nowadays. An ugly, ragged, nine-inch scar on a hairless patch of shin where the fractured tibia poked through the skin over a year ago.

+

Ten days earlier
1st July

'Aw'right, Stevie?'

'Aye, fine, Alf. Yersel?'

'Monday mornin', eh?' Alf shakes his head like a working man rueing the start of another week at the coalface. But he doesn't work. The days must all be the same to him.

'Aye, Alf. Bloody Mondays. Who needs 'em?'

Both men reach down for a milk bottle and the papers. Both grunt their exertion. But one is twenty-five, the other seventy-five.

'How's the leg, son?'

'Aye. Gettin' better.'

'Ach, ye'll be takin' on the dugs at Shawfield in nae time, lad.'

'World loves an optimist, mate.'

'Ye heading out later?'

'Ah am, Alf.'

'Mibbe get us some baccy an' some good butter? Put a coupon on for us?'

'Aye. Nae bother. I'll pick up the slip when ah'm leavin'.'

It is the same conversation every weekday. Give or take. But there's a variation today. Stevie Milloy has a job to go to.

'Fancy comin' ower later? *The Man from U.N.C.L.E.*'s on?'

'Dunno, Alf. Ah'll see how ah feel when ah get back.' Stevie pauses. 'Fae work, y'know?'

'Ach, son – ah went an' forgot. Sorry.'

'It's fine, Alf, honestly.'

'Ye need tae come ower noo, then. Tell me aw aboot yer first day. Ah'll make ye yer tea.'

Stevie smiles.

'An' then we can watch wee Kuryakin fae up the road there, smashin' they Russians.'

Stevie laughs. Alf's amazement that a lad from Maryhill appears on his television set once a week, never mind his role in one of the biggest Hollywood films of all time alongside Steve McQueen, James Garner and Richard Attenborough. Alf talks about David McCallum as if he was a favourite nephew. Alf and McCallum's family lived in the same tenement for the first three years of young David's life, before his father's job took them all to London.

'He belongs tae Glasgow,' says Alf whenever Stevie takes a playful rise out of the old man.

It's hard to say no to old Alf. Spam and chips again, no doubt. He's a one-trick host. But he'll have beers in, and Stevie doesn't.

And it's always good to see David McCallum on screen. Despite the brevity of his tenure, he's a Glaswegian who escaped. Who made it out.

'Aye, aw'right, then,' says Stevie.

'See ye later, son,' says Alf. 'An' good luck th'day. Cannae wait tae see yer name back in the paper.'

Their doors close simultaneously. Stevie sits to finish his tea and burnt toast. Significance is everywhere: 'the death in the dream represents the death of a time of your life, of a hope or a dream, or the end of a relationship.' The first words read from a horoscope on a page in the paper published by his new employer, opened at random.

The record player chips in:

'He's a real nowhere man...'

He looks at his wrist. His gold watch – a retiral gift from his team-mates, which he has regularly resisted the urge to pawn – has stopped.

'Fuck this,' he mutters.

He grabs a jacket and leaves.

Nervous initially, Stevie Milloy relaxes a little when he smells the newsroom. He has missed the dressing-room stench of alpha-male body odour. But it's present here, and it's comforting to him. He sniffs it all in, the stinking socks and putrid farts. The hair tonic and Brut 55. The cigarette smoke and alcohol stench. And, bizarrely, the Algipan. For the lumbago, most likely.

Introductions over. The odd handshake. Nods from some. A squad of fifteen here. Almost obscured by the fog of fag smoke. Everyone stooped and out of shape, and looking a decade older than they probably are. He sees monochrome tones. Frayed, off-white shirts. Trussed-up ties. Regulation short back and sides. Cheapside Street formality. In comparison he's a peacock.

For half an hour there is an impromptu press conference with his new teammates:

'Ye ever kick a baw these days, Stevie?'

'Wis it sair when the leg went, Stevie?'

'Did that cunt Geordie McCracken ever say sorry, Stevie?'

'How much wid ye have been on at Stamford Bridge, Stevie?'

'Who d'ye think'll win the World Cup, Stevie?'

'How the fuck did ye end up here, Minto?'

The last one was a question he has been asking himself since waking up in the Victoria, left leg in plaster from ankle to thigh.

He should have moved to England the previous season. Everybody said so. But he stayed. Because Denice didn't want to go. London was so far away, she'd said. He stayed at Thistle. Turned down Chelsea. Turned down the chance to play with Ron Harris, John Hollis, Eddie McCreadie. Buying his clothes from King's Road boutiques. Drinking in Soho pubs alongside The Beatles and The Stones. He decided to wait until Denice was ready. And while he waited, she was warming the bed of two of his international teammates.

After the injury, the Chelsea deal was off, naturally. Thistle stood by him. But he knew it was over the minute he looked down at his snapped leg. You don't come back from a compound fracture like that. A rapid descent. No fans standing him a drink anymore. No handshakes at the players' entrance. No requests for autographs. Not even the baiting from rival supporters. Just pitied looks and weary shakes of the head. Nowhere to go except the boozer. And the bookies.

Then the money ran out.

Luckily, he pulled out of the tailspin just in time. Took old Alf's advice and joined a local library. Found the days disappearing. But in a good way. Time spent in the stimulating company of George Orwell. D.H. Lawrence. Barry Hines. Colin MacInnes. Time spent being inspired by words. Sentences. Paragraphs. Chapters. Fiction. Non-fiction. Values. Ideology. Social justice. Reconnecting with an education he had left behind. Spirits lifted instead of lifting spirits.

His was a life of two halves.

The whistle sounds.

The second half begins.

'Milloy!' A howitzer voice. A six-letter shell. Cascading off the walls. Even though its owner isn't in the room. It puts a stop to the questions from the assembled hacks.

Stevie follows the reverberation to its source: a small office off the press room.

'Jesus Christ, whit the blazes are you wearin'?' asks Gerry Keegan as Stevie enters. Keegan runs the press room.

'Casual, boss,' says Stevie.

They size each other up. Both wondering if the other will be too much trouble for the wages.

Keegan shakes his head. 'Ye done much writin' before?'

'No' really, Mr Keegan. Notes in the Thistle programmes, that sorta thing. But ah'm a quick learner.'

'That right?'

'Ah've still got the contacts, an' obviously ah've played the game.'

'Mibbe so. Playin' fitba an' writin' aboot it, they're worlds apart.'

'Did ye see me play, Mr Keegan? Mibbe the Scotland games?'

'Look, Milloy, ye're here cos some high heid yin oan the top floor vouched for ye. No' ma idea, obviously, but ah'm nothin' if no' fair-minded.'

'Ah understand that, Mr Keegan.'

'That's ma squad oot there. They might no' be up for a Nobel Prize for Literature but they put a decent shift in. They know how tae get the job done. Tae cut corners. Tae file copy oan time. Tae work tae The Man's plan. Ah trust every single yin ae them.'

'They look like a decent bunch, Mr Keegan.'

'Trust has tae be earned, Milloy.'

'Totally agree, Mr Keegan.'

'Havin' an ability tae kick a baw willnae make ye a sportswriter.'

'Aye, ye said.'

'Aye. Ah did.'

'Well, proof's in the puddin', Mr Keegan.'

'The proof's in the *eatin'*, son. If yer gonnae use expressions, use them right.'

'Appreciate the tip, Mr Keegan.'

'Aye. Right. Well. Then.' Gerry Keegan sits. 'Noo' that we've got that oot the way, ye're goin' tae Ayrshire on Thursday. The Brazilians are there. Get some exclusives. How's Pele feelin' about their chances? Who's starting against Bulgaria. Who's injured? That sorta thing. Elsie's got yer pass, an' ye can take one ae the motors.'

'Great,' says Stevie.

'An' then, if ye dinnae fuck that up, ye're shadowin' Meikle for the rest ae the month. Got it?'

'Aw'right, Mr Kee—'

'An' drap aw that "Mr Keegan" stuff, right? It's "boss", or "gaffer".'

'Got ye, gaffer!' says Stevie. 'Oh an', gaffer...'

'Whit?'

'You can call me "Minto".'

Gerry Keegan's hardman exterior crumples. He rubs his chin. He sniggers. 'Aye. Right.'

Stevie Milloy smiles. He winks at his new manager.

He is back in the first team.

Inside left.

Socks rolled down.

The baw at his feet.

Goal gaping.

+

3rd July

Stevie Milloy has ditched the beatnik look, for now. He's in a light suit. The only one he has. Tonic. Sleek. Shiny. A white shirt and thin tie. Fitting in rather than standing out. Or trying to. Connery in *Goldfinger*, rather than Lennon in *Help!*

He takes the car. It's nice to be behind the wheel again. He misses driving. He heads to Ayrshire. Rugby Park. It's a quiet time for the domestic game. The close season. Scottish players are on holiday. Blackpool or Skegness or Butlins down the coast for the part-timers. Only the well-paid players – the ones like Geordie McCracken, the Rangers and Scotland captain who ended Stevie's playing career – can afford to go abroad.

The Brazil national squad are training at Kilmarnock's ground. Preparing for the defence of their World Cup in England. Bidding to win the trophy for a third successive time. Nearly seventy-five thousand spectators watched them draw 1 – 1 with Scotland in a friendly at Hampden the previous week.

Stevie watches Garrincha, Silva, Tostao and Jairzinho pass and juggle the ball effortlessly. He watches the lesser-known Manga,

Rildo and Fidelis defend crosses fired in from left and right by Gerson and Silva, respectively.

The other squad members stand or sit on the pitch. They look bored. Uninterested. As do the onlookers. Cameras click occasionally but just to provide the photographers with their own view-finding practice before the star man shows.

And then suddenly, he does.

Poised. Confident. The balance of Nureyev. Like Cassius Clay entering the ring at Lewiston last year. Or Elvis Presley walking onto the set of *Viva Las Vegas*. The most famous footballer in the world strolls out from the Rugby Park changing rooms. It's a walk Stevie Milloy has done countless times himself.

Everyone stops what they are doing. Even his team-mates on the pitch. Time itself seems to pause, acknowledging the presence of genius. He is dressed in a blue tracksuit. *BRASIL* on his chest. Arced. Three letters either side of the zip. Perfect symmetry. He brushes against Stevie's shoulder.

'*Desculpe*,' he says. A voice deep and sonorous, despite his small stature.

He wanders over to the left goalmouth. The players surround him.

He lines up a few balls. He fires rapier shots at the goal. Minimum effort. Unerring accuracy. Stevie counts them. Nineteen hit the net before Gilmar even comes close to saving one. When the keeper eventually does, that's the signal for Pele to stop.

He then juggles the ball. Hundreds of times. Black Puma boots. White flash. Knees. Head. Shoulders. All working in perfect co-ordination. Keeping the ball in the air as if God himself was suspending it from a heavenly wire.

But as the showboating for the cameras continues, Stevie notices something. Distinct factions. Only a former professional would recognise the subtleties. Training in separate groups. Little conversation or eye contact between the squad members. Disgruntled reactions when Vincente Feola, the manager, cajoles them, insisting they run across the Ayrshire pitch. Only Pele doesn't. He doesn't have to.

Signs of a discontented camp.

Feola has won the World Cup before. He gave the seventeen-year-old Pele his debut. But the manager left the national side five years ago to coach in Argentina. Considered a betrayal back then. His return has been seen as something of a desperate move by the Brazilian FA.

'Are you more confident now than in Sweden in 1958?' Stevie asks him once they're back inside. He waits for the translator. A language so impenetrable, and without pauses, that it sounds like one ridiculously long word. And then a response from the manager that is just as long. A shorter version is the English outcome.

'No.'

'Will Pele be fit enough to start against Bulgaria?'

An even longer description, and some shakes of the manager's head.

'Yes.'

'How have you found our Scottish hospitality?' Stevie consciously pacing the words. Big gaps in between. Overcompensating.

Feola stands before the translation is given.

'Yes. Very good. Very happy to be here.'

And with that, he leaves. Back to the pitch. There will be no interviews with the players. Although Pele is the only one anybody wants to speak with.

Stevie leaves the ground. The piece forms in his head as he drives back to Glasgow across the moors.

'Brazil will not win this World Cup', is his closing sentence.

He files it late that same evening.

Across the hallway from Stevie's empty flat, Alf eats spam, drinks beer, and watches the famous blonde-haired boy from Maryhill on his own.

+

Eight days later
11th July

'Uruguay play at a walking pace,' says Kenneth Wolstenholme, the BBC's stiff-upper-lipped complainer-in-chief.

'Jesus, nine-men in defence, these yins!' says Alf.

'It's just a difference in styles, Alf. Uruguay like to play slow. England fast.'

'It's borin' tae watch, son.'

'Aye. But that's the modern game. A lot more technical. No' just kick it an' run.'

Stevie and his elderly neighbour eat spam and chips. They drink beer. Stevie's treat. They watch a dour and lifeless 0 – 0 draw kick off the World Cup.

'Think they'll win it, Stevie? The whole thing, ah mean?'

Alf's question goes unanswered. Stevie Milloy is miles away. His mind no longer occupied by the trivialities of football.

If crime reporting is as procedural as Meikle says, what is there to learn about it? Ask the right questions, listen closely to the answers. Observe the body language of all involved. It's not rocket science.

Stevie examines the notes he took earlier that day at the briefing on the murder. Writes new ones and underlines them all.

The pastor and the copper know each other.

First-name terms.

She was a lovely girl. Hard-working. Polite.

Death.

Not murder.

As if it was accidental.

A brown car.

Stevie is intrigued by Jock Meikle. A man so obviously disenfranchised, despite his obvious talent. Why is he festering at the *Star*? Where few rate, respect or even like him? Why not move to another newspaper? A broadsheet, perhaps. Somewhere his writing would have the space to breathe.

Could Stevie do his job? *Fuck, yes.*
Jock Meikle is an enigma.
But so is Stevie Milloy.

She Said, She Said (1966)

*Stevie hopes for a reconciliation – Denice Milloy delivers some
shocking news – Geordie McCracken crosses Stevie's path.*

26th July

A tune he can't get out of his head.
Sunny, yesterday my life was filled with rain,
Now the dark days are done and the bright days are here...
If only.

Stevie is nervous. His palms are moist. He pulls at the top
button of his shirt. He loosens his tie. He checks his watch frequently. Tapping its face with an impatient finger. Furtively
glancing towards the door. Fidgeting with the salt cellar. A dense
cloud of cologne hanging over him. It's a show for someone important. A woman. And he's not sure she will turn up.

'Get ye another tea, love?' asks the waitress. She's been watching him.

'Eh ... aye, aw'right.'

This will be his third. The waitress knows. She's seen enough
young men stood up by a female to recognise the signs. She
decides: one more cuppa. On the house. And then she's going to
tell him, *Look, son, she's no' comin'.*

But by the time she returns, the young man has been joined at
his table. If anything, though, he looks more nervous now. The
waitress waits, allowing them time to talk.

'Ye look...'

'Nice?' Denice smiles.

'Well, aye. Different,' says Stevie.

She does. Something – or someone – has changed her. Her hair's longer. Darker. Cut straight. Subtle make-up, but heavier on the mascara. She's wearing a short, pale-blue raincoat. Buckle tied across her middle. The Biba dress or skirt she's presumably wearing underneath is so mini it can't be seen. Pale-blue matching shoes with a tiny heel. She is fashionable. Stylish. Like Cathy McGowan or Twiggy. Although that doesn't mark her out as different. Not nowadays, when it seems that all young women look to Mary Quant for direction. He means different from when she was with him. The gold band missing from her finger the clearest indication.

She leans across to kiss him on the cheek. The whisky whiff hits her.

'Dutch courage?' she smiles.

'Could say, aye,' he replies.

'What'll ye have, hen?' asks the waitress. She sees his new companion is nervous too.

'Em ... a tea please? No milk.'

'Right ye are, love.' The waitress leaves them to whatever it is that is unnerving them.

Stevie flips open the engraved cigarette holder. Offers Denice one.

'Oh, you've still got that,' she says.

'Aye.'

'Thought you'd chucked them?'

'Aye, ah have,' he replies, her importuning for him to stop being one good thing that stuck. He lights the one she puts in her mouth. 'Knew *you* hadn't though.'

She rolls her eyes. She turns her head to the side but keeps her gaze fixed on him. She blows the smoke away. It wafts. Rises. Clings to a formerly white ceiling.

'How've ye been, Stevie?'

'Aye. Good. Ah'm good.' He doesn't ask her the same question. 'Been workin' on a murder case.'

'Ye have not!' She says it like a proud mother. 'Well, that's excitin'.'

'Aye. Mibbe. Eveythin's gone a bit cold, though, this last week.'

He fidgets. She clasps and then unclasps her hands on the table in front of him. There's an awkward silence until she finally breaks it.

'Ah saw the articles ye've written for the *Star*. They're great. Everybody in the office said so.'

An ambulance speeds up Victoria Road. Siren blaring. They both turn to look at the diversion.

'Never a good sign,' says Stevie.

'No ... it's not. Hope whoever's in it is fine,' she says. Then: 'It's great that the job's working out for ye. Ye always wanted to be a writer, remember?'

'Hmm.'

'All those book ideas ye had.'

'Aye.'

The waitress returns. 'A black tea. Here ye are, hen.'

Both are glad of her interruption. Wishing they could get past the pointless small talk. Wishing they could begin again. Stevie especially.

'Look Denice...'

He pauses. He thinks of the scenarios he's imagined since she called him a week ago, agreeing to meet. The optimism Alf's counsel has built. The words he rehearsed in his head last night. The sentences he wrote. But with her here, sat in front of him, they've all evaporated.

They've both put on a little weight. But while she carries it well, he doesn't. He needs her guiding him. Looking after him. He didn't realise it until she was gone. He wants to tell her how much he misses her. How the time passing since his injury has changed him. How lonely he is. How much he wants her to come back. To give their relationship another chance. To put the past behind them.

'Stevie—'

'We made mistakes—'

'Stevie. I'm pregnant.'

An uppercut lands. His guard was down. He didn't see it coming. He's struggling to recover. Head swimming in watery images. The room starts spinning. He grips the table's edge.

Six years ago, almost to the day, they sat here in the Queens Café. Holding hands. Their first date. Both anxiously sipping cups of tea, then as now. The Curzon afterwards, to see *Psycho*. A full cinema seated before the film started. No rolling screenings. No-one allowed to arrive in the middle of a showing. Ramping up the tension. That unprecedented audience reaction. Denice screaming. Whispering that she'd never shower again. *Baths all the way!* Cuddling into him. Her heart pounding through her cardigan. Her perfume weaving its spell. Then as now.

'Stevie...'

'Aye. What?' He swallows hard.

'Did ye hear me? I'm pregnant.' She speaks quietly. Trying to reach for compassion. She knows how badly he will take this. Their inability to conceive was the wedge that drove them apart. The arguments. The desperation. The expectations of friends and family.

When will we be hearin' the patter of tiny fitba boots, then?

Well-meaning. But brutal when they don't know the truth.

Ach ... Stevie's career. We don't know where it'll take us. The schools, ye know? Ye have to think carefully about these things.

For years, this was Denice's mantra. Repeated so often, it might as well have been tattooed on her forehead to save the bother. Eventually people stopped asking. The only person who really cared was Stevie's mum. Wanted them settled. After she and his dad died, things went downhill fast. Stevie spent more time in the pub after games. More time with other men. Reinforcing a false masculinity. Unable to cope with his grief. Unable to confide in anyone. Bottling it all up. The realisation that he was somehow less of a man if he couldn't provide his wife with children.

What kinda man is that, eh?

He clung to the selfish hope that the problem was Denice's. But here she is proving it's not her. It's him. It must always have been him. No-one is in his corner. He wants to know who the father is. But what difference would that make now?

She sees the change. His fingers ball up. Make tight fists. But not in rage. Digging fingernails into his palms to distract from thoughts that will bring tears.

'Everythin' alright?' The waitress is good at reading body language.

'We're fine, thanks,' says Denice. 'Maybe another tea? I'd like another tea. Stevie, d'ye want another—'

'No.' Shut down.

The ref steps in.

A mandatory count.

Denice looks at the waitress. She shrugs almost imperceptibly. But the waitress sees it. Equally imperceptibly, she raises eyebrows in response. Female sixth sense.

'Comin' right up, love.'

The intervention works. The air has gone out of him.

'Whose is it?' Stevie mumbles. What other question is there?

'That's not any of your business.'

'How's it no'? Course it is.'

'We're not together anymore.'

'We're still bloody married!'

'In name only, Stevie. Come on.'

'Where's yer ring?'

She covers her left hand with her right. 'Stevie, ah want a divorce.'

'Jesus Christ, Den – the jabs keep comin', eh?'

He laughs. If he didn't, he *would* cry. He shakes a sarcastic head. Slim hopes he had clung to lie shattered and broken at his feet. The waitress may as well come over now with a brush and shovel.

'Fuck's sake, Den.' His hands cover his face. 'How did we get here, eh?'

'We were over years ago,' she says. Not bitter, just matter-of-factly. 'We were makin' each other bloody miserable. Both wantin' different things in the end.'

'Ah wanted *you*!' he protests. 'Ah wanted you, Denice.' Quieter this time. He is losing her. And for good. And he knows it now. But still he says: 'Ah still dae. Ah put the move tae the English First Division oan hold for you. Because you didnae want to leave here.' Hands open. Pleading.

'The cracks were there long before that, Stevie. An' you know that.'

She looks around. No easy way to say this.

'When yer mum an' da were killed, ah stayed. Ah stayed for you. How could ah have left ye then? But Stevie, ah was stayin' in the marriage for the wrong reasons.'

His head slumps into his hands again.

'Pity ... is that really a good foundation for happiness?'

He knows she is right. He has nothing to counter this with.

His mum and dad were the very best people Stevie knew. Never a harsh word heard between them. Hard-working, conscientious, supportive – of each other and their boys. A railwayman and a secretary. Stevie's dad never let shift patterns get in the way of watching his sons play football. John was less naturally gifted. A hard meat-an'-tatties defender, his dad called him. He was proud of both. But Stevie played the game the way his dad taught him to.

Head up, son. Be confident. Trust yerself. Ye know where the baw is, ye dinnae need tae waste time lookin' doon at it.

His father's face, beaming with pride that night Stevie got his first Scotland cap. His mother in tears. They were so happy. Fit to burst, they were. And then, weeks later, some careless young bastard wipes them out. Both parents killed in the same accident. Only three streets away from where Stevie and Denice are currently sat. A young copper on his first driving assignment. No criminal consequences. No reparations. Barely an apology.

An unfortunate accident sustained in the pursuit of a crime.

His brother couldn't get out of Britain and away to Australia quick enough after the funeral. John, his wife and three kids. Barely a backward glance as they boarded the ship. A player-manager position with Port Adelaide Pirates waiting for him. A new life away from the emotional turmoil of Glasgow.

Stevie wanted to do the same when the Chelsea opportunity materialised. To escape the memories. To try and outrun the dark thoughts – the nightmare visions – that haunted him. Why couldn't Denice have understood that?

'If we'd gone to London, you really think we'd have been happy?'

'Aye. Mibbe,' he says. 'Ah don't fucken know, do ah? But it might've stopped you divin' intae bed wi' that cunt McCracken behind ma back.'

'Yer tea, darlin',' says the waitress.

Immaculate timing. An elderly couple return to their newspapers. A young mother resumes tending to her baby. Denice stubs out the fag. He doesn't offer another.

'And young man,' says the waitress with quiet menace, 'I understand that ye're upset, but that kinda language won't be tolerated in here, do you hear me?'

She is just like his mum, this waitress. A kind face. Firm but patient.

'Ah'm sorry,' says Stevie. Sheepish.

'Ah know ye are, son,' says the waitress.

Denice mouths *thanks* as Stevie looks away ashamed.

The reality of her request is only just dawning. His senses are swimming against an emotional tidal wave.

He is like a small child faced with a complex algebraic equation.

$X + Y \times Z = ?$

What are the defining factors, Milloy?

Ah don't know, miss.

You're not trying hard enough, boy.

It's too hard, miss.

If X is Pregnant ... and Y is?

Ah dinnae know, miss.

Y is The Father. Come on Milloy, try harder. Apply yourself.

Yes, miss.

Z is...

Z is Divorce, miss.

That's right, Milloy. So, what's the answer?

She's gettin' remarried, miss.

That's correct, Milloy. Well done. See, that wasn't so hard, was it?

Why are you crying?

Why are you crying, Milloy?

'Stevie. *Stevie!* Don't cry? Please don't. People are lookin'.'

He wipes his eyes with a handkerchief. He glances left and right, suddenly embarrassed.

'Yer gettin' married again, aren't ye?'

Her turn to swallow hard. 'Stevie.'

'Just tell me.'

'Yes. I'm engaged,' she says.

He sighs. He sniffs. He wipes his nose on a sleeve like a child would.

'Ah still love ye, Denice. Ah should've told ye that more, when ... y'know.'

'I care about ye, Stevie. Ah really do. I want ye to be happy, but it can't be with me.'

He snorts. Wipes his nose again. Now indifferent to the voyeurs' stares. 'Fuck sake. Look at the state ae me, eh?'

She smiles. 'Ye're gonna be fine.'

'Is it McCracken?'

'No.' Her upturned expression tells him the truth. As if she's just smelt something foul.

'Well, that's somethin', ah suppose.'

'He's an arsehole. He was just a stupid mistake.'

'Somethin' we can agree on.'

'He was never goin' to leave Carole.'

Stevie sniggers. 'Maybe me an' her should've got th'gither then.'

'Aye, you had yer hands full already though.'

Stevie looks up. Bemused.

'The team nights. Up the dancin'. Young girls throwin' themselves at the star players. Those nights you didn't come home?'

Her head tilts. His drops.

'Come on, Stevie. Don't be a hypocrite. Not now. Ah knew all about that.'

Geordie fucking McCracken.

This is how the insidious cunt inveigled his way in.

Stevie's back on the ropes. 'Christ, Den ... that was ... they meant nothin'. It's a fitba team thing. Changin'-room bollocks. Ye've got tae fit in. Be one ae the herd.'

These words. The insincerity of them. Especially now. When he's no longer a part of that world. He's done. Nothing left to counter with. Nothing to salvage. Only the realisation remaining that at least she doesn't hate him for it.

Minutes pass. No words said. Neither sure how to end what will be their last date.

'You still buyin' yer records?'

'Aye,' he says. 'They've been a comfort since...'

'Ye'll have no need to sneak them into the house now,' she says.

'There is that, ah suppose.' He tries a smile, but it looks awkward and forced. Because it is.

'I got a new job too,' says Denice.

'Whereabouts?' Trying to fake interest.

'I'm workin' in the campaign office of Mr Campbell,' she says.

'Who's he?'

'The shop steward, y'know – the one that's in the papers all the time. He's goin' to be sittin' for election as a new Labour MP. Shettleston ward.'

'Aw ... aye, him? *Big Jamesie* Campbell? He's in the press office every now an' again. He seems like an arsehole. Talkin' doon tae everybody. Swans aboot like he owns the place.'

'Well, he kinda does, in a way. You know he's married to Maude Denton-Hall? Her dad's company owns yer newspaper.'

'Yeah, ah know that.'

'Anyway, Mr Campbell's actually quite nice, as it happens.'

'Ah saw him give the gaffer a right roastin'. Couldnae hear what he was sayin' cos the door was shut, but he very nearly had him by the throat. Ye mibbe better watch yersel'.'

'Well, he's never been anythin' other than a gentleman to me. Your boss must've done somethin' to deserve it.'

Stevie hesitates a moment. This could be an opportunity. He's not sure it's one he should take, though. He looks out of the window. Makes a decision.

'Listen, can ah ask a favour, since ye brought it up?'

'Depends what it is, Stevie.'

'Ah'm workin' on somethin'. An investigation intae the murder ae a young woman fae Lithuania.'

He pauses.

'For the *Star*?' she asks. 'What's that got to do wi' sports reportin'?'

'Nothin'. Ah'm just interested, that's aw. Anyway, Janina was workin' at Raskine House when—'

'Janina? Who's that?'

'The wee foreign lassie that wis murdered.'

'So what are ye askin' me, Stevie?' Denice is annoyed.

'Well, Big Jamesie Campbell and his missus own that place, Raskine House. That's right, int'it? And it seems like there's a connection there somehow. Ah'm sure ae it.'

'You want me to snoop about in the private affairs ae a man ah've just started workin' for? Is that the reason you asked me here?' Stevie tilts his head. 'No chance, Stevie. Mr Campbell is a respectable man. An' you're accusin' him of...' She stops short.

He sighs. 'Naw, sorry Denice. Yer right. Forget it,' he says.

Minutes pass with no words. Only looks. There's little left to be said. Other than:

'How did ye get that job?'

She looks down. No easy way to say it.

'Bobby works there too.'

He doesn't need to ask. Her face says it all.

He settles with the waitress. Outside, Denice watches through the window. She waits. He joins her on the pavement for the final awkwardness. Him offering a handshake. Her reaching past it for a hug. She kisses him on the cheek and then turns away to the left. But he remains. Standing in the doorway of the Queens Café. Watching her walk down Victoria Road and out of his life for good.

He reaches inside his jacket. The silver cigarette case. Engraved in a complicated Edwardian script:

To Stevie, on the occasion of our engagement. From Denice

Fuck it.

He flips it open. Takes one out. And lights it.

+

11th September

'Meikle's phoned in,' says Keegan. 'He's off oan the Pat an' Mick again. Nothin' movin' on the crime desk. So get yersel ower tae Ibrox for the Old Firm presser.'

'Right, gaffer,' says Stevie.

It has been a rough week. Left to his own devices. Meikle is softening but still holding back. A modicum of grudging respect. But they don't trust each other. It's hard to build trust between two avowed loners.

Stevie opted for a weekend-long bender. Saturdays are the worst. What to do with your time when 3pm comes? Drifting from Maryhill boozers to West End pubs. Indulging fans' reminiscences, listening to them describe in minute detail matches he's long forgotten about. Living – and still playing – vicariously.

Mind ae that turn? That way ye swivelled an' beat three ae them? Left them needin' to buy a ticket tae get back in tae the ground? Ye 'member, Stevie, son? An' then that shot ... Wid've been headin' tae outer space if the net hudnae stopped it. Whit a goal that wis. Lemme buy ye a drink, eh? Least ah could dae.

Weeks after Denice's bombshell, he craves this. Needs it. It is all built on a lie, of course. On a partisan perspective. For every game being lauded from the terraces there was another where a lingering, painful death from cancer was wished upon him. For a misplaced pass that led to an opposition goal. For missing a sitter. Those important things in the life of a football fan. The fine line between a fiver won at the bookies and a wife needing thicker make-up to conceal her black eye.

Fuck it! Take the drink. And another. And another. Take the money they can't afford. The rent money. The family food money. The kid's birthday present. The stupid bastards.

The weekdays since, though. A cold realisation. She's gone. She's not coming back. She's having a baby. She's engaged. She's getting married to some cunt called Bobby. Some *Bobby* cunt who, it transpires, is Geordie McCracken's cousin.

She left that bit out. Conveniently.

Stevie walks along Edmiston Drive towards the imposing entrance of Ibrox Park, home of Rangers Football Club; one of the unshakeable pillars of west of Scotland life. The self-confidence he displayed here as an opposition player has gone. His hand shakes as he reaches for the brass handle.

Any hope that an awkward encounter can be avoided dies the minute he climbs the marble staircase. The door to the Blue Room on the first floor is open.

Geordie McCracken, club captain, is on pre-match press duty.

Of course, he is.

+

If ye know yer history...

Early season, September sixty-two. Stevie Milloy's debut. Thrown in at the deep end, away to Rangers at Ibrox. He was twenty-one years old. Brought to the Jags from the Juniors. A very promising inside left.

Geordie McCracken was marking him. Tactically and literally. Intimidating him. Fair enough, that's the game.

'Think yer a big shot, wee man?'

'Think yer a fancy Dan, eh?'

'Ye're just a wean.'

'Ah'll fucken snap you in two, ye try an' go by me.'

A running commentary, all through the first half.

Geordie McCracken 1 – 0 Stevie Milloy.

Half-time team talk over, and Stevie returns to the pitch a different player. Demanding the ball. Dummies. Stepovers. Running at the defence, with the ball at his feet. Finding wingers with clever passes.

Thistle score. Then score again. An upset on the cards. The discontent from the home support.

'Ah telt you, ya wee cunt! Ah'm gonnae fucken do you!'

Hairs pulled from Stevie's legs when the ref's not looking. Nutted in the back of the head when he was.

'Play on, son. No foul!'

Ten minutes left. Stevie picks up the ball. Flicks it up. Balances it on his forehead for a second. The crowd boo. Anger floods down from the terracing. The fucking cheek of it.

McCracken runs forward. Out of defence. Stevie spots him coming. Drops the ball. Drops a shoulder. Anticipates the launching two-footed tackle. Slips the ball between McCracken's legs. Makes the Rangers and Scotland captain look like a Sunday League player in his own backyard. But rather than advance toward goal and score a third, Stevie stops. Puts his foot on the ball. Waits for

McCracken to recover, get up and advance again. Through those big, lumbering, tree-trunk legs again. With the right foot this time.

'Too fucken slow, auld man!'

Then Stevie's down. From a punch, not a tackle. The ref left with no option. The Rangers captain is sent off. Stevie hears the ref say, 'Sorry Geordie.' *Apologetic? Jesus Christ.*

Scot Symon, the Rangers manager, shook Stevie's hand at the end. Ushered the remaining Rangers players away from him. 'Ye played well, son.'

'Thanks, Mr Symon.'

'A word to the wise though: the enemies ye make on the way up, they'll be waitin' for ye on the way down.'

+

Scot Symon is around, but he's not participating in this media preview. Stevie spots him through a side door. He has his back to Stevie. Talking to other men. But Stevie knows the profile. The impressive stature of the man.

Stevie always liked Scot Symon. He is a gentleman in a sport where the characteristics that make one are disappearing. After McCracken broke Stevie's leg, Scot Symon was the only person from Rangers F.C. who visited him in the Victoria Infirmary. Apologetic on his captain's behalf. Hopeful that Stevie could come back, better than before. He stopped short of confirming that Stevie had been a transfer target for the Ibrox club. That might only have made things worse. But he did say how much he admired Stevie's ability. Rumours have now reached Stevie's ears in the *Star* press office suggesting that it was Scot Symon's connections that brought about the job offer.

The manager turns. Spots Stevie. Nods politely. The big man just beyond Symon seems familiar to Stevie, but the light in the corridor is insufficient to see who it is. The three smaller men beyond are mere silhouettes.

Stevie touches his forehead with two fingers. Symon goes back to his conversation as George Young, Willie Woodburn, Alan Morton – the giants of Ibrox – look on from their picture frames.

Stevie sits at the back. A few seasoned hacks notice him. There are nudges and nods. *This'll be interesting*, the unsaid subtext.

It starts softly enough.

The dinosaurs lob easy shots for McCracken to bat away with ease.

'Good start tae the season, Geordie. Ye must be pleased, eh?'

'Aye, Jock. A great performance last week. Six goals at home in the first game ae the season is a good start by any standards...' McCracken looks to the back of the room. He knows Stevie Milloy is there. 'Even if it was only against the Thistle.'

Laughs from the assembled pack. Bluenoses to a man.

'They'll struggle this season,' adds McCracken. 'Nae bite. Nae hardness in their midfield. Soft as a builder's putty.'

There is an intake of breath. A collective *wooo-oh-ing*. Followed by sniggers. As if the audience on *The Good Old Days* has just heard Leonard Sachs describe the Jags team as a 'panoply of pluranimous mountebankery'.

The game's changing. Nonetheless, it is unusual to hear such overt criticism of opponents. Especially for a team that don't comprise the next fixture.

'Thistle are just a team full ae women's hairdressers. Pansies.'

Nobody knows what it means, but it's going to be tomorrow's back-page headline. Even though the game they should be asking about is the first Old Firm match of the season at Celtic Park on Saturday.

'Ye worried about the Celtic this season, Geordie?'

'No. Not at all. They had a good run last year, fair enough. But we finished the season stronger. We're the cup-holders. Cup Winners' Cup starts in a month. We're feelin' confident.'

'Stein's buildin' a good team though ... Johnstone, Chalmers, Lennox. They play good fitba.'

McCracken's annoyed. 'So dae we, Harry. Ye suggestin' we don't?'

'Em ... no, Geordie. Ah didnae mean...' The *Evening Times* reporter fades to silence and visibly slumps in his seat.

'1967 is gonnae be Rangers' year,' says McCracken. 'Celtic'll win nothin'. There's a predication ye can put yer drink money on!'

The air in the room returns. Until...

'You're what, thirty-three now. Gettin' on a bit for a defender at the top. Game's gettin' quicker. Are ye worried your lack ae pace is gonnae be a big problem against Celtic?'

There's silence for what seems like minutes. The quickened breathing of the pack is almost audible. McCracken's face reddens. The hacks' pencils are poised. This. This right here – *this* is the pre-match story.

'Gents,' says McCracken. Calm. Composure regained. 'It's a good enough question from ... what was yer name again, son?'

Stevie concentrates, mainly to control the shakes.

'It's Milloy. Stevie Milloy. The *Star*. Ah'm sure ye'll have heard ae it.'

'Aw, aye. The *Star*. Ah don't read that myself, but ah know of it.'

The smug bastard, thinks Stevie. *Sat there holding court. The cousin ae the Bobby cunt.*

'Two bookings already this season, Mr McCracken, an' only two games played, eh? The years catchin' up wi' ye, are they? Just no' quite quick enough for the youngsters?'

McCracken is rattled. The hacks' heads turn. Back and forth. Observing a tennis match. Milloy smashing the defensive lobs straight back at McCracken's baseline.

'Well at least ah'm still playin' eh? Still quicker than you ever were, Minto,' says McCracken. 'How's the leg, by the way?'

'It got me up the stairs just fine. Ah dinnae type wi' it. The hands an' fingers are aw ah'll need for this report.'

It is going to be a fucking hatchet job. No holds barred. If

Celtic win on Saturday, there's going to be no hiding place for this lead-footed cunt.

'Well, we better give ye a positive result tae write about then, eh boys?' McCracken is trying to rally the troops. Put a flame under the Protestant ranks that run – and report on – the game.

A standing man in a hat leans in. Whispers to McCracken.

'That's it for today, fellas,' says the captain. Then beckons the man in the hat. Whispers again.

The man in the hat looks to the rear. To where Stevie is sat.

The hacks file out.

The man in the hat approaches Stevie. 'Mr Milloy, could you wait behind please?'

'What for?'

'Mr Symon would like a word.'

Stevie sighs. An apology will be hard to give. Even to Scot Symon. He would be apologising for something he isn't sorry for.

'This way.'

The man in the hat guides Stevie towards the corridor. Scot Symon and his colleagues are not there. A room to the left has its door open. A brass plate reads *Manager's Office*. Voices can be heard from inside.

'This way, Mr Milloy.' The man in the hat is ushering Stevie past Scot Symon's room.

'But...'

'This way.'

Stevie glances into the room as they pass. Four men. Three standing. Symon seated at his desk. The big man, familiar from earlier ... Jamesie Campbell. Denice's new boss. The other two. Also familiar.

They are the top copper from the Cranstonhill murder briefing. And the anxious pastor. *What the fuck is going on here?*

<u>*Death. Not murder*</u>, he wrote in his notebook.

'Mr Milloy? Please.'

Ushered along the corridor. Through a door. Into a staircase. Door closes behind him.

'Hullo, Stevie. Long time, son!'

Stevie turns. A flat, solid forehead thumps into his nose, bursting it and cracking the bone.

He might be as slow as a week in Barlinnie, but McCracken was always a good header of the ball; you had to give him that.

Stevie's on his knees. His blood speckling the landing. The pain starting to ratchet up several notches.

'Ungrateful cunt!' spits the raging Rangers defender.

Ungrateful?

McCracken volleys Stevie in the ribs. This puts him down. Flat and defenceless. A cheek cold on the concrete. Eyes closed, anticipating another kicking.

'Don't ever come back here, ya manky bastard,' warns the Scotland captain. Mainstay of the footballing community. Hero to thousands. Leader of a nation. 'Or ah'll have ye fucken wiped oot, ye understand me?'

Stevie gurgles. Wincing. Blood running into his mouth. He reaches for the railing. Anything to anchor himself. To prevent him capitulating completely.

'An' stay away fae Denice tae. She's nae need tae be seen wi' a fucken loser like you.'

The staircase door opens.

'See yersel' out, ya useless prick,' he whispers.

The door slams.

+

13th September

'Jesus. Whit happened tae you?'

'Walked intae a door.'

PC Dennis Dryburgh might be wet behind the ears, but he knows this cliché only too well. He doesn't press it. Stevie side-eyes him. Plain-clothes awkwardness drapes Dennis Dryburgh now. The type of young copper who embraces the uniform like it's a shield. Feels naked without it.

'Want a pint?' Stevie asks.

'Naw, sorry. Kinda still oan duty, y'know?'

'Fair enough,' says Stevie. He's already four pints and a whisky chaser deep, and the money saved will fund another. 'Look, sit doon, will ye. Dinnae draw attention tae yersel.'

Dennis Dryburgh sits. Stevie wonders what kind of copper he will make if he's perpetually this nervous.

'Ah cannae really wait. Got tae get back,' says Dennis. This favour goes well beyond the terms of his original offer.

'This'll no' take long. Find out anythin' for us?'

'No' really. Forensic report's locked up tight. Cannae get a look, an' the top brass are the only ones dealin' wi' the case files. Inspector McCracken's on top ae everythin.'

'Fuck.' Stevie drains his glass. 'Aw this secrecy no' seem a bit strange tae you?'

'Dunno, ah've no' been in the job long.'

'An' nane ae yer comrades talkin' about it?'

There's a pause. Dennis's hand reaches up to his face. Rubs his eyes. Stevie leans forward. Seizing on it. 'Well?' Prising the naïve copper open.

'Ach, ah dunno. There's a couple ae things, mibbe,' says Dennis.

His eyes dart around the pub's back room. Four drinkers check the scores in the evening *Pink*. Two argue about Wilson's attitude to Vietnam. One struggles with folding the *Citizen* into a small enough shape to fit into his coat pocket. No-one cares about Stevie and Dennis, and the subject of their meeting.

'Aye?' Stevie prompts him.

Dennis hesitates.

'Well, one ae the lads said that apparently she didnae die where the body was found. She was murdered somewhere else, an' then shifted.'

'An' the other thing?'

Dennis puts a hand over his mouth and whispers, 'The post-mortem found this rubber thing, jammed right up inside her arsehole.'

'Eh?' Stevie leans closer to hear him. 'What kind ae rubber thing?'

'Like a stopper thing off the end ae table leg, or a walking stick or somethin.'

+

18th September

'MINTO!'

'He's in the bog, gaffer.'

'Ah want him in here the minute he's wiped his fucken arse!'

There's no need for the message to be passed on. Stevie hears it.

'Gaffer?'

'For fuck's sake, son – whit happened tae you?'

'Fell doon the stairs, gaffer.'

'Were ye bloody drunk...?'

'Naw.'

'...when ye wrote *this*?'

'Eh?'

Stevie sees the leader; the only part he didn't write.

RANGERS FLOUNDER AT PARKHEAD
CELTIC 2 – 0 RANGERS
League Division One.
Saturday, 17th September 1966.

'We're no' runnin' this!'

'How no'?' asks Stevie.

'Because it's a fucken slatin', that's why no'!'

'But Rangers were rubbish, gaffer. Two down inside four minutes. It could've been six or seven if Celtic—'

'Ah'm no' talkin' about the match, son. These extracts are aw about Geordie McCracken. It's a personal agenda ah'm readin' here.'

'And?'

'*And*?' Gerry Keegan shakes his head. He laughs sarcastically. 'Ye know the cunt's connected to the proprietor ae this paper?'

'Does that mean he's untouchable, then?'

'Well, in a sense, aye.'

Stevie sniggers.

'Look, son, ah didnae want ye here at the beginning. Thought ye'd be trouble. But fair's fair, these last few months, yer writin's been good, on the whole. No' just the fitba stuff, either.'

'Aye, well ... thanks.'

'But Minto, son, there's always limits. Editorial lines ye cannae cross. This is one ae them. Keep yer personal grudges out the paper, okay?'

Editorial. A mysterious Oz-like crypt hidden somewhere inside this urban rabbit warren.

Dinnae get oan the wrang side ae Editorial, Stevie has been warned. *Eddie Pink'll get ye.*

Eddie Pink, the *Star*'s legendary bogey man.

Gerry Keegan hands Stevie the draft. Blue pen lines run through the sentences with Geordie McCracken as their focus. The initials *E.P.* are scrawled at the bottom.

'Reduced piece. A thousand words. That'll dae.'

'Want me tae change the score, tae? Award Willie Henderson a wee phantom hat-trick?'

'Just caw canny, son. Dinnae be makin' yerself a target. Heid doon, an' get the work done. Pick up the wage at the end ae the week. That's it. Take it fae me. Or fae Meikle. He'll tell ye.'

Stevie is walking away ... but when children are warned about sticking their fingers in an electrical socket, it is amazing how many are magnetically drawn to it. Tempted by it. Just to find out what will happen.

He turns back in the office doorway. 'Gaffer, why was ah sent tae the Janina Žukauskas murder briefin' back in July?'

'Whit?' It's not a question Keegan was expecting. 'For experience,' he suggests, as if he's not entirely sure either.

'There's somethin' odd about that whole case, d'ye no' think?'

'Naw, ah dinnae think – an' neither should you,' says Keegan.

'But no' think it's bloody weird, that Geordie McCracken wis hangin' aboot in the background ae a murder presser?'

Keegan slams a hand on his desk. It causes raised heads from the press room.

'For fuck's sake, son, gie it a fucken rest wi' this McCracken obsession. That's a life-limitin' condition, you've got there. So, for yer ain good, get ower it. He's off limits fae now oan, right?'

Stevie spends the rest of the afternoon thinking about the crime. The trivial task of reshaping a report about a recent football match lies undone. Instead, diagrams emerge. At their centre is the name of a young woman: Janina Žukauskas. Brutally murdered and her body dumped across the river. Other names encircle hers: McCracken. Campbell. McTavish. Meikle. Dryburgh. Keegan. Arrows point in and out. He writes the words SCOTLAND and LITHUANIA. And the letters U.S.S.R. And draws a box around them.

There's something going on here, but he doesn't know what it is. Just that it's more important than football.

'Ah'm Stevie, by the way. Stevie Milloy. Ah buddy wi' Jock Meikle on the second floor.'

'Ah know who ye are, son.' The man sniffs.

Both look straight ahead. No eye contact and no downward glances. The man is big. A head above Stevie. Seems safe to imagine that his cock is like a fireman's hose. Don't want to get caught eyeing – and gasping at – it.

'Minto.' The man smiles dismissively and shakes his head. 'Aye, ah know all about you. And Captain Paranoia.'

Stevie ponders this. He's obviously referring to Meikle.

'You're Eddie Pink, aren't ye?'

'It's Pinkerton tae you, ya cheeky wee cunt.'

'Aw, right ... like the detective agency.'

'Look ah'm havin' a fucken piss in peace ... or ah wis tryin' tae.'

'Sorry.' Stevie finishes and zips up. He then extends a hand. It is ignored.

'Did you follow me in here?' asks the man.

'Naw ... Well, aye, but no' like that. Ah wanted tae ask you somethin'.'

'In the fucken bogs?'

'Yer a hard fella tae pin down.'

Eddie Pink pours cold water on his hands. Dries them with a paper towel, which he then screws up and fires at a bin in the corner. He misses the target, like several before him have.

'Right then. Whit is it?'

'Keegan told me you were the guy that recommended me for the *Star*. Is that right?'

'Naw, it isnae.'

'Well, he showed me your signature on the contract.'

'Want tae see it again? Along wi' yer P45? Stop fucken askin' questions.'

'That no' the main part ae the job?'

'Writin' tae order – that's the job, son. Dinnae deviate fae that path if ye want tae keep it. An' anymore hatchet jobs on Geordie McCracken an ah'll bury ye face doon, right?'

'Hey ... can ah call ye Eddie?'

'Naw.'

'Mr Pinkerton, ah'm no' a daft lad. Ah mighta played fitba for a livin', but ah'm educated. Ah can string coherent sentences th'gither. An' ah can form an understandin' ae most complex situations. But y'know, Mr Pinkerton, one situation completely baffles me. Dae ye know whit that is?'

'Enlighten me?'

'How did ah end up gettin' offered a sports reporter's job at the *Star*, when ah've had zero trainin', an' ah never even applied for one?'

'Fuck knows, pal. Friends in high places? Who fucken cares. Ye want the job or no'?'

'But it's no' *that* job though is it – the sports yin? Ah'm being manoeuvred intae the crime job. Meikle's.'

'Meikle, fuck sake. He's protected, the crocodile-faced cunt. Look, son, ah've nae time for this. Ah'm needed back upstairs.'

'Protected by who? "Editorial"?'

Eddie Pink looks straight at Stevie. Stares him out. Leans down into him. Foreheads almost touching. Mismatched boxers squaring up before the bell.

'Pftt!' says Eddie. He sniggers. 'Aye, as it happens.'

'Figures.'

Eddie Pink has a look that sits squarely between pity and rage. Like he would pummel this cocky little bastard through the nearest window, but then sling a silk hankie after him to clean up the blood.

'Gonnae just tell me? Who recommended me for this job?'

Eddie Pink laughs at the question. The unexpected open-goal opportunity to have fun with the answer.

'It was Geordie McCracken. He felt sorry for ye, after he ended yer career an' fucked yer wife. So lay off the personal attacks. Ye owe him for ye bein' here.'

Eddie Pink sticks a sausage-sized finger in Stevie's chest. As if a further warning is about to be delivered, But it doesn't come. Stevie wouldn't have heard it anyway. Those words – 'ye owe him' – like a punch to the face. Filling his eyes, ears, nose, and mouth. Blocking all his senses. Until he can't see, hear, or speak.

Stevie slumps. Only the windowsill catching his arse prevents him from sliding to the floor.

Eddie Pink strolls away whistling. He reaches the stairs. He turns and looks back.

'Mind how ye go, son,' he says.

EPISODE THREE:
TOMORROW NEVER KNOWS (1966)

Stevie visits Meikle in hospital – Stevie gets a glimpse into a lonely future – Gerry Keegan delivers a harsh lesson.

20th September

Ward 6E.

He has been moved again. And there is a familiarity to this new location. 6E is the ward Stevie recuperated in following the surgery to set the bones in his leg.

The ward demographic is markedly different from his time here. Elderly and barely conscious men. Unlikely to leave here other than feet first. It's a relief to see Meikle awake and breathing on his own.

Meikle's lying on the bed this time. Not in it. Shorn of his black uniform, the thin suave veneer has cracked. The teeth are lacking their usual lustre. Hands bruised and pockmarked by clinical needles. Eyes sagging from lack of sleep. Hair wild and feathery like he's been caught in the downdraught of a jet engine. Still, he looks marginally better than on Stevie's previous visits. But that might be down to the afternoon sun shining across his face. Three pillows propping him up. Feet crossed. Scarf defiantly round his neck despite the blistering hospital temperature. Pyjama legs riding up. Pale, veined, bony ankles on show. An old wound on the sole of his left foot. Like a pellet hole. Stevie sits on the bedside chair. He notices blistered flesh on the top of the foot too.

'How ye feelin'?' asks Stevie.

'Aye ... aw'right, aw things considered,' says Meikle. 'An' you?'

'Aye, fine. The swellin's away. Still look like a panda though.'
Stevie takes off the dark glasses.

'Christ,' says Meikle. 'Mibbe ah should shift ower a bit.'

Stevie puts the glasses back on. 'Share a bed wi' you, ya aul'
poofter? No thanks.'

An older nurse tuts loudly. She is tending to an old man in the
bed adjacent. Stevie puts a hand up in silent apology.

'Pull the curtain ower,' says Meikle.

'Brought ye some grapes. An' Lucozade.'

'Ye didnae stick a drap ae vodka in it, by any chance?'

'That allowed, is it?'

'Who cares. Ah'm no' gettin' ootae here anyway.'

'Ach away. Ye'll be right as rain in nae time.'

'Aye. Keep haudin' on tae that optimism, son. It'll bode ye well,'
says Meikle. 'Listen, before ah forget, can ye dae me a favour?'

'Aye,' says Stevie. 'Whit is it?'

'Keys tae the motor are in the house. Kitchen table. Can ye get
the fan belt replaced? Fucken thing's a pain in the arse.'

'Sure,' says Stevie. He takes a house key from Meikle with a note
of the address. Given their initial misgivings, it is strange that they
are now ostensibly partners.

Meikle reaches for a newspaper. One from a couple of days ago.
He folds the pages back. Stevie's Old Firm match report faces up.
Meikle knows it has been cut and reshaped. Like an elderly pro-
fessor admonishing an underperforming student, Meikle's face
assumes a weary 'told you so' expression.

Stevie shrugs.

'Join the club, son,' says Meikle.

'Well, ah suppose ye did warn me, eh.'

'You're a reporter, son. The job, as they see it, is for you tae
report what they want ye tae report. Your opinions, perspectives?
None ae that matters. Aw they want is compliant company men.
Fucken stooges, like Gerry Keegan.'

'Seems so.'

'Or me,' Meikle whispers.

Stevie is rustling the pack of grapes. He doesn't hear Meikle confess this.

'The paper's owners urnae interested in anythin' insightful or controversial. "If ye want tae write an opinion piece, some other cunt can publish it." That's the attitude at the *Star*.'

'A wee edge in a fitba report's hardly rockin' the establishment boat, though, is it?'

'For fuck's sake, have ye no' listened tae anythin' ah've told ye? The establishment in Scotland is the media, the judiciary, the polis and the clergy – aw "follow follow", and funny handshakes an' Sunday sash bowler hats. An' the public fulcrum ae that is?'

The sound of pennies dropping. Stevie nods. 'Glasgow Rangers.'

'Right first time, Mr Milloy. Go tae the top ae the class.'

Stevie laughs. Meikle does too, but a guttural, painful-sounding cough curtails it.

'Ye have a dig at the Rangers, ye're havin' a dig at the establishment. An' that's a vested interest for the *Star*. An' the interests they're protectin' are the very ones we should be investigatin'.'

'We?'

'Reporters, son. The yins that are in it for the right reasons, that is.'

'Us, ye mean.'

'Follow the line ae influence fae the top doon, an' just see what criminality it uncovers. That's the job they dinnae want us doin'.'

Stevie scratches his chin.

'Bumped intae Eddie Pink,' Stevie ventures. 'Fae Editorial?'

'Ah'm familiar wi' the cunt's work. What of it?' Meikle's tone hardens.

Stevie contemplates the next sentence. How best to phrase it. *Fuck it.*

'Says you're protected. Whit the fuck does that mean?'

Meikle coughs again. Louder this time. As if the establishment gods are constricting his windpipe for his insolence.

'Gie's some ae that juice, then.'

Stevie unwraps the orange paper. Unscrews the cap. Then pours a couple of inches worth of the Lucozade into a teacup.

'Christ, that tastes like pish,' says Meikle.

Stevie smiles.

'Looks like it tae,' says Meikle. 'Well, mine at least.'

'So, what's your story, then?'

'Whit d'ye mean?'

'Ah mean wi' you. Aw this antipathy for the *Star*. Yet ye're still there. Still writin' for them.'

'Still pocketin' the wages, ye mean? Takin' the devil's money?'

Stevie shrugs. 'Ye just dinnae seem like a company man, if that's the right term.'

'Aye well. Every cunt's got tae put food oan the table, eh?'

'Work for somebody else, then?' Stevie suggests. 'Or write a book?'

Meikle laughs at this. It is a laugh forged over decades. Cut. Bent. Heated until soft. Deformed and hammered into shape. A laugh that knows its place.

'What's so funny?' asks Stevie.

Meikle sighs deeply. Weighs what he is about to say.

It has taken a couple of months to reach this position with Stevie Milloy. The unlikeliest of comrades. Old debts seen as now paid, Meikle knew the *Star* were gradually phasing him out. Realised they were phasing Stevie Milloy in. Grooming him to cover the crime stories too.

After that difficult first week, Stevie has become someone Meikle feels he might be able to trust. And he trusts damn few people. Meikle has come to wish he had met Stevie Milloy years earlier. When there was still some fight left in him. Before he became the acquiescent lackey he despises himself for being. Nevertheless, Meikle remains guarded. Especially where the Denton-Hall newspaper-publishing estate is concerned.

'It's complicated, son,' is all that comes out.

'Very cryptic,' says Stevie.

'There's bad history there,' he adds.

'Be keen tae hear aboot that someday – that protection. Ye still huvnae answered me aboot that.'

'Aye, well. Someday. Mibbe.' He sighs. 'How is the murder story goin'?'

'Strange,' says Stevie.

'How come?'

'Everythin's went quiet. There's been nae press briefings for weeks. The story's dyin'. Naebody seems interested. The body's been buried already.'

'Where?'

'Where was it buried?'

'Aye?'

'Wee graveyard at the back ae the Sovereign Grace Mission, ower in the East End.'

'Surprised it wisnae shipped back tae Lithuania.'

'Aye, me tae,' says Stevie. 'Then right out ae the blue, a suspect's been arrested.'

'When?'

'Monday, ah've heard. Early mornin'.'

'Bank Holiday. Quiet day for the papers. Typical.'

'Whit d'ye mean?'

'Somebody's hidin' somethin'.'

Stevie has suspected this from his first day. So has Meikle. But Meikle has kept such thoughts to himself. Has encouraged Stevie to do the same.

Meikle fingers the grapes. Finds one that interests him. The bell rings. Visiting time is over.

Stevie stands. 'Aw, somethin' ah meant tae tell ye,' says Stevie. 'When ah wis Ibrox for the ... y'know?' He points to his face. 'That top copper an' the nervous pastor fae the murder room briefin', they were there in Scot Symon's office. An' somethin' else tae – yon Inspector McCracken? He's Geordie fucken McCracken's uncle.'

'Connections, son. Aw these establishment cunts are involved somehow.'

Meikle fingers more grapes. The action distracts Stevie. A thumb and first two fingers. Rolls the fruit. Pops it. Then licks the three digits in order. The other two remaining raised throughout like they had been trained at a Swiss finishing school.

'An' that politician, Jamesie Campbell. He was—'

'Big Jamesie Campbell?'

'Aye. Ye know him, dae ye? My missus – well, *ex*-wife soon tae be – she's went tae work for him. An' she's marryin' that bastard McCracken's cousin tae.'

Meikle puts the grapes down. He licks his nicotine-stained fingers.

'That's a lot ae weird connections, naw?' asks Stevie.

'Ye start movin' in newspaper circles, son, that's whit happens.'

'The *Star* fucken loves Jamesie Campbell though, eh? No' read a negative word about him in aw the time ah've been there.'

Meikle takes a deep breath. Leans toward his younger colleague. He pulls Stevie's sleeve. Draws him closer. He lowers his voice.

'Jamesie Campbell has nae sense ae right or wrong. The cunt's a moral vacuum. If ye were tae look up the word "venal" in the dictionary, Jamesie Campbell's name would be beside it.'

'Ah think ah might have tae,' says Stevie.

'Ah'm tellin' ye straight. He has nae regard for anybody but himself. No' the people he was supposed to lead. Tae protect. The union interests he was charged wi' lookin' after. No' the people he does business wi'. No' the people that follow him in politics. Aw these daft wee twats, blind an' loyal tae a fault. No' even the ones that think ae themselves as his friends. He has a contempt for aw ae them. He's married intae a wealthy clique that thinks every scandalous action, every crime, every life they destroy can be swept under the carpet by writin' a cheque. The bastard thinks he's fucken untouchable. An' the sad thing ... he probably is.'

There's that word again ... 'untouchable'. Stevie has hit a nerve. 'Ye know a lot about him then?'

'Aye, ye could say.' Meikle scribbles on a piece of paper and hands it to Stevie. He takes it and reads:

PROTECTION – Desperate to fire me, but they can't!

'Fuck does that mean?' His desire to interrogate the words is cut short by the ward sister.

'Time to go, love,' she says. 'You can visit yer dad again tomorrow,' she teases. 'He'll still be here then, won't you, Mr Meikle?'

'Depends. Tomorrow never knows anythin', does it?'

Stevie has so many questions to ask his experienced colleague. But perhaps it's better to go home and work them into his growing portfolio of diagrams. So they make a bit more sense. Then he can return and lay it on Meikle, his wild theory about how Janina Žukauskas was murdered by someone who was at the Cranstonhill presser.

Stevie turns at the entrance to the ward. He waves his colleague goodbye.

Meikle nods softly. 'Watch yersel, son,' he says. But Stevie's too far away to hear.

The ward sister ushers Stevie down the corridor.

'So, what's the likelihood ae him goin' home soon, sister?'

She sighs. 'It depends, Mr...?'

'Milloy. Ah'm no' his son, by the way. Just work wi' him.'

'Mr Milloy, he suffered a massive myocardial infarction – a heart attack. If the bus driver hadn't brought him straight here, he wouldn't have survived. He has responded reasonably well, but he's far from out of the woods yet. The next thirty-six hours or so is vital.'

'But he looks fine,' says Stevie, appreciating the relativity of the statement. He means fine compared to the poor sods in the other beds of ward 6E.

The ward sister smiles. She leaves him with no further elaboration.

Meikle's close smells of piss. Nothing remarkable in that. Most do. If old Alf wasn't so diligent and house proud, Stevie's would too. But a different smell assaults Stevie's nostrils when he opens Meikle's door.

There was this one time, Stevie would have been about nineteen, not long in the Thistle first-team squad. A wet, muddy pre-season training session. His team-mates dumped him in the dirty kit basket and padlocked it. The soaking socks and stinking shirts. Muddy shorts and skid-marked pants. Left him in there for over an hour. Meikle's hall smells like the contents of that basket. A contributory factor is the dead mouse. Neck snapped by the trap's hammer as the rodent pursued mouldy cheese that has turned the same colour as the deceased.

Meikle's tenement flat is remarkably like Stevie's. In layout and personality. Cold, sparse and masculine. Stevie recognises what it must have taken for Meikle to expose his austere lifestyle to him. He'd have known that a journalist – even one as new to the trade as Stevie – couldn't resist the urge to investigate. To make assumptions and draw conclusions. And he does.

A wooden kitchen table. One seat. No need for any more. Stevie finds the car keys early. Next to a dirty plate and the crusts of burnt toast. A chipped china cup with an inch of clear liquid in it. He picks it up. Smells it. It's vodka.

Over on the cooker, a frying pan with solidified lard. A fingertip's depth. The sink next to it full of unwashed dishes. Water from a dripping tap forging a determined trail through a dam of ketchup. The window looks out to the back court. It is a shared space clogged with engine parts and rusting sections of bodywork. Unlikely to be Meikle's, Stevie guesses. Three unruly kids bounce on an old mattress. He watches them until one cuts a leg on an exposed spring.

Stevie finds the bedroom. Flicks the light switch. A bare hanging bulb fails to illuminate the room. He opens the mustysmelling, orange-patterned curtains. He sits on the bed. It is firmer than his own. Newer. The old mattress outside is probably Meikle's. Although it would have been a struggle for him to wrestle it out on his own.

Thick leather-bound titles line a bookcase. The only thing in the room demonstrating order, a sign that someone loved them enough to organise them. Alphabetical by title.

Next to the bed there's an odd pile of magazines: *Tomorrow's Man, Health & Strength, Physique Pictorial.* All their covers are adorned by young, smiling, muscle-bound men in tiny swimming trunks assuming Charles Atlas poses.

Stacks of old newspapers line the bedroom walls. Three to four feet high for the most part. A fire hazard.

Stevie riffles through the drawers of a tallboy. Various papers, loose and without any obvious system.

He finds a page bearing a list of names and dates connected by arrows. Notes in the margin signify what the dates mean. Born, married, worked, died – the significant stages of a life. At the top is written *Albert Raskine.* The dates start at 1769 and run down the page to 1935. Other names appear as the dates progress. He spots one – De Maupassant. Halfway down the page, the Maupassant becomes Maupauy. Near the bottom, the tree branches into Malpas, and locates the descendants in Clydebank in the early part of the twentieth century. All of this is written in Meikle's cursive handwriting. Sweeping loops on the l's, dipping curls on the g's. The letters flowing effortlessly. A man who enjoyed the process.

'Hullo?'

A voice wafting through the letterbox. Stevie hears a key turn and the door opening. It catches him off guard. Like a teenager caught looking through his sister's underwear. Stevie shuts the drawers and stumbles over a discarded shoe.

'Hullo, Mr Meikle? Is that you?' It's a woman's voice. Elderly.

'Hi there. Mr Meikle's no' here the now,' says Stevie. 'Ah work wi' him. He's in hospital. Ah'm here tae pick up his car keys.'

'Aw no ... The hospital? Whit's happened?'

'Are you a neighbour, Mrs...?'

'Ah live upstairs, son. Ah heard a noise, an' it's been quiet for days.' The fish aren't biting. 'Is he alright?'

'Heart attack – start ae the week. Ah think he'll be fine though. Just needs to watch his self, y'know?'

She shrugs. They can't be close then. Although she does have a key.

'Tell him ah wis askin' for him.'

'Ah will ... Mrs...?'

'Cheerio, son.' And she's gone.

Stevie takes a last look around the flat. At the cumulative shit lying everywhere. The dirty linen hanging from a broken pulley suspended over a scummy bath. Empty soup tins discarded because there is no-one to tidy up for, so what would be the point? If he was as well paid by the *Star* as everyone hinted, what the fuck did he do with the money?

Stevie leaves. Pulls the heavy door behind him and locks it. Meikle's environment is a product of choice. Stevie's is one of neglect. He shakes himself, determined that this is not going to be his future.

+

21st September

Stevie lays the crumpled newspaper on the table. Yesterday's news. He unwraps the package. Steam bursts from the fish supper inside. He pours a whisky. Half fills a pint tumbler.

He turns on the television set. He turns the sound down before the picture emerges and he picks at the battered cod.

Finished, he licks his fingers in much the same way as Meikle did the previous day. He finds a bin sack. Throws the papers in it, and the remnants of today's, and yesterday's, food.

It's time.

He takes the bag, walks down the corridor and opens the

bedroom door. The putrid stink of decay and disregard hits him hard. He has barely been in here since Denice left. He sees the tiny room now for what it is: a columbarium for a failed marriage.

The bed left the way it was when she last got out of it. The depression in the patterned pillow slip. The bedsheet in which he can almost trace her foetal outline. Her back arched into his chest. That was before they began facing away from each other. And before he began to sleep on the settee while she stayed in the bed. In every part of the room, on every surface, in every corner, fragmentary remnants of a now-broken relationship.

On the bottom corner of the bedspread, three wooden coat hangers.

A magazine. *Woman's Own*. A smiling, beautiful Audrey Hepburn on the cover. The actress is holding a little dog. It reminds him of Denice's inability to conceive, and his thoughtless suggestion that she get a pet instead.

The withdrawn contract offer from Chelsea. Unsigned.

The bedside tables. A sewing kit on hers. A pencil and betting slips on his.

A bedside lamp with a head square draped over it because the light hurt her eyes.

A book. His. *The Blinder* by Barry Hines. There were times when Stevie identified so much with Lennie Hawk that it read like his autobiography.

In the far corner of the room, a tailor's mannequin rescued from a January skip overflowing with other people's festive regrets. Wrapped around it, a sleeveless cardigan she had been knitting.

Her dressing table. Open lipsticks. Discarded lids. A mascara brush welded to the surface by the hardened gloop.

A string of pearls that he had bought her. She professed to love them but months later said she hated them, and him.

There is a small handheld mirror with the words *FUCK OFF* capitalised in lipstick. Stevie cannot remember them being written. Or by whom.

Tellin' her she should get a dog. That might've been the FUCK OFF *moment.*

A teacup. Like Meikle's. Could almost have come from the same set. Cracked. Quarter inch of whisky still in it.

Three little brown pill bottles, all empty.

Two framed pictures. A happy couple in happier times.

Pushed into a corner of the dressing table's mirror, a postcard from Australia sent by his brother via air mail.

Wish you were here.

On the floor, a newspaper clipping from Stevie's Scotland debut.

His international cap. She wore it when they had sex after returning home on the night of the game.

An unopened pack of chocolates.

Tampons.

A 45rpm record she bought him for his twenty-fourth birthday. 'She's Not There' by The Zombies.

A birthday card:

> *Don't worry, I love you. And I forgive you.*
> *Happy birthday, Stevie.*
> *Denice X*

A cinema-ticket stub for the Odeon. *Dr Strangelove*. They'd both hated it.

A collection of Thistle programmes.

Whisky miniatures.

A screwed-up cigarette packet next to the bin.

A matchbook. Hers. An address written on the inside of the card. Geordie McCracken's. The catalyst for the final fight.

A woman's shoe. Hers. He threw it at the wall. It broke the glass on a picture. Fuck knows where the other one is.

On the wall above it, the picture – behind the cracked glass, a copy of a painted landscape of a Scottish island, a wedding gift from Denice's mother.

A wardrobe. Emptied. Not by her on the night she left. He had dumped everything in a suitcase and left it at the front door. Alf told him she'd picked it up the following afternoon.

She left. She took the car. Fair enough – she used it more. And he had struggled to drive it after the injury.

He kept the telly and the radiogram; he used *them* more.

He makes a start. He picks up the framed pictures of them; smiling, or at least prepared to portray temporary happiness for the camera. Binned, all of them.

However painful it is to admit, she isn't coming back. Time to get on with his life. And let her get on with hers.

It will be difficult, but he'll sleep in this bed tonight – the one in which they spent years trying to conceive – and maybe, if he fills the ghostly shape of her, the emptiness of it won't haunt him.

The clear-up takes over an hour. Bags of rubbish. Bags of clothes. Bags of memories. He feels lighter somehow. One step at a time. He'll dispose of them at the weekend, he promises himself. He'll dust and hoover tomorrow. Scrub the sinks and the bath the next day. It's a new beginning. Every journey begins with one step, and he has just taken the hardest one. All that therapeutic rubbish addicts gird themselves with when trying to free themselves of their demons.

He pours another whisky. Lights a cigar that he found at Meikle's place.

Such clarity of thought he would not have considered possible a month ago. He looks for the right record. Finds it.

'What can I say, she's walking away.'

Stevie smiles wryly. But a tear escapes. It surprises him. Moving on will not be easy.

'How can we hang on to a dream?' sings Tim Hardin.

Stevie wipes his face. Drains the glass. Pours another.

To distract himself, he unrolls the dusty, sepia-faded newspapers he signed out from the *Star*'s archive. Everything he could find covering Jamesie Campbell.

Stevie suspects there's much that Meikle is not telling him. About the *Star*. About Jamesie Campbell. Maybe even about the murder of Janina Žukauskas.

Aw these establishment cunts are involved somehow.

Stevie's convinced that Geordie McCracken's involved.

Revenge is a dreadful motivator, but he wants so much for that to be true.

+

22nd September

Stevie heads for the bus stop. Torrential rain pours onto the Glasgow streets. Small rivers of dirty, oily water line the pavements as the drains overflow. There is no space under the shelter. He catches a 61 outside George Dougan's newsagent's on Maryhill Road, even though that will leave a walk when he gets off. The rain might have abated by then, he reasons. He rattles a shin on the footplate. A grimace mistaken for a smile prompts a wink from the conductor. Stevie contemplates the elderly downstairs contingent. He takes the stairs instead to a smoke-filled top deck. He picks the last fag from its silver container. The smog inside gets a little denser.

'Single,' he says. He hands over the wet 4d.

'Here ye go, Minto,' says the conductor. 'How's the leg, son?'

'Aw. Aye ... fine, mate. Thanks.'

The clippie winks again. Moves up the aisle. Leaves Stevie to his paper. Stevie opens the *Star* he picked up at Dougan's.

Avoids the damp back pages.

Skirts the celebrity focus of the cover.

Lands on page seven.

At the bottom, a picture of Janina Žukauskas. Smiling. Happy. Alive.

She has been placed under a story about LBJ; the American

president flying to Honolulu for an emergency Vietnam conference. Opposite a column confirming that the latest talks to avert a planned strike by the National Union of Railwaymen have stalled. And beside a half-page advertisement for warm plaid travel rugs retailing at 13'6 each...

CHRISTIAN EXCHANGE STUDENT MURDER:
SUSPECT ARRESTED
By John Meikle
Crime Writer

Stevie reads the perplexing text. A thousand-word piece. Attributed to Meikle but obviously not written by him. Limited in detail, but enough to indicate that the police have their man. A twenty-four-year-old mute of no fixed abode. Living rough. Psychiatric issues in the past. Identified after an anonymous witness came forward.

It is not only the girl's body that's been buried with indecent haste.

'What the fuck's this, gaffer?'

Stevie slams the paper down on the untidy desk. A paper cup holding lidless biros topples over. Sheafs of notes fly like birds after a shotgun blast. A dust cloud rises.

'Never heard ae knockin' first, son?'

'The door was open.'

They both look down at the morning edition. At the young Lithuanian girl smiling back at them.

'Shut the door over,' says Gerry Keegan.

'Why? Ye got somethin' tae hide?'

'Don't fucken push it, Minto.'

Stevie closes the door. Stares hard at his nosy colleagues through the glass. Blank expressions. No clues.

'Sit doon.'

Stevie takes a seat as Gerry Keegan returns his desk into an approximation of its previously disorganised state.

'Questions?' asks Gerry.

'Fucken loads,' says Stevie.

'Shoot.'

'The boy – "no fixed abode", but he's got a swanky, new broon motor?'

'He's a drifter. Pillar tae post.'

'Mute? That's bloody convenient.'

'His haun still works though.'

'Psychiatric issues?'

'Unfit tae stand trial. Insanity plea. Carted off tae Carstairs.'

'An anonymous witness materialises out ae thin air, months after the murder?'

'Memory must ae got jogged. It happens. Folk don't like tae get too involved. Whit the fuck dae you care?'

Stevie shakes his head.

'Madness is usually the emergency exit for evil bastards like him,' offers Keegan.

'C'mon gaffer.'

Keegan shrugs.

'An' Meikle, for fuck's sake. He didnae even write this!' Stevie jabs a finger at the page.

'Aye he did. His name's right there, look.'

'Ah was wi' him two days ago. In the hospital. He couldnae have written me a fucken bettin' slip, ne'er mind file a murder report.'

'But he did.'

'Gerry, for Christ's sake, eh? These urnae his words.'

'He phoned it in. Editorial filled in the gaps.'

Editorial: Eddie Pink's domain. A closed-door office on the top floor. Of the second-floor press office scribes, only Gerry Keegan has been up there. He never talks about what he sees.

Stevie puts his head in his hands. Something is happening here, but he doesn't know what it is.

'Look, son,' says Gerry Keegan. 'You an' me – an' Meikle, an' they dumb fuckers oot there – we work tae the agenda. We don't set it. We don't question it. We just work tae it.'

It has the rehearsed tone of an edict Gerry Keegan has delivered many times before.

'An' we get paid for it. *Meikle* gets paid for everythin' that's got his name attached. He probably needs the cash, just like the rest ae us. That credit? Ah'm doin' him a bloody solid here.' He folds his arms. 'Dinnae rock the boat, son. There's no' enough lifebelts for everybody if it tips ower.'

'Y'know, gaffer, if ye see wee brown chunks oan the floor...'

'Where?'

'...never confuse the chocolate an' the shite. They might look the same, but they taste totally different, right?'

'Dae whit everybody else here does then, Confucius – walk round it an' don't get any on yer fucken loafers.'

Stevie heads to the Victoria. A fast black taxi. Quicker than the bus.

Stevie is angry with Meikle. He had trusted him. Divulged his suspicions about the McCrackens. And the pastor. And Big Jamesie Campbell. If Keegan was telling the truth, the devious old cunt has sat on vital information even as they've shared Stevie's bloody grapes.

The lift's out. The burn from a welder's soldering iron illuminates the opening. Its hot-metal vapours overwhelm the disinfectant. God help the poor bastards – and porters – needing transferred to an operating theatre.

Six flights up. Pain throbbing from his head *and* his leg. The metal chairs at the landing are occupied by those waiting for their laboured breathing to return to a normal rate. An older man amongst the seated recognises Stevie but says nothing. Just points at him and whispers to a woman adjacent:

'Minto Milloy ... whit a player he wis. Could trap a baw

dropped fae outer space, him. Look at him noo – blawin' oot his arse.'

Stevie puffs out his chest. Strolls away. Embarrassed.

It is a different ward sister. Older. Less patient. And less interested in anyone no longer on her ward.

And Meikle is no longer on her ward.

'And you are Mr...' She thumbs the papers on a clipboard. Terse.

'Milloy.'

'Are you a relative?'

'No, ah'm ... Ah work wi' him.'

'Then I'm not a liberty to—'

'Has somethin' happened? Tell me, for Christ's sake!'

'Mr Meikle died yesterday evening, Mr Milloy. Another heart attack. I'm sorry for your loss.'

'But—'

'Excuse me, I have to get on.'

'Hey, haud oan a minute.' Stevie follows the ward sister.

She turns. Her stare halts him in his tracks. 'I'm sorry, Mr Milloy. There was nothing that could be done for him.'

The Sound of Silence (1966)

Stevie discovers an uncomfortable truth about Meikle –
Denice cuts all ties – Stevie spirals out of control.

1st October

Stevie sits in Meikle's car. The fan belt Meikle asked him to attend to remains loose and squealing. No point now. Someone else's problem. He takes the keys. Pulls up his collar to shelter from the driving rain. And tips his hat respectfully as the hearse passes him. As a further mark, he pops two mints to mask his alcohol breath.

Stevie walks into the crematorium, hoping to find that 'someone else'. But it is a sparse turn-out. Meikle was a loner, everybody said so. Unsurprising then that his funeral is attended by fewer than ten people, not counting the minister. The ten are spread out – either side of the aisle; different rows – they're strangers to each other. Stevie is alone in representing the *Star*. A major story has broken. Multiple deaths following a landslide at Aberfan in Wales. A spoil tip has collapsed and destroyed a junior school. It seems certain the dead will include small children. Fair enough, although Stevie thinks it's a convenient excuse for his colleagues to avoid Meikle's last farewell.

He guesses that the slight woman in the front row is Meikle's upstairs neighbour. Then she turns to the side and it's not. His mother, maybe? An aunt? Or a nurse from the Victoria, as unlikely as that seems? Across the aisle, three rows back, another woman. She too is familiar. She's dressed so differently from when he last saw her, it takes Stevie a moment to realise it's Mags from Blythswood Square.

He glances at the order of service. At the photograph on the front. Black and white. Meikle as a much younger man. Smiling. Unrecognisable. Shirt and tie perfectly arranged like it was his first day of work. Maybe it was.

John Meikle
4th January 1923 – 24th September 1966

'Forty-three? Fuck me!' mutters Stevie. Much louder than he intended, as he draws an irritated *tut-tutting* from across the aisle. Meikle looked at least ten years older than that, thinks Stevie. Particularly in his final days.

The minister asks for all present to stand. The coffin is brought in by six pallbearers. Slow-paced, down the aisle. Everyone glances to the side but tries not to make it obvious. Stevie imagines all are thinking the same thing as him: *One day that'll be me … and surely to God more than ten strangers will turn up.*

'Please be seated.'

And then the minister delivers the first surprise.

'We are here to celebrate the life of John Meikle, born Andrew John Donnachie, in Glasgow on the fourth of January 1923…'

Eh?

'Our opening hymn is "The Lord is My Shepherd". Could you please be upstanding.'

An out-of-tune organ leads the lacklustre singing. Stevie tries to remember the names and details on the papers in Meikle's bedroom.

The brief service passes in a blur. A piece of classical music – 'Nimrod' from Elgar's *Enigma Variations*. A prayer. A reading from the Gospel according to Paul or John … or George *or* Ringo. And when it comes to the eulogy, it is clear the minister has little source material to work from. He briefly embellishes this adult life with the few facts he could determine. Supplements those with a positivity that those here are unlikely to challenge.

Well liked.

Respected.

Diligent.

Industrious.

A reputation for detail and determination as a journalist.

Will be sorely missed by friends and colleagues alike.

Oh really?

A curtain slides for the committal. And then it's over. The mourners file out to the soothing sound of Sinatra singing. 'Strangers in the Night', appropriately enough. Stevie is at the end of the line. Watching for any indications of emotional closeness. But there are no tears from anyone. No-one dabbing a hanky at moist eyes. No obvious person to whom Meikle's car keys should be given.

There is a small woman in front of him. She carries herself differently to everyone else. A camel-coloured coat. Fox fur decorating the neck. She smells of expensive perfume. Her make-up is professionally applied. Hair carefully coiffured. With a black-leather-gloved hand, she touches the hand of the minister, who says:

'Thank you for coming, Mrs Denton-Hall. And your generous donation is, as always, gratefully received.'

She doesn't reply. Just a slight nod in acknowledgement. Then takes a small bouquet of flowers that she's been holding and places them against a wall in the modest remembrance garden near the entrance.

'Minto?' A voice Stevie doesn't recognise. 'You're Stevie Milloy, aren't ye?'

It's a man who was sat two rows in front of Stevie, across the aisle.

'Eh, aye,' says Stevie. Distracted. He is watching the woman in the camel coat take the arm of a suited man. He watches them walk away slowly, respectfully.

'Whit a day, eh?'

'Aye, miserable,' says Stevie, not sure if the man is referring to the proceedings or the weather.

'Ye were some player, son.'

'That wis a while ago, pal.'

'Afore that bastart Geordie McCracken crocked ye.'

Stevie smirks. 'Sorry, ah didnae catch yer name.'

'That's cos ah didnae throw it.'

Stevie laughs.

'My name's Archie Blunt. It's a real pleasure tae meet ye, son.' Archie Blunt removes his bunnet. They shake hands. 'Ah've mind ae ye at Parkhead a few seasons back. Scored twice against us. Ye ran Benny Rooney an' Boaby Murdoch ragged that day.'

Stevie smiles at the memory. 'Aye, that wis a good game.'

'Ah wanted ye tae sign for us … when Chelsea came in for ye, like, y'know? Ah telt ma da, "That boy's a Celtic player every day ae the week," so ah did.'

'Thanks, sir,' says Stevie. Life might have been better if he had landed at Parkhead. 'So how did ye know Jock?' he asks.

'Ah didnae know him that well, tell ye the honest truth. He'd come doon tae the Barnabas once in a while. Ah dae turns there. Singin' an' that, y'know?'

'Aye.'

'He wis a Sinatra fan. So am ah. We got talkin' between the sets. "Strangers in the Night", that wis his favourite.'

'Ye know the story ae him changin' his name?'

'Naw, ah don't. Like ah says, we didnae know each other that well…'

'Aw, right.'

'Which is why it was weird that he took the heart attack oan my bus.'

'Really? That wis you?'

'Aye. Anybody else, an' they'd probably just've waited tae somebody went intae a shop or somewhere, an' phoned 999. But ah took him straight there. Nurse said it probably saved him. For a coupla days, anyway. Ah'm lookin' at a disciplinary for goin' off route, but ah couldnae have left him oan the bus.'

'Ah'm sure yer gaffers'll appreciate that,' says Stevie.

The camel coat is still in sight. Sheltering under a large umbrella until her car pulls up.

'Ach, ah hope so. Cannae afford tae lose any shifts.'

Stevie notices the envelope Archie is holding.

'Oh aye, there's this,' says Archie, spotting his gaze. 'Nearly forgot. Ah wis tae gie ye this. He had it wi' him oan the bus.'

'What is it?'

'Dunno,' says Archie. 'Didnae open it. Nane ae ma business, like. Ma Bet says tae have a swatch, but ah says naw, nae way.'

'Bet?'

'The wife. We fell oot ower it. Went wi' nae tea 'cos ae the row. But she's just a nosy besom, that yin.'

'How did ye get it?'

'Ah went intae the Victoria that night. Tae check he wis aw'right, an' that. He telt me he worked wi' you at the *Star*. Says that ah'd tae gie you this if anythin' happened tae him. Said ye'd know whit tae dae wi' it.'

Archie hands the bulging envelope to Stevie.

'It's mibbe his last will an' testament. Everythin' he had's yours noo, mibbe.'

Stevie looks at the keys in his hand. 'Ah doubt he had anythin' worth leavin',' he says.

Archie Blunt departs smiling. He has an autograph from a once-famous young football player scrawled on Jock Meikle's order of service.

Stevie wanders over to look at the flowers left by the tiny woman in the camel coat.

The writing on the card reads:

With sincere condolences.

And then typed underneath:

`From the office of James Campbell.`

Fuck sake, Meikle. What were you intae, eh?

'Excuse me, missus,' Stevie shouts. He breaks into an awkward, painful jog.

The woman in the camel coat disappears into the back of a large car with blacked-out windows. A suited man with a peaked cap shakes the water from the huge umbrella. He puts it in the boot. The car door remains slightly open.

'Missus ... Denton-Hall, is it?'

The door closes. But then the window rolls halfway down. She peers out. She lowers her glasses to look at Stevie over the horn-rimmed frame.

'Can ah ask ... about your husband – Jamesie Campbell, isn't it?'

She raises an eyebrow. The man in the peaked cap moves towards Stevie.

'Ah'm lookin' for an opportunity tae talk tae him,' says Stevie. 'An interview, like.'

'Fuck off, pal,' says the peaked cap's owner.

Stevie ignores him. 'Any chance?' pleads Stevie. 'Ah'm a re-porter ... wi' the *Star*. Ah want tae ask him about the Raskine House parties. The Weekenders yins.'

The peaked-cap owner looks behind him. As if waiting for the woman's signal to pummel this insignificant bug into the fine dust this place specialises in.

'What's your name, young man?' asks Maude Denton-Hall.

'Milloy. *Stevie* Milloy. Ah'm Meikle's buddy. Well, ah wis anyway.'

'And what do you know of Raskine House?'

'No' much, just that a young woman fae Lithuania was there before she turned up dead in a field.'

The peaked-cap driver takes a step towards Stevie. He instinc-tively drops a shoulder, as if a ball was at his feet.

'And you are investigating this crime, are you, Mr Milloy?' asks Maude Denton-Hall. She draws out his surname. She won't forget it.

'Tryin' tae,' says Stevie.

'For the *Daily Star*?'

'Well ... aye, just like ah said.'

'And Gerard Keegan is your boss?'

Stevie didn't anticipate being the subject of the questioning.

'Yeah,' he mumbles.

'Well then, I'll be sure to let my husband know you approached me.'

The window closes. The peak-capped driver winks and mouths a silent 'fuck off'. He gets in behind the wheel and drives away. A smaller black car follows them, like it's the woman's security detail.

Fuck.

Stevie parks Meikle's car around the corner from his flat. He abandons it in a dark corner not covered by the streetlights. Hopefully, someone will steal it. Save him the hassle and expense of dealing with it.

He puts on the new Simon & Garfunkel record. He pours a whisky. Three fingers' worth.

He opens the envelope and pulls out the contents.

There are long-form pieces on lined, yellowed paper.

Beautifully hand-written. No mistakes. A proper writer was Meikle.

'*July, she will fly...*

And give no warning to her flight...'

He lifts the needle. It is too distracting. Too personal. Still too raw.

He discovers less-tidy notes. Scribbles. *Aide-memoirs*. Short-hand, which he has now learned to decipher. An elaborate depiction of the life of Albert Raskine, the trader. Notes on the architect of Raskine House. And notes on his barbaric demise.

Stevie finds diagrams. Little sketches. And a more considered drawing entitled 'Raskine House, 1947'.

There are copies of birth certificates. Death certificates. Marriage certificates. And handwritten notes regarding a tragic accident that killed the builder of Raskine House, a man named Jeremiah Hall. But nothing on Albert Raskine's descendants.

Another collection of papers bound with elastic bands reveal that Meikle's mother died in childbirth. Her name was Katherine Margaret Donnachie. She was twenty-one years old. His father, also John Meikle, died in 1928. Cause of death: cirrhosis of the liver.

And then there is a list of female names. First names only and mainly of English origin. But at the bottom there's:

Janina Žukauskas.

Stevie's hand shakes, holding the paper. The poor girl. It seems obvious to him that her murder was covered up, and that the perpetrator didn't die in police custody. Meikle knew that from the very beginning, and these papers prove it, he's sure. As for finding evidence that someone will believe, that's a totally different challenge.

Stevie continues to sift through, and uncovers a *Daily Star* front page from 1945. The copy describes a tragic attack at Raskine House. A nurse killed with a knife by a soldier rehabilitating there. He was disarmed by a fellow soldier; a decorated war hero of the Italian campaign:

Lance Corporal James Campbell.

The photo accompanying the story has a smiling Campbell with an arm around his buddy:

Private Michael McTavish.

Holy fuck! The fucken pastor.

All these connections orbiting around Janina.

Stevie pours another stiff drink. He downs it in one before tipping the contents of the envelope over the floor in front of him.

Elsewhere, there is an arrow-marked map of Kaunas, the second city of Lithuania. A collection of photographs of a prominent red-brick building in the old town area.

The torn, sepia-tinted print of a big, smiling, bearded man

amongst some children; *J.C. – Dec. '53 at House of Perkūnas*, written on the back.

'Jamesie fucken Campbell', Stevie whispers. He pours another stiff drink. Downs it in one. The tremors momentarily subside.

He examines an intriguing page entitled 'Epilogue'.

> *A house is more than the bricks and mortar and wood and glass it is made from. It is imbued with the personality of those who give it life. From the owner to the architect, to the builder, to those who occupy and pass through it, leaving their essence. Genetic molecules that help the organism function and develop. I find that fascinating.*
>
> *Before Raskine House existed on this land, a solitary oak marked the spot she had chosen. She had choices. She picked well. She too was a gardener once upon a time. When the world was young, and all the earth was hers. Life-affirming beauty has not always been the domain of the demonstrably good.*
>
> *'All things bright and beautiful, the Lord God made them all.'*

Stevie is perplexed. At a loss to understand what the contents of this envelope mean. And why Meikle would want him to do something with it.

There's another list of names among the pages. He wonders about their significance.

Bell.

Goldberg.

Guthrie.

Wechter.

All have the word 'deceased' adjacent.

Continuing his trawl, he finds more detail on these names.

Stubby Goldberg

*In 1926, the American silent movie star Noam 'Stubby'
Goldberg rents Raskine House. Stubby is an acquaintance
of Sir Donnachaidh Denton-Hall, and godfather to his son,
Finlay. Stubby is recuperating in Great Britain after badly
damaging a hand while filming with a faulty explosive
prop. Two weeks after taking up residence he returns from
an unsuccessful hunt on the local moors in a fit of rage. He
assaults a housemaid, breaking her jaw. As the stricken
maid raises a hand to defend herself, Stubby's hunting rifle
discharges. The maid dies instantly. Her body is removed
and disposed of by Denton-Hall's people. During a lavish
party the following evening, thrown to celebrate an
Academy Award success, a drunken and coked-out Stubby
accepts a wager from a co-star that he can't reproduce a
stunt from the film. The inebriated star leaps from an
upper landing and catches the outer iron ring of a chandelier. But his broken hand fails him. He loses his grip. He
falls thirty feet, his head hitting the marble flooring before
the rest of him. He dies instantly.*

Patrick Guthrie

*Raskine House is hired in 1957 by the eccentric filmmaker
Patrick Guthrie. Guthrie is a close personal friend of Finlay
Denton-Hall. They met as seven-day-a-week boarders at
Glenalmond College. Guthrie distributes his 8mm 'glamour'
home movies discreetly by mail order. His clientele includes
several government ministers and their opposition shadows,
as well as high-ranking members of the British judiciary.
Guthrie's latest film is to be entitled* The Lady and the Lay-
about. *It will contain a scene featuring a suspended harness.
In testing the harness, Guthrie forces a Raskine House
servant to perform fellatio on him. Under stress, the hook detaches. The ceiling – rose and all – comes down. Guthrie*

overbalances, falling backwards out of the swing. He breaks his neck. He dies instantly.

The Denton-Hall organisation cleans it up and buries the story. Like it never happened.

They have become adept at this.

<u>*Wilhelm Wechter*</u>

In 1941, Wilhelm Wechter pilots a Messerschmitt Bf 110 stolen from somewhere in Bavaria. The plane crosses the English Channel, miraculously avoiding RAF manoeuvres. Flying at low level over the Scottish borders, the plane runs out of fuel, crash-landing in a field near Eaglesham. Wechter's passenger, Rudolf Hess, breaks an ankle on impact. Unable to escape, Hess is found and detained by an Ayrshire farmer, but Wechter disappears into the thick gorse, eventually finding his way to Raskine House. The high-ranking SS officer – known as the Butcher of Krakow – initially holes up in the woods on the Raskine House Estate, living off animal scraps. Forty-three days after Rudolf Hess is imprisoned in the Tower of London, a parlour maid discovers his fellow Nazi stealing a ham hock from the Raskine House kitchen. He drags her into a milking shed. Convinced no-one has seen or heard the incident, Wachter rapes the girl. She jabs him in the cheek with a concealed fork. His agonised howl alerts a stable groom. Wechter escapes, running to an adjacent field, where he is gored by a black bull. He dies instantly. His body is never found.

Stevie thinks it's safe to assume Bell has a story too.

While looking for it, he discovers an envelope inside the bigger envelope. It contains a few pages of typed script on good-quality, embossed paper.

The Origins of Raskine House (1769)
by Andrew J. Donnachie

Jeremiah Hall is a busy man. His fingers invade many pies. Since he first established himself through brute force and fortuitous opportunity, he and his four sons have monopolised the construction and expansion of Glasgow's West End, which has been funded by the proceeds of trade: whether it be slavery or other commodities. He doesn't need the Raskine House commission – this challenging vanity project for a foolish rich man with suspect judgement and abhorrent morals. And he fears Albert Raskine, the naïve merchant whose house and estate Hall is building, will run out of money before his bill is settled.

Any fiduciary concerns vanish when Albert Raskine pays in advance. £15,000 in cash. An enormous sum of money. Jeremiah Hall appreciates, more than most, the opportunity to separate a fool from his wealth. So he and his sons accept this commission, primarily as a way of teaching this dissident libertarian an expensive lesson about free enterprise. About a righteous imperialist worldview. About right and wrong. Raskine is far travelled, Hall acknowledges, but it is well known that he shares his house, and it seems, his bed, with an outspoken black woman who sailed to Glasgow on Raskine's ship on its most recent return from the Americas. His mind and faculties have obviously been poisoned against God by the barbarous primitive practices Raskine has witnessed there.

The house, designed by architect Jefferson

McGovern, has a typically symmetric square floor plan, predicated on the classical H-shape proportions. In the centre of its formal front-facing facade, four rounded Corinthian pillars support a substantial entablature. To his chagrin, Jeremiah Hall is instructed by the dominant black woman to find a craftsman who can sculpt the modillions in the shape of mandrake leaves. Struggling to contain his rage, the builder ignores the black woman's command. His stonemasons carve column brackets formed in acanthus-leaf designs. Desultory and discourteous, Hall then charges Raskine eight times the normal rate. When challenged, he will not rectify the work.

Months pass with no contact between client and constructor. A day after the building and its immediate estate infrastructure is completed by his craftsmen, Hall returns to Raskine House for the remainder of his remittance. Albert Raskine is already gone. At sea. A short trip to Spain this time. The dominant black woman is home, clearly pregnant, and refusing to accede to Hall's demands.

How objectionable for a God-fearing pillar of decent society to be spoken to so disrespectfully. By what heavenly rights are Albert Raskine and his pregnant Caribbean whore able to challenge him?

Jeremiah Hall is convinced Albert Raskine is the father of the soon-to-be-born bastard. God's natural hegemony being flouted so outrageously in front of him.

The builder's contemptible disgust for this immoral parvenu is complete. His tumultuous fury cannot be contained. He yells aggressively. He demands his money. Raskine's limited household staff cower. His horsewhip finds the face of two females and a male. Blood is drawn. The black woman intervenes. She lays hands on him. She invokes Satan. She lays a de Maupassant family curse on Jeremiah Hall, his children, and his children's children. The Devil will take his yard, she tells him. Snakes and demons will torment his progeny for all eternity, she claims. And finally to Jeremiah Hall himself, she foretells of a painful, sudden death.

She points at him, a long-nailed finger lingering in the air inches from his face.

He steps backward, shocked at the effrontery. The horsewhip cracks on the black woman's cheek. She staggers but remains upright. Hall drops a shoulder and lands a sharp southpaw jab. A gold ring bearing the face of the sovereign cuts deep into the corner of her mouth. She pitches backward from the former streetfighter's blow. She steps on her dress and trips. The back of her head hits the marble with a loud, dull crack. As she lies on the floor, her dark-red blood spreads until it laps against the enormous Far Eastern rug that perfectly complements the vast reception room's impressive volume.

Jeremiah Hall staggers back. He wipes a dry mouth with a silk handkerchief. His hand tremors. He is suddenly shocked and fearful. His breathing is erratic. He looks up and around the vast reception hall. He feels eyes on him, but it seems that no-one has witnessed the brutal act of violence. He needs to be gone from this place.

He reassures himself, tries to compose his mind. Adjusts his attire and quickly leaves. Outside, his horse is gone. Its reins were tied tightly around the stone newel cap. But the animal is nowhere to be seen. There is no sound outside Raskine House. No birdsong. No breeze blowing tree branches. No livestock mooing from the byres. Nothing other than Jeremiah Hall's laboured wheezing.

A thick fog is descending. He feels the intense tightening of his chest. The hunger for air that is thinning around him. The panic of being found here, miles from civilisation, the stench of a dead, pregnant black woman clinging to him like a skin he now can't shed. Suddenly, he hears a voice. Angelic. Youthful. Soothing. It is calling him.

'Mr Jeremiah Hall, Mr Jeremiah Hall,' the siren repeats.

He spins around. Looking forlornly. But there is no-one there. He is alone, in the middle of a nowhere that even God has forsaken.

'Mr Jeremiah Hall, Mr Jeremiah Hall.'

The voice; beautiful and hypnotic. He lifts his head. That glorious voice is coming from the upper window. From the salon on the first floor. The room containing nothing but an unusual white, card table whose marble top bears a distinctive hoof mark.

Jeremiah Hall looks upward. An odd light penetrates the fog. He lifts a hand to shade his eyes. A heavy piece of the portico's stone architrave detaches. It falls squarely onto the head of Jeremiah Hall, smashing through flesh and

bone and bursting the builder's head as if it
were a ripened tomato flattened by a cook's
mallet.

Jeremiah Hall is killed instantly, his
features unrecognisable. His body, remarkably,
is not damaged.

By some preternatural miracle, the unborn
child being carried by the dead black woman –
whose blood has infused the enormous and
sumptuous Far Eastern rug – survives.

You may run on for a long time but, sooner or
later, God will cut you down.

Stevie bypasses the glass and reaches for the bottle. He takes
on a mouthful and swiftly swallows it. He shakes his head at the
papers strewn around him. He doubts himself; his ability to piece
together what Meikle was pursuing.

And then he spots a smaller envelope. A white one. Newer than
the rest. It has slipped into a grooved joint between the floor-
boards. Unsealed, and with *MILLOY* scrawled on the front.
Stevie's heartrate increases. He opens the envelope and pulls out
a folded note, grubby, but in Meikle's perfect handwriting:

*As inconceivable as it seemed, I knew it was him. The moment
I saw him, standing in front of me, dogs straining on a leash
to get at me. A shotgun crooked over his arm. Before he said
a word. Before he grabbed my jacket. Before he let the dogs at
me. Before he punched my face. Before he put me in a head-
lock, just like he did regularly when we were children.*

*St Mary's Roman Catholic Industrial School was where,
from 1927 until 1932, he and I were inmates. Two out of
thirty-three little bastards. He was not the oldest of us, but
he was the biggest. The strongest. The most forceful. Those terrible things, the sins of the flesh, that were visited upon him*

by those voracious priests, he inflicted on several of us. The youngest. The smallest. The weakest.

I stood in front of him that day in 1950. Trembling. Fearful.

'What's your fucken name, you little prick?' he yelled at me repeatedly. It had been nearly twenty years. He did not recognise me. Given what he then did to me, I often wonder what difference it would have made if he had.

'Jock Meikle,' I lied.

'Ye're tresspassin'.'

'Ah'm a writer.'

'Think ah gie a fuck about that, son?'

Would our previous association have made him more lenient, or less? Less lenient could only have meant death, because he dehumanised me that day. Took me to the very brink of dying. When all I wanted was to ask some questions. About the building. About those who owned it now. About the people I was interested in tracing.

He dragged me back to the house. Not through it though. I saw a woman's face at a window. I don't know if he knew we were being watched. He pushed me into a remote shed about a hundred yards to the rear. He smashed my mouth. Broke my teeth. He tortured me. He repeatedly strung me up by the neck. He drove a garden fork right through my foot. Thankfully, I passed out.

I awoke in hospital. Driven there, I was told. An envelope addressed to Mr John Meikle was given to me. It contained a handwritten letter apologising for any misunderstanding, a ten-pound note, and the offer of employment writing for the Denton-Hall group of newspapers.

My abuser's name is James Campbell, and he is married to Maude Denton-Hall, the daughter of Lord Finlay Denton-Hall, proprietor of the newspaper group that I still take wages from.

You asked about protection?
I take their money – and they pay very well – in return
for my silence.
A modern-day slave with secrets of my own.
That is my hypocrisy.
My shame.

Stevie's eyes hurt. His head's sore. A vehicle and voices out in street interrupt the silence. He looks at his watch. Ten past six. It's the milk float.

A full shift studying photographs and maps, and reading notes and clippings and the structure of … what? An autobiography? A fiction? Evidence of criminality? Whatever it is, it appears to be a picture of an establishment covering up historical scandals at Raskine House that include religious cults, drug-taking movie-makers, and the fucking Third Reich. If even a fraction of what Meikle has written is true, what else were they concealing? The truth about a young woman's murder?

And Big Jamesie Campbell. What of *him*?

Abused abuser from a Roman Catholic school for orphaned boys.

Married to Maude Denton-Hall.

Son-in-law of Lord Finlay Denton-Hall.

Army comrade of Pastor Michael McTavish.

Employer of Denice Milloy *née* Rodman.

Associate of Scot Symon and Geordie McCracken.

At the fucking centre of everything.

A cog in the wheel?

Or the one who makes it turn?

+

14th October

'No' sure ye'd remember me?' says Stevie.

'Pretty face like yours? How could ah forget.'

'Ah saw ye at Meikle's funeral a coupla weeks back. Didnae get the chance tae say hullo.'

'Aye, well ... He was a decent man. Dug me out a hole a few times.'

Stevie leans over and sparks the lighter. Mags hold the fag over the flame and draws heavily. Half an inch of it lights and instantly becomes ash. She flicks it out of the window. But it lands on the door handle of Meikle's car. Stevie lights his own. Their smoke coalesces in front of their faces.

'Ye looked different,' he says.

'No' like a hoor, ye mean?'

'Sorry. Ah didnae mean it like that.'

'It's a uniform, son. Just like a nurse, or a fireman. They dinnae sit in the hoose wearin' it. Neither dae we.'

'Ah just meant that ah didnae recognise ye wi'...'

'Ma clothes oan?'

'Ach, naw,' he says. Wishing he hadn't started. 'Yer hair wis different.' He struggles to rescue the situation. 'Ye looked nice.'

'An' whit – ye sayin' ah look like a bowl ae dug meat now?'

'Aw for fuck's sake.'

She laughs. He does too.

'Can we start ower?' he says.

Mags adjusts her skirt. Pulls it down, but it still leaves the top of her pink thighs showing. She is aware of Stevie trying not to look.

'Meikle bailed me out a time or two. But he wisnae a punter.'

'Did he go wi' any ae the other girls fae the square?'

She laughs. He isn't in on the joke.

'Naw, naw,' she says. 'Yer man liked the men, y'know? The *young* men. Wi' the dark skin.'

'Jesus. Yer jokin''

'See that tan he had? They teeth? Got them in Morocco.'

'Whit?'

'Spent aw his money ower in Tangiers. Went there regular, so he did.'

'For sex?'

'An' sunshine ... an' cosmetic dentistry.'

'Fuck sake. Secrets of his own, right enough,' says Stevie. 'It wisnae the weights he wis interested in liftin' then.' He smiles and shakes his head. 'This motor an' the manky flat – ah wondered whit he wis doin' wi' aw his wages.'

'His business. Ah didnae ask. He telt me. We dinnae judge folks' weird kinks. No' doon here.'

'Naw,' says Stevie. 'Me neither. Each tae his ain, eh?'

'Meikle wis a good man. He wis ay' helpin' the lassies oot when they were short.'

'So did he dole oot cash roon' the square for favours, or information?'

'Bit ae both,' she says. She stubs out the butt. 'Whit's wi' aw the questions? Has he left a will?'

'Naw. Ah'm just tryin' tae clear up somethin' he was workin' on, that's aw.'

He hands her another cigarette. Lights it.

'He had this list ae names. Bella, Evie, Angie, Sadie, Sophia ... Mags.'

She looks up.

'Ah'm assumin' that's you. An' other lassies fae the square.'

'Well, it's no' oor real names, obviously, but, aye, what of it?'

'There's a *Janina* tae...'

'Unusual name. Foreign?' asks Mags.

'We were investigatin' a murder. Victim's name was Janina Žukauskas. Odd that he had the same name oan a list ae prostitutes.'

'You're startin' tae sound like a polis, son.' Her tone suddenly serious.

'It's no' that, Mags. Honest. Ah cannae get this lassie Janina's face out ma head. It's there aw the time, hauntin' me. Meikle was on tae somethin' that links her tae a raft ae Glasgow bigwigs. He left me wi' ... ah dunno, clues. Lists an' pictures an' maps...'

'Maps?'

'Aye ... Kaunas.'

'Where?'

'It's in Lithuania.'

'Nane the wiser, luv.'

'In Russia.' She shrugs. 'Like odd bits ae a jigsaw puzzle, an' ah cannae work out whit the full picture is,' says Stevie.

'Ah'm no' sure ah can help ye.'

'Ye ever heard ae a place called Raskine House?'

Mags turns her head. She looks at him strangely. 'What did he know about up there?'

'That's what ah'm tryin' tae find out.'

'Look, son, ah need tae be headin'.'

'Ah think Meikle might've been related tae the folk that built the place. He was doin' family trees an' aw sorts, right back tae when the place was built.'

'Fascinatin'.' Her eyebrows arch. The eyes below them widen. The sarcasm hammered home.

'Did ye know that wisnae his ain name?'

'Naw, ah didnae. No' until the minister mentioned it, anyway.'

'Donnachie wis his ma's name,' he says.

'Mibbe just didnae want folk tae know he wis born a bastart, eh? How should ah know?'

'Look, aboot Raskine House ... dae ye know what goes on there, Mags?'

She draws in deeply. He senses that she is weighing the risks of telling him what she knows. And that it isn't simply about the right price for the information. She puts a hand over her mouth.

'Tell me, will ye?'

'Look,' she says. 'Sometimes yer nose gets ye intae trouble, right? Ye see an' hear things in this game that ye dinnae want tae hear. Wish ye hudnae heard. Ye know what ah mean?'

'Aye,' says Stevie. But he doesn't know what she means.

She rolls the car window up. Turns the volume dial on the radio sharply to the right. If she suspects Meikle's car is bugged, The Lovin Spoonful are going to give her a degree of plausible deniability.

'There's a group ae posh folk...' She is whispering. Stevie leans closer, unable to hear over the American group's din. 'Rich men mainly. The lassies call them "the Weekenders". Every month they haud a big boozy shindig at that place. Been goin' oan for years.'

'At Raskine House?'

'Aye. The Denton-Hall place away out oan the moors. Ye know him, right, Finlay Denton-Hall? ... He owns the paper ye're workin' for.'

'Ah know who he is, aye. Never met him though.'

'Well, him an' aw his posh, wealthy pals. Judges. Politicians. Actors. Folk off the telly. Fitba players. They're aw there.'

'Fitba players?'

'Aye. Ah wis telt that the Scotland captain wis there once.'

'So whit happens at them?'

She shrugs. 'Ah don't know, dae ah? Ah've never been asked.'

'Whit d'ye mean *asked*?'

'Some ae the lassies – the young yins – they get invited up.'

'For sex? Is it an orgy or somethin'?'

'Ah telt ye ah don't know. We dinnae talk about hires an' business. There's a bloody code here, ye know.' She says this unconvincingly. The queen's head on a sheet will break this code as easily as Stevie's passes used to break a stubborn defensive line.

Stevie shifts the focus. 'Ye hear ae a Janina Žukauskas? Is she fae the square?'

'Never heard that name before.'

He holds up a five-pound note. It's been a while since she's seen that much money.

'Ah've nae change for *that*, son.'

Having tempted her with it, he withdraws it. He's learning the game.

'Look Mags, thanks anyway. Ah'm just tryin' tae dae the right thing for Meikle.'

'Ach, for Christ's sake,' she says. 'No' a word ae this tae anybody else, right?'

Stevie nods. He gives her the cash.

'Ange telt me it wis great up there. They'd send a taxi. Pick the lassies up. Take them away oot there oan the moors. Get them dressed nice. Feed them an' water them, an' it wis just a party. Champagne, chocolates, the works. Serious drugs tae, but naebody forced tae take anythin' they didnae want. There wis sex, aye, but nae weird shite. Well, no' at first. An' no' outside in the cold an' the rain like here in the lanes. Inside. In the warm. Oan eiderdown blankets or animal-skin rugs in front ae a log fire. The ones that went loved it. Ah wis as jealous as fuck.'

'You never went?'

'Too auld, son. They only wanted the young lassies, the yins wi' nae pimps,' she says. 'Anyway, them that went got paid a fortune. Same deal every time. A bloody great hustle, Angie said. That's aw ah know.'

Stevie pulls out another fiver. It is all he has. He might need to scadge food from old Alf for a few nights. Nonetheless, he dangles the bait.

'Ye sure?' he says.

'You're just like the rest ae them,' she says. 'Think money'll get ye anythin' ye want.'

'An' will it?'

She snatches it from him, thinking, *Ten quid? Just for providing some gossip?* Equal to her weekly wage at Betty's Hair Salon. And when compared to her night-shift job, she doesn't have to get some dirty aul' beggar's smelly cock shoved into her mouth.

Okay. Deal.

'A few months ago, it aw stopped up there. Ange says it wis because this foreign lassie starts a ruckus in one ae the bedrooms. A right rammy, Angie says. Screamin' and yellin' like she's been chibbed or somethin'. The men start panickin'. Gaun absolutely tonto at this wee minister.'

'A church minister?'

'Aye, a wee holy Wullie.'

'An' then what?' asks Stevie.

'So the game's a bogey. Everybody gets huckled oot, quick smart. Drapped back at the Anderston Bus depot. Nae money, nothin'. Just a serious warnin' about spillin' the beans tae anybody.'

'That's weird, naw?'

'Well, the warnin' would've been a bit pointless, ah suppose. Where were the lassies gonnae go? The polis? Nae chance. The papers? Denton-Hall owns them aw. But the threats – they were enough tae put the shits right up ye, Ange said.'

Stevie mulls this over.

'Look son, ah need tae go.'

'One last question?'

She sighs deeply. 'Value for fucken money, eh?'

He smiles. 'Dae ye know Big Jamesie Campbell?'

'Aye.'

'Is *he* a punter?'

She looks at the two fivers in her hand. She folds the cash and puts it inside her bra.

'He's the one that pays the girls. He was the one that threatened them.'

+

20th October

'Ah'm sorry, we don't have anyone here of that name.'

Fuck sake.

He's in a phone box. He's had a drink. Followed by three more. At the end of a full week's indulgence. Sustenance for the job at hand.

'Rodman, then? Denice Rodman. Can ah speak tae her?'

'Ah, okay. Hold on. Who should I say's callin'?'

'It's her husb— ... Tell her it's Stevie.'

Stevie watches three gulls attack chips that a lolloping drunk has dropped. They finish and fly off before the drunk notices the chips are no longer in his hand. Stevie takes his coins and puts them on the top of the phone.

'Hello?'

'Denice, it's Stevie.' He is slurring his words.

She can tell immediately. 'Is everythin' okay?'

'Aye. Fine. Ah got the papers. Ah'll get them signed an' back tae yer solicitors.'

'Thanks, Stevie. I appreciate that.' Stevie notices her diction. The rough edges of their last exchanges before she left him all gone. Smoothed out. 'Are you alright?'

'Look, Den ... that's no' why ah'm callin'. Ah'm lookin' for a favour.'

'What kind of favour?'

'Ah'm tryin' tae get a word wi' yer boss.'

'Mr Campbell?'

'Aye. Is he in?'

'No, he's out at Sovereign Grace all of this week – for their fundraisers. Is it an interview? For the *Star*?'

'Naw ... no' that exactly. It's more ae a ... a private word. Jis' him an' me, like.'

'I told you before, Stevie, you can't just use me like this. It doesn't work like that,' she says. 'Look, is everything okay?'

'Tip-top, Den. Can ye sort it, eh? It's important. Ah need this.'

'What's it about? I need to know what the subject is, an' even then...'

She's being paid to be suspicious. If Stevie wasn't sure what her job was, he now knows. Denice is Big Jamesie Campbell's secretary.

'Denice, have ye ever been up at Raskine House?'

'Mr Campbell's home? Yes, why?'

'At the weekends?'

'No, of course not.' She is annoyed. It is beginning to feel like an interrogation. 'Look, Stevie, what are ye askin' me that for? Are you investigatin' him?'

'Naw...' The pips. 'Ach, fuck sake ... hullo? Ye there? Wait a minute.' He forces the coins in. 'Den? Denice?'

Silence.

'Are ye still there?'

'Yeah, I'm still here. Now, tell me. What are you doin'?'

He dithers. He hasn't thought this through properly. Hasn't considered how it sounds. He's forced to acknowledge that he doesn't know what he is doing. The booze emboldened him, but now it is polluting the messages leading from his brain to his mouth. He fights the impulse to set them free and say: *Ah think yer new boss was involved in the brutal murder ae a foreign lassie. Aye, she might've been a prostitute. Killed an' dumped, an' now the murder's bein' covered up ... so, any chance ae ye organisin' a wee word wi' him for me?*

He takes a breath. 'Sorry, ah just need to talk with him. Is he there?'

'Stevie, if this is a proper press request, it needs to come through from the *Star* in writing. Ye should know this already. Mr Campbell only deals with certain contacts from the Denton-Hall Group.'

'It's no' an official request. Ah just want a word—'

'He's not here, Stevie. He's out.'

A voice in the background. Male: 'Denice. Everythin' okay?'

'That him? Shoutin' ye?'

'What?'

The male voice again: 'Denice.'

'I need to go.'

'Yer man, the Boaby cunt?'

'Look Stevie, ah'm goin' tae bloody hang up. Don't call me here again!'

She's back; the Denice he remembers.

'Denice! Hang up the phone. Now!'

'Ah can hear him there. Is that him? The fucken Boaby cunt?' Stevie shouts.

Click.

+

23rd October

'Ye aw'right there, son?'

'Aye, Alf, never better.'

'It's just ... ah huvnae seen ye aboot as much lately.'

'Been busy, pal. Work's a bit mental, y'know?'

Alf stands in his doorway. Like an old shopkeeper out to greet his customers. Hair combed, side-shed perfect. Blue V-necked jumper over shirt and tie. Dress trousers with creases so sharp they could cut a block of cheese. A pair of old slippers peek out from the bottoms, but other than that, he's prepared for anything.

'Fancy nippin' in, Stevie? Ah'll fix ye a sandwich. Mibbe some tea.'

'Ah've nae time. Thanks though.'

Stevie hunts for his key. He can't find it. He has to put the carrier bag down to search his pockets.

'Got somebody over?' asks Alf.

'Eh?' Stevie turns and sees Alf clocking the three whisky bottles in the bag.

'Aye ... somethin' like that,' adds Stevie.

'Best be layin' off the booze, son,' says Alf quietly. This meeting in the hallway is not coincidental.

'Whit?'

'Ah'm worried about ye, Stevie, son. Yer hittin' the bottle pretty hard.'

'Christ's sake, Alf. Mind yer ain business, mate.'

Stevie pats himself down.

'It's no' gonnae bring her back, son.'

Stevie halts the search for his key. 'Whit did you say?' He takes a step towards the old man, fist clenched before he gets a grip of himself. He uses the hand to point instead. 'Ah dinnae bloody want her back. Ah'm fine oan my own.' He knows he isn't. 'She can go an' fuck herself for aw ah care.'

'Ah just dinnae want ye tae throw yer life away, Stevie.'

'Well ah'm no' gonnae, right. You awa' an' bother about yersel, granda.'

'Stevie...'

'Look, just butt out, Alf. Understand? Or ye'll be pushin' up the daisies quicker than ye think.'

The door shuts. Stevie is left out in the close. Alone.

Something is happening here, but he doesn't know what it is.

He finds his key. Back trouser pocket, left-hand side. Snagged in the torn lining.

He thinks about chapping Alf's door to apologise. Decides to leave it for now. Best to do it later. When his head's right.

He stumbles over the threshold. Into the toilet. The person looking back at him is someone he doesn't recognise. The sharp clothes. The Tonic suit. The cool hair. The trim physique. All gone. In their place, a shirt missing two buttons because a constrained belly is trying to burst out of it. Stained trousers; piss and booze. A fortnight's stubble. And hair like a school janny's used sick mop.

'Ach, Alf,' he mutters. Embarrassed. Ashamed. 'Fuck.'

The drinking is getting too much. But he can stop. Anytime. Just better to be when this obsession with Geordie McCracken is done. When Stevie proves the cunt is in up to his eyes in a murder that the cops are covering up.

He puts on a new record. And sniggers as Bobby Fuller sings, *'I left my baby and it feels so bad. I guess my race is run.'*

He slumps in his seat. Slurps the booze from the bottle. And falls asleep.

+

24th October

Stevie wakes. A bin lorry outside. The whisky bottle is on its side. Capsized in a puddle of its own contents. Stevie breathes in and the fumes catch his throat. Luckily, he didn't have a fag in his hand last night or the whole block would be up in flames right now.

He feels the pain. The ghosts of old injuries returning to ache his entire body. Tremors rolling in waves down to his fingertips. He gingerly washes the stink off himself with a cold, wet flannel. First time clean water has touched his skin in a week.

He forages for food. Finds only stale bread and a tin of corned beef. Beggars can't be choosers.

Somewhat revived, Stevie files three stories. The shakes subside. The brain is sharp enough for the tabloid task. And the words still flow mechanically, if a little cliché-ridden. An easy procedural Celtic home win against Aberdeen. A brief interview with Celtic manager Jock Stein, previewing the club's European Cup second-round tie away to Nantes. And a court report on the sentencing of Bernard Rayner, a Duntocher dentist convicted of sexually assaulting three women while they were under anaesthetic. What he can't recall, or decipher from his notes, he fabricates. These get Keegan off his back and provide the window he needs.

He heads to the East End for the second time in a week. Four days after Denice hung up on him. Meikle's car spits exhaust fumes into the already polluted Glaswegian air. He pulls up across the street from the mission. Fifty yards along London Road from the cop shop. He rolls the window halfway down. It won't go further.

He watches upright, uniformed bobbies coming and going in packs. Travelling the beat from the station to the Sovereign Grace Mission. Hard to imagine that religious succour is their purpose.

Half past two. A miserable, grey Glasgow afternoon. Big Jamesie Campbell's car appears. Same time as yesterday. A Jaguar. Black. Film-darkened windows. A driver opens his door, and Campbell gets out of the vehicle like a mob boss. All heft and substance.

Big Jamesie checks the street. Both ways. Secure in the knowledge that he is the biggest threat around. He strides up to the arched opening, driver a pace behind. Big Jamesie glad-hands two elders. Leans down. Kisses a small woman on the cheek. Passes a white envelope to another man. All five disappear inside the Sovereign Grace Mission's substantial wooden doors. The doors close with an audible thud and the driver returns to the car.

The booze is still in Stevie Milloy. It never leaves his system these days. Just gets replenished when the tank is running low. He shouldn't be driving. Yet here he is. Half-cut in the middle of the afternoon. Again. The whisky encourages him. Goads him.

Ye're close, Stevie boy. The last lap. Go on, son.

He reaches for the silver case. Flips it open. No fags left. Typical. He drops the box. Can't reach it under the seat.

If yer half the man ye think ye are, fucken show it, Minto.

C'mon, son.

Fucken do that McCracken cunt.

Show him up for the murderin' bastart that he is.

Bring this whole protected racket down like a house ae fucken cards.

Show Denice.

Show her yer better than him.

Better than aw ae them.

The best there is.

Stevie shouldn't be here. He shouldn't be creeping around the rear of this house of God.

Looking for answers to questions he cannot properly form.

Looking for revenge.

Looking for Meikle's denouement.

Looking for his own purpose.

Looking for a life less lonely.

Looking for a fucking way in.

Caught in a cleft stick.

Stevie takes a breath. It's as if he knows that the direction of his life will change irrevocably if he enters this building. He thinks about Meikle. What he went through as a younger man, and then the choice he made to suppress that knowledge. But was that really a choice? If Meikle had turned down the job at the *Star* and the paid protection that went with it, Jamesie Campbell could've – *would've* – made him disappear. Maude Denton-Hall's conscience wouldn't have saved him. But Meikle undoubtedly wanted to do the right thing. Particularly when it became obvious that poor Janina Žukauskas was a victim of Campbell's crime syndicate.

Like it or not, Meikle had chosen Stevie to do what he couldn't. Maybe he had been too ashamed to tell Stevie directly. Maybe he'd trusted him to figure it out from the assembled clues. Stevie owes it to Meikle to bring it all tumbling down. He owes it to Denice to make sure she gets out while she still can. But above all, he owes it to Janina Žukauskas, and however many other missing or un-identified young women there might be. He unscrews the top of a silver hip flask. Luxuriates in the warm, throaty burn. And then pulls on his gloves.

He forces a window. Clambers through it, catching his trousers on the head of a nail sitting an inch proud of the sill.

Fuck it.

He pulls up the ripped trouser leg, surprised to see blood dribble down his scarred shin from a deep cut just below the knee. Booze and adrenaline are doubling up to anaesthetise what would otherwise have hurt like fuck.

He looks around himself. He's in a cold, empty kitchen. A tap drip-drips determinedly onto disregarded crockery. He pulls a door handle, but it only reveals a cupboard with buckets and mops lined up. He pulls another. There's activity beyond, to the right. He follows the distant sounds of voices. Down a dark, unlit corridor with walls painted with sickly Corporation-green emulsion.

Two left turns. Through two open doors. And he's standing at the edge of a church hall containing almost fifty people, buzzing like flies around the big man in the centre. The Labour Party candidate for Shettleston East. Jamesie Campbell.

Stevie stays in the shadows, like he imagines Perry Mason would. He watches a range of activities play out, Big Jamesie Campbell the focal point of them all. Talking, gesticulating, to men in suits mainly. Autographing photographs. Posing for flashbulb pictures. Patting the heads of small children. And the white envelopes: collecting them and then passing them, via an intermediary, to the man from outside, who is now sitting at a table in the far corner of the room.

Stevie hears the faint sound of a cistern flushing. It comes from behind him. And then:

'Can ah help ye, son?' The voice, soft yet firm. It's the pastor from the police station. McTavish. 'Ye look lost,' says Pastor McTavish.

If he recognises Stevie from the Cranstonhill presser, he isn't showing it. It is dark in the hallway. Stevie's grateful for the cover.

'Ah wis just at the loo. Got a bit lost on the way back, that's aw. Thanks,' says Stevie.

'Are ye a volunteer?'

'For the church?' Stevie replies.

The pastor smiles. 'No, for the campaign?' He considers Stevie's perplexed look. 'Are ye one ae Big Jamesie's team?'

'Em, no' exactly.'

'Well, what are ye exactly?' A shift in tone.

Stevie shuffles. 'Ah'm a reporter. From the *Star*. Ah'm lookin' tae get a wee word wi' Mr Campbell.'

They move into the light. Examining each other's faces for clues.

'Well, let me see if ah can help ye there, then.'

Stevie watches the pastor walk away. He limps badly. He requires the aid of a stick. The stick is wooden. It strikes the concrete floor like a drumstick hitting a paving slab. There's no rubber stopper on the end of it to dampen the sound.

Reaching the big man, the pastor leans in and whispers to him. As he listens, Campbell's gaze fixes on Stevie.

Stevie's senses might be blunted by the booze and the insomnia, but Meikle's muddled pieces are slowly falling into place. McTavish and Campbell. Army comrades. Raskine House inpatients. The Denton-Hall Russian connections in Lithuania. Young women being trafficked from behind the Iron Curtain for protected, privileged men of the Scottish establishment to abuse. Traded like modern-day slaves and with the Church providing cover.

This is too big for him. These ruthless people will squash him like a fucking beetle crawling across the floor.

Seconds pass. They feel like hours to him. The exits are at the other end of the hall – beyond the group of men now staring at him like he was naked. A leper. His horrible afflictions exposed for all to see.

For Stevie, time seems to stand still. The movement of all others in the room temporarily paused. The four men facing him fan out slightly and contemplate him, this novice acting only on his inebriated wits.

Big Jamesie's head tilts slightly. Hands now down by his sides. Like this is a gunfight in a Hollywood western and he is preparing to draw.

The big man nods. And the slow walk towards Stevie begins. Big Jamesie's bulk blurs Stevie's peripheral vision. The three deputies drop back a step, but their sheriff's advance is all Stevie can focus on. The hat tipped back, Sinatra-style. The black jacket. The pin-striped waistcoat. The gold watch chain. The black tie, harnessing a wide, white shirt collar. The dark-grey trousers turned up and sharply creased. The black brogues, polished to pass even the most stringent army barracks inspection. The beard. Thin lips parting confidently for the tongue to lick them. The beady, narrowing black eyes. Closer. Coming close. So close now that Stevie can feel Jamesie's hot, fetid breath.

'Stevie, int'it?' says Big Jamesie. 'Milloy. The fitba player turned rovin' reporter.'

The three who have accompanied Big Jamesie across the church hall snigger. One of them with a face like a human Spirograph, so densely interwoven is the pronounced scar tissue.

'Ah saw ye play a couple ae times. Decent left foot.'

'Aye, well ... no' anymore,' says Stevie.

'Workin' wi' the *Star* now ah hear? How's that goin'? Eddie Pink an' that lot aw lookin' after ye?'

Stevie's not sure how to answer. How to behave. How to extract himself from a situation that he's so ill-prepared for.

'Are yer hauns cold?' asks Big Jamesie. 'Or just worried aboot leavin' yer dabs when ye broke in earlier?'

Stevie removes the gloves. He jams them in his pocket.

'So, whit can ah do ye for, son?' asks Big Jamesie.

Fuck it!

'We're lookin' intae the murder ae Janina Žukauskas.'

'We?' asks Big Jamesie. 'Or just you?'

'She worked at Raskine House. That's your place, isn't it?'

'Why don't we take this intae a side room, son.'

'So ye can batter the fuck out ae me?'

Big Jamesie laughs. Looks back at his comrades as if Stevie had just farted.

'Well, only if that's what yer intae, Stevie,' he says. 'An' ye've got the readies tae pay for it.'

They all laugh. Big, deep, guttural laughs. The laughs of men who know they are untouchable.

'Boaby?' ushers Big Jamesie, with a sweeping arm.

Boaby? The Boaby cunt?

The Boaby cunt drapes a massive arm around Stevie's drooping shoulders. He escorts him back up the dark corridor. Stevie's heart is trying to escape through his ribcage. Thumping against the sides. Skull aching as his brain tries to rid itself of thoughts of this six-foot-plus gorilla's massive cock all but splitting Denice in two. And of her lapping up the pain, screaming: *Stick it tae me, Boaby, ya massive big cunt ... you're twice the man Minto is.*

'In here,' says Big Jamesie.

Stevie is huckled into a tiny, windowless room. There's a table and two chairs.

Stevie is guided towards one. Big Jamesie takes the other. He sits, one flared trouser leg folded over its partner. His hat dropped onto one knee. He fingers the brim. Laconic. Relaxed. Untouchable.

Stevie coughs. Palpitations interrupt his breathing. He tries to regulate it. He pants. Like a man who has just single-handedly pushed a piano up a hill.

'Get him a drink,' says Big Jamesie. 'Looks like he could dae wi' a stiff yin.'

'Ah'm fine,' says Stevie, not fine.

A flex with a bare bulb hangs from the ceiling. No carpet. No sound absorption. Surely somebody in the big church hall will hear the screaming when they start pulling out his fingernails and teeth.

'That poor wee lassie's murder ... they got somebody for it. He confessed, did he no'?' Big Jamesie looks behind himself for assurance. 'Detained at Her Majesty's pleasure oot at the Carstairs loony bin, naw?'

'Aye, he is boss,' says the Boaby cunt.

'So, where's the story, son?' asks Big Jamesie. 'Whit's yer alternative theory?'

The politician is calm. Unruffled. The opposite of the shambolic ball of twitching anxiety sitting across the table.

'Janina lived here ... in this mission,' says Stevie.

'Aye. Ye've got that right,' says Big Jamesie.

'An' she worked up at Raskine House, cleanin' an' that.'

'Two out ae two – though ah dunno what "an' that" refers tae.'

'An' she was at one ae yer Weekenders parties. She was heard screamin'. An' then she turns up deid – sexually assaulted an' dumped in a field just a few days later?'

'Weekenders, ye say? That sounds like a cult or somethin',' says Big Jamesie. Arms folded.

'You tell me,' Stevie ventures. But his voice wavers. It betrays him. He's an easy target for this opposition. Gallusness with a ball at your feet in front of four slow, muscle-bound defenders while a capacity Hampden crowd roars your name is one thing. Sat here, outnumbered four-to-one, sapped by Johnnie Walker, exhausted by the emotional carnage of losing his parents, his brother, his wife, his career ... He's fucked, and he knows it. Stevie's in deep now. Too deep, and too sozzled to admit to himself that he can't prove any of this.

But still with the presence of mind to hold on to the one bit of physical evidence he knows of:

The rubber stopper that surely must have come from the tip of the pastor's walking stick.

He's reluctant to play that card though. Fearful of what it might mean for him if he does.

The four don't move. They register no emotion. Stevie's fingers drum the table to conceal their shaking. One of Big Jamesie's gull-wing eyebrows rises slightly. It draws Stevie's attention to the yellowy rheum collecting in the corner of each eye. Big Jamesie lifts a clammy pink hand up to a crook of a nose that could smell a Sunday roast from the previous Thursday. The hand moves to his ear. Fingering the plastic hearing aid that wraps around the helix.

'Did ah hear you properly? Are ye suggestin' ah should have ma lawyer present, Chief Superintendent Minto?'

There's a pause. And then Big Jamesie turns to his colleagues again. Smirking. The standing men laugh, like this is the funniest joke they've ever heard.

'Ah like you, son,' says Jamesie. He puts his hat on the table and pulls his chair in. 'Ah dae. Ye had a lot goin' for ye. The fitba talent.

The looks. The lovely missus ... But they've aw gone. An' ah get that's gonnae sting. That must be a fucken bitter pill tae swally.'

Stevie leans forward to speak. But Big Jamesie's wrinkled paw elevates and stops him.

'Ah listened tae your wild accusations – it's only fair you listen tae ma response, naw?'

Stevie's shoulders slump. He's a novice, and they all know it.

'So, acceptin' that yer no' thinkin' straight. That the booze is helpin' ye forget everythin' an' everybody that ye've lost, ah can forgive this wee lapse in judgement. We're aw men ae God here, after all. Forgive us our trespasses, an' we'll forgive those who trespass intae the Sovereign Grace withoot permission, as the good Pastor McTavish would say.'

McTavish. The pastor. Accusatory words form, but Big Jamesie anticipates them. He hypnotises Stevie with a chubby finger raised to lips buried in that thick, black wiry beard.

'Noo, let's say ah phone Eddie Pink, or even that wee prick Keegan, an' ah tell them you're here on *Star* business, spoutin' off about circumstances ye know fuck all about,' says Jamesie. 'Are they two gonnae say "Aye, Jamesie, that's right, he's there cos we encouraged him tae be. We're runnin' a story oan you, pal." Or are they gonnae say "Jamesie, we've nae idea what yer talkin' aboot, son. Minto disnae even work wi' the *Star* anymore"?'

Stevie feels like that mouse in Meikle's flat. Just before the hammer dropped.

'Now, whit's it tae be, son? Ye can drop this pish now, walk ootae here an' get back tae the job, an' the wages, an' we'll aw forget this conversation ever happened. Or else ye can take this half-arsed, fucked-up an' genuinely insultin' theory tae the polis. See how ye get oan there. An' meanwhile, a lawsuit'll be headin' yer way afore ye can say "Mister, can ye spare a few bob?"'

The remaining air goes out of Stevie Milloy. Like someone taking a knife to a leather bladder. The one thing he hadn't given any thought to was the end game. What did he expect? For

Jamesie Campbell to admit that Janina Žukauskas had been so-
domised with a walking stick by a Glaswegian pastor during a
weekend party held at a house owned by the Denton-Hall family?
The young woman's body then dumped on remote moorland, and
an innocent man framed for her murder. An event that had sub-
sequently been covered up by the Glasgow police and the
judiciary. And underlined by a news report written by a dead man?

Stevie Milloy confronts the stark reality that he has been so
desperate to pin this on Geordie McCracken, or even just connect
him to a high-profile public scandal, that he hasn't covered the
basics. Investigated the circumstances. Researched the background. Established the facts. Assembled the evidence.
Double-checked everything, like Meikle would have.

Big Jamesie sits back. His outsized hat returns to his outsized
head. The three maintain their standing, arms-folded henchmen
pose.

If the next move is Stevie's, he can't immediately connect the
actions to the consequences. His sclerotic responses focus only on
the most likely scenario: the big man will leave, then the three
others will wade into Stevie with fists and feet and bats and maybe
even a razor.

Big Jamesie stands. Statesman-like. Untouchable.

'Like ah says, son, ah like you. Ye deserved a break when the
fitba finished. This job wi' the *Star* was yer break. Don't fuck it up.'

'Ah dinnae want any favours off that cunt McCracken,' says Stevie.
Tears are welling in his eyes. 'He can shove his pity up his arse.'

'Whit ye talkin' about?' asks Big Jamesie.

'He ends ma playin' career, an' then fixes me a fucken paper-
boy's job at the *Star* tae ease his guilt?'

The four standing men look at each other, puzzled.

The Boaby cunt leans forward. 'It wisnae Geordie that sorted
the job. It wis Denice.'

'Whit?' Stevie can't decipher the words quickly enough.

'Denice felt sorry for ye. Pleaded wi' Geordie for him tae reach out tae Maude, Big Jamesie's wife,' says the Boaby cunt. 'Maude's Geordie's godmother.'

Big Jamesie nods. Slyly winks.

'Geordie was against it, but Denice went ahint his back, anyway,' adds the Boaby cunt.

Denice. Fuck sake.

'Yer makin' an' awfy cunt ae yersel', son. But, *que sera*, eh? So, drop aw this shite about the wee foreign lassie, get back tae writin' about Jim Baxter boozin' and Jimmy Johnstone jinkin', an' we can put aw this unpleasantness behind us, right?' says Big Jamesie.

Stevie says nothing. His head slumps.

'The boys'll drive ye hame. Away an' sleep if off.'

The Boaby cunt reaches into Stevie's pocket. He draws out Meikle's keys. 'That wee rusty banger outside, int'it?' he asks.

'Ah can drive maself,' mutters Stevie.

'We'll take ye. We know where ye live, son,' says Big Jamesie. The threat is left hanging. 'Plus, we cannae run the risk ae some poor innocent Shettleston wean gettin' killed oan the roads cos you're fucken blootered, can we?' says Big Jamesie. 'That widnae be good for the campaign noo, would it?'

The Boaby cunt and the other two haul Stevie to his feet.

'Ah'll be seein' ye, son,' says Big Jamesie. He smiles and holds his massive bear-paws outstretched. 'An' remember...'

Stevie turns.

'Vote Campbell.' Big Jamesie laughs.

They drag him out to the corridor and turn left. Away from the main church hall. Stevie Milloy looks briefly over his shoulder. Pastor McTavish smiles. He lifts a hand to wave. The hand is holding the walking stick.

Big Jamesie also lifts a hand, motioning to the Boaby cunt to telephone him later.

Big Jamesie Campbell drapes an arm around Pastor McTavish and ushers him back inside the Sovereign Grace. Business as usual.

FORMER THISTLE & SCOTLAND STAR KILLED IN CAR CRASH

By Gerard Keegan
25th October 1966

DRAFT: For Editorial

Stevie Milloy, known to Partick Thistle fans as 'Minto', has died in a tragic motor-car accident. The twenty-six-year-old former Scotland international's car was pulled from the Clyde in the early hours of this morning. Mr Milloy's body was recovered from the vehicle. He was pronounced dead at the scene.

'Our investigations are at an early stage, but it appears that the car driven by Steven Milloy left the Broomielaw at the section underneath the Caledonian Railway Bridge,' said Inspector David McCracken of Glasgow Police. 'For someone so young, and with their whole life ahead of them, to perish in this way is a tragedy. Our thoughts and condolences are with Mr Milloy's family and friends at this difficult time,' Inspector McCracken continued.

Police are appealing for any witnesses but have confirmed that no-one else was in the car with Mr Milloy at the time of the accident.

After his playing career was over, Stevie Milloy took up a post in journalism with the *Star*. Colleagues at the newspaper have expressed their shock. James Campbell, former National Printworkers shop steward and prospective MP for Shettleston East said: 'This is devastating news. I met with Stevie only yesterday. He was interested in contributing to the Sovereign Grace Mission, where I am a patron. He was a lovely lad, although his demons often got the better of him. I really hope his troubles with alcohol didn't play a part in this terrible accident.'

Mr Milloy's estranged wife Denice was unavailable for comment.

GK
(250 words)

part 02

JAMESIE

EPISODE FIVE:
The Liberation of Jamesie Campbell (1943–44)

Lance Corporal Jamesie Campbell meets Private Michael McTavish – The unit is separated from their platoon – Jamesie forges a plan to get back to Scotland.

December 1943

'Fuck's goin' on?' asks Jamesie Campbell. He has been wakened by raised voices. He wipes at the dribble escaping the corner of his open mouth with a mud-encrusted sleeve.

'A fight? Ah dunno,' says the man seated to his right. A Glaswegian, like him, going by the inflexion. But not a man he has seen before. 'Michael,' says the man. He tentatively holds out a hand, which Jamesie ignores. 'Michael McTavish.' Jamesie notices the hand shaking as it is withdrawn.

'Where's...' Jamesie tails off, forgetting the name of their senior officer from the north-east of Scotland. Jamesie had helped the Aberdonian back to his feet after a gangplank cleat sitting proud had brought him down.

'Who?' asks Michael. 'Who ye lookin' for, pal?'

'Ah'm no' yer pal, son.'

'Sorry.'

Jamesie leans forward. Michael glances at the single chevron on Jamesie's jacket. Jamesie sees Michael's head droop in apparent embarrassment.

Jamesie sighs. *Dinnae be so aggressive.*

'Jamesie Campbell,' says Jamesie.

Private McTavish offers Lance Corporal Campbell a smoke.

The younger man sparks a light off his helmet. Jamesie accepts the lit roll-up reluctantly.

'Fifty-first Highlanders,' says Michael.

'Aye,' says Jamesie, without saying his regiment in return.

'Were ye in North Africa, Jamesie ... wi' Monty?' asks McTavish. As if recalling a fond night out carousing the Duke Street boozers. Getting the pints in at the Dunchattan Arms with thirsty mates after a long shift.

'Naw,' says Jamesie.

'Wher'abouts then?'

It is normal patter. Jamesie Campbell knows this. Soldiers meeting. Comparing their stories. Their campaigns. The cunts that have commanded them. Their fallen comrades. It's only natural to share such experiences. It keeps the dead alive. But Jamesie Campbell won't be sharing his story.

That doesn't stop Michael McTavish. Anxiety is making him talkative. This is his first tour. Six months ago, he prayed to God for guidance. The Lord answered. Michael enlisted in May. On his eighteenth birthday. His minister reiterated that it was what God would have wanted. Basic training in Perth. Billeted briefly in Southampton. Shipped out to Tunisia, and then on to Tripoli. God willing, he will finally see some action in Italy.

Half listening, Jamesie half hears Michael.

May. Perth. Tripoli. God.

There is a lot of God. Young, naïve Michael McTavish has an unshakeable faith in some invisible guardian fucking angel watching over the British brigades, to the exclusion of all others. But Jamesie Campbell knows different: that since he first set foot on foreign soil in 1940, God – or whatever manifestation prayers are directed towards – has forsaken all of them. The Tommy. The Yank. The Nazi. The Russki. And every other stripe of unfortunate fucker in between. God, Jamesie has decided, couldn't give a fuck about man. He imagines God, sitting up there on a cloud, laughing Himself silly as angry wee, power-hungry men make ill-thought-out plans that obliterate millions.

Aye. God ... what a fucken comedian he is, eh?

The earlier kerfuffle starts up again. On deck, and from the other side of the cruiser. Jamesie and Michael stand, rifles deployed as crutches. The emotion rippling towards them isn't anger. It is joy.

'The Eighth have taken Bari!'

'The Eighth have taken Foggia!'

What sounded like wanton aggression earlier is now boisterous jubilation. Like fans on the Hampden terracing celebrating an unexpected last-minute winner against the Auld Enemy. A chorus strikes up:

'Last night as I lay on my pillow,
Last night as I lay on my bed,
I dreamt Mussolini was dying,
I dreamt that the fat cunt was dead.'

A few at first. Growing to a majority.

'Send him, Oh send him,
Oh send Mussolini to Hell, to Hell,
Oh keep him, Oh keep him,
Oh keep the fat bastard in Hell.'

Michael notices that Jamesie isn't singing. 'Mibbe we'll be goin' home soon,' he says.

Lance Corporal Jamesie Campbell has not been home in more than two years. He's been everywhere else it has seemed. All the weathers of hellish imagination. Every mud-drenched, blood-soaked, rotting carcass shitehole from the frozen trenches of France to the blistering dunes of Algeria: all making Bridgeton look, smell, sound, feel, taste like fucking Xanadu.

'Will we fuck, son,' Jamesie says.

He heads off in search of a quieter corner. The cruiser is half an hour from docking in Taranto.

+

'Hey, Jamesie ... How ye, big man?'

Jamesie Campbell recognises the voice despite having spent limited time with its owner.

'Aye,' he replies. Languid. Indifferent. 'How's yersel?'

Michael McTavish sidles over. 'Good. Bloody cauld though, eh?'

'It's winter, int'it? Whit d'ye expect?'

'Italy though. Thought it'd be sunny.'

Jamesie Campbell can't decide whether McTavish is joking. Or a halfwit. Either way, he is the first person to have spoken to Jamesie with any civility in weeks. They are to be together for the time being.

The unopposed advance through the heel and up the lower calf of Italy began in icy winds and torrential rain. It has ended a week after it started, in freezing-cold blizzards. Jamesie has kept his head down. Apprehensive of those who might have heard about his history. The army's version, as opposed to his own. The mutiny at Salerno. Shipped back to Algeria. Imprisoned. Court-martialled. Facing nine years penal servitude. Repealed at the last minute. Commuted to continuous duty in the frontline. And now, re-turned to an operation he and 190 other mutineers had allegedly refused to join only two months earlier.

The massed troops of the Allied Forces' Eighth Army hit German resistance near Campobasso. They attempted to cross the River Sangro. Heavy rain burst the banks and they are now forced to construct a new means of doing so. The exhausted ranks have dug in. They are occupying the buildings and outhouses of a small school and are awaiting further orders about the advance north. Jamesie Campbell, Michael McTavish and a handful of others are directed towards a block of toilets.

'There you go, ladies.' Their new sergeant is a thick-lipped, moustachioed bull. Like so many who occupy the rank, not one to be messed with.

The men file in. The tiled floor is ponding in the middle. They shuffle and jostle for the drier edges. Including one along the trough urinals.

'Right, you dozy fucktards. Oh five hundred hours. Up and at these Kraut bastards!'

'Sir, yessir!'

'This should suit you down to the ground, Campbell.' The sergeant points at Jamesie. He knows what coming. 'A shitehouse for a fucking cowardly shitebag, eh?'

Too close to the bone. But Jamesie internalises the rage.

'Sir,' Jamesie acknowledges. The sergeant leaves.

'What's that mean?' Jamesie hears it. Whispered but audible.

Cat's out the bag. His new comrades eye him suspiciously. Jamesie has the rank. His shoulder proves it. But the sergeant has just stripped him of his advantage. Only one thing for it.

'Afore any cunt wants a pop, here's the real story.' Jamesie is still standing. Still wears full battle dress. Helmet on. Backpack on. Rifle – a soldier's closest friend – by his side. Arms straight. Fists balled. Ready for a fight.

The other men are now seated. Prime spots already taken. It means he will need to bunk down on the deepest part of the puddle, but compared to what he has been through recently, that is almost literally just a piece of piss.

'Ah was wi' the Fifty-First, in Sicily.'

'Were ye?' says Michael McTavish. 'Didnae know that. Me tae.'

Jamesie stares. Holds the stare. Daring another word. Silence.

He continues. 'Caught fucken dysentery. Sent back tae hospital in Tripoli. Then oan tae transit camp 155. While ah wis there, wi' aw the injured, an' the nearly deid, Wimberley shows up.'

'The major-general?' A Scots accent. Northern. A proper fucking Highlander.

'Aye,' says Jamesie. Irritated tone elevated to head off any further interruptions. 'Wimberley says that his men should be returned tae their units. We fucken believed him. Why would we no', eh?'

Jamesie notices a couple of head-nods in the gloomy darkness.

'We get fixed up. Joined the draft in the middle ae September. Shipped oot an' headin' back ower the Med. Only nae cunt had a clue where their regiments were. Jist that they were somewhere here in fucken Italy. Right up until the boats dock, naebody tells us fuck all. But it comes clear soon enough that we're no' gaun back tae the units we aw came fae. We'd been fucken lied tae. Half ae they poor cunts were barely fit tae walk, yet they volunteered for that fucken draft oot ae loyalty tae their mates. Tae the Fifty-First. An' aye, tae wee fucken Monty, the devious wee bastard.'

'Steady on, Jock.'

'Naw, you steady oan, sunshine. Ah've bottled this fucken anger for long enough. If you want the brunt ae it, then fucken come ahead!'

'Simmer down, fella.' An Irishman. 'Lookit, Montgomery's been good to many of us here.'

'Aye well, no' tae me, son. No' tae me.'

Jamesie rubs his mouth. Takes water on board. Screws the lid back. Continues.

'We're oan the cruiser. Nae cunt knows where the fuck we're headed, but it's no' bloody Sicily, that's for sure. The first that any ae us knew the true destination wis aff the west coast ae Italy when the message comes ower the ship's tannoy system. Gaun tae the Forty-Sixth, fightin' alangside the fucken Yanks at Salerno. Ah cannae believe whit ah'm hearin'. Nane ae us can. We'd been taken for mugs. When we disembarked, the new recruits were marched away, an' the veterans like me, cunts that had been fightin' non-stop for fucken years ... we were aw herded intae a field. Stuck there for three days like fucken sheep. Limited rations.'

Jamesie's neck stretches. As if his head is trying to escape the rest of his body. He sniffs. Carries on.

'We were convinced that some stiff fucken public-school chin-strap somewhere wid realise that there had been an administrative mistake an' sort it aw out. But naw. We get ordered tae parade.

There's been nae mistake. We're gettin' telt tae prepare for the orders comin' doon the line.'

Jamesie pauses. He's out of practice. It is the most he's spoken in weeks. He feels the rasping tickle that usually precedes a sore throat.

'Captain Albert Lee.' Jamesie spits the name out. One he won't forget. One that might be getting a few visits paid down Civvy Street. If the dishonourable bastard lasts that long. 'He shouts, "Fall in." Hunners dae whit they're telt. A few ae us decide we've had enough. Three times Lee commands us. Fuck that! Three times the cunt's denied. A sergeant sits doon in the field. Soon every bastard left is sittin' doon.'

Jamesie pauses. His audience waits, uncertain if the testimony has reached an end. Silence. A low-pitched chitter-chatter from the far corner fills it. The rats' cover is blown. Nocturnal creatures: rats, and soldiers in wartime.

Jamesie breathes deeply. Inflated, he continues. He needs to get it off his chest. They will think differently of him then.

'Three fucken days. Stuck in a coo'field. Nae food. Nae shelter. Gettin' barked at fae every C.O. cunt there. Whipped across the face. Battered and booted fae heid tae foot. Two hunner men, near enough. Aw got arrested for disobeyin' orders. For refusin' tae fight. But we wurnae refusin' tae fight. We just wanted tae fight wi' oor ain comrades.'

More neck stretching. More involuntary sniffing.

'So, you're one of the Salerno mutineers?' A quiet Midlands voice. Its owner sounds impressed.

Jamesie nods. Still unsure of his audience.

'Marched tae a POW camp. Locked up alongside fucken Krauts. Shipped back, tied up. Fucken Algeria again.'

He scans the shelter. Eyes have adjusted and he can see them all. Even the rats in the darker corners.

'So that's ma story. Any bastard in here says ah'm a coward, they're gaun tae be oan the other end ae ma bayonet.'

'Your *pork* bayonet?' The Irishman.

Sniggers follow. And it breaks the ice. The sniggers turn to laughs. And Jamesie laughs too. For the first time in months. It is not only when faced with an enemy that soldiers learn how to survive.

'Fair enough, Jock,' says a Cockney accent.

'Tough break, cocker,' adds a Lancashire one.

'Gor any chocolate?' Liverpool this time. It brings another laugh. Any tension there might have been condenses and vanishes along with Jamesie's breath.

Jamesie smiles. Then laughs again. Relieved. His commanding officers can think what they like. Only the acceptance of his comrades matters.

'Aye,' says Jamesie. He opens his backpack and throws a tiny square wrap into the dark corner where the Scouse accent came from.

Jamesie puts his pack down. Two inches of it disappears into a broth of sludge and pish.

He takes the helmet off. It makes a seat on top of the sodden backpack base.

The soldiers don't sleep. They rarely sleep. Minutes stolen here and there. That's it. They do not yet know it, but those who make it back home will never sleep soundly again.

The soldiers sit up. In the darkness. Distant church bells ringing. Even more distant gunfire. The Bible and the bullet. Italy's dissonant bedfellows.

Jamesie's confession has loosened lips. They keep it low. Whispering. No-one wants to be up on a charge. They talk of war experiences in the present tense. Chapters they will not return to once the madness is over. If it ever ends. No-one else would understand. Only comrades.

Life during wartime: only comrades matter.

Jamesie Campbell is learning the value of comradeship. And what – when fully exploited – it can achieve. He first understood its power when in the field in Salerno. Despite the knowledge that it would lead to court-martial, and, for the officers at least, the likelihood of facing a firing squad, a stance taken against perceived unfairness was a powerful galvaniser. Without leadership and direction, it would have halted at gossip in the ranks about the idiocy of the current orders. For most of the mutineers, dislocation from their own regiments – their comrades – only exacerbated their sense of injustice. Many simply bottled up their anger and accepted the order. But some remained seated. Defiant.

Jamesie watched all this unfold with interest. He had no desire to be returned to his regiment. He'd had his fill of war. He had killed, and almost been killed. Several times in each case. Any duty he felt towards the British military and its allies had run out. He wanted to go home. To whatever that concept even meant. Time to look after number one. So Jamesie stayed in the field as one after one, 191 disobedient men – including him – dropped to their arses. Immovable objects. Theirs, Jamesie considers, was the victory. There is power in a union.

Jamesie Campbell has a new union now. There are only ten of them, the toilet-block outcasts. But Jamesie has assumed control. He is the oldest. He's the most experienced. Regularly demeaned by his sergeant, he has used that brutal treatment to build loyalty. To demonstrate leadership. Just as the sergeant who sat down in protest did.

Seven weeks pass. Seven weeks of military stalemate. Seven weeks hunkered down in a freezing, rat-infested outhouse. Seven weeks incorporating Christmas Day and Hogmanay, the birthdays of Jesus Christ and Jamesie Campbell; indistinguishable days save for an extra tin of bully beef from the dwindling compo ration crates. One tin to be shared between two.

+

14th February 1944

Fall in. Move out!

The orders come. The bombers have peppered an advance towards Cassino. The Eighth Army's objective? To break through the Gustav Line and clear the way to Rome and the liberation of Italy.

+

Early May 1944

Jamesie's gang of four is dislocated. Disconnected from their platoon. Disorientated by the mountainous terrain, the relentless rain and the sporadic overhead bombardment. For three days, they have hidden in the scattered debris of a jagged, stony wasteland. Drifting through the rubble. Sticking to the shadows. Lost. Directionless. Running. Running out of food. Running out of ammunition. Running out of time.

'Think he's deid?'

'Aye.'

'Must be deid. It's been hauf an' hour.'

'Fuck's sake!'

Jamesie Campbell has been gone too long. His three comrades fear him killed. Their leader took it upon himself to rush out of the foxhole without warning. His depleted unit suspect German troops are surrounding them. Playing the waiting game. Toying with them.

'Whit we gonna do, Scouse?' Deek O'Hara. Soft, trembling Irish brogue. Thinking of Alison. The sheepdogs. His mammy's stew. His papa standing him a half-and-half down at Canty's bar after the harvest fete in Piltown. Uncle Jimmy singing 'The Old Galway Bay' during the lock-in. He's likely seen the last of all of them. It's an icy splinter to the heart.

'Fuck should I know, la'?' Benny Robertson, nineteen years old.

The eldest of the remaining three. Stoic, but doubting he will reach twenty.

The third is on his knees, quietly praying.

'Tav,' says Benny. 'Give tha' a fucken rest, willya?'

Michael McTavish's hesitant, desperate pleas to his God are replaced by boyish sobs.

'Ah'm not gettin' captured. No way,' says Benny. 'Ah'd rather fookin' end it here. Now. Myself.' There are tears in his eyes as he asks his comrades, 'Well, you'se wit' me?'

Deek and Tav look at each other. Is Benny suggesting a pact? One for all and all for one?

'You serious, Benny lad?' asks Deek.

A slow trembling nod is the response.

'Suicide is a sin,' says Tav. He is shaking uncontrollably. 'Ah ... ah couldnae.'

Benny's breathing is rapid. Deek is crying now too.

'Then ah'll do you, then, la,' says Benny. 'Want me to do you too, Deek?'

Deek cannot believe it has come to this. It is one thing copping it in the battlefield, but swallowing a comrade's rifle? Waiting for your mate's trigger finger?

'Oh, Jesus! Oh, God ... my Saviour in Heaven. Please save me!' Tav loses control. He pisses himself. Eighteen years old. Still a virgin. Never even kissed a girl, never mind killed a man. 'Please,' he shouts. 'God! Save—'

Benny slaps him hard across the face. 'Shut th' fuck up, Tav.'

'Benny,' Deek appeals to him.

'We doin' this, then?' Benny has decided. Distant gunfire won't stay distant for long.

Benny grabs Tav. Moves his hands upward from trembling shoulders. Cups his colleague's face. Wipes the tears. Leans in. Kisses his forehead. 'It's gonna be fine,' he tells him.

Deek sees Benny reach behind for his bayonet. Benny maintains eye contact with Tav.

'Benny, wait,' says Deek.

'It's all fine, Tav. God loves you, la.' Benny grips the bayonet. Manipulates it so that Tav won't see it going in under his ribcage.

'Wha' if you don't go through with it?' asks Deek. He is shaking.

'Go through wit' what?' says Benny, distracted.

'The suicide, like?'

'Eh?' Benny pulls his arm back. Like uncocking the hammer. 'Wha' d'you mean?'

'You do us ... but then don' do yourself.'

'Well, what fookin' difference will that make to you? You'll be fookin' dead, la'!'

'Exactly,' says Deek.

'Shh,' says Tav, quietly. 'Hear that? Somethin's movin' out there. It might be Jamesie.'

Jamesie Campbell is an accomplished drifter. A loner. He was born in the freezing outside cludgie of an East End slum tenement teaming with paupers. His mother cut the cord with a rusty pen knife and left him in there.

Happy Ne'erday. 1921.

Abandoned minutes into life. Paupers found him. Kept him. One with a lactating tit fed him. Another tried to sell him. When that failed, he was left in a battered pram outside the Parkhead Citadel Salvation Army Hall. Abandoned again. Three weeks old.

Pillar to post until St Mary's Roman Catholic Boys' Industrial School in Bridgeton became home. By the age of seven he had a new name. James Campbell, named for the first priest he had seen naked. By ten he had sucked his first cock. By thirteen he was kicked out. St Mary's – and his namesake – had done with him. Wandered the East End streets. Hiding in the nooks and crannies. Adjusting. Enduring. Hustling pool and people. War, when it arrived, held few fears for Jamesie. It was an escape. It offered regular food, drink and a route out of the dangerous streets where his actions were beginning to catch up with him.

Home? Jamesie Campbell has not been home in almost three years, because he has no home. Enlisting was a life-limiting career move. But Jamesie Campbell jumped at it. Because beyond all else, Jamesie Campbell is a survivor.

They hear him before they see him.

He approaches from behind their shelter.

He lobs his helmet towards them.

Benny raises his rifle.

Cocks it. Breathes heavy and loud, like an elderly asthmatic at high altitude.

'Boys! Dinnae shoot, boys. It's me.'

'Holy fuck. Jamesie?' Benny Robertson, relief, and disbelief. His heartrate slows, but only slightly.

Jamesie Campbell vaults into the crater. Michael McTavish bursts into tears again. Wherever Jamesie has been, it has been rough. He is leopard-spotted, head to foot in blood stains. Some might even be his. Blotches and spills. Splatters and sprays. His pigsticker has been working overtime. He wipes it carefully on his ripped sleeve. The slaughterman and his tool.

'Jesus Christ,' says Deek. 'We thou' ye wis dead!'

'There's deid yins aw ower the place, aye. Bodies piled up.'

There's blood on his teeth. Dripping down his chin, as if he might've eaten one of them.

'But Jamesie Campbell's no' deid, naw!' Jamesie laughs. 'Fuck that, boys. Still too much livin' for big Jamesie tae dae.'

Tav turns back to God. Ignorant of how close he has just come to being killed.

Benny looks at Deek. He shakes his head – a silent appeal for Deek to keep schtum.

Jamesie stands tall. He is somewhere else. Exalted. He punches the air. Blade still in hand. It glints in the southern-Italian sunshine. A gift for even the most mediocre of snipers. He is still in shock, and overcompensating.

Benny tries to pull him back down. But Jamesie will not yield. It is not his first kill – far from it. But this feels different.

'Fuck Italy's liberation. The fascist cunts sided wi' Hitler, for fuck's sake.'

No, Jamesie Campbell is the one liberated.

'Jamesie, get down mate,' Benny pleads.

Jamesie remains upright. Looks down at his comrades. At the frightened looks on their faces. Not sure whether to be more afraid of their hidden enemies or this insane Scotsman.

'Nae need, Benny boy. They're aw deid. Ah kilt them aw, son.'

'But ... but ye'd no bullets,' says Deek.

'Bare hauns, ma friend. Wi' these bare hauns,' says Jamesie.

Tav lifts his discarded bayonet. He attempts to attach it to his Enfield. It takes too long with quivering fingers.

'A whole section, ah took them aw oot,' says Jamesie.

'Jamesie, please.'

'Ah runs at them. Screamin' blue murder. Facin' them doon, the shitebags. A buzzsaw pointed right at me, tae. Must've fucken jammed, cos ah wis able tae launch maself right intae their fucken bunker. The look oan they Kraut faces, ah swear tae God.' Jamesie laughs like a maniac. 'They must've thought *whit the fuck kinda madman is this*? Me slashin' awa' at them afore they could reach for a pistol. Faces, necks, bellies. Destroyed. Four deid Huns.'

'Four of 'em?' asks Benny.

'Aye. Four. An' then another four. Separate fae the first four.' Jamesie pauses. Twists his neck. Sniffs.

'That no' enough for ye, eh?'

'Ah just meant there might be more out there, tha's all, la.'

'There isnae. Only deid yins. Ah fucken telt ye this.' Jamesie is irritated. The three should be grateful. He has just single-handedly freed them.

'We heard gunfire...'

'Look, Benny...' Jamesie's free hand makes a fist.

'AAHHH!'

Tav moves instinctively. His body and arms raised in self-preservation. 'Watch out!'

'Stirb, du verdammter Bastard! Ich werde euch alle toten!'

Tav pushes Jamesie backward. Caught off guard, Deek falls forward. The German slashes downward. Tav's elevated rifle. The German's body falling. Tav's bayonet goes straight through the German. Through the ribcage and into a soft heart. The sharp point punctures the soldier's back. A hot knife going through butter. No resistance. A hole in his fraying uniform. Blood seeping and spreading along the threads. The German falls on top of Tav.

Falling.

The German looks younger than him.

Both terrified. Of dying. Of living through this. So close they could be kissing.

'Mama!' Gurgling.

Trying to swallow.

German hands on the Scotsman's throat.

Tightening.

Clinging to life.

Failing.

McTavish doesn't struggle. The shock has enveloped him. The Scotsman feels the last of the German's hot, sulphurous breath on his face. He gags. Blood trickles from the dead mouth. It drips on Tav's lips and into his own mouth, onto his tongue, and it is this that finally makes him scream.

Jamesie drags the dead man off and away. The German soldier bellowed too soon. His inexperience showing. He should have waited. A second or two would have done it.

Tav is still screaming. Hysterical. Jamesie hugs him. Muffles the screams. Grabs him so tightly Benny briefly thinks he is suffocating him.

The screaming subsides.

'Ye saved ma fucken life, Tav,' says Jamesie. The wide-eyed loon of only minutes ago is gone. 'Ah'll never ever forget it, pal.'

Tav hyperventilating like he might combust.

'Breathe, son. Dinnae forget ... deep breaths,' says Jamesie.

Benny puts his hand to his mouth. Pulls Jamesie's trouser leg with the other.

'Ah think ah'm in bother, fellas.' Deek is speaking calmly.

They turn. The German's knife is buried in Deek's neck. Only the handle is visible. Blood is oozing down the Irishman's left side. He shudders.

'Does it look bad, Benny?'

Benny cannot answer. The words are stuck behind a trembling hand. The wide eyes tell Deek the answer.

'Aw fuck,' he wails. The colour drains from his face. The blood rushes to the hole in him. He begins to cry. He begins to shake.

'Ah don't wanna die here,' he sobs.

'Jamesie?' Benny appeals. But Jamesie shakes his head.

'Ah wanna go home,' Deek says.

Jamesie Campbell moves from Tav to Deek. 'Ah know, son. Ah know ... an' ye will.'

Comfort in the last moments. Jamesie takes his flask and un-screws the top.

'Drink it in, son,' says Jamesie softly.

The whisky dribbles.

Most of it dripping off Deek's chin.

Jamesie touches the knife's handle. The crimson spreads. The whole of the left side now. Deek shudders and the blood starts spurting under the pressure of Jamesie's fingers trying to stem it. Like a dam bursting.

'Ah'm cold, Jamesie.'

'Ye'll be fine, son. Dinnae be feart.'

'Mammy! Help me, Mammy!'

The Irishman's eyes flicker. He misses a breath. And then four come rapidly. And eighteen-year-old Derek O'Hara dies, having never shared a Black an' Tan with his papa. Having never told Alison he loved her. Thinking of his mama's stew.

+

They look back only once. Deek two feet under rocks and mud. The dying and resting place marked by his helmet perched on a tiny wooden cross fashioned from whittled branches. His name, and *15 MAY 44* inscribed on the metal using the blade that killed his killer. It is a rough estimate of the date of death, nothing more. Thirty feet to the right, the killed killer lies dumped. A grey wolf waits on the edge of the undergrowth beyond. Tongue hanging to one side. Panting in anticipation. There is a fresh human carcass in the ditch. War is bountiful for the wild animals of Italy.

The three British soldiers head east. Jamesie, driven and determined. Benny, submissive; content merely to follow. Tav, lost in a chimeric dream of home and safety, in which the last two months haven't happened.

They track the sun's rise over the Adriatic. They keep to the forests during daytime. They only break cover to pilfer from grain silos and cowsheds. They hunt rabbits. They steal chickens and bread and the clothes of farmhands. They bag the regulation army issues. They have officially absconded. The war seems to have moved north. The aerial bombardment of Lazio has been brutal. They encounter a country in desperate hiding. Surviving in the shadows. Afraid to come out into the light. Those that do are female and elderly. It is as if every male over five and under fifty has been wiped out.

The three fugitives parade around bombed-out graveyards. Give wide berths to hunks of abandoned military equipment, their metal skins twisted and open like discarded rationed-meat tins. They would make good places from which to launch ambushes. They file past shelled Renaissance chapels and Benedictine abbeys missing buttress walls and pan-tiled roofs. God's estate targeted from both sides. Reduced to fractured stage sets in the war's theatre. A country of artists and poets and beauty and colour and passion and faith, rendered ruins.

Benny hotwires a truck. Much of the journey along the coastal tracks towards Pescara is conducted in silence. Grieving for Deek O'Hara is taking differing forms.

For Jamesie, it is rage.

For Benny, guilt.

Tav is in denial.

+

June 1944

Jamesie Campbell is wired. Adrenaline is coursing through him. He cannot sit. It is as if the stolen dungarees and dirty checked shirts and indigenous flat caps are acting as invisibility cloaks. Maybe the Holy Spirit is with them. Protecting them as they motor through deserted villages and alongside sun-bleached sand. No-one here to stop them. No checkpoint challenges. As if they have been granted the freedom of Italy. Incredibly, they haven't needed to speak to anyone else in months.

They bypass Ortona. Three army renegades with no definitive sense of time or current understanding of place still have knowledge of the carnage that took place there. Six months earlier, over eight days either side of Christmas, Ortona witnessed brutal close-quarters combat. Staggering casualty numbers, worsened by the chaotic rubble of the town and the countless catastrophic booby traps used by both sides.

It is unlikely that the ease of passage they have experienced so far will continue in Ortona. The locals will be less submissive. More suspicious. More desperate. The line of the conflict may have been redrawn around Rome, but the deepwater port is still strategically important for the Allies. And, in any case, Jamesie isn't ready to surrender yet. Even to his own side. Only to be interrogated? Accused of desertion? Court-martialled again? Or best outcome … immediately despatched to yet another frontline death zone? *Fuck that.*

They veer off towards the comparative safety of the Teatina hills. Dirt tracks and barely formed mountain roads. Benny is astonished at the durability of the stolen truck's axles. But the sputtering engine gives up before the suspension. Steam billows from a cracked radiator and they are forced to abandon the vehicle. They ascend the shallow peaks around Tollo, climbing higher until they can see the shimmering Adriatic on their right. And the snow-covered Apennine massif away to their left. For the first time, the three are simultaneously struck by the untamed beauty of this country.

High up above the slaughter.

Breathing pure air.

Closer to Heaven.

Maybe there is a God after all, Jamesie muses. This is as far from the destitution and deprivation of slum Glasgow as his imagination can stretch.

'Think we'll be safe here, Jamesie?' asks Benny.

'We're only safe in this life by the grace of God,' says Tav.

'An' the will ae strong men,' adds Jamesie.

They meander through the verdant olive groves and vineyards of the upper plateau. Untouched by war. Five miles or so away, they can make out the smoking remnants of the edge of Ortona. It's like another country altogether. They have become so used to the grit, the decay and the mud – the desaturated greys, beiges, browns and blood-reds of that world – that this new spectrum of vibrancy dazzles their eyes. A hazy sky of purest blue melts into the jagged horizon. The grass is green, and leafy trees waltz to the tune of the breeze. Birds sing. Bells chime in the distance. Life in its simplest form. A surrealist vision of Paradise.

It seems false. Tav wonders if it is only him who sees the sharp contrast of the colours. Fluid and swaying as if this liquified landscape was being stroked by God's painterly brush in front of his eyes.

They build a shelter in dense woods on the outskirts of a hamlet.

A handwritten sign reads: *Colle Secco.*

An initial recce offers encouragement that food and drink can be easily procured in the environs. There is activity here, but Jamesie considers it to be non-threatening. Provided they keep their heads down and take no risks. That attitude, he hopes, could see them outlast Hitler and Mussolini.

The weeks pass. The three play cards for imaginary money. They tell stories. Describing the naked bodies of Vera Lynn or Hedy Lamarr as if they were right in front of them. They masturbate. Separately at first, but then together. And on the odd occasion, each other. Each man secretly wondering how far the others might go to release sexual tension.

The late-summer heat intensifies. Jamesie's bravado grows and energises him. But there is a restless boredom growing inside him. Benny, on the other hand, is buoyed by their repetitious regime. Even Tav harbours optimistic notions of his God eventually delivering him from the evil pit of Hell that war-torn Italy has become.

+

September 1944

Tav hears the dull, coded thuds.

It's Jamesie.

Seconds later, the Glaswegian appears. Light from a sparked match guides him.

'Christ, where've ye'se been?' asks Tav.

His tone is a mix of annoyance and relief. Like an impatient wife interrogating the holder of a broken pay packet. His colleagues left him ages ago, in daylight. They have been gone for hours.

'Where's Benny?'

Jamesie ignores the question.

'Get up Tav, son,' Jamesie commands. 'Let's fucken go.'

Tav looks around apprehensively. What's happened to Benny Robertson?

'Battle dress oan. We're movin' out.'

'Th' night, Jamesie?' Tav asks.

'Aye.'

There is something different about Jamesie. He has had alcohol, for one thing. But he isn't celebrating. It is not the end of the war. Or if it is, that's not propelling Jamesie Campbell. Something more malign is driving him.

Benny has noticed dips in Jamesie's mood of late. He asked Tav if he had detected it too. But Tav's constantly on the verge of a breakdown himself. Tav sees it now though. Jamesie Campbell has the devil's fire in his eyes. A switch has been flicked.

'Where's Benny?' he asks again.

'Ah'm here, Tav.'

He's outside the shelter. Quiet. Head down. Keeping his distance.

'But ... but it's pitch-black, Jamesie,' says Tav.

'Scared ae the dark, ya cunt?' Jamesie Campbell is not in the mood to be challenged.

And Tav doesn't have the belligerence for a confrontation. He is like putty; pliable and lacking in the substance needed to resist.

Benny Robertson sighs. He'd hoped the war would be over before they needed to leave this sheltered eyrie. He's just turned nineteen years old and is ignorant of the fact.

'Tav ... c'mon! Move yersel.' A command this time.

Their dirty khaki fatigues replace the faded denim dungarees. That brief period of anonymity that their disguise offered them has gone. All pretence that they might have passed as locals if observed from a distance has been stripped away. Once more, they are desperate soldiers. Fugitives in a foreign land where their presence isn't welcome.

They quietly gather what little things they have. Tav concealing anxiety for the unpredictability of what lies ahead. Suspecting Benny already knows. Jamesie Campbell, for reasons that seem unfathomable to his comrades, is going on the attack.

The walk through the undergrowth towards the hamlet is brisk. Jamesie Campbell leading. Loud, strident provocations challenging the evening calm. Benny Robertson, head down. Bringing up the rear. Tav ahead of him despite struggling with a blistered foot. A tight boot only making it worse.

Into the dark, narrow passages. Easy pickings for an attack. Three pairs of eyes scan the closed shutters. Peer upward towards chimneys and belltowers. Two still fearful of a sniper, however unlikely that would be. Habits that will take a lifetime to eradicate. Tonight, Jamesie Campbell fears no-one. He taunts the cowardly.

'Gaun, ya fucken cunts, ye'se! Ya shitin' bastards,' Jamesie yells into the gloomy recesses between low-rise stuccoed masonry.

His voice reverberates. No responses to his call. Minutes pass. There is no sound. Tav contemplates the horrific thought that Jamesie and Benny have executed the entire village. Even the crickets are suddenly silenced.

'Ah freed ye'se!'

Tav has heard the stories of sane young men turned mad by the atrocities they have seen. Is he witnessing it now?

Jamesie stops in the middle of the little village square. He looks around. He walks to the centre. He takes out his cock and pisses in the small fountain. The sagacious strategy to remain inconspicuous is dead. And now Jamesie Campbell is urinating on its corpse.

'Get it right up ye'se. The lot ae ye!' he drawls, an arm outstretched. Cock-spraying like a hose with the other. 'An' ye dinnae even hae the common decency tae welcome us in. Tae offer us a wee dram.' Jamesie Campbell spits his disdain. 'Greasy *tally* bastards!'

Maybe Jamesie Campbell has been on the edge of this explosion for months. Bottling up the anger. Hiding the rage.

Perhaps Benny and Tav have been too preoccupied with their own demons to see the threat mounting.

There is movement. Slow and hesitant, but Benny Robertson notices it. Something, someone, trying to sneak away. To escape Jamesie Campbell's wrath.

'Jamesie.' Whispered.

Jamesie hears it. He's noticed it too. Jamesie draws a pistol Tav didn't even know he had.

He fires it low. Not aiming. Guesswork. The bang ricochets off the walls.

Tav shakes. He rocks back and forth. He makes a murmuring sound. 'Please, God, save me. Please, God, save me.'

The movement has stopped. A cat lies dead. A dog barks in the distance. Jamesie, alert and razor sharp. Like a wild beast sensing prey. His nose protrudes. Elevated. Sniffing. He leads them towards the sound of the animal. He appears to know the route. A corner turned. Halfway along an alley with enclosing walls that can be touched without stretching arms. The faintest, flickering light from a loose-fitting timber door.

Behind it, Benny and Tav discover a well-stocked cellar doubling as a tiny bar for those who knows of its existence.

'So, whit we got here, lads?' says Jamesie. He has been here before.

Two old Italian men lift their heads. Slowly. They sit hunched in a corner. Under the worn brims of identical pulled-down *berretti* craggy lines on pitted, pockmarked, leathery faces are illuminated only by the flame from a candle with a limited lifespan. A dusty bottle sits between them.

Two glasses.

'Mind if we join ye'se, aul' yin?' says Jamesie.

A shrug indicates indifference or incomprehension.

'Get the fucken drinks in then!'

Benny Robertson glances at Tav. Tav cannot decipher the look. Benny walks behind a makeshift counter. The reluctant Scotsman drags small stools to the Italians' table. The Scouser plays barman.

'Anythin' decent, Benny boy?'

'Cognac, Jamesie. Loads ae it.' Barely audible.

'Speak up, son,' says Jamesie. 'That'll dae fine, son. Let's hae a party. Got anythin' tae scoff?'

'Bread. Lots of it. Some cheese here too.' He sniffs it. 'Smells like scabby feet, mind.'

'Gie's it ower. Killin' the Krauts makes ye hungry, eh, aul' yin?'

Another shrug from one of the Italians. The slightest of movements. Not discernible to Jamesie, but Tav notices it.

'Fucken stinks, this,' says Jamesie. But he devours the cheese anyway. Tears at the bread with his teeth. He slurps from cognac bottle number one. He belches.

Benny laughs, but it is not the laugh of a contented man. Tav notices Benny's leg shaking under the table.

'Siamo circondati da uomini morti.'

'Whit's that, granda?' Jamesie questions the elderly farmer. Jovial enough, but Jamesie's comrades know an escalation is coming.

Jamesie tops up the glasses of his captive audience. He swigs straight from the bottle. All drink, except Tav.

'Get it down ye, ma man,' says Jamesie. 'Mr Michael McTavish. Ma saviour.' He wraps a left arm around Tav's shoulders. The right arm lifts the bottle to Tav's face. 'Here. This is aw for you,' says Jamesie.

Tav's tongue probes the bottle's rim. His eyes are closed. Like a child being force-fed pungent medicine. Jamesie suddenly angles the bottle. Tav coughs. His face screws up. He gags. His forehead ripples like corrugated metal. Cognac soaks his chin and runs down his neck and inside his shirt collar.

Jamesie laughs. 'Never had a cognac afore, boy?'

Tav coughs again. 'Ah've never had booze before,' he splutters.

'So?' Jamesie will not be put off.

Tav takes a proper sip. 'It's burnin' ma throat.'

'It's a good burnin' though, int'it?'

'Aye,' Tav says. 'Suppose. It's okay.'

'Hear that, Scouse?' shouts Jamesie. 'He's one ae us noo.'

Time passes slowly. One empty bottle in front of Jamesie quickly becomes three. Four men watch his rapid inebriation.

'Ah'm gaun outside for a pish an' a smoke,' Jamesie announces. 'Watch these aul' wop cunts. Ye cannae trust anybody in this fucken bastart country.'

The wooden door rattles. They can hear him whistling outside. Not a care in the world.

'Tav,' Benny whispers. 'We need to get gone from him. And now! Jamesie's fucked in the head, mate.'

'Whit happened?' asks Tav. 'Where did he get the pistol?' He is on the verge of tears. Wanting, but not wanting to hear the answer.

The Italian farmers stare. Like they can read Tav's mind. Eyes boring into his soul.

'We came into the village,' says Benny. 'Ah told him it wasn't safe, but he wouldn't listen. Said he needed to fuck somethin'. This first place down near the chapel, there's a man. Carryin' a bucket. He's just got one arm. Jamesie speaks to him. The guy drops the bucket. Tries to reach for the gun in his belt. Jamesie rushes him. Takes the gun off him an' then fookin' throttles him. Dead.' Benny is breathless. 'Jamesie goes fookin' berserk. Screamin' about freedom an' liberation an' shit.'

'My God...'

'There's worse than that.'

'Hurry up, he'll be back,' pleads Tav.

'We found an air-raid shelter...' Benny speaks quickly. 'In a basement, round the back. Jamesie's wild wit' the rage. Hears somebody coughin'. We jemmy this lock. Pull open the doors. There's seven or eight folk huddled inside. Women, kids.'

Jamesie's whistling outside turns to singing:

'Ah'll be seein' you, in all the old familiar places.
That this heart of mine embraces. All day through...'

Tav stares at the old farmers. Do they already know?

Their vacant gazes continue.

'He drags a young one out ... by her hair. Then he shuts the door. Tells me to sit on it so they can't get out.' Benny shakes his head.

'Ah'll find you. In the morning sun. And when the night is new. Ah'll be lookin' at the moon. But I'll be seein' you.'

'Whit, Benny? Whit happened?'

'Jamesie ripped her dress off an' fucked her ... in the bum. He lay on her an' raped her. Right there in front of me. She was jus' a kid, Tav!' Benny wipes a tear away. 'She looked like my lil' sister, Jeanie.'

Tav doesn't know what to say. Or do.

The old farmers still stare. Their glasses untouched since the soldiers entered.

'Whaur is she now?'

'He threw her back in the bloody cellar, Tav. Made me lift boulders onto the hatch doors.' Benny shakes his head. 'They're still down there.'

The two old farmers. They must know. They *must*.

The metal lock rattles. Jamesie's back.

'Had yer fill yet, boys?'

'Think we should get outta here, Tav, eh?' says Benny.

'Prob'ly right, Scouse,' says Jamesie.

He lifts a cognac bottle by the neck. Left-handed. Drains it. Then brings it crashing down on the skull of the closest Italian farmer. The old man collapses. Jamesie sticks the serrated end into the face of the other. Punctures the leathery skin. Blood flows. The old man makes a horrible, guttural howl sound. Like a stuck pig.

'Jamesie! Fuck's sake, man. Wha' d'you do that for?'

'Are you next, ya fucken English bastart?'

Benny and Tav are on their feet.

Stools overturned.

Glasses smashed.

Cognac bottles rolling on the floor.

One Italian unconscious.

The other down on his old knees. Hands failing to stem the blood from oozing through his thick, dirty fingers.

'Ah says let's fucken go!'

And the three soldiers leave.

Dogs bark.

Candles light.

They disappear.

Through the vineyards.

Hidden by the olive trees.

Thieves in the night.

Dawn breaks. The depleted unit numbers only two now. Both Scotsmen. Benny Robertson has snuck away. Taken his chances alone. Tav watched him go as Jamesie slept off the booze. Tav knows that the Englishman has gone back to Colle Secco. The need to atone is powerful. Tav wishes he was as courageous.

'Fuck him,' says Jamesie. 'He was just an English cunt anyways.'

A plan for their repatriation has been fermenting. Benny Robertson doesn't feature in it. It will involve some personal pain but that is all just in the mind. Six months after drifting away from their platoon, the two remaining soldiers head back down the steep slopes toward Ortona. Towards the Allied Forces. In the opposite direction from a war that has moved on without them.

Jamesie, pistol in hand.

Dragging Tav as if he was a captured prisoner.

Two hours of marching.

Two hours to get the story straight.

Persuading Tav to remain silent.

Let Jamesie do all the talking.

They will be fine and heading home to Scotland if Tav trusts Jamesie. If he lets Jamesie look after him.

For now, and for the rest of their lives.

War 'Heroes' (1944)

Jamesie and Michael return to Scotland – Jamesie meets Maude Denton-Hall, proprietor of Raskine House – An opportunity emerges for Jamesie and Michael.

October 1944

Taped to the walls there are colourful maps with folds and torn edges. A small map of the world, almost inconsequential in comparison to the others. A larger map of Europe, which has been vandalised by thick pen arrows and divided up by strings held in place by drawing pins. Front-line positions after five years of conflict. Michael McTavish wonders if the faint lines and colour changes marking the boundaries of countries he learned about in school might be redrawn when the fighting finally finishes. Whether that is the purpose of war, the perpetual redrafting of power and control.

The largest map is one of Italy, the country they are in. A proliferation of angry red pins surrounds the word *ROME*. Michael McTavish is struggling to orientate himself in this map. Despite being in the country for a year, he has no idea where he is relative to the capital. His ignorance may yet save him.

'At ease.'

Tav's rigid torso relaxes noticeably.

'Sit down, Private.'

'Sir, Ah'd prefer tae stand, sir.'

'Sit, soldier. That's an order.' Not commanded. Said softly and with a concern for the soldier's wellbeing.

'Thank you, sir.'

Michael McTavish drops off the crutch and onto the wooden chair. He winces. He spots a large, scuttling blister beetle heading for a hole in the skirting board. A door opens behind him. A tray carrying a silver teapot, sugar bowl, a milk jug and three china cups is brought in. All present silently observe the ritual of a private pouring tea and adding sugar and milk, in memorised order, for the officers. Michael McTavish is not offered anything. The conversation only resumes when the tea-pouring private has left the room, closing the door behind him.

'Quite the adventure you and Lance Corporal Campbell have had.'

'Yes, sir.'

He doesn't lift his eyes upward to meet the officer's gaze. It will look disrespectful. But he can't look away from the beetle.

'How is Campbell?'

The beetle is nearly home. Just a few inches now.

'McTavish!'

'Sir?'

Only two inches more. Then safety.

'Lance Corporal Campbell – how is he?'

Someone else has noticed. A boot slams down. The beetle is crushed. Yellow secretions pop. The beetle was so close.

Why not just let it go?

'McTavish!' Loud. Impatient. Angry now.

McTavish looks up sharply. Peering, as if trying to focus. To recall the question.

'He's no' good, sir.'

McTavish is breathing deeply. He looks down again, before remembering his place. His head lifts and he makes eye contact again, as Jamesie has instructed.

'He can't sleep for the nightmares. Wakes up screamin', sir. There's a lot ae screamin' in the field hospital. Jamesie ... Lance Corporal Campbell usually kicks it off. Loads ae poor buggers in there, sir. Once he starts...'

'It must be difficult.'

'He's confused, sir. Hears these ringin' noises that nobody else can hear.'

There is a silence as the major-general reads from the papers on his clipboard. He flips the page.

'You were in North Africa, Private?'

'Yes, sir.'

'See much action?'

'No, sir. No' until landin' in Italy.'

'That must've been a shock to your system.'

'Yes, sir. Definitely.'

'And they tell me you're a man of faith.'

'Oh yes, sir. My Lord kept me an' Campbell alive through those bleak months, sir.'

'Your capture and imprisonment – tell me about that. What happened?'

Jamesie Campbell has prepared Michael McTavish for this:

Remember, a liar needs a good memory.

Think ae the key points in the story as dots.

You just need tae join them usin' different words.

Every story needs a structure. Tav has rehearsed it relentlessly. It is as familiar to him now as the Lord's Prayer.

Our Father who art in heaven,

- Dug in for weeks with the Eighth at Campobasso.

hallowed be thy name;

- Moved out in November. Advanced north towards the Gustav Line.

thy kingdom come;

- Came under heavy fire at Cassino ... must've been early February.

thy will be done;

- Multiple casualties. Separated from our unit.

on Earth as it is in Heaven.

- German and Italian resistance pocketed all around.

Give us this day our daily bread.

- Four of us: Lance Corporal Campbell, Privates O'Hara, Robertson, McTavish.

And forgive us our trespasses,

- Lance Corporal Campbell took out a machine-gun post, single-handed.

as we forgive those who trespass against us.

- In the fighting, O'Hara's killed. We're captured.

And lead us not into temptation;

- The Lance Corporal ... tortured. Starved. Blindfolded. Kept in darkness for months.

but deliver us from evil.

- We managed to escape.

For thine is the kingdom and the power, and the glory,

- Lance Corporal Campbell gets shot. I break an ankle falling from a roof.

for ever and ever.

- Lance Corporal Campbell carries me on his back. For miles. Here. To Ortona.

There is a long silence. Four people in the room. No-one speaks. The three facing McTavish write simultaneously. McTavish can't see what forms they are filling in. Evaluating his story? His honesty? His sanity?

'You know of Campbell's past? His ... involvement in the mutiny at Salerno?'

Jamesie has prepared him for this too.

'Eh, no, sir. Ah first met him on the sailin' from Tripoli, sir.'

'And how did you find him?'

'Sir?'

'Did he strike you as an honest man, Private McTavish? Someone a man might put his trust in?'

'Oh, yes. Yes, sir. Very honest. A quiet man, but someb'dy who'd do anythin' for his comrades.'

'I see.'

'Ah owe my life tae him, sir.'

'Hmm.'

'And the other private...' The major-general consults his notes. 'Robertson. What became of him?'

McTavish grimaces. 'Ah don't know, sir. We got out ae the base-ment at night. It was in the woods, sir. Pitch-dark. One minute he was behind us – the next he wisnae. There was a lot ae shots fired. One ae them hit the Lance Corporal but we just kept runnin', sir. Found a water tower, climbed up it, an' hid in there for a day or so, sir.'

'You think Private Robertson got away?'

'Ah hope so, sir.'

'And the leg?'

'We shinnied down an overflow pipe, sir. Onto a metal roof attached tae the tower. Ah fell off the roof an' the ankle snapped inside ma boot, sir.'

The constant pain in his left leg is not fake.

'Wait outside, Private.'

'Sir.'

McTavish stands. Leans on the crutch with a left arm. Salutes with his right. Turns. Hobbles away.

Making for the rectangular hole in the wall before a British Army boot squashes him into oblivion.

The door closes behind him.

Sitting immediately outside, he can hear snippets of the delib-erations. But nothing specific. He's participated in three of these debriefings in the month since they got here. Each conducted by a person of increasing rank. Each taking less time than the one before. He watches a clock on the wall. A quarter of an hour passes before the door opens again.

He doesn't sit this time. Is not offered the opportunity.

'Private McTavish, you and Lance Corporal Campbell are being repatriated. You will be stationed in Scotland for a period of rehabilitation. Following which you will be assessed for fitness to return to the front line.'

Amen.

'Thank you, sir.'

A colonel leans in. He whispers in the ear of the major-general. The eyebrows of the seated man raise.

'And McTavish...'

'Yes, sir?'

'Lance Corporal Campbell is being recommended for a Distinguished Service Order, for his commendable leadership during active enemy operations. You, Private McTavish, will receive the Conspicuous Gallantry Cross for actions of conspicuous gallantry during the campaign to liberate Italy. Congratulations, soldier.'

The major-general stands. Salutes. Nods in McTavish's direction. 'God save the king!'

'God save the king, sir!' says Private Michael McTavish, war 'hero'.

The dead blister beetle has gone. The ooze from its stamping gone too. As if it never existed.

+

March 1945

The formality of Raskine House is mirrored by its grounds – generous green lawns, spacious gardens and fruited orchards, all laid out with geometric precision. Of course, it wasn't always this sylvan. Raskine House endured decades of climatic exposure in a barren landscape. Now though – when the smoke relents and reveals its secrets – the house benefits from rich pasture lands and well-wooded screening.

The estate's balance and order are reinforced by an avenue of regularly spaced stately limes. Following this line to the left until the house is almost out of sight, a small grove of trees can be found. A picturesque woodland path winds away, punctuated with steps hewn from natural rock. There are trailing ferns and lichens on either side. Beyond the steps, the path branches off in two directions. One way leads to a substantial rock abutment. Massive though the rock is, a narrow access route has been carved through. It leads to a tennis court, where, when the weather permits – as it does today – those able to undertake group recreation.

Jamesie Campbell and Michael McTavish watch some of their fellow patients head off to the court. Several nod in Jamesie's direction. A nurse waves, but in a discreet way she hopes won't be noticed by anyone other than the recipient.

When they've disappeared from view, Jamesie leans back and lifts his feet up onto the timber bench that faces the front of the old house.

'This is aw'right, Mikey boy. Could definitely get used tae this life.'

'Hmm.' Michael McTavish is not a convert. Not yet anyway. 'Ah'm glad tae be back hame, Jamesie. Nae danger there. But *this* ... ah dunno.'

'Whit? Yer kiddin', son. Three meals a day. Nane ae them eaten oot a rusty metal tin. We get oot in the sun when it's warm. Sat inside listenin' tae *Desert Island Discs* when it's cauld. Nae cunt gie's a fuck about sendin' us back to thon Italian hellhole. Fuck me, Mikey, whit more could ye want?'

'Aye. Suppose.' Michael McTavish ponders this. 'But whit'll we dae when this is over?'

'Whit, the war? Fuck knows, son. The Lord'll provide, an aw that shite. Live for the day, no' the morra.'

Jamesie Campbell is sitting in a wheelchair. His left arm supported by a sling, He doesn't need the sling. The bullet-wound in his shoulder is healing well. He doesn't need the wheelchair for mobility either. Even if he did, his tanned, muscular arms can manoeuvre it. He just likes the power the sling and the chair gives him over the nurses. He can yell or wave or snap fingers, and one of them will come running.

Jamesie Campbell is a decorated war hero. His story has featured in some newspapers, so he is a celebrity around these remote parts. Jamesie feels like the king of this Scottish castle. He has sussed the staff; assessed points of weakness. Manipulating those to his benefit, as well as exerting his alpha-male authority over the recovering soldiers.

Jamesie has what is being described as 'post-concussion syndrome'. He is a plausible performer during his weekly medical assessments. And a few tactical fits thrown from time-to-time help. Some nocturnal 'madness' – ripping at his clothes and hair. Scraping bitten fingernails on the heavy panelled doors of this old house. It is a small price to pay for the stress-free lifestyle he and Michael McTavish now enjoy.

Michael McTavish is sitting on the wooden bench. From time to time, he does require the wheelchair. Even with a cane, walking any distance is a struggle. Two months of painful rehabilitation and joint manipulation since he arrived here from Italy. The nurses at Raskine House treat him as a war hero too. But that doesn't soothe the pain. Can't erase the dishonesty. Because Michael McTavish knows that Jamesie Campbell's bullet wound was self-inflicted. And that he deliberately hobbled his younger comrade with a mallet to sustain a fabrication.

'Ah mean, look at this place,' says Jamesie. 'We could've been sent tae some fucken loony bin wi' nae windows, an' doctors that shove thermometers up yer arsehole every ten minutes. This is like a classy hotel.'

'But ye surely dinnae want us tae be here forever, Jamesie.'

'For Christ's sake, relax. Away in an' listen tae that Beethoven thing, or yon Messiah piece ye like. Calm yersel' doon. Ah told ye ah'd look after ye, didn't ah?'

'Aye.'

'Well then. We're no' goin' back tae the fightin', that's aw ye need to know for now.'

The patients here are housed in the newer extension. It was

added to the right of the main house a decade ago, as part of a wider refurbishment following a fire. The residents of Raskine House are all male, and are divided by physical ability –the 'wheelers' and the 'walkers'; and mental capacity – the 'screamers' and the 'dribblers'.

The dribblers are beyond rehabilitation and kept upstairs. Occasionally, one can be spotted at a window. Ghosts. Men who are there, but *not* there. They won't be leaving Raskine House unless it's in a pine overcoat.

The wheelers and the walkers and the screamers are encouraged to congregate. They share the ground floor's big, high-ceilinged rooms. All participate in group discussions and therapy sessions conducted by the all-female nursing staff. They listen to Beethoven's 'Ode to Joy' and Handel's *Messiah* on an almost daily basis. Those that retain the attention span for it read news and current affairs reported in pro-Attlee newspapers owned by the Scottish press baron, Lord Finlay Denton-Hall. These are the titles that lauded Jamesie Campbell on his return from Italy.

'Good morning, Mr Campbell.'

Jamesie didn't see her approaching. 'An' a lovely mornin' tae you too, miss.'

Maude Denton-Hall's family owns Raskine House. The building has been part of their estate since it was built in 1769. Her father is Lord Finlay Denton-Hall. Jamesie Campbell has met Lord Finlay before. In 1933, the orphan boys of St Mary's were presented to Lord Finlay and the patron of the institution, his father, Sir Donnachaidh Denton-Hall. The boys were cleaned up, lined up and handed a number. Jamesie wasn't given a number. Jamesie was told to stand at the back. At the end of the line. When Lord Finlay reached the last boy, Jamesie pushed forward with an outstretched hand.

'Campbell, where your manners, boy? Dinnae be so aggressive.' Jamesie's face was slapped by the priest whom he was forced to wank off on a weekly basis.

'He's trouble, that one,' Lord Finlay was informed.

Jamesie Campbell has never forgotten that day. Nor the suspicion that boy no.8, who was the one selected out of the St Mary's line-up, has been living the Denton-Hall life of Reilly that by rights should have been Jamesie's. How strange that fortune has brought him to the Denton-Hall family pile now – over a decade later?

Maude Denton-Hall doesn't come here often. But Jamesie is always interested when she does. An increased application of disinfectant to all surfaces usually presages her visits. This time, though, it must be unplanned.

Jamesie studies her, making a mental list for recall later, when he is alone:

Full face.

Perfect make-up.

Thick eyebrows.

Dark eyes.

The hint ae a wee bit ae menace.

Light-powdered and blushed cheeks tae accentuate the bone structure.

A dimpled chin.

Glistenin' Rita Hayworth red lips.

Wee body.

Stooped back.

Odd proportions.

Thick black hair piled high in fat, pompadour rolls tae add three inches.

Big tits an' an arse stickin' oot more than they should for the height.

Perfect wank material.

'Are we feeling fit and healthy, gentlemen? Is this beautiful, pure, west of Scotland air helping to cleanse and invigorate?'

The rare smell of her – patchouli, carnation, vanilla – an enticing mixture of fragrances that Jamesie and Michael have never experienced before. Such a stark contrast to the exaggerated chemical odour on the wards.

'Most certainly, miss.'

'And how about you, Mr McTavish? Becoming more capable with every passing day, I see.'

'Em, aye. Still really painful though, Miss Denton-Hall.'

'Oh, come now, you two can call me Maude. You are bona fide Raskine House celebrities.' She laughs.

Then she spots Michael absentmindedly picking at an unusual burn mark on the surface of the bench.

'Did you know that bench is said to belong to the Devil?'

Michael looks up sharply. His fingers retract as if the mark has emitted an electric charge.

'Yes, it's true,' says Maude. 'The original owner of the house brought it here from the West Indies.'

'Ach, there's nae such thing as the Devil,' says Jamesie. 'Just an excuse for bad men tae justify the evil inside their selves.'

'That's not true,' says Maude. 'Is it Michael?'

Her stare drills into the young soldier. And he feels exposed. And guilty. Accused of something but not sure what. He slides along the bench. Maude smiles and the panic he feels dissipates. But only slightly.

Jamesie lifts himself out of the wheelchair. His left arm breaking free of its sling. He leans closer to the bench. Investigating it like he's Sherlock Holmes.

'Aye, mibbe ye're right, miss. That burnt mark looks like a horse's hoof.'

'There's another one of them inside,' she says.

He drops back into the chair.

'Mr McTavish, could you let us have a few minutes, please?'

Michael looks at Jamesie. Jamesie subtly nods. Maude notices but says nothing until Michael McTavish is inside Raskine House.

'He needs your permission for everything he does.'

'He disnae need it.'

'Craves it then,' says Maude.

Jamesie shrugs. 'We aw need a wee bit ae assurance fae time tae time.'

'Hmm. Will you walk with me, Mr Campbell?'

'Em ... ah'm a bit...'

'Oh, your secret is safe with me.' She glances at his legs. She winks.

He scans the windows of the house and then the grounds. There is no-one watching. No-one in sight. She touches his arm. He rises slowly, like Lazarus. They turn towards the tennis court. He limps dramatically. She lets him take an arm.

'That burn on the bench – let me tell you the story,' says Maude. 'Deacon William Bell led his Brotherhood of God followers to Raskine House in the early 1930s. The group had been ostracised from religious circles in the west of Scotland...' She notices Jamesie's puzzled expression. 'Ostracised, Mr Campbell ... excluded. Shunned. You understand?'

'Aye,' says Jamesie. 'How come?'

'It was due to the deacon's strict adherence to polygamous teachings and practice.'

Jamesie's puzzlement continues, but Maude presses on this time.

'The group initially found refuge here at Raskine House. To enter the order, members had to turn over their entire wealth to Bell, so he was in a position to agree to a hefty up-front rental payment for some space here. They were permitted to stay in the outbuildings, but they were prohibited from using the main house. The deacon had few options, so he reluctantly accepted the terms.' She pauses.

'So whit happened next?'

'Someone broke into the house. On discovering stores containing large amounts of cocaine in the basement, an irate Deacon Bell barged into the salon.' Maude points up to the window over the portico.

Jamesie's eyes widen and she picks up the pace:

'My grandmother was playing solitaire up there. He accused my family of funding sinful and satanic activities with the Lord's money.' Maude smiles. Takes a breath. 'The deacon raised a hand to my grandmother. And he overturned her marble table. The next day, a fire destroyed part of the house. Following the blaze, skeletal remains of thirty-three adults and children were discovered in the basement.'

Maude, almost breathless. Jamesie's breathing accelerating in sync.

'It is almost certain they were the disciples of the Brotherhood of God. It is unlikely they died instantly. No-one knew they were inside Raskine House. As I said, they were supposedly restricted to the outbuildings.' A deep, satisfied breath. 'No-one investigated their disappearance.'

Sated.

'Whit happened tae aw the drugs?' asks Jamesie.

Maude laughs. 'A man after my own heart,' she says. 'Don't worry. All safely removed and distributed to the *demi-monde* of Glaswegian high society before a match was lit.'

'Fuck me,' says Jamesie. He crosses his legs to conceal a developing erection. He turns to look back up at Raskine House. He coughs. Then corrects himself.

'Sorry about the language, miss.'

'Please, it's Maude ... and don't worry, I've heard much worse.'

'Your family ran a drug supply chain fae that basement! Jesus.' Jamesie rubs a hand across his chin.

'And we may well again. Soon. I had hoped you might be interested, Mr Campbell.'

'Jamesie, miss. It's *Jamesie*.'

'Raskine House contains multitudes of unusual stories. Strange happenings. When the basement was cleared, that wooden bench was recovered exactly as you see it now. The whole underground space was incinerated, but the upper floors only suffered smoke damage. No interstitial charring at all. And the bench was unmarked apart from the unusual burn impression in the shape of a hoof.' Maude smiles. 'That's why it's known as the Devil's seat.'

'Who knows aboot aw this?'

'Very few,' she confirms, adding: 'My father's a very powerful man.'

Jamesie is confused.

'Our family is adept at concealing secrets and burying unfortunate news,' she says.

But covering up the mass death and burial of an entire religious congregation does not seem like the sort of knowledge that should be shared with someone like Jamesie.

'So why ye tellin' me?'

'You're a man of interest, James.'

'Of interest tae who?' With big secrets of his own to conceal, Jamesie's senses are permanently attuned to others doing the same.

'To us.' She looks into his eyes. 'I think we can trust each other,' says Maude. 'You don't want to return to the front, I presume.'

Jamesie sniggers. 'Would *you*?' he says.

'I can ensure that you don't.' Maude stops. She turns and looks straight at Jamesie.

His eyes narrow. Disbelieving. Suspicious. He is momentarily speechless.

Then: 'Whit aboot McTavish? Him tae?'

'Your little lap dog?'

'Whit d'ye mean by that?' Jamesie bristles.

Maude smiles. Her gloved hand touches his hairy forearm.

'Don't take offence. There are leaders, James ... and there are those who are only fit to be led.'

'So, Michael stays tae?'

'We need someone here we can trust, James. A capable man. The war will not last forever. Raskine House needs a new purpose.'

She hands him a sheaf of papers.

'You might find this of some interest,' she says. 'It's some collected notes on the history of Raskine House.'

Jamesie takes the folder. Flicks through the pages, and then hands it back.

'Nae use tae me. Sorry,' he says. 'Ah cannae read, miss.'

'Oh,' she says, more embarrassed for forcing the admission than he is for admitting it. 'We'll need to address that then.'

'Aye. Aw'right,' says Jamesie. As long as it's her doing the teaching.

'In the meantime, I want you to do something for me,' says Maude.

'Aye? Whit's that then?'

'There's corruption in this house, James. One – or more than one – of the staff is taking money from the men.'

Jamesie stretches his neck. He swallows. He sniffs through flared nostrils. It's a tell. It's hard to prevent when he's confronted with potential exposure. He tries to suppress it.

'Is that right? It's no' happened tae me.'

'A visiting relative has raised a concern. I would like you to find out who is involved and how many of the men have been affected. Can you do that for me, James?'

'Eh, aye. Ah think ah could do that for ye, miss.'

The *quid pro quo* can be revisited later.

'Maude, James. It's Maude from now on.'

She smiles. She reaches into her bag and takes out a bar of chocolate. She hands it to him. He takes hold of it, but she delays letting it go. Her eyes; reading him, boring into him.

'Let's head back. Let us take some tea, James.'

Maude Denton-Hall might know more than she is letting on.

Jamesie knows all about the service-pay scam, because he instigated it. From the moment he was wheeled through its heavy timber doors, Jamesie detected the sexual frustration of those residing here – both the cared-for and the carers. He could smell it. Almost taste it. It was present in every look. Every glance. Every caress of a rubber-gloved hand during a bed bath. Even the wiping of a shitty arse could result in a forlorn, frustrated soldier's hard-on. If testosterone had been flammable, one spark of his lighter could have blown the structure and everything inside it to kingdom come.

Jamesie has been fucking Alice Wilson, the most senior of the nursing staff from the night duty. He also fucks Nurse Mary from the day rota, but less often. Neither nurse knows about the other. A little bit of warmth and companionship during the dark, de-pressing days of a Scottish winter. Where's the harm? The Alice liaison began during the week he and Michael arrived. Where Mary gives it away, Alice now charges Jamesie two shillings a nip. Fair enough. Alice is younger and more sexually adventurous. Better value. But he recovers this by pimping her to the other men for three shillings. He keeps one, she gets two. There are fourteen men in this arrangement. Michael McTavish is not one of them.

The men are ignorant of each other's activities with Alice, and Jamesie and Alice have been careful to keep them that way. Only the wheelers and the walkers are involved. The screamers are too much of a risk. And the army doesn't pay anything to the dribblers directly.

Ending this financially beneficial arrangement will not be easy. Alice Wilson is married. Apart from the public shame, if it is dis-covered, she will be dismissed at best, arrested at worst. And she has no obligation to Jamesie, so she might well be tempted to expose his part in the affair to lessen her punishment. He assumes Maude doesn't know any of what's been happening. He will need to trust his instincts.

When they arrive back at the bench, Michael McTavish has re-turned to it. He is reading from his Bible.

'Mr McTavish,' says Maude, with a slight tilt of the head. Her hand rises. It lightly brushes Jamesie Campbell's shoulder. 'I shall see you both later, I hope.'

The earlier casual offer of tea has been forgotten. A white-gloved hand waves royally as she departs.

'Jesus … whit ah'd give tae fuck her,' says Jamesie.

Michael McTavish says nothing.

'Imagine that life, eh? Fucken loaded. Never has to work a day. Handoots an' inheritances fae the aul' man. Fuck!'

He breaks the chocolate and hands a third of it to Michael McTavish.

'Ah want a bit ae that life,' says Jamesie as he watches the woman's slow sashay until she vanishes.

Jamesie licks the chocolate saliva from his lips.

Two weeks pass. Jamesie Campbell is distant and withdrawn. Whatever Maude Denton-Hall said to him that afternoon at the tennis courts has had an effect that is making Michael McTavish paranoid.

'Everythin' okay, Jamesie?'

'Aye. Why would it no' be, eh?' Jamesie's tone is short.

Michael McTavish begins to panic. Their discussion must have been about him. Jamesie has turned on him.

The lies told at the debriefs in Italy are surely being investigated and unravelled.

Jamesie Campbell watches.

Jamesie Campbell makes mental notes.

One woman. Fourteen men.

One of the men is more malleable than the others, Jamesie has established. Young. Innocent. Impressionable.

Only four years separate them, but the boy looks up to Jamesie Campbell like a naïve teenager hanging on the every word of a worldly-wise uncle. His name is Frank Ross. He was the first Jamesie pimped Alice to. The guinea pig. Like another four damaged young men at Raskine House, his virginity was taken by Nurse Alice. In an upstairs broom cupboard, next to where the dribblers sleep.

Him dabbing shaking, inexperienced fingers inside her knickers.

Her spitting on her hand to lubricate his penis.

Him hyperventilating.

Her straddling him.

Less than a minute of his cock inside her wet fanny before he was done, while Jamesie kept watch outside. It cost Frank two shillings and his sugar ration for the week. The price has since risen. Three shillings. The add-ons now include tea, coffee, cigarettes, a pair of socks.

'How's it goin', son?'

'Aye. It's good. It's good, Jamesie. Aye. Good. Good. Aye.'

'Ye seem a bit rattled, Frank.'

'Naw, Jamesie. Naw. Naw. No' me. Naw.'

'Ye seen the night nurse this week?'

Frank's head dips. 'Naw, Jamesie. Naw.'

'Ye still got tae pay though. That's the deal we made.'

'But, Jamesie, naw ... it's different. Different noo, Jamesie.'

'Is it, though?'

Frank looks up. Uncertain.

'Sup', son?' asks Jamesie.

Frank's voice cracks. 'She says we have tae ... have tae stop. Stop seein' each other. Stop, an' that.' He is close to tears. 'She told me she loved me, Jamesie. Loved me. She *telt* us.'

'Hmm. That's a bit ae a problem, Frank.'

'Aye. No' good, Jamesie. No' good. Naw.'

Jamesie ratchets the pain. 'You know she tells everybody that, don't ye? You're nothin' fucken special there, pal.'

Frank's eyes moisten. He starts sobbing.

'Fuck sake, son.' Jamesie leans in. A hand reaches under the bedsheet. He feels for a wrist. He twists it. 'Get a fucken grip ae yersel, Frank, son.'

A low grumble. Undetected by those around them – all lost in their own mental pain.

'Jamesie! Sorry, Jamesie. Sorry. Whit ah'm ah gonnae dae, Jamesie?'

'No' sure, son,' says Jamesie. 'But ye still owe me the debt.'

'But Jamesie—'

Jamesie puts a finger to his lips. 'No' my problem, Frankie boy. Ye need tae sort this yin out yersel.'

'Ah'm sorry, Jamesie. Sorry, big man.'

Jamesie puts an arm around the younger man's shoulders. Frank continues to weep.

'It's fine, son. Ye're in a corner, ah get that,' he says. 'C'mon noo, pull yersel th'gither. Stop blubbin' like a wean an' take control ae the situation.'

Frank wipes his face. His expectant eyes longing for fatherly advice.

'Ah'd confront her,' says Jamesie. Frank nods meekly. 'Although ah will say this. Any bitch did that tae me, an' she'd know aw aboot it.'

'Jamesie?'

Nothing.

'Jamesie, please. Tell me whit ah've done.'

Michael McTavish is ignored.

Michael McTavish is devastated.

'Jamesie!'

Nurse Mary's brother has died. She has a week's compassionate leave. Nurse Alice is on time-and-a-half to cover Mary's day shift. Perfect timing. It's as if Jamesie has scripted the opportunity.

A quick visit to the kitchen. Unseen.

The implement, wrapped in a kitchen towel. Unseen.

Placed in Frank's bed while he was in the toilet. Unseen.

Another quick word in the ear of the desolate young man on his return. Unseen.

Good to go.

Music plays from the tannoy. 'Don't Fence Me In' – Bing and the Andrews Sisters. An exercise-session favourite. The song wafts and bounces across the tennis court. Like the ball in a doubles match.

Twenty-four men are seated. Four rows of six. A military formation. Sharp shadows on the court's gravel. Arms waving from side to side. Aping Nurse Alice's own movements. Perfect obedience.

'Oh, give me land, lots of land under starry skies above...'

The tranquillity is disturbed. A distant rumble can be heard. Jamesie sees it before anyone else.

'Let me ride through the wide-open country that I love...'

A low-flying Lancaster bomber flies over the Campsies. It heads towards Raskine House. Jamesie sees the panic rising in the ranks.

'Don't fence me in.'

Some of the men shake. Some wail. Some scream as the aircraft gets louder. Jamesie Campbell can't believe his luck. Maybe there is a God. Or gods. If there are, they're shining down on him now.

'Let me be by myself in the evenin' breeze...'

The screaming intensifies. The military formation abandoned as escaping the inevitable bombardment becomes the only motivation. Nurse Alice tries to calm them.

'And listen to the murmur of the cottonwood trees...'

The neurasthenic men flail. Wheels crash together. Fragile bodies upended. Several crawl as best their weary bodies allow, like they are back in the muddy, sodden, death trenches of Italy.

Nurse Alice. Losing her patience. Losing control.

'Don't fence me in...'

Nurse Alice shouts. Louder than the men. The bomber banks left, over their heads. One purposeful soldier leaps screaming from his chair.

'Send me off forever, but I ask you, please...'

Frank Ross stabs the nurse in the chest with the kitchen knife that he has concealed inside a sleeve.

Nurse Alice dies instantly.

A fortuitous fly-past. A coincidence such as Jamesie Campbell could never have conceived even in his wildest dreams.

'DON'T FENCE ME IN!'

The Fat of the Land (1948–52)

Jamesie and Maude grow closer – Jamesie faces a test of character – Jamesie's temper gets the better of him.

October 1948

In the aftermath of the events at Raskine House three years earlier, Jamesie Campbell managed to land on his feet. His involvement in the soldiers' 'fucks-for-folding' fraud remains unknown.

For his part, Lord Finlay was able to manipulate the awkward situation at his property to his advantage. Armed-forces chiefs were forced to accept culpability for the scandalous actions of their nursing staff once the other men – encouraged by Jamesie – claimed the dead nurse had taken advantage of them too. And those chiefs also publicly apologised for a low-flying aircraft veering off course. Substantial reparations were paid. And Jamesie was rewarded for his silence.

Raskine House estate is now back in the family's full control. Jamesie's bedroom is the second largest in the house. And he has money – earned not stolen. His job is to manage the estate – its grounds and its staff. That staff includes Tav, Jamesie's general assistant, and Nurse Mary, now head of the kitchen staff. He still fucks her regularly.

The job comes with a shotgun, which he is rarely without. And a car, which, although not specifically his, no-one else uses. Jamesie Campbell has come a long way from the stale bread and cold porridge of the mission. The kitchen is always fully stocked. Venison, pheasant, rabbit from the fields. Salmon and trout from the streams running into the loch. The cook knows Jamesie's favourite dinners. And Maude visits him on the weekends. She is teaching him to read and write.

Jamesie likes Maude. And he knows she likes him. But there is a darkness to her. He recognises it because it's inside him too. They take regular walks across the estate's moorland. Growing closer and more comfortable in each other's company.

'Hurry, James. Look!'

Maude has run ahead of Jamesie. She's looking for something but won't say what it is. The early-autumn light is disappearing fast. The tree canopy above him is still clothed in auburn leaves. He can no longer see her. Only hear her excited cries. He follows the sound of her through the woods.

He curses her. Agitated. He's cold. And bored. They have been out here for hours. Miles from Raskine House yet still within the bounds of the estate. His belly rumbles its discontent.

'Where are ye?'

'Down here. Quickly, James. Come.' Less faint now, but still fifty yards or so away from him.

He spots her red woollen bobble hat. It blends with the burnt oranges and yellows shed from the dense formation of sentries towering over him.

The red bobble vanishes from Jamesie's sight.

'James!'

Jamesie turns left.

'James. Hurry.'

'For fuck's sake, ah cannae fucken see ye!'

And suddenly she's there. Twenty feet in front of him. Perfectly camouflaged. The faintest glimpse of red spilling from her coat pocket.

'It *is* here. I have found it,' she says. 'And don't be so brusque,' she scolds.

Jamesie looks around and beyond her. He doesn't know what she has been searching for, so it could be anything. Some daft fucking plant? Buried treasure? Or the bones of some poor cunt she's had buried?

'Down in the hollow, James.' She sets off ahead of him, gesturing for him to follow.

He hesitates. He likes her, but he cannot be entirely sure there isn't an animal trap down there, primed and waiting for his leg.

She stops and turns. 'James,' she says softly. 'What are you waiting for?'

'Whit the fuck is it, Maude? C'mon ... ah've nae time for this nonsense.'

'You scared, James? A big muscly man like you?' She giggles.

He cocks the shotgun. 'Christ's sake, ah'm cold an' starvin'. Hurry up then.'

Jamesie wanders down the slope. Slipping a bit. Almost falling. Gun helping to balance him. He passes her. Gives her a suspicious glance. She sticks out a tongue.

'Whit ah'm ah lookin' at here?' Agitation is becoming anger.

'Keep going,' she says.

And then he begins to see it. The camouflage collage of branches and leaves is at odds with the fabric of the rest of the woodland floor around them. This is familiar to him from years of hiding from assailants with rifles. It's a shelter. A dug-out. So well constructed and concealed as to be almost invisible, even when standing only a few feet away.

A shudder shakes its way through his core. Jamesie is momentarily dazed. His head is swimming. Senses blocked. He's back in the dark, dangerous woods outside Ortona. Exhorting Benny and Tav to dig fucking faster.

'James? What's wrong? Go inside.'

And he wonders what fucked-up game she is playing. This manipulation of his fragile emotions. His trembling finger rests on the trigger. But he likes her. And he knows she likes him. Jamesie Campbell is a survivor. Jamesie will do what it takes.

'James!'

Suddenly her voice irritates. Boring its way into his brain. A maggot that won't stop chewing.

He peels back a corrugated sheet, weighed down by turf cuts and heavy ferns. It slides back enough for him to glimpse inside.

'What's in there, James?'

He's on his knees. Leaning down. Peering in. The light almost gone. He pulls out his torch but it fails him. He has no perception of the depth.

Fuck sake!

He reaches inside. Feels around in the darkness. Heart pounding. Expecting something to bite. Or to drag him in. Down into the bowels of Hell.

'James?'

The disturbed edge of the excavation gives way under Jamesie's bulk. He falls into the pit. Six foot down. Like a grave, but wider. His head throbs. He feels a wetness with his fingers. He smells the coppery odour of his own blood. He has cut his forehead on the rusty metal corrugations.

'James!'

'For fuck's sake, shut it will ye, eh?'

He stands up straight. The excavated foxhole is smaller than theirs was in Italy. Claustrophobia grips him. He gulps in air like he is about to dive underwater. His leg stretches out. Feels something rigid. Maybe a bed frame. He bends and gropes around further. And then he feels something else. A rectangular shape. Small. Hard. A book? He puts it inside his coat.

'What is it, James? What have you got?'

She's on the edge now. Peering down at him.

He stands on the frame. Levers himself out using the heavy corrugated metal as a pivot. He's on his knees in front of her. Panting at the exertion.

'This,' he says.

He brushes the muck and the spiders and damp off the book. On the cover, there are gold letters.

'I knew it,' Maude announces. 'This proves it.'

'Whit?' says Jamesie. 'Knew whit?'

She takes the book from him. She flicks through the pages. A card falls out. Although faded, a handwritten note can still be deciphered. If the reader understands German.

'The German High Command was trying to get a message to my father. During the war.' She is breathless. Struggling to contain her excitement. 'My father's convinced they wanted his help to broker a peace deal with Westminster in 1941. Rudolf Hess didn't fly here alone. He couldn't have.'

'What are ye talkin' about, Maude?'

'The Germans were looking to end the war in forty-one, James. They needed a powerful advocate. Someone trusted and respected in political circles. Someone who could control the propaganda.'

Jamesie's head is swimming. His forehead throbs with the pain of the cut. He doesn't understand what he is being told. He is like Alice from that book Maude gave him when she was teaching him to read. Everything in the Denton-Hall orbit is upside down. Back to front. Fucked-up and frivolous. Yet at the same time, Raskine House seems at the centre of it all. He can't entirely believe anything he is told. Everything is a test. Of his loyalty. His honesty. His commitment. His sanity.

'You found it, James. I cannot believe it. My father's been searching for this for years. And *you* found it. Have you any idea how priceless this book is? ... Maybe you should keep it for now.'

And there it is. Jamesie still struggles to read words. But he can read between the lines. Maude has planted this artefact. She intended for him to discover it. To see what he'd do next. This is a personal test. Can he be trusted? Or will he fuck off over the nearest hill, looking to sell the book to the highest bidder?

Jamesie is going nowhere. There is money and power in the Denton-Hall circle. There is madness too, but he has seen enough of that during his twenty-six years to know how to take advantage of it. And besides, he likes her. And he knows she likes him too.

He brushes the caked muck off his knees, and when he looks up, she is already halfway up the path.

'James.'

He can barely see her. She is hiding again.

'Where are ye, this time?'

She keeps him on his toes, that's for sure. A life being around her won't be boring.

'Will you fuck me, James?' Posh Edinburgh English asking politely.

This is an unexpected turn.

He sees her outline. She comes towards him. Her hot breath on his neck. The intoxicating smell of her. Her fingers reaching for his belt. Then his trouser buttons. There's jeopardy in every exchange.

He stops her. 'Ah dinnae have a johnny,' he says.

She laughs. 'It's okay, my love,' she says. 'I don't have a uterus.'

Jamesie doesn't know what this means. His instinct tells him that, for now at least, it means sex with no consequences.

+

May 1951

Bad timing.

'Something wrong?'

'Fucken cunts!'

'Jamesie? What is it? What's that article you're reading?' Maude's hand rests on his shoulder.

'Stay oot ma fucken way, Maude.'

'But Jamesie...'

'Ah'm warnin' ye, right?'

She is taken aback by the sudden rage.

He throws the newspaper across the room and storms out, booting the kitchen door in the process. Maude picks up the paper and reads the offending article:

In late September 1943, nearly two hundred veterans of Montgomery's Eighth Army were arrested for refusing orders to join units of the US Fifth Army at the Salerno beachhead in southern Italy. Within six weeks, all but one had been found guilty of mutiny, their sentences ranging from five years' penal servitude to death.

Almost a decade later, the *Herald* can now reveal how the defence team at the trial were given adequate time and full access to witnesses, and yet offered a case based on no evidence and which was doomed to fail. Public pressure has been building, with correspondence submitted to the House of Commons calling for the dishonoured mutineers to have their war pensions rescinded. As a result of their convictions, the former war heroes are to be rightly stripped of their campaign and gallantry medals and branded as cowards.

'Jamesie?' She looks for him, but he's gone. Out to the wilds. Gun loaded and looking for something to kill.

Jamesie has controlled and maintained this estate for the past six years. He is well paid for a relatively stress-free lifestyle largely spent in the open air. But he is also Lord Finlay's muscle. His enforcer.

On several occasions during his tenure, he has come across trespassers wandering the grounds. Raskine House is so remote that those caught here without permission to be so must have an ulterior motive.

Each time, Jamesie took them back to a shed. Battered them senseless then dropped them on the other side of the boundary wall nearest to Barrhead. Left them at the base of the sign that reads:

RASKINE HOUSE ESTATE: STRICTLY PRIVATE PROPERTY
NO TRESPASSING – BY ENFORCED ORDER

Jamesie spots the man in the distance. Too far to hit with a shot from here, but he's still inclined to do so: aim at him and fire in hope. But that would only alert the trespasser, and what good would that do Jamesie? He needs to hurt something, or someone. He needs to feel that release.

Jamesie skirts the trees. Gaining ground. The man is heading in the direction of the house but with the uncertainty of someone who doesn't know exactly where it is.

After following him for twenty minutes, Jamesie is close enough to be heard. And close enough for a cartridge to hit the target.

'Can ah help ye, son?'

The young man is startled, and even more so to see a shotgun aimed at him.

'Aw, Christ! Don't shoot me, mister,' he says, arms aloft. He's holding a satchel. A white-bread sandwich falls out of it.

Jamesie pauses. A voice in his head says, *Shoot the cunt, then eat his sandwich*. Another one says, *Take him tae the sheds*.

Bad timing.

Jamesie leads the young man to a barn.

'Mister, ah just want tae talk tae Lord Finlay. He owns this place, right? Ah'm a history student. Ah'm researchin' Albert Raskine ... the story ae Raskine an' his descendants an' their part in the Glaswegian slave trade.' Talking a mile a minute. His dread increasing.

Bad timing.

'Shut the fuck up, son!' says Jamesie. The butt of the shotgun rattles the young man's jaw, and he's down, holding dislodged teeth in his bloody hands.

Jamesie strips him naked.

Jamesie takes the young man's belt.

Jamesie ties the belt round the young man's neck.

Jamesie uses it to hang the young man from a hay-bailing hook.

And it's only when the young man is up there, swinging, that

Jamesie feels a release of the tension that has been building up inside him. He can't put his finger on it, but something has been irritating him. It might've been Maude. Or her father. Or Tav. But whatever it is, it culminated in that fucking newspaper article.

These cunts that manipulate the truth to further some politician's agenda. Cunts that have never served. Who weren't there. Who've never had to look some *other* poor cunt in the eye as you take his life to stop him taking yours.

Just bad timing.

Jamesie observes the young man like a scientist conducting an anatomical examination. The bizarre contrast between the terror in his wide, bulging eyes and the thrust of an unexpected erection. The ejaculation. The defecation. The saliva. The body's fluids squeezing out of him like someone wringing out a sodden flannel. Every time the young man comes close to suffocation, when his desperate hands can no longer grip the tightening belt, Jamesie lifts him down. Drenches him in trough water. Then hangs him again. And again. And again.

Jamesie watches the torso contorting as the limbs stretch. The toes grasping for any surface that can take the weight. The eyes pleading for the strangulation to stop. Jamesie finds it fascinating. Regardless of the exhaustion, the survival instinct of the human body remains intact. Jamesie understands that only too well.

Before depositing him at the usual spot, Jamesie takes a pitchfork and rams one of its sharp points through the young man's foot. The young man lies moaning at his torturer's boots. Whimpering. Empty. Completely at Jamesie's mercy. Genitals wrapped in an old grain sack. Arms outstretched. Blood pouring from the hole in his foot. Consciousness fading.

Brutal violations. History repeating.

He tells Maude. When he's calmed down he feels he owes her an explanation. Plus, there is something about the young man. Something oddly familiar. And there was something about his interest in the estate – something more than the usual public nosiness or professional intrigue Lord Finlay has warned him about. Jamesie told Lord Finlay about all the other times. All the previous invaders he dealt with. But not this one. Maude tells him not to. She knows he has gone too far with this one. But fortunately she also knows how to tidy up this mess Jamesie has made. The young historian will soon find himself set up for life in a newspaper job.

Now that he can read, Jamesie is interested in history. The Denton-Halls' history, primarily, and how he can subsume himself into it. He has looked through the books in the Raskine House library. If it interested a young history student enough to risk the consequences of trespass, there might also be something of interest to a man like Jamesie.

He spends a lot of time there with Tav, who helps him understand antiquated words written in a different era. Although, unlike Tav, Jamesie believes that knowledge rather than faith is the route to salvation.

They absorb the stories of Britain's history. Of Scotland's slave-trading past. Of how the spoils of empire built this place. Of the brutal violations that occurred in the pursuit of that empire. More recent violations too.

Jamesie has participated in some of them.

A Marriage of Convenience (1953)

Jamesie and Maude's Wedding Day – Lord Finlay Denton-Hall spells it out for Jamesie – Jamesie adapts to his new status.

April 1953

Jamesie Campbell thinks back to those days often. Particularly the day when he discovered the shelter in the wood. The German book. The first time he fucked Maude. He thinks of that pivotal day regularly. Never more than when out walking the estate with his future father-in-law. Their guns cocked. The dogs meandering. Waiting for shots. Excited about recovering dead grouse.

'Jamesie, I've got something for you,' says Lord Finlay.

'Aye? Whit's that, sir?' Jamesie doesn't reciprocate Lord Finlay's informality. He knows his place, and his forthcoming marriage will not change that.

'It's a job, son,' says Lord Finlay. 'A far more important one than you have now.'

'Ah like it oot here. Wi' the dugs. The fresh air. The wind in yer hair, y'know?'

'You're marrying my daughter, son. You can't remain a bloody gamekeeper and be marrying a Denton-Hall. You need to be moving upward. Moving into political circles. Alongside men with power and influence.'

'Dinnae know much about politics, other than both sides seem like a bunch ae cunts.'

Lord Finlay laughs at this. 'And that's all you need to know, Jamesie,' he says. 'We use politicians to manipulate things.'

'Fair enough, sir.'

'The electorate are comprised of idiots and servants, Jamesie. "The puppet on the right ... he shares my beliefs," they'll say. Then, "No, wait a minute, the puppet on the left is more to my liking." They're too stupid to appreciate that there's one man holding the strings of both puppets. That man is me.'

Jamesie purses his lips. Raises an eyebrow. Not sure whether to speak in the gaps or not. He decides not.

'We are going to move the publishing arm into a place where it has more political influence, son. That's where the real power lies. The potential for a newspaper to pick and choose the government of the day – that's *real* democracy!'

Jamesie nods. Interested but not yet understanding.

'Churchill's done. He should never have come back. The welfare state goes against Conservative principles. It means high taxes, large-scale government spending and government interfering in the lives of the public. But how could he dismantle it?'

Jamesie isn't sure if he is expected to have an answer to this question. He doesn't.

'Prosperity might well rise, son, but so will prices. Elderly people are going to struggle with their pensions.'

Jamesie strolls on, unaware the old man has stopped. The gunshot shakes him. The shells whistle past his right ear. So close that he could easily have been hit. The ringing renders him temporarily deaf. The dogs bark and chase away in the direction of the shot. Maybe this was a warning discharge. A reminder to pay full attention.

Jamesie turns. Expressionless, but as always, weighing things up.

Dinnae ever fire a gun withoot warnin' near a man that's been in a war, ya stupid aul' cunt.

Jamesie visualises taking the rifle and repeatedly ramming it into Lord Finlay's face until flesh, meat and bone are reduced to one pulped substance. He could batter seven shades of shite out of this privileged old ponce. With one arm restrained, too. No danger there. He could bury the body. Return weeks later to exhume it. Carve it into pieces and feed it to the pigs.

But what would that profit him? This old fucker is his route to riches. Maude, his only child, will not provide a grandson. If he plays his cards right, Jamesie Campbell will be *de facto* heir apparent.

'When simple folk get desperate, they get angry,' Lord Finlay continues. 'Angry at rich people proclaiming there's no money left for them. You understand?'

Jamesie paces his breathing. Calming himself. 'Ah'm beginning tae, aye.' And he is.

'We're part of the establishment, son. I won't deny that. Always have been. But we weren't born to it.'

Jamesie raises an eyebrow.

'From right back to the beginning of human existence, anyone of means stole their wealth from someone else. The ancient Greeks, the Egyptians, the Romans ... the Normans. In the aftermath of 1066, a handful of noblemen took the land from the people. They just took it, and assumed it as their own. Civilisation invented the concept of money as a mechanism of wealth control. Nothing more. And those in power used indoctrinated muscle to keep it. And wrote new laws and legal titles to maintain it. They became the landowning classes. They didn't earn it, son. They just had the balls to steal it. Jeremiah Hall, my ancestor, the man who built this estate three hundred years ago, did you know *he* stole his fortune?'

Jamesie contemplates this.

'Yes. Hard to believe?' asks Lord Finlay. 'Mark my words, son, at the root of every fortune is a crime.'

Jamesie shrugs.

'Jamesie?'

'Who knows, sir. Ah'm just a poor man fae...'

'So was Jeremiah.' Lord Finlay stops again.

Jamesie stops too. He won't make the same mistake twice.

'He was an uneducated streetfighter. Down on the Clydeside docks. Battered a man to death in a prize fight. The man had no money, so my ancestor took the man's construction business as payment. He learned to read and write. Built the company up. Ruthless, he was. Uncompromising. A real man. Enforced his honour when he had to. He left his family very wealthy, Jamesie. Made them part of the social elite of the day. The house and everything you see around you became theirs when the owner, Albert Raskine, couldn't, or wouldn't, settle his debts. Jeremiah's sons simply took the estate from him.'

Jamesie Campbell and Lord Finlay Denton-Hall walk on.

'Sir ... the book? The German High Command? Wis that genuine?'

'Genuine, in so far that it happened?'

'Well ... aye, but the links tae your family? Ah mean, it just seems a bit far-fetched that fucken Nazi high-heidyins would fly here, tae bloody Scotland, tae...'

'To reach out to us?'

'Well...'

'During the Great War, my father made political friends, all over Europe. And in our most recent war, while you were fighting in Italy, I was negotiating deals with our country's allies, and its enemies. Commerce doesn't stop just because politicians go to war with each other. These overseas connections are essential, son, as you're going to find out. The Germans needed my influence, my contacts. They knew of my father's personal friendship with Churchill. But my father and I always preferred the Soviets. They know how to trade.'

'Trade?'

'Trade ... yes. In valuable things. Goods. Secrets.' Lord Finlay turns to look at his future son-in-law. 'People.'

The dogs weave crocheted patterns around them.

'We've made valuable long-term friendships with those behind the Iron Curtain,' says Lord Finlay. 'As you'll soon find out.'

Lord Finlay lifts an arm and puts it as far round Jamesie's shoulders as it will reach.

'The British aristocracy has always been brittle. It's never been about bloodlines, always about money for the ruling class. Our family prospered in the Industrial Revolution. We sent our children to the best schools, to become part of the establishment. A nefarious past didn't matter if you had money, and lots of it. Do you understand what I am telling you?'

Jamesie nods.

'And the best schools constructed barriers. They did it through language, pronunciation, confidence and most importantly, by creating an elite network of relationships. You scratch my back, I'll scratch yours. A knighthood here, a life peerage there – that's how *we* maintain control. Favours. As long as we have wealth and the land we stole from them, the working-classes – *your* people – cannot touch us.'

Jamesie scratches his beard.

'It's only natural for superior peoples to dominate inferior peoples, Jamesie. It's our God-given right.'

There is a gulf between them that matrimony won't bridge. It's as wide as an ocean. Jamesie understands this. He'll always be an outsider. But that's alright. Opportunity is only what you make of it, right?

'You don't have access to that traditional superior network, son,' says Lord Finlay. 'They'd never accept someone like you. Someone with no pedigree. Scum, from the gutters.'

If there is a compliment hiding here, it's taking its time to show itself, thinks Jamesie.

'So, you must build a network for yourself. You need to create a circle … a group with political influence and new wealth. Cultivate relationships with people who crave the same power, the same access, the same desires as you. And know how to protect themselves.'

'Cunts that'll steal the land fae other cunts, ye mean?'

Lord Finlay cocks his shotgun. He aims. Fires. And another of God's creatures dies. The spent cartridges fly backward. Lord Finlay is a seasoned hunter. Killing is as intuitive to him as it once was to Jamesie.

Lord Finlay laughs. 'In a manner of speaking, yes. Once inside the circle, simply being there is usually enough to maintain control.'

Jamesie Campbell sees opportunity where others wait for it to announce itself.

'So, what ye're sayin' is ah need tae be as ruthless an' devious as your aul' ancestor, Jeremiah?'

'A man is whatever room he says he is in, yes.'

Jamesie senses an opportunity. A chance. He just needs to make it count.

'Right then. Ah've got a favour tae ask.'

'Okay. What is it?'

'St Mary's Roman Catholic Boy's Industrial School ower in Bridgeton – you're the owner?'

'Of the building, yes. My father was patron of the institute. Why?'

'Let me take control ae it. Let me run it. Ah'll convert it tae a religious mission that makes money.'

'There's no money in religion, Jamesie. And that building is shot to pieces. Simply maintaining its upkeep is a drain on our finances.'

'So, let me take it aff yer hands. Prove tae ye that ah can be worthy ae Maude. Worthy ae you an' yer establishment circles.'

'But you're already marrying into the establishment. You'll never want for anything ever again. That's what you are joining, son. Privilege. Aristocracy. You'll be one of the elite, albeit an interloper.'

'But ah want tae prove ah can make a success ae this on ma own terms, sir.'

Lord Finlay looks at Jamesie closely. The request confuses him, but it seems to matter to the young man. And since he has no loyalty to the priests who run the school, he concedes.

'Fine. It's yours. I ask only two things in return.'

'What's that, sir?'

'If you raise a hand to my daughter, do it in private, behind closed doors, where such things between a man and wife should remain.'

Jamesie nods. His focus momentarily diverted by thoughts of the day when he will appear with his squad unannounced at St Mary's. He'll bolt the doors behind him and force the priests inside to suck each other's cocks at gunpoint before putting the rancid cunts out on the street.

Remember me, ya evil bastarts?

Ah'm Jamesie fucken Campbell.

An' ah'm here tae send aw you dirty child-fuckers tae Hell.

'An' the other?' he says, still grinning.

'Don't ever fucking betray me, son. Or you'll vanish like mist in the morning sun...'

'Ah won't, sir.'

'Or like your young Scouse comrade, Benny Robertson.'

Lord Finlay Denton-Hall turns and strolls away. Weapon crooked over his elbow. Barrel open. Muzzle pointing downward.

He whistles the dogs. They run at his command. He is a small man, but with that last sentence left hanging in the breeze for Jamesie Campbell to digest, the full extent of Lord Finlay's reach and power lands. The only person alive that could contradict Jamesie and Tav's version of events during those final weeks in Italy was Benny Robertson.

But how could Lord Finlay have known about him?

And then slowly it dawns. The dots gradually join. After the tennis-court incident, Jamesie Campbell became something of a newspaper celebrity once again. Columns fabricated Jamesie's selfless disarming of young Frank Ross, saving several of his infirm comrades in the process. Subsequent front-pages reprinted previous stories of Jamesie Campbell's war heroics in Italy. A public hero was being carefully manufactured. In the aftermath, Benny – on reading this fiction – must have gone to the papers with his own version. The populist ones published by Lord Finlay Denton-Hall. Probably the last thing the former soldier ever did, Jamesie thinks.

Jamesie is awestruck by the power he's witnessing. And, although he is a hard bastard, he is fearful of being on the wrong side of it. He rushes to catch up.

'The job, sir,' he says. 'You mentioned a new job?'

'So I did,' says Lord Finlay. 'You'll be going to Lithuania for a while. After your wedding day.'

'Lithu— ... *where*?'

Lord Finlay smiles. 'We're setting up the Donnachaidh Denton-Hall Trust. In Kaunas. Look it up. You'll be there for six months. Our friends in the U.S.S.R. will look after you.'

Jamesie breathes heavily. This does not sound like a promotion.

'Then, you'll come back into the newspaper industry, son. I need a man on the inside. The Conservatives are going to wage war on the unions, and that's not good for business. You're going to learn the trade. Work your way up. Take control of the print unions. And then we use that foundation to get you into politics.'

Jamesie looks bemused.

'Labour politics, obviously.' Lord Finlay snorts. 'No chance of us passing *you* off as an Old Etonian, eh? Not with the untamed manners of a savage.'

Jamesie Campbell sees his life being mapped out in front of him.

'Does Maude know aboot this?'

'It was her idea, Jamesie,' says Lord Finlay. 'It's a substantial pay rise. And you'll stay in the best hotels. Eat in the best restaurants. Conduct important business for the Denton-Hall family.'

Lord Finlay thumbs cartridges into both chambers.

'Well, interested?'

After the brutality of his childhood. Then the ensuing chaos of the war years. The British army betrayal, stealing his fucking hard-earned pension...

'Aye, fuck it, sir. Aye,' he says. Six months *R&R*, eating well and sunbathing in Lithy-*whereeverthefuck*? 'Too right ah am.'

'We're not so different, you and me,' says Lord Finlay. 'Men who understand human nature.' He cocks the gun again. Aims. 'And how to fucking exploit it for our own ends.'

He fires. A young deer collapses in the distance. The dogs race each other for the prize of ripping the carcass apart.

+

2nd June

Raskine House has rarely looked better. The sunshine helps. But only a select few will bear witness to it on this, the wedding day of Maude Denton-Hall and James Campbell.

Lord Finlay will shortly transfer ownership of Raskine Hall to his daughter and her new husband. It is a one-sided deal. A huge dowry. Jamesie Campbell brings nothing material to this marriage. Only his word. And his commitment. And his willingness to be moulded and manipulated. The father of the bride trusts his own judgement. Always has done. He is sure this will prove to be a balanced transaction.

The vast, blackened-timber doors, resembling those of a baronial castle's keep, are open. Ornamental balconies extend to the edges of the front facade. Blood-red roses climb all around the lower windows, clustered thick, and enlivening the otherwise plain stonework.

Once inside, a marble staircase rises from the right of the vaulted reception hall. Lilies drape and coil their way along the stone balustrade's mahogany capping. The staircase's three wide flights create a voided well for appreciating the entrance centrepiece: a cut-glass chandelier, twenty feet in diameter.

The interior of the hall smells of fresh paint.

The layout of the upper floor of the house mirrors that of the lower. The drawing rooms of the ground level are the bedrooms of the first floor. All have attendant toilets. All contain large fireplaces with inner hearths a man can easily stand in.

These bed chambers have elaborate cornicing with sensual patterns and carnal figures that seem to dance and sway and gyrate in the corner of your eye when your gaze is averted. All but one of the upper rooms – the salon – has an ornate ceiling rose.

The ceremony will take place in the salon. It's an eery room, not least because of its spartan arrangement, the echoes created by the cold, hard surfaces.

Michael McTavish has always disliked this room. There is something menacing and other-worldly about it. And for the newly installed Pastor of the Sovereign Grace Mission in Bridgeton, it feels doubly dangerous. It is a challenge to be conducting a ceremony that celebrates two people coming together under God, bestowing God's blessing upon them, when the presence of evil is almost palpable.

Pastor McTavish stands patiently behind the card table. He cannot avert his eyes from the hoof print in its corner. He has brought a beautiful lace cloth from the Sovereign Grace Mission to cover it. But the lace isn't big enough. It doesn't conceal the mark.

A wooden lectern holds the Pastor's Bible, open at Corinthians 13. Two elaborate candlesticks stand on either side. The reduced height of the candles indicates the lateness of the bride. Almost three hours since they were lit. The eight wooden seats in the salon are empty. Those here to witness the wedding are elsewhere in the house. Lord Finlay is in an adjoining room. He can be heard barking orders to someone down the telephone.

'A full issue dedicated to it ... Yes. You heard me,' he commands.

Pastor McTavish wanders closer to the door. His empty stomach threatening to expose his nosiness.

'The *Telegraph*, definitely. Less for *The Times*. Sixteen-page extra. A pull-out. Yes. Full front-cover photographs.'

A long pause.

'Of course. It's a massively significant event in this country's history.'

A shorter pause.

'Something simple like "Elizabeth the Second is Crowned", with "Splendour in Abbey Seen by Millions" as sub-head.'

A pause.

'No, for God's sake ... the *Telegraph*! Jesus Christ, do I have to do everything myself?'

The receiver slams down. Pastor McTavish rushes back to his place behind the table with the distinctive hoof mark.

He hears a piper outside.

Action stations.

Five kilted men file in. The last of them, his friend, the groom. The other four look like they have been hired for the day. And are being paid by the hour.

The piper leads the bride up the staircase. Pastor McTavish glimpses another woman meet the bride on the top landing. Bridesmaid for the day. He sees Lord Finlay take out his fob watch and stare at it. The point theatrically made.

Maude Denton-Hall takes her father's arm, and they approach slowly to the sound of Mendelssohn's *Wedding March*, adjusted for the pipes. This music, which portrays fantasy, murder, sex and other delights, was chosen by the bride. No-one else will appreciate the association, she suspects. To them, it will just be noise, akin to a bag of cats being hit with a cricket bat.

Jamesie lifts the veil. He winks. Maude grins like a lovestruck girl of thirteen.

'Dearly beloved, we are gathered here in this place to bear witness to the marriage of James and Maude, and to celebrate the deep love they have for one another.'

The pastor spots another melodramatic check of the fob watch.

Quite why Lord Finlay insisted on the ceremony being held on the same day, and at the same time, as the coronation of Great Britain's young queen is baffling. Still, here they all are, the invested and the instructed.

With no-one objecting, God the ventriloquist says his piece:

'Love is patient. Love is kind. It does not envy. It does not boast. It is not proud. It does not dishonour others. It is not self-seeking. It is not easily angered. It keeps no record of wrongs. Love does not delight in evil but rejoices with the truth.'

The pastor delivers it perfectly. He conceals a trembling hand.

Both participants vow to love and honour. Jamesie to cherish. Maude to obey. Until death parts them.

And with the briefest of kisses, they are married.

The assembly silently mouths 'The Lord of All Hopefulness', but only the bride and the pastor sing the words.

The bedroom at the northernmost corner of the house has a different ceiling rose from the others. This room contains the marital bed. The domestic staff have been given the night off. The guests left after the one glass of Champagne they were offered. Like it was being grudged them.

Lord Finlay and Tav have departed too. Only the newly Honourable Jamesie and his newly obedient wife remain in the house

The fire in the bedroom is raging. Winifred Atwell's plinky-plonk 'Coronation Rag' plays in the corner. It is headache-inducing, but Maude likes it and the seventy-eight shellac disc is rarely off the Marconi. Candles burn, dozens of them. Jamesie has been left momentarily to the slabs of venison and the bottles of port he has brought with him from downstairs. It feels like a sacrifice might be about to take place. He laughs at the thought of her coming through those vast double doors brandishing a sword.

He swigs laconically from the bottle. He's rapidly acquired a taste for the finer things in life. Who fucking cares if the Denton-

Halls are as mad as March hares. If there is a price to pay for social acceptance – and there always is for the likes of Jamesie – he's happy to pay it.

The blood-red liquid spills down his chin. Runs through his beard. He watches it accelerate down the trough between his pectorals. And then just as it looks to be heading for a hole-in-one, it swerves his belly button and streams into his pubic hair.

Jamesie laughs again. His teeth tear at the red meat in his hands. He tips the bottle and pours the alcohol on his chest until it floods his abdomen and his genitals and turns the white bed-sheets crimson around his body.

These rich cunts ... like Roman Emperors and their Domina.

Not giving a fuck.

Untouchable.

Fucking brilliant.

The doors open.

Jamesie looks up.

Maude is naked. Just like him.

Except for the black mask she wears.

Jamesie considers the mask unnecessary. There's only two of them in the house, after all. And he fucking knows it's her.

A black leather strap is buckled tightly around her waist. The strap has a big black plastic piece attached to it. She turns side-on. Showing it to him. The extent of it. The elevation of its upward arc. It's shaped like a cock – ripples and veins and all. In fact, it's shaped and sized like Jamesie's cock.

'Can you turn around for me, James? On all fours. Like a dog.' She says it politely. Quietly.

He wonders where she learned about depravity. Not the same places as him, that's for sure. And he wonders why the wealthy version is somehow different. More acceptable compared to the experiences he endured as a child.

Their sex was relatively traditional until a few weeks ago. He fucked her – usually in the open air; she has a weird thing about that – then when he couldn't come inside her, she sucked him off. What her vagina lacks in spatial volume, her mouth and her throat make up for.

But in the run-up to the nuptials, he's noticed increasing adventurousness on her part. A finger up his bum. Then two. Her big toe. Then the introduction of a cucumber, which he grabbed from her before it entered him.

Fuck sake!

What is it about posh cunts and religious zealots, and their obsession with arseholes? They are not so different, he thinks. Maybe the aristocracy and the Church are collaborators in this regard. Maybe they practise their fucked-up shite on the defenceless. The homeless. Those without a voice. Those too small and powerless to fight back. Given the power Lord Finlay exercises over everyone, who would listen to a child's complaints? No-one listened to him, after all. They just beat and whipped him more than the compliant ones.

There is a definite darkness to Maude. A dangerous edge. An attraction to inflicting pain. It's in Jamesie too, to be fair. They are a match for each other.

'Ach, fair enough,' he says. It's her wedding night too, he acknowledges.

He turns and assumes the position she's described. He's had stuff put up his arse before. But never plastic, or rubber, or whatever the fuck that thing is made of. And this one won't spunk in his arsehole, or hurt as much as the first time the chaplain did it.

Maude climbs onto the high bed. She's on her knees behind him. The dummy cock touches his lubricated anus. Lightly, at first. Tickling him. Then she draws back. She adjusts her position.

She moves to the left-hand side of his hairy back. Finds the clearing in it. The part where hair no longer grows. Her hand rests over the exit wound. She softly caresses the rough edges of cratered skin. Touching each angry ripple of scarred tissue in turn. Like an obsessed geologist returning to a volcano, determined to prove it remains active. She digs a nail into the softer centre. He winces, not because of the wound; the nerve endings there are long dead. He winces because he recalls the inconceivable pain of his own bullet leaving his body. He adjusts his position to distract her.

Jamesie feels Maude's dainty fingers going up inside his arsehole. The oily smell of petroleum jelly wafts from between his legs.

'Christ, hurry up, eh?' he tells her. 'That good meat's gonnae be cauld.'

'Are you ready, boy?' she asks.

Fuck sake!

'Aye. Geezit.'

She does. His sphincter expands to take the dummy cock. She pushes as hard as she can. But there's little purchase on the soft bed. And his bottom is too high for her. She pulls out after a few thrusts. She reaches for a pillow. Silk cotton from Egypt, she's told him. She puts it down and kneels on it.

'Boy, I'd like you to beg me, is that understood?'

Aw for fuck's sake.

Sticking a plastic cock up him was one thing, but making him beg her for it is another thing altogether.

'Maude, gimme a break, will ye? Jist fucken ram it in an' be done wi' it, eh? It's been a long day!'

'BEG!' she screams. She slaps his arse cheek hard.

This is too much for Jamesie. Supplication has its limits.

He turns round sharply. The windmilling back of his newly ringed left hand rattles her jaw. It sends her tiny body crashing into the bed's carved corner post. She careers off it. She lands on the carpet. She rolls onto her back. A smile slowly emerges on her face.

Fuck sake!

She lifts her head. Smiling broadly. Taunting him now.

Fortunately, the ring didn't cut her.

He quickly unstraps the fake plastic cock. He looks at it. The anger in him builds. He considers battering her with it.

She moans. Just as she did that first time in the woods. And all the other times.

She likes this, he realises, the anticipation of his violence. It hasn't happened before. The fear of excommunication from a comfortable future at Lord Finlay's table has always stopped him. But no longer. He's in the fold now. They are behind closed doors. But something still holds him back. An uncertain feeling he can't fully comprehend. As unlikely as it appears, *she* has the control. Jamesie is embarrassed. He tries hard to control the temper but sometimes, just sometimes, he gets pushed too...

'I love you, James,' she whimpers.

He sighs.

He takes the fake plastic cock in one hand. Looks at it. Looks at his bride. He casts the dildo into the flames of the open fire.

'Just don't forget all about me when you're gadding about in Kaunas.'

He wipes his jellied arsehole on the Egyptian cotton.

part 03

DOODLE

Life During Wartime: (1941)

'Little creature, formed of joy and mirth,
Go love without the help of any thing on earth.'
  – William Blake

The sirens have been warbling for hours. The boy, initially excited by being woken in the middle of the night and rapidly evacuated from the Clydebank tenement, is now crying. The incessant noise of bombs hitting and missing their intended targets is terrifying. The chaotic carnage being wreaked is far beyond the boy's imagination. He knows only what his father has told him of the war. That Adolf Hitler is a bad, bad man. And that the Germans want to kill us all. And that those of us that survive will be their slaves, kept in dark, freezing basements and tortured for their entertainment.

The boy is scared of Germans. Although he does not know any. He only knows his mother and father, the boys and girls in his classroom, his teacher, the people upstairs, the people downstairs, the woman with the walking stick across the landing, Paddy Sullivan – the rag and bone man – and his horse, Neddy. And his little brother, Malcolm. The boy is seven years old. He knows little of the world beyond Dumbarton Road.

His mother has let go of his arm. She yells at him to move quickly. And not to let go of his brother. Tells him not to look at the people lying awkwardly in the street as he runs past them.

The string around his neck breaks. The box drops to the ground, falling open. He looks down at it to make sure the mask is still in there. He will die without that mask, his father has warned him. His mother screams his name. The scream is cut short, replaced by coughing. He can hear her, but he can no longer see her. There is too much smoke in the street.

A blast from an explosion to his right knocks the boy off his feet. The wind is taken from him. He cannot breathe. The sirens have stopped. But so has every other sound. Only a dull ringing in his ears remains.

Lying on his back. Staring upward into the black night sky. He watches the tiny lights move from left to right. They are following the line of the river. Occasionally a searchlight will catch a cluster of the bombers. The boy can see hundreds of them. Like that time a wee while ago when his father took him to Greenock for chips. They sat on the dockside. Legs dangling over the side walls. And they watched the birds flying in steady formation, tracking the steam drifters as they came in up the Firth of Clyde with a full haul. The most birds he had ever seen in one place. Those birds were white. These ones in the sky above him are black.

Another explosion. Closer this time. The boy senses the force of the blast pass over him. He feels the heat of the flames. Searing his face. He turns his head to the side. A burning football rolls awkwardly from the furnace. It trundles closer.

It is not a football. It is a head. It stops rolling. Comes to rest over a drain. The hair is on fire. The face blackened. Skin melting. He smells burning. He has a strong sense of smell, but this is not a smell familiar to him. It smells thick and rich and sweet and musky.

A new smell reaches him. On top of the other smells, this one is far more powerful. Like burning toast. His mother makes him eat the toast whether it is burnt or not, so as not to waste anything. The boy hates burnt toast. It looks like coal from the grate. Suddenly, that is all he can smell. He lifts his scarf up to cover his nose and mouth. It's a jaggy scarf and it annoys his neck. But he is glad of it for now.

His father is a volunteer air-raid warden. He has been called away to provide first aid to injured civilians and people rescued from the rubble of ruined buildings in Burns Street. Now the boy has lost his mother *and* his father, and although his brother remains beside him, that is of little comfort. Neither has any real idea of what is going on. Neither fully comprehends the danger that the Luftwaffe bombers flying overhead present.

The boy gets to his feet. The ringing has reduced. Another bombardment brings yet more screaming. Huge flames burst skyward. He watches the outline of the roofs on Castle Street sink down. Slowly at first. And then more rapidly as the stone structures that hold them up crumble.

He runs in the direction of other grown-ups. He hopes they will know his father or his mother. He hopes someone will help him find them. The desperate adults run into Burns Street. The boy is not allowed to go as far as Burns Street, although he has been here once before. There are more explosions. Regularly spaced, seconds apart. Getting louder. Becoming closer. Someone grabs him. Lifts him from behind. He drops the box again. The boy tries to look around to see who has picked him up, but his scarf is too tight and prevents the rotation. He can tell it is a man. Beer breath and cigarette smoke.

'Get oot this fucken street, son!'

It isn't the boy's father. It is an older, gruffer voice. The man runs. The boy is being carried horizontally under a beefy right forearm. He has lost his gas mask. He starts to cry. He will surely die now. His father told him he would. Tears drip sideways across his face. From this peculiar vantage point, he watches a bomb drop into a group of people. He watches flames rise from where they were. He watches one stagger out, ablaze. He watches men take their coats off. Watches them try to get closer. Watches them beaten back by the intense heat. Watches the staggering person stumble and fall. Angry orange flames rising. And that acrid, sulphurous smell wafting across Burns Street.

Inside the shelter, women weep inconsolably. Children stare

at them. Some children rest their arms on the women. A comforting action they have seen adults perform. As if knowing something terrible has happened but not entirely sure what is to be done about it. This role reversal is odd, the boy thinks. But it stops his tears. Makes him feel that he should be a big boy down here. Just like his mother told him to be the first day he went to school.

The boy looks around for his little brother. Takes him by the arm. Speaks reassuringly to him.

'There, there, it'll be aw'right.' Echoing what he is hearing from these older children. The girls, mainly.

He looks for a small space. He drags his little brother into it. He curls up into a ball. He resolves to never go outside ever again.

The thumping and crashing and banging and shattering noises continue until early morning. And then there is calm. The sirens stop sounding. The crying women are silent. Sandbags are moved. Doors are opened. Barricades are lifted. And faint shouts are heard from the street outside. The boy hears screams and despairing voices.

'Aw naw.'

'Watch!'

'Fuck sake!'

Structures collapse around him. He is pulled backward. Trapped by his scarf. Straining his neck to free himself, but he cannot. Struggling for breath. The scarf seeming to tighten.

An almighty pounding, and then nothing.

No ringing. No noise of any kind.

Just black silence.

The boy is dragged out. Lights from dancing torches blind him. He smells the charred wood. The cordite. Glimpses a pile-on of people like the ones the bigger boys orchestrate in the playground. But this one has motionless bodies and blank faces. Limbs contorted and stretched, with blackened, burned muscle and sinew exposed.

That smell.

Men in sodden greatcoats blow their whistles through the smoke. Some of them lean over him. Their lips move. Talking to him. A silent language he does not understand. Torrential rain raps a determined rhythm on their steel helmets. The dirty water bounces up and lands on the boy's forehead, running grit into his eyes.

Shortly after that, the boy's father pushes his way through the rescuers. He holds his lamp up to his son's face and quietly says, 'Aye. That's him.'

The boy is laid down on the rubble. Water from a billycan is poured on his face. He tries to blink the dust out of his eyes. He coughs. Chokes.

'Da, where's Malcolm?' the boy croaks. He said it, but he cannot be sure anyone heard it.

His father doesn't answer, his attention is elsewhere. His father moves away, out of sight. His father leaves him. The boy turns his head to the side. He cannot move anything else. Only his head. Lying near to him is a girl he recognises. From his school classroom. She sits at a desk to the left of him. He cannot remember the little girl's name. Rose? Or Rita, maybe? He is sure it begins with an 'R'. Her face is dirty. Her eyes are wide open. Staring. Broken teeth and cracked lips thick with dark, dirty blood. He tries to shout to her, but no sound comes. His throat aches from the effort. Her mouth is open too. But she isn't speaking.

A woman pushes through the crowd and falls to her knees. She drapes her body over the girl's. Still, the girl does not speak. The woman opens her mouth wide. The boy expects her to scream but nothing comes out. The little girl just stares. Stares back at the boy. Wide-eyed. Lifeless.

In that moment, the fingers of a soft, warm hand caress the boy's cheek. He smells something wonderful. A mixture of leeks and hot butter. Like when his mother saved up the rations and made his favourite oatmeal soup. He closes his eyes and sees a woman, more beautiful than any he has encountered before. Although admittedly, that isn't many. Her black wiry hair falls across dark skin. But not blackened like the ones lying in the street. This woman's skin is brown. Deep and rich and comforting, like chocolate. The boy has never seen a person with such extraordinary skin before. Her fine clothes are clean. Untouched by the carnage. Amid the wailing and the despair and the anger and heartache all around him, no-one but the boy is paying attention to the woman and the soft, comforting song that she gently sings:

'Little creature, formed of joy and mirth,
Go love without the help of any thing on earth.'

The boy reaches out to her. But she pulls away, withdrawing quietly into the maddening crowd of bereft survivors.

'My name is Birgitte. Don't forget me. I will see you again...' she whispers, and then just loudly enough for him to hear it, '... someday.'

There are so many things going on around him. But hers is the only sound he hears.

The boy turns his aching head again.

A dirty, wet blanket covers the little girl.

The boy can no longer see her broken face.

His eyes close, and he blacks out.

EPISODE TEN:

A Man Of Constant Sorrow (1969)

Donald 'Doodle' Malpas recovers from a beating –
Denny Dryburgh has a proposition – Doodle has sinful thoughts.

27th July

It's the smell that rouses him. Always the first of the senses to get up. Always awake before the others. Shaken into life by that distinctive *pish* smell. Acrid ammonia attacks his nostrils like pungent smelling salts. Revives him from the state he's been in. The other four sensations creep out slowly from the shadows. One more slowly than the others.

He has defective, or, rather, selective, hearing. For the last twenty-seven years, his deafness has been a manufactured pretence. His hearing is like an out-of-condition relay runner, relying on the other team members to up their game.

The vibrations. A dog barking, muffled by the dull ringing admittedly, but he can tell it's big. And close by. He tastes his own blood. Moves his tongue around, probing.

No missing teeth. A busted nose and a split lip appear to be the primary causes of the blood loss. He reaches down towards his groin. No wetness. He hasn't pissed himself. Not this time at least. He's been pissed *on*.

Could've been that same passing dog relieving itself in the dark corner of this unlit city-centre lane. But more likely, he's drenched in the stale beer *pish* of the angry men who did this to him.

One eye opens slowly. Fearful of any remaining threat. Human or canine. The other eye stays closed. He flexes the painful blue fingers of his left hand. The brown fingerless woollen glove is shredded and hanging uselessly around his bony wrist. He glimpses the deep tracks of tackety boot segs still imprinted in his hand's reddened flesh. That same hand rises slowly to the closed eye. Arm shaking out of control. The muscles of the limb register-ing their protest. It's as if the arm is attached to a novice puppeteer's string. When it eventually reaches its destination, the trembling fingers feel the lump. It's impressive. The size of a hard-boiled egg. No wonder he can't force the lid open. He presses the hardening flesh. Winces. New pain registers around his head. Sharp stabs on top of the dull ache.

He drags himself up in instalments – concrete Corporation housing blocks have been erected quicker. He catches sight of his wooden board lying in two pieces behind the bin. Split down the middle. *JES* and *SA* on one, *US* and *VES* on the other. Red spots and dribbling blood stains have seeped into the grain on the square timber post the board was nailed to. He's been battered with his own message of salvation. An indictment of these immoral times. Not for the first time, he was set upon by agnostic men smelling of pubs and nicotine and engorged with sectarian violence.

No-one listens to God anymore.

Reality dawns gradually. His brain processes it at the only pace it can currently cope with. He's shivering with cold or shock, but at least it hasn't been raining. He can't recall when it last rained. That's unusual for this city. It must be Monday. Still early morning. He has no idea of the time. The face of his watch is smashed. The little and big hands bent shapeless. Ends fixed at the *11* and the *9*. Could mean that was a pre-midnight, Sunday-evening battering, if anyone asks. But he won't be encouraging questions. Plus, he can't say for certain that the watch was working properly before-hand.

Just to his left, a clump of greyish paper moves suddenly. Then comes into sharper focus. It's not paper. His heart rate accelerates.

It's a pigeon. A big one. A dead one. It's being pushed and dragged. By three black, hairy rodents. The biggest of them must be a foot long. Two, from head to tail. His musophobia overcomes the muscular aches. He's upright sharply, staggering away from this nightmarish scene.

"'And these are unclean to you among the swarming things that swarm on the ground; the mole rat, the mouse, the great lizard of any kind...'" He says these words aloud for reassurance. "'Whoever touches them when they are dead shall be unclean.'"

He won't be unclean.

Along the lane, a baker loads his van with trays of fresh bread. This new smell intoxicates. The scripture has worked its magic. He is suddenly hungry.

'Ye aw'right, pal?' says the baker.

He reads the man's lips. He nods weakly in response.

'Too much ae the bevvy?'

He doesn't acknowledge this assumption. He doesn't drink alcohol. He doesn't admit that though. It's none of the baker's business. Glasgow's not a city where abstention is lauded.

'Here.' The baker hands him a bottle. 'Get that doon ye. No' hair ae the dug, but it'll settle yer belly,' the baker adds, without any further inquiry.

The creamy milk slides down easily.

'Thanks,' he tells the baker.

Now the baker hands him a brown paper bag. There are four warm rolls in it.

'I don't have any...' He exaggerates the monotonous delivery. Redacts all intonation. Sees the baker's understanding dawn and demeanour change. He's become adept at this manipulation since those received-pronunciation staccato speech lessons he received at the Deaf & Dumb Institute in West Regent Street.

'Fine, son,' the baker shouts. 'Nae charge the day.' He forces a crooked smile. 'Mind yersel, now. Mibbe see the doctor, eh?'

The baker bids him a farewell with a comforting hand on the

shoulder. The contact is such a rare occurrence that he feels revived. And this feeling is sustained by the thought of fat, greasy bacon and good butter filling the rolls when he gets home.

+

1st August

His name is Donald Malpas. But you can call him Doodle. Everyone he knows does, although that doesn't amount to many people. He's a month short of thirty-five. He lives alone. In a crumbling Bridgeton tenement that has recently been sentenced to death. He has known no other home as an adult. He took on the rent in the winter of 1952. Seventeen years ago. His mother lived there. Although 'existed' there is a more honest description. His father drifted in and out. They endured a violent, unhappy marriage until their last evening together. That night of the burnt food. Burnt toast. Doodle hates burnt toast.

His father came home drunk. And later than expected. A big football match hadn't gone his way. His tea was incinerated. Deliberately, he felt. A predictable man-and-wife argument built. It quickly escalated.

That burning smell. Almost like charred flesh.

Doodle's father complained about the meal. His mother hit her husband across the jaw with a heavy pan. That usually ended their fights. But not this one. Not that evening. His father snapped. Stabbed his mother eighteen times. Coincidentally, once for every year of Doodle's life to that point. Doodle didn't think his father was counting. He was probably just done in from the exertion, or Doodle was sure he'd have kept going. When Doodle's father stopped stabbing, his mother grabbed the legs of his father's damp long johns as they hung around the pulley. She held on and for a few minutes they kept her upright. Doodle could see the hook slowly working free from the ceiling. A strange expression on her face. It wasn't pain, or anger, or shock or fear. It was more like her feelings had been hurt.

Doodle has endeavoured to capture that look in numerous sketches he's drawn since. Never quite managed it though.

They watched her. Doodle and his father. Watched her let go of the long johns before the ceiling let go of the pulley. Watched her drop right back onto her fat backside. Sitting up, legs spread, balancing her. Watched her face lose its structure as the dentures fell from her mouth into her lap. Watched her gurning, crumpling skin age ten years in two seconds as a result. Watched her look down at the shredded pinnie. Watched it turn crimson. Watched her topple back in slow motion. As if the blood had rushed up to her torso. Leaving those thick white legs hollow. The dull *thump-bump* as her head hit the lino and then bounced a bit before hitting it again, but softer. They watched the blood pool around her as she lay face up, struggling for breath. Watched it spread slowly, covering that horrible sunflowery pattern that Doodle loathed. The uneven flooring driving it towards the years-old crack that all three still regularly tripped over.

There was not a word uttered between them.

After the last spluttering sigh, father and son watched the woman's muscles relax. Her tortured soul leaving for its next destination, presumably. And then the pulley's hook did give out. The wooden slats dropped, one of them cracking her nose. Washing fell on top of and around her. Some of it soaking up the blood. They'd have a real job on their hands, cleaning the clothes again on the washboard with the soap and the scrubber. It'd be a steamie job, for sure, Doodle thought.

His mother died that night. Slowly. Right in front of him. And although it was a shock, he was glad she did. She'd taken the heavy pan to his head many a time too. She wouldn't be doing that again.

His father opened a window. The smoke cleared. The stench of burning dissipated. Doodle calmed himself. His father went into the front room and turned the radio on. *Life With the Lyons* on the BBC's Light Programme. A favourite escape for the older man. He turned it up loud. From the kitchen, Doodle imagined Ben and Bebe's American accents and their adopted English children and their Scottish housekeeper and their perfect London life, and how it was so much happier than his.

Doodle sat until the crimson puddle touched his feet. Then he got up and moved his seat back a couple of feet. He got his pad and his pencil and started drawing. He knew old Edith across the landing would've phoned the coppers. She always did when the big fighting started. She was at that phone box across the street so often people called it 'aul' Edith's private lavvy'.

There wasn't much unbloodied lino left when the front door was smashed in. Doodle's father had locked it behind him when he came in. The sound surprised Doodle's father, a second before the action surprised Doodle.

It was funny watching them. Their detection cogs working at various speeds. Their confusion clearing. A woman had been killed, sure, but they didn't know which man had done it. Doodle's father was a big man. And blood splattered. They went for him. There was no resistance. He went quietly. The coppers leathered him anyway. Just to be sure.

'I'll die ... I'll just die!' said scatter-brained Bebe, over and over. Doodle didn't hear it clearly of course. Just assumed it. And the uproarious laughter from the big gramophone's speakers in the other room signalling the end of the drama.

From a very young age, Doodle's father had made sure Doodle knew that *he* was the reason they had been rehoused in Glasgow's deprived East End after the Clydebank Blitz had destroyed their Dumbarton Road tenement. As a child, Doodle's father largely ignored him, other than the occasions when the boy offered his father a convenient outlet for his anger. But that only lasted for a couple of years or so. It stopped when Doodle went to the special school near Bridgeton Cross. His father wasn't around much after that. He would return home sporadically. When he needed money. Or needed fed. Or wanted free sex. They were the reasons he was back at MacKeith Street in the months leading up to the stabbing.

Doodle was pleased his father survived the coppers' beating. His mother, though, had it coming, he felt. Doodle didn't see his father from that night until the trial. Doodle wouldn't see him again once he had left the dock. His father escaped the hangman's noose on a legal technicality. But he succumbed to a massive heart attack six months into his sentence. He was a bastard; in that he never knew his own father. Doodle's granny whored herself about the Clydeside shipyards until the syphilis put her in the ground. There may have been siblings. But Doodle's parents didn't talk about them. He didn't observe them talking about anything. Not really.

Doodle's only living relative that he has knowledge of is his younger brother. Malcolm. Malcolm spent much of his youth living elsewhere. Doodle didn't ask where. Or why. Despite his mother's denials, his father was convinced Malcolm wasn't his son. Doodle's uncle and his family emigrated a month before the stabbing. They left for a better life, his mother said, but a better life than theirs could've been found in Motherwell or Hamilton or Irvine or Saltcoats. The uncle would've been a bus ride away though. And that was too close for Doodle's father. He hated his brother-in-law. Malcolm, this damnable product of an incestuous relationship, he believed was the real reason for their leaving Scotland for Canada.

Doodle's itinerant brother didn't attend the funerals of his parents alongside Doodle and old Edith from across the landing. He also didn't witness the killing of his mother. But he adopted the trauma. Absorbed it, wholesale. It became an excuse for his reckless addictions. His criminality. His drift towards the razor gangs that he said gave him an identity. A purpose.

The Lord is waiting for him to return, and Doodle prays for

that daily. But Malcolm is lost. Spiritually and literally. Doodle hasn't seen him since the night he pulled him, drunk, off a terrified woman. Malcolm told Doodle he was going to kill him. That was more than four years ago.

The following day Doodle went to the Sovereign Grace Mission for the first time. A forthcoming sermon trailed on a board outside, *Abstinence Is next to Godliness*. A universal truth. He went in. Poured his shattered heart out. Pastor McTavish and the elders offered him succour. There was no judgement. No homily – not at that point. They've been Doodle's family ever since.

He doesn't need to lip-read. Not anymore. His hearing has been gradually returning. A little better every year. He puts it down to God's intervention. But others need not know that. For many years, others have thought him stupid because he's deaf, and he's learned that there are advantages to this misapprehension.

He's always been good at watching. Observing. Memorising.

'For fuck's sake, get outta here, awa' from under ma feet, ya wee cunt. Awa' ootside an' play like a normal wean!' his mother would yell. It was a release for her. She thought he couldn't hear her. She was wrong about that.

'Ye'll niver amount tae anythin' scribblin' in that bloody pad mornin', noon an' night,' she'd say. But she was wrong about that too.

An unexpected, if pitiful, life-insurance pay-out bought a few months' grace on this flat. And since then, Doodle has been self-sufficient. He lives off his earnings from making courtroom sketches and working as a composite artist, creating artist's impressions from police witness statements

It's steady work. Lawbreaking is a growth industry down here in the Glasgow slums. Violent crime is spreading like a communicable disease. Its hosts are typical. Young, sullen working-class defendants fill his sketchbooks. Many bear the tell-tale cheek slash of the Glasgow kiss. Defiance is their marker. Only occasionally does the profile change. Age or accent, mainly. But sometimes attitude too. The remorseful show it by their posture. Shoulders slumped. Heads down. No eye contact made with their victims. Those fearful of the consequences are betrayed by their tears. But these are the minority. The guilty are invariably proud of the status.

The broadsheets pay more for Doodle's work but take longer to settle. The local newspaper editors give cash on delivery. A higher price if it's the High Court. Even a bonus for murder trials. If the accused is in the public eye, a court artist can occasionally name his – or her – own terms.

+

4th August

The flat is freezing. Doodle is glad to be leaving it. It'll be marginally warmer outside, he hopes. Work has been surprisingly scarce of late. He must feed the meter as infrequently as possible.

A furtive man moved in across the landing two months ago. He knows how to fiddle the disc. 'Stoap's it spinnin', but ye'll still get the leccy,' he says. Told Doodle he would show him how. For the lesson, though, Doodle would have to pay his neighbour more than he'd save.

He closes the door on the walk-in cupboard. It's his private space, where he pins or tapes his sketches of suspects that don't make the cut. Or of victims in imagined crime scenes.

Doodle has a vivid imagination for such things.

A glance at the mirror near the front door to check his tie is straight. The eye socket swelling has gone. The ugly, black-and-blue stain has spread across his face. It's yellowing at the edges. But for this painful colouring, the hollowed-out husk of a compulsive blood donor stares back. Questions may be asked.

The court officials will have seen far worse. It's the enquiries at the mission Doodle dreads more. The sepulchral shame he'll feel in lying to them. Denying that he was beaten in the service of the Lord. The brethren are unsympathetic in such instances. Especially if donation money has been taken. Which it was. His wallet's gone. There was little in it. Few passers-by will give a street preacher cash in these days of hardship. Nonetheless, he can't return to the flock empty-handed. Not again. So, as a result of having to replace the stolen donations out of his own pocket, he'll be going without until his next wages.

'It's a holy war we are fightin', Donald Malpas. Against evil. Against Satan,' Pastor McTavish sermonises weekly. 'And wars need committed soldiers. Soldiers with fortitude. Wi' strength ae character *and* ae body. Do ye have the necessary fortitude, Mr Malpas? Do ye have what it takes tae be a Sovereign Grace disciple of Jesus?'

Doodle knows these words – and the upward intonation of their challenge – by heart. He knows they are intended to lift his spirit. To inspire, like those used by a steely football manager to an out-of-form, low-on-confidence defender. Or a brutal sergeant major forcing a cowardly sapper out of the trench and towards the line of fire. But mostly, they just serve to reinforce his failure.

Hopefully, the bruising will fade before Sunday. He tilts his hat down. Folds up the collar of his coat. Tightens his scarf. Pulls the door closed behind him.

The boarded windows across MacKeith Street now outnumber the glazed ones by three to one. These Victorian buildings will be gone soon. But slowly, like a cancer eating their insides until their shells collapse. The local children play in the evacuated husks, but children are resilient. Anywhere can be a playground. The adults know better. Uncertainty awaits them. A future removed from their communities is now certain.

Along London Road, this process is more advanced. But fixed hours and job cuts are slowing progress. What the Luftwaffe achieved in a night, thirty years ago in Clydebank, will take Glasgow Housing Corporation months, if not years. Their operatives are like a team of archaeologists. Carefully peeling back walls to examine how another civilisation lived. Uncovered tenements with their innards on show. Fireplaces. Panelled doors. Wallpapered living rooms. Carpeted floors with exposed joist ends. The demolition ball is waiting, and the East End of Glasgow is its target.

'Haw there, Doodle-de-doo,' says a high-pitched voice.

It's one of the boys from the flat below his. The oldest one. The one that reminds Doodle of Malcolm at that age. Not yet a teenager but possessing the gallusness of one. Future trouble, no doubt.

'Deef, deef, the Doodler's corned beef!' the boy sings in a nasal whine.

Doodle sees the boy's mother come out of the newsagents on the corner of the street. He waves to her.

'Hey, ya cheeky wee get. Tell Mr Malpas yer sorry,' she commands. The boy ignores her. 'Ah'm really sorry,' says the mother. Lips exaggerating the shape of the words.

'He's fine. It's no problem,' says Doodle.

The boy runs away, kicking a can and singing a song about the Celtic.

'How are you, Ms MacDonald?'

'Aye, fine. Same aul', y'know,' says the woman.

'And how's your sister?' asks Doodle. He thinks of the woman's sister often. Mostly at night, when he can't sleep.

'Aye, Magret's braw. Hopefully startin' a new job, soon.'

'Ah, that's good.'

'Well, it's better hours, an' that. She'll be able tae help oot more wi' the weans,' she says. 'An' that means ah'll be able tae head up the dancin' more,' she adds, laughing. 'Mibbe get maself a proper lumber.'

'Can you pass my regards to her, please?' asks Doodle.

Mima MacDonald's sister, Margaret, lives in the same tenement. She and Doodle meet every now and then. Usually heading in different directions on the close stairs. A conversation with Margaret is tougher to strike up than with Mima. Because he doesn't know how to conduct it.

'Will do,' she says. 'Be seein' ye, Mr Malpas.'

And off she goes, full of life and well turned out for someone who doesn't work and has no residing husband or father for her three. She's always pleasant and talkative and interesting, and Doodle imagines her better-looking sister will be similarly so. One of these days, he'll summon the confidence to find out.

His route takes him past the Barrowland Ballroom – 'a den of iniquity' Pastor McTavish says. He hears those words in his head as he cogitates on Mima MacDonald in there, three nights a week. Gyrating with different men every night. Enjoying their attention. Enjoying herself. Loving life. While Margaret stays at home. Looking after six children. Much though he likes Mima, Doodle knows which sister he'd rather be with.

It takes him half an hour to walk to the High Court. He does it briskly to fend off the determined chill that still hangs in the morning air. He's early. The business of the day inside this imposing, black, soot-stained stone temple won't begin until 10am.

'Haw, Doodle. You been oot oan the randan again, son? Steamin' drunk an' then a wee bit ae boxin'?' Charlie Duke. He says this as he searches Doodle. The guard knows Doodle doesn't drink but it's any excuse to poke fun at the younger man.

'I fell, Charlie.' Doodle illustrates a fall with his hands.

'Were the polis staunin' behind ye?' Charlie Duke teases.

Doodle shakes his head, sighing. Charlie Duke pats him down, lingering a little too long around the crotch.

'Ye dinnae need tae lie tae me, boy,' says the guard. 'God's lonely men ay the worst when the Devil gets a haud ae ye'se an' pours the demon drink doon yer thrapple.'

Charlie Duke pushes Doodle in the chest. Playfully, but he's a big man and Doodle's ribs still hurt from the beating in the lane. Doodle ponders his description.

God's lonely men.

It's a new one on him. But Charlie is correct to a degree. Those venturing out in the streets to proclaim God's word do so alone. There may not be many men of Christ out there on the frontline, but those that are require resolute commitment. Not just Sabbath soldiers, congregating out of duty. Or habit. Or because there's little else to do on a Sunday. Or in the misguided belief that six days of sin can be erased by one hour of perfunctory worship. Donald Malpas is a devoted disciple of Christ. It's a full-time calling. And that calling takes courage. The Baptists at the Sovereign Grace Mission demand the Good News be spread to everyone. At all times. And that often means dispersing to the shadowy extremities of a brutal city. Ultimately, it's not the exhortations of Pastor McTavish that will get Doodle back out on the mean streets. It's his own devotion to duty. He takes a little comfort from that.

'It's not too late for you to be saved,' he tells Charlie.

'Aye, righto Moses.' Charlie Duke laughs dismissively. He gestures Doodle towards the stairs. 'Only the upstairs gallery's oan the day, Doodle. Nae scribblin' in session, mind.'

Charlie Duke hands Doodle a note, as he often does. It has the number of the courtroom and the name of the judge who is presiding written above the words *Murder* and *Female*. A high-profile trial is starting today. One Doodle hasn't been aware of. Normally, there's a buzz around the place for days – sometimes weeks – before a murder case, and especially one where the victim was a woman. Perhaps he's been too absorbed in his own trials and tribulations around his imminent rehousing. A recent suggestion that Bridgeton decants to Springburn is his latest perturbation.

Officials crowd the stairs. Perhaps anticipating trouble from the public. Doodle skirts around them, eyes down. Ghost-like. Nodding only to a nervous young 'A' Division copper he knows from the Central Police Office at Turnbull Street.

The young copper opens the door for Doodle, and that

pungent, waxy, turpentine smell that pervades the wooden interiors of his church slaps him around his face. The same cleaners may work at both venues.

Inside the courtroom, the high corner perch is free. This is the vantage point from where Doodle watched his father take his punishment. He prefers it if he's forced up to the gallery, to be honest. He has heard it referred to as 'Doodle's doocot' by some officials. He likes that.

Looking down to the left, the rear benches are full of sober-suited pressmen. Squeezed in, sardine tight. Like they're in Church of Scotland pews on an Easter Sunday service. Doodle recognises many of them. They sit behind large defence and prosecution teams. Like rows of supporters sat behind uniformed management at an international football fixture. Doodle sets his notepad down next to him. Pencils and chalks on top.

He has sketched hundreds of the accused in this courtroom. Imagined numerous murderous crime scenes. Visualised countless dead bodies – usually female. Observing, as these sins against God are laid before everyone. Making notes about features. Gestures. Remarkable expressions. Mentally drawing as quickly as possible. It's a rapid process requiring the memory of an elephant. Which, fortunately, he possesses. Capturing a defendant. Composing the courtroom context in his head. Then running outside to an available press room or hunkering down in a quiet corridor. Pencils, chalks, charcoals. Often less than an hour to meet print deadlines.

Occasionally, a rough representation can be created covertly. But only when the upper benches aren't occupied. And only when out of the main line of sight of the judge or a court official. Less chance of a warning or a fine for contempt up here. Unquestionably, the gallery is the best place from which to view – and read – proceedings. But a glimpsed eye-level view through a dark frame of shoulders is often more dramatic. A representation like that can place the viewer at the heart of the trial. Particularly when something noteworthy happens.

Doodle was sitting downstairs when he sketched his first court-room scenes. A nineteen-year-old and a sixteen-year-old had been accomplices in a robbery that ended in the death of an older man. It was understood by the court that the younger man had been responsible for the action that led to the death. The older – due to his assumed responsibility as an adult – was the one being sentenced for murder. The nineteen-year-old was a handsome lad. Angular jawline. Pronounced cheekbones the defining characteristic. And with that lacquered style of wet, swept-back hair favoured by the American actor Montgomery Clift.

Doodle regularly notes resemblances to famous people he has seen in the newspapers. It's how he recalls a particular look or attitude. It gives his drawings personality.

The accused shook and wept and frequently cried out for his 'mammy' during the three-day trial. He didn't conduct himself as a man should, in Doodle's opinion. Doodle was embarrassed by the loss of control. And when Lord Wheatley reached for his black tricorn and sentenced him to death by hanging, the nineteen-year-old accused collapsed. There was no noise after the judgement was delivered. No cheering from the public benches, where the relatives of the victim sat. No clamour from the pressmen to get back to their typewriters and type up an exclusive.

A sympathetic shockwave crashed on the lower public benches. Acknowledging the jury's verdict, and supportive of an appropriate punishment, but nonetheless, hoping for mercy. The young man was carried from the dock, out cold. His baggy grey trousers stained with urine. It took a few minutes until the ammonia overwhelmed the beeswax. But when it did, when it too rolled back towards Doodle, he felt sick. Disgusted by the indignity.

Doodle's pencil captured three policemen lifting the condemned man by his arms and a leg. His shiny, oily hair lopping to the side like the thick strands of a dripping mop. His free foot catching on the carved mahogany of the defence benches and dislodging a slip-on shoe. Doodle spotted dirty toes protruding from a holed sock. He knows the importance of noticing the smallest of details. The shoe might've loosened because he'd borrowed, or stolen, all he was wearing from a bigger man. Doodle knows that such details matter.

His drawing was run by four newspapers. All front pages. That was almost nine years ago. They don't hang guilty people anymore. Maybe they should, he considers.

Such daydreaming happens often in the languorous legal process. Little runs to time. Today Doodle has become so absorbed in his thoughts that he's barely noticed the central figures in today's proceedings taking their places.

A man is in the dock, unsurprisingly. He wears an unkempt beard. A collarless shirt. Strings of beads drape to his mid-torso. Inappropriately vibrant tied-and-dyed colours clash. Doodle can't be certain, but he suspects the sacrilege extends to bare feet, and the type of open-toed shoes once favoured by Doodle's Lord and Saviour. A different type of sweet pungency emanates from this accused. He resembles those wandering student agitators responsible for the disruptive anti-war protests in America that the newspapers have been so full of lately. Shambolic, unclean, dirty, drugged-up tramps. Faces painted with peace symbols. Bringing shame on God with their free-love promiscuity. Doodle will be astonished if he isn't found guilty of something serious.

All are commanded to stand. All do. The judge appears. Lord Balcombe; known to be a tough disciplinarian. Doodle has seen him in action on a few occasions. All resulting in convictions. The disrespectful hippy before him today will have little chance of acquittal.

The judge sits.

Everyone else sits.

Unexpected footsteps tapping the terrazzo draw the collective attention towards the rear of the room. Doodle is late to notice. A big man, head down, strides towards some vacant seats just behind the prosecution benches. Doodle anticipates the reverberating ire of Lord Balcombe all but stripping the varnish from the wainscoting. But it doesn't come. A few steps behind the big man, a woman follows. She stands out from everyone else due to the colour of her skin. It's a deep and rich shade of brown. Comforting, like chocolate. Doodle has rarely seen a person with such extraordinary skin before. Before taking her seat, she glances up towards the gallery where Doodle sits.

A nod from the judge to the big man is reciprocated – the acknowledgement made because this particular big man is Jamesie Campbell; the Labour Party politician commonly known as Mr Glasgow. Photographs of him feature in Scottish newspapers regularly. Making a rousing speech here, downing a pint of beer in a public house there. Baby-kissing and glad-handing in between. His unforeseen presence will elevate the press interest to a different level. Yet it's the woman who captivates Doodle and sparks something in him that has lain dormant since he was a child.

Doodle knows the woman isn't Campbell's wife. Doodle has been introduced to Big Jamesie and Mrs Campbell previously. Neither would remember the meeting. It was at Turnbull Street Police Station a couple of years ago. Mr and Mrs Glasgow were at the station to commend the squad on the conclusion of a high-profile murder case.

Mr Campbell's wife is a stout woman, as wide as she is small. Expensively dressed, no doubt, but on the day of her official visit to Turnbull Street, she smelled of lentil soup, which, when mixed with the distinctive aromas of an unventilated police-station basement, forged quite the memorable, heady brew. She spoke to each man in turn. Her painted smile perhaps betrayed her true feelings about this excruciating duty.

'And you are, young man?' she'd asked Doodle.

'Aw, ne'er mind him, ma'am. He's just Doodle. He's a deaf an' dumb mute. Draws pictures ae suspects fae witness descriptions.'

'A very important job, I'm sure,' said with a pitying head tilt.

Doodle imagined Big Jamesie Campbell lying on top of her, how he would compose such an illustration. The bloated belly flattening her. Sweat dripping onto her face from his brow. The dry, dead skin from his hairy chin flaking into her mouth. His big fat penis juddering into her tiny body. Threatening to split her apart. Just like the poor unfortunate woman whose murderer's conviction they were celebrating. Doodle felt sorry for her. That God hadn't graced her with better looks. An attractiveness that would have provided better choices than having to settle for a clammy blob of avarice like Big Jamesie Campbell.

This woman, though, the one who glanced up towards Doodle, is, by contrast, uncommonly beautiful. Going against the mandate of the court, he scribbles impressions of her. These will assist his compositions later, even though this woman is not one of the central characters in today's spectacle.

Strangely, the elegant woman with the skin like chocolate is dressed exactly as the dirty hippy in the dock should've been. A man's pin-striped suit; grey, three-piece and with a dark-blue daisy-patterned tie finishing the buttoned-down collar of a brilliant white shirt. Her black hair is partially tied back but still caresses her shoulders. She carries no bag. No other female accoutrements either, as might be expected. She is a remarkable sight.

Big Jamesie Campbell coughs and clears his throat. It breaks the spell and Doodle's focus returns to the proceedings.

The session begins, and it appears that the wretched hippy has confessed to the brutal murder of a young waitress. Her body was discovered by a man walking his dog across remote moorland hills on the outskirts of the city. Doodle now recalls hearing young coppers discussing the case. He didn't realise the trial was beginning today.

'Gentlemen of the jury, the prosecution will prove to you that this...' an elongated pause deployed with disgust '...man, Abraham Blair, did murder Miss Emilija Baltakis...'

Doodle's pencil drops to the floor.

Emilija? One of the girls from the Sovereign Grace Mission? Good God in Heaven, not Emilija Baltakis.

'That he abducted her against her will. That he viciously raped her. And that he strangled her, before brutally and callously caving her skull in with a hammer, in an attempt to conceal the young woman's identity.'

Oh, my dear Lord! That poor girl.

'Furthermore, the prosecution will prove that Blair then defiled Miss Baltakis's dead body by gouging out her eyes and so-domising her with a wooden pole, and that his belated confession was made purely to lessen his punishment, not out of any humanitarian remorse.'

There are gasps from the assembly.

Glasgow is the murder capital of Great Britain, and its citizens acknowledge this. Almost pride themselves on the city's brutal reputation. 'Only hard bastards welcome here,' they'll joke. But occasionally, a crime will brush right up against them. And they are reminded that a perpetrator isn't always a drunk, violent husband. Or a spurned lover. Or a thuggish neighbour. The victim of the random attack – usually a woman – is someone exactly like them. Or their wife. Sister. Daughter. Mother.

True-crime stories are the tabloids' daily fodder. Yet this one didn't register. Doodle didn't even know the girl was missing from the Sovereign Grace Mission. No one had even mentioned she'd been found dead. He'd assumed she'd simply gone home to the U.S.S.R, to Lithuania. She was a lovely young woman, he recalls. Their interactions might've been few, but Emilija Baltakis was vibrant and vivacious. Curly blonde hair tied up with a ribbon and a beaming smile like Shirley Temple. A very similar personality to his neighbour, Mima MacDonald.

Doodle scans the courtroom for Pastor McTavish. Emilija was one of his favourites from the mission's foreign-exchange programme. The pastor will be truly devastated. Maybe he is too devastated to attend.

Abraham Blair violently vomits. It's almost as if the enormity of the situation facing him has only just dawned. As if any substances intended to blot out the memory of what he has done have abruptly worn off.

The case is briefly adjourned for him – and the dock – to be cleaned up.

The door is held open. It's the young copper from Turnbull Street.

'Thanks,' says Doodle.

It's Doodle, right? The young man signs this with confident fingers. It catches Doodle off guard.

'Yeh,' says Doodle.

I have the station seen around you. Hope you mind me not asking, but I was in the church interested ... the Sovereign Grace Mission, okay?

It's a spirited attempt, but Doodle puts up a hand. 'You sign?'

'Aye...'

Doodle points to the young man's lips.

The policeman nods and drops his hands by his side.

'Ma da ... in his last years, y'know. It was the only way tae communicate wi' him. I'm Denny, by the way. Denny Dryburgh.'

'Oh, right. Hello. The church ... how can I...?'

'Ah'm interested in joinin' it. Ah overheard ye tellin' somebody about it.'

'Okay, yes ... of course.'

Doodle is taken aback. His determined attempts to convert others usually result in ignorance or injury. Never interest.

Amidst his despair over Emilija, Pastor McTavish will at least be pleased that one new soul is looking to be saved.

Poor Emilija Baltakis. He thinks about her again. Her smile as she asked him for help in lifting a heavy, leather-bound book from a high shelf in the Sovereign Grace Mission library. *Atlas Shrugged* by Ayn Rand, a gargantuan tome that Doodle wasn't aware of despite having taken on responsibility for the library's inventory and administration. It was to assist with her English, she'd said, although her English was perfect. Often more understandable than the careless demotic of many locals.

She was a lovely girl, yes. She was. Attractive. Considerate. Kind.

God's plan is very hard to fathom at times.

'These tests of faith will visit ye at the most unexpected of moments,' Pastor McTavish has warned. But it's still shocking when they do.

Doodle spends that first evening of the trial listening to gospel music being performed on a radio channel he's had to search for. He uses the hearing-aid at home sometimes. Purely to amplify his favourite programmes or music. Nowhere else. No-one even knows he has it.

He pins his rough sketches of the beautiful woman with the skin coloured like chocolate onto a wall. Underneath one, he writes:

Little creature, formed of joy and mirth,
Go love without the help of any thing on earth.

He turns the radio's volume up, and begins drawing.

'*Oh Happy Day...*'

Gradually though, he's not in full control of his pencil. His sketches form a picture of the woman from the courtroom's naked body.

'*When Jesus washed...*'

The roundness of her breasts. The slight swelling of her tummy.

'*When Jesus washed...*'

The athleticism of her thighs. The delicacy of her fingers and toes.

'*When Jesus washed...*'

Her dark hair cascading down wildly. The coiffured bushiness of her pubic hair.

'*He washed my sins away...*'

And suddenly he is naked. Only a scarf around his neck. He pulls the scarf tightly. Falls to his hands and knees. Rolls to one side. Tightens the scarf's knot with his right hand. Grips his hard penis with the left. Throttling it until he is in pain. Staring wide-eyed at the drawing. Thrashing violently until the devilish spunk spurts from his cock and all over his sketchpad.

'*Oh happy day.*'

And he lies there in the dark, crying. Choking. Out of breath. On his back. He hears Mima MacDonald's sister, Margaret, moving around downstairs. She shouts, but it's not clear what. Or at whom. He hates himself. Prepares to self-flagellate for granting these impure thoughts entry and allowing them to take root. Tears flow.

For the first time in months, Donald Malpas reaches for the whip and repeatedly whispers, 'I chastise my body.'

EPISODE ELEVEN:
Alone (1969)

*Doodle becomes suspicious – Denny meets Pastor McTavish –
Jemima MacDonald extends Doodle a kindness.*

6th August

Confusion reigns at the High Court. The officials are flustered.
Directing people here and about, but in a disorganised way. The
trial of the hippy, Abraham Blair, has been adjourned. Suddenly
and unexpectedly. A plea change is speculated. *Not guilty*, claim-
ing the confession was beaten out of him in the gloomy underbelly
of the City of Glasgow Police HQ. Disgruntled reporters are
having none of this.
   'Hippy scum.'
   'Filthy wee bastart.'
   'String him up.'
   'Fucken guilty as the day is long.'
   'Polis should've battered the cunt stone deid when they'd the
chance.'
   Doodle spends the afternoon in Court Three, following the
case of the assault on a dancehall doorman by a young man connected to an East End razor gang. It's his least favourite chamber.
A phalanx of beefy columns obscures the action from much of the
public gallery. Nevertheless, he captures the young man's 'duck's
arse' hairdo and massive quiff from memory later, then walks
briskly to the offices of the *Evening Citizen*.

+

10th August

He hears it eventually from the most reliable of sources, the BBC. Eventually, because the Saturday news update on Radio 4 is dominated by an emerging story from America: the brutal murder of a pregnant Hollywood actress and four of her friends. Some words are harder for him to decrypt due to the accents. But he understands that five victims were stabbed multiple times and, according to unconfirmed reports, the word 'pig' was written in blood on the walls of the young actress's Los Angeles home. The world has become an unrepentant cauldron of deviants and reprobates, he concludes. The actress is named as Sharon Tate. Doodle hasn't heard of her, or of her apparently more famous husband, Roman Polanski. Polanski, a European film director, wasn't home at the time of the attack. That must make him the prime suspect, Doodle thinks.

As shocking as that news story is, the cold formality of the final item shocks him more:

'...Archibald Blair, the man charged with the murder of the exchange student Emilija Baltakis, has been found dead in the holding cells of Glasgow's Central Police Office, where he was awaiting the restart of his trial. On Tuesday of last week, Blair stunned his legal representatives by altering his plea to not guilty. The trial was adjourned to allow prosecution and defence teams time to respond to the change.'

He picks up his sketches of Archibald Blair. There's good work here. Under normal circumstances, he'd get a good return for his efforts – the last images of a suicidal killer unable to come to terms with what he had done. But he's sure the Sharon Tate story will dominate the newspapers for days. The morbid fascination with the murder of a celebrity. Doodle knows the Archibald Blair suicide could be relegated to a page in the double figures. The likelihood of a picture credit reducing along with the public's interest.

There's a knock at his door. So unusual an occurrence is this that he waits for it to happen again before responding.

'Hullo, Mr Malpas, how are you th'day?' It's Mima MacDonald. Vibrant red lips. She's holding a plate.

'Oh hello,' says Doodle. He sticks his head out and looks beyond and around her. Hoping her sister is there too. She isn't.

'We made a wee bit too much cake for the wean's birthday. Ah just wondered if ye'd like a slice tae have wi' yer tea.' She smiles.

He does too. He is unprepared for this act of kindness. Doesn't know how to react. The world *is* a cauldron of deviants, but very infrequently, something happens to remind him that all isn't lost.

'That's thoughtful. Thank you.'

'Yer welcome, Mr Malpas.'

He takes the plate from her. 'I'll hand this in to you later.'

'Ach, nae rush, honestly.'

'I'll say an extra prayer for you. And for Margaret,' he says.

'Oh, aye, right ye are,' she says, laughing. 'If ye're puttin' a word in wi' the big man, could ye ask him tae send a tall, dark, handsome fella in ma direction?'

'I'm sure he'll see what he can do, Miss MacDonald.' He smiles.

She's a lovely woman. Attractive. Considerate. Kind. She makes him feel less alone.

+

11th August

The *Star's* Monday morning edition runs a piece supported by Doodle's sketch. It's a page-four, side-panel five-hundred-worder written by Gerard Keegan. Doodle has met Keegan on several occasions. Keegan is a brash, obdurate man, disdainful of those who practise religion. An argument looking for a reason. Doodle doesn't care for him.

The article portrays Blair as a dangerously unpredictable man with a mental age of ten. A man who – according to police sources – showed no emotion when confronted with the acts he'd been accused of. A hippy loner whose illegal drug-taking made him dangerously paranoid. Someone for whom remorse came too late, and only after long discussions with a minister while in custody.

Doodle shakes his head. The words don't square with his impression of the young man he witnessed in the dock. Damaged and degenerate, he might've been, but Doodle saw the face of someone unable to comprehend the details of the charge. Not immature. Not emotionless. More that he was hearing them for the first time.

+

14th August

Denny Dryburgh seems to have shrunk. It's amazing what stature the uniform adds, even without the bobbie's hat. Denny sees the surprised reaction and acknowledges it:

'Expectin' somebody else? Somebody taller?'

'No,' says Doodle. But he was. 'Not at all. Come in.'

Denny feels the cold air inside hit him. It's as pronounced as a slap in the face from one of his constabulary colleagues. It's considerably warmer outside. But the mission building doesn't offer the welcome relief of a cooling shade. It's more like finding himself inside a large, refrigerated storeroom. Or a morgue.

Doodle conducts an impromptu tour. The mission is – as usual on weekdays – vacant.

After an hour or so, they reach the library. Doodle makes tea.

'So, what's the story wi' students that live here?' asks Denny.

'What do you mean, story?'

'Where do they aw come from, the foreign yins?'

'Pastor McTavish has connections in outreach institutes in various parts of Europe.'

'Religious outreach programmes?'

'Yeh. It's an annual exchange programme that brings young

people here from those countries to learn better English, and to learn the word of God, obviously.'

'Aw, aye ... obviously,' says Denny. 'But it's only females, right?'

'Yeh. The pastor is looking to expand the programme to young men in the New Year.'

'So how many go back there fae here?'

'What do you mean?'

'Exchange ... that's a two-way street, naw?'

'I don't know of any.'

Denny reflects on this. He seems anxious. Carefully assembling the words that he'll say next.

'Nothin' about that seem odd tae you?' he asks.

Doodle hesitates. He experiences a strange sensation. A paranoia grips him as he struggles to recall anything incriminating that he might've said in the past hour he's been with the policeman.

'You said you wanted to join our church. Is this why? Was it just an excuse?'

Tables turned. It's now Dennis on the defensive. Neither has experience in the art of show and tell.

'Look, Doodle, ah joined the polis because ma da was a copper. An' his da before him. That wis before he took the stroke, like. Always talked it up. "Comrades for life," he'd say. Everybody lookin' out for everybody else. Turnin' a blind eye, here an' there, know what ah mean?'

Doodle nods. Although he's not entirely sure what it means. The odd free bottle at The Bells? A share of some contraband goods? Or more serious bribery and corrupt practices?

'Great pension tae, if ye can see oot the term. Intae the fitba for nothin', aw that kinda thing,' says Denny. 'But ma da wis still a principled man. Strong as an ox. Always at the centre ae things. Always in control, y'know? An organiser. A fixer. Knew where the line wis an' knew never tae cross it.'

Doodle nods again.

'This current crop, though...' Denny shakes his head. 'Ah'm no' one ae the lads, ye understand me?'

'Yeh. I think so.'

'But ah'm nothin' like him either, ma da,' Denny admits. 'Ah'm a different sort aw th'gither. Ah'm soft. They batter an' bully me doon the station. Ah'm called a poofter. "Penis Dry-bugger".' Denny Dryburgh swallows hard. Lowers his voice.

Doodle concentrates on the lips. Detects the pain that they are describing.

'Ah've tried tae get a transfer fae Central but it'll be the same everywhere.'

'My God,' says Doodle.

'They aw say ma da wis a bloody grass, an' that ah've got tae account for him.'

Doodle watches the tears well in Denny's eyes.

Denny takes a minute. Composes himself.

'But ah'm a Christian, Doodle. Just like you. We cannae look the other way when we know somethin's rotten.'

Denny gets up. Walks across the library floor to the open door. Doodle assumes he's leaving. That this admission has been too much for him. But Denny stops. He scans the corridor beyond. Then closes the door quietly before returning to the table.

'Can ah trust ye, Doodle?'

'Yeh.'

'See the Baltakis lassie – the one that wis stayin' here.'

'Yeh.'

'D'ye no' think there's somethin' weird aboot the way her murder trial ended?'

Doodle wants to agree. To acknowledge aloud that he knows something is amiss. But it would feel like he'd be going behind Pastor McTavish's back. Betraying the open arms that took him in nearly five years ago. When he was at his lowest ebb. But it can't be denied that Denny has struck a chord. Doodle has observed hundreds of accused men face their crimes in the dock. And amongst them all Abraham Blair stands out. Not because he pleaded his innocence – most do – but because Doodle had the distinct feeling he was completely ignorant of the details of the brutal crime to which he'd apparently confessed.

Denny now reinforces this: 'He didnae confess, that Blair laddie,' he says. 'They picked him up near this travellin' commune. Brought him in, back door, middle ae the night. Nae fuss. Discrete, like. Stoned oot his mind. He'd nae idea who he wis, never mind *where* he wis. Held him for a week straight. Nae lawyer present. Everythin' covered up because they'd fabricated the confession. CID battered the bones ae him. Tortured him for hours oan end. Denied him water, food. Painkillers. Tied him tae a metal chair. Let him shit an' piss aw ower himself an' then left him sittin' in it. The poor bastard.'

'There were no marks on him at the trial.'

'Torso only. Body shots,' says Dennis. 'Bags full ae snooker balls. CID are experts at that kinda treatment.'

'What was being covered up?'

'No *whit* – who.'

'Who?'

'There's the question, eh?'

'How do you know this?' asks Doodle.

'Ah'm like you,' Denny replies. 'Ah spend ma life tryin' tae be invisible. Blendin' intae the background. Hidin' in the shadows. Avoidin' bein' a target. Ye become human wallpaper. Eventually folk don't notice ye. They drop their guard. They loosen their lips when they think naebody's listenin',' says Denny. 'Or when they think somebody's deaf an' cannae hear them anyway.'

Doodle finds himself surprised by Denny's insightfulness. It's rare someone sees inside Doodle's mind like this.

'Aw ah want is for somethin' that would make ma da proud if he was still here,' says Denny.

They stare at each other. Neither man says anything. Neither has the social skills to navigate the chasm that lies between them. To construct the bridge to the other side.

Doodle feels dejected. 'You're not here to join the Sovereign Grace Mission, then?' he asks.

The tension is broken. Dennis laughs, until realising that Doodle is being serious.

'Look, ah think we can help each other,' says Denny.

'How?'

'The Baltakis case – it's almost identical tae another one. Three years ago, Janina Žukauskas. Were you here then? D'ye remember her?'

'In 1966? Yes, I was. But only at the Sunday services and out in the community. The name isn't familiar,' says Doodle.

'There was this reporter, Stevie Milloy – the fitba player, re-member?'

Doodle looks baffled.

'Yer no' a fitba fan, are ye?' Doodle shakes his head. 'Well, he ended up at the *Star*. Investigatin' this murder. A foreign lassie. A Christian, she was. She was residin' here tae. Murdered. Sexually assaulted. Similar attack tae the Baltakis lassie. Strangled. Skull caved in. Buggered wi' a big stick ae some kind.'

'My God,' says Doodle. 'An' what happened?'

'Exact same thing. The polis arrested a suspect. Some loner naebody knew or cared about. Extracted a confession. Then the poor bastard gets declared unfit for trial. Claims insanity, for Christ's sake.'

'Where is he now?'

'He was detained in Carstairs Mental Hospital.'

'Have you spoken to him?' asks Doodle.

'Well, here's the thing – a few days after he went there, he hung himself in his cell.'

Doodle mulls this over. His head hurts. White lightning bursts are converging around the edges of his vision. The fragments of these cases. Both involving young women temporarily living at the mission. Both dead. Murdered. Sexually assaulted. Both, osten-sibly, in Pastor McTavish's care prior to their deaths.

'Ah know Abie Blair didnae kill himself while in police custody.
I was there that night, drivin' the inspector. There was nothin' in
the bloody cell for him to dae it wi'. They'd stripped him again.
Taken aw the bedding away fae him. They caw'd him Abie the baby,
sayin' he was that immature his food had tae be liquidised. He
couldnae even choke oan a chicken bone, for God's sake.'

'What about the reporter – Milloy. Is he still tracking the case?'

'Guess whit – he's deid tae. An' accordin' tae the notices in the
Star, the last place he went before his motor tumbled intae the
Clyde was here – meetin' Big Jamesie Campbell.'

It's a lot of information for Doodle to absorb. He's still not entirely sure what Dennis Dryburgh's angle is. Is the young copper
implying that Pastor McTavish knows more about these events
than he has let on to the police? Or, conversely, that the police
know more about Pastor McTavish's involvement in them than is
being made public? But why? Who benefits from a cover-up?
Surely an unassuming man of God wouldn't be embroiled in a
murderous scandal. Then again, what do we really know about
those close to us? We are born alone, and we die alone. That's the
universal truth. Some people – like Doodle's brother Malky –
might share our genetic formulation, but we're all ultimately
strangers when it comes down to it.

'What d'you want from me?' asks Doodle.

'No' sure. Just do whit ye're good at – what *we're* good at –
blendin' in. Be invisible. Take advantage ae the disability, an' keep
yer eyes open.'

Doodle nods.

'Ah'll be in touch soon,' says off-duty PC Dennis Dryburgh.

They leave the library. They take the stone stairs briskly. Two
at a time.

'Hullo, son.' A voice reaches them at the bottom. Its owner
remains in the shadows.

'Eh, hullo,' says Denny.

Doodle sees him. 'Hello, Pastor,' he says.

'This our new convert, then?'

'Yes, Pastor,' says Doodle. 'This is Dennis.'

The pastor hooks his walking stick over a forearm and takes Dennis's hand within his two. They are bloodlessly cold. His eyes close. As if he were offering a blessing.

'Dennis, my son. You'll dae well here, ah'm certain ae that. Ah can feel it.'

'Aye. Thanks,' says Denny.

The pastor's eyes open. Little, dark intimidating spots. Unblinking. Casting a spell.

'Doodle tells me you are a Christian man,' says the pastor.

'I am, yeah.'

'An' your family, Dennis – are they believers?'

'Em, no. No, they weren't. Da wis an atheist. Ma just went along wi' what he said most ae the time.'

'Ah, okay. That's understandable. I too have had struggles wi' the existence of God at times. When ah served in the war, y'know?'

'Aye,' says Denny. His own detestable National Service term springs to mind.

'Ah experienced so many things that had me questionin' God's plan ... or even if there wis one. Do you see what ah mean, son?'

'Ah do.'

'These days, so many atheists are well versed on scripture an' the contradictions ae the theological struggle. More so than the slavishly dogmatic' – the pastor glances at Doodle – 'who meekly accept God an' their religious calling without any doubting. You understand?'

'Yes, ah think so.'

'It's often healthy for us to admit to doubts in our faith. It oftens strengthens our conviction an' helps us when we face those out to harm us or destroy our beliefs. Don't you agree?'

'Aye, ah hadn't really thought about it, like...'

'So, our challenge, young Dennis, is tae be completely sure ae those that walk amongst us. Tae be certain ae the pureness ae their hearts, an' convinced ae the veracity ae their intentions. Ye get my drift, Dennis.'

'Aye.' Dennis withdraws his hand.

The pastor relinquishes it reluctantly. He rests a hand on Doodle's shoulder. 'Simple, accepting innocence – it's laudable, aye, but easily taken advantage ae. Innocence an' naivety represent the cracks. There's cracks in everythin', son. This city. This building. This poor deaf believer, here. An' while the cracks are where the light gets in, that's also where the Devil prises an' openin'. Unless we're constantly on guard. Can ye hear what ah'm sayin' tae ye, Dennis?'

'Aye. Ah hear ye, Pastor McTavish,' says Denny Dryburgh.

'As Christians, we benefit from divine grace, Dennis. As long as our faith sustains, God permits us certain freedoms ... tae set our own moralities. Our own rules of behaviour, so tae speak. But with that comes a huge responsibility to bind with others like us, do you see?'

'Ah think so, aye.'

'Good. We understand each other, then.' Pastor McTavish smiles. 'Ah'll hopefully see ye in the congregation oan Saturday an' Sunday.'

Dennis takes a step backward.

'We live for the weekends, don't we Doodle?' The pastor pats Doodle's shoulder. 'The opportunity tae come together an' express our love for God an' for each other.'

Doodle nods.

'An' tell me one last thing, my son,' says the pastor. 'Dae ye earn a wage?'

'Ah'm a PC,' says Denny. '"A" Division.'

'Ah, that's very good.' Pastor McTavish's eyes light up. 'I'm sure you'll know Inspector McCracken then, an' he you ... a good man. A real supporter ae this mission.'

The pastor turns. That odd irregular heartbeat of shoe heel and cane on the stone floor fading into the darkness.

Baby, Let Me Follow You Down (1969)

*Doodle befriends a new girl at the Sovereign Grace Mission –
Denny plants a seed of doubt – Doodle witnesses a shocking event.*

15th August

He hears someone approach. But he doesn't turn immediately. He
feels the vibrations too. It's either a slim female or a child. Something tells him it's almost certainly the former. She reaches out
past him. Places a note on the table in front of him:

*Hello, my name is Biruta Kruze. I'm new here. It's nice to meet
you.*

'Oh, hello. It's okay. I lip-read,' Doodle says. Voice low and
nasally exaggerated.

'The pastor told me you were deaf,' she says.

His initial assessment was correct. On both counts. A slim
female *and* a child. The girl is very slight. Elfin-framed. Bones that
might break under the pressure of even the tenderest of hugs.
Short, boyish hair. She can't be more than sixteen.

'When did you arrive?'

'Yesterday,' she replies.

'From?'

'I'm originally from Kaunas,' she says. Her smile is constant.
'Lithuania.'

'And your parents, your family, they're back there?'

'Oh, no. No, I have no family.'

Her English is perfect. As good as his. Better than most he
has to decipher. She is educated. And the way she holds herself

indicates a maturity that Doodle has rarely seen from other European girls in the mission's care. Older than she looks, perhaps.

'I was born in House of Perkūnas, in the centre of town,' she says. 'My mama died having me. I had no father.'

'You must've had a father – *everybody* has a father.'

'I mean that I didn't know my father,' she says. The smile never leaves her lips. 'I grew up being cared for by chaplains and then, two months ago, selected to join the Christian Fellowship serving God with Pastor McTavish here in Scotland.'

The girl is beaming. Like she's just hit the final thread on *The Golden Shot*.

'I'm so very lucky to be here,' she says. But it sounds rehearsed. Something she's been taught to say.

'Would you like a tea?' he asks her.

'Yes,' she says. 'Thank you.'

She follows him to the kettle.

'I'm still not sure what I'm to do here yet,' she says. Her smile has dimmed, and for the briefest of seconds he sees the frightened little girl that she's struggling to conceal.

'The pastor will know,' he says.

'Yes. The pastor.' Her smile returns. Her youthful composure regained. 'He will know.'

She takes the tea from him. Holds the cup in both hands. She sips from it as if it was a friendship quaich.

'How long have you been working here?' she asks him.

'Oh, this is not my work,' he says. 'I just like being here. I do another job.'

'For the pastor?'

'No. My job is illustrating court scenes.' He sees her confusion. 'I'm a courtroom sketch artist. No cameras allowed in a courtroom, so to record what happens, I sketch the proceedings. The sketches are featured in newspapers.'

'Only newspapers?'

'Mainly,' he says. 'To give the public an idea of what happened in a trial.'

Her eyes widen. It's as if she's drawing all this information into her brain via her sight.

Doodle opens his sketchpad. He lets her look at it.

'These are all criminals?' she asks.

'Yeh,' he replies.

She stops at the pages that he has paper-clipped together. The ones that feature Abraham Blair's trial and the woman with the dark-brown skin and the black hair. She glances up expectantly, an impressionable pupil looking for a teacher's permission. He nods. She pulls the clip away.

'These drawings are beautiful,' she says of the woman's likeness. She touches the pencil markings delicately. He watches her finger trace the outline of the woman's face. Page after page of detailed study.

'She is lovely,' she says.

'Yeh, she was,' says Doodle.

'What was she on trial for?' Biruta asks.

Doodle is distracted by reflections flashing across the ceiling. He takes the sketchbook from her. He walks over to the window. Three big cars outside. The sunshine hitting their shiny wing mirrors as the doors open. Heavy-set men clad in black and wearing brimmed hats get out. Sombre expressions. All here for serious business of some sort. Unlikely to be the salvation of their souls.

He hears them storm the stairs like bailiffs. Segs sparking off the concrete. The library door opens. One greasy head leans in. He sees Doodle seated. Back to him. The girl on the other side of the table. Smiling. Facing the door.

'He's no' in here, Jamesie. The wee lassie is though. An' that daft mute yin tae.'

Mute? My God.

Doodle doesn't look up. Face down. Writing whatever generality occurs to him.

'Hello,' says the girl. Still smiling. Still anticipating the best of human nature.

'You,' says the booming voice Doodle knows to belong to Jamesie Campbell. 'Lose yersel', hen.'

The girl looks puzzled. Until Bobby McCracken comes in. She waves in acknowledgment. He takes her gently by the arm and escorts her out.

'Whit aboot him?' asks a new face.

'He's fine,' says another. 'He works here. The cunt's deaf as a fucken post. Look...' The man tiptoes up behind Doodle. 'Haw ... CUNTYBAWS!'

Doodle anticipates well. He doesn't flinch. They leave him alone in the library, the main doors slightly open.

Listening as best he can through the inch-wide gap, Doodle still can't distinguish the content of the conversation happening further down the corridor, in Pastor McTavish's office. But it involves raised voices. He risks widening the gap and even progresses to the other side of the door.

'...were ye fucken thinkin', Tav, eh? She's fucken sixteen, for Christ's sake.'

The response is muted. Hesitant. Unclear. Only Big Jamesie Campbell's voice – capable, some political opponents have said, of stripping paint at two hundred yards – is audible to Doodle. The tone, the timbre. The anger. Clear as a bell, even to a partially deaf man.

'An' you – he's a fucken balloon, but you, Boaby, *you* shoulda fucken known better.'

A dull noise. Something heavy hitting a wall.

'Eighteen, we said, did we no'? Minimum age limit. The age ae legal fucken consent. They aw have tae be fucken eighteen tae come here. Classed as adults. That wis the rules fae the bloody start.'

Indistinguishable.

'How the fuck did ye even get her oot the country?'

Indistinguishable.

'For fuck's sake. Whit if some nosy wee passport cunt at the border had checked closer, eh? Get yer collars felt, an' aw this traces back tae the fucken Denton-Halls. An' then it leads tae me. An' ah'm no' havin' that. You dozy wallopers know this aw'ready, an' yet ye'se went ahead anyway. Well, that's it this time. Ye're fucken barred fae up the road. Nae mair Weekenders.'

Indistinguishable.

'Dinnae gie me that bollocks, son. Ah sick hearin' aw yer excuses.'

Indistinguishable.

'Aye, fucken right ye are. "Ah'm sorry, Jamesie ... It'll no' happen again, Jamesie." Until it does an' ah'm left moppin' up aw the shite ahint ye. Well, that's it. Fucken finito. Wilson's got me oan the fast-track tae a cabinet post an' ah cannae afford any fucken spot-lights shining oan us cos ae your dirty business.'

Indistinguishable.

'Tav, listen son, that's enough fae you, right. Ah've gie'd ye too many chances. It's done. Ye've "loved them aw"? Big fucken deal. Didnae stop ye doin' away wi'—'

The door along the hall closes. The argument is only tremors now. Doodle returns to the library. He makes notes. Tries to fill in the gaps – for Dennis Dryburgh's benefit.

+

16th August

He has moved the table closer to the window facing MacKeith Street. In this position, it benefits from the orange glow of the streetlamp outside the entry to the close. He can draw, write, or observe through the night without drawing the attention of nocturnal passers-by.

It's still daylight when she leaves. The third night in a row. She's wearing a black dress of the type worn by Japanese women. A white ruffled blouse underneath. Tan stockings. High-heeled shoes. A headscarf over new curls. Bright lipstick, the physiognomy of female fashion. Dressing to impress an as yet unknown man. Details matter.

She turns and waves with her free arm. Brown coat and matching handbag draped over the other. She isn't waving to him, but towards the flat below. To her sister. Possibly even to her children. Doodle can hear them bouncing around downstairs, so at least three out of the six cousins are up. It's a warm Saturday night. No school in the morning. Margaret's oldest is probably still out. Playing kick-the-can, or British bulldog, or hide-and-seek in the derelict tenement husks. His Auntie Mima is off out to play adult games in the bright lights. The Majestic Ballroom, or the Barrowlands, or somewhere else music and dancing happen. So many in this city living for the weekend, regardless of their means.

He watches her disappear. Turning right at the end of MacKeith Street. He wonders what his life might've been like if it had been as conventional as hers. If her favourite bandleaders conducted the pattern of his week rather than his pastor. Were their lives so different? Both enduring the weekdays, anticipating the weekends. A different type of Weekender. Could he ever have been the man she'd be returning home with later tonight? Or would he have been one of the absent fathers she's left in her wake?

The hours pass. He tunes the transistor to a mainstream station. Turns it up louder to hear it better. Popular music, for popular people?

'The moment I wake up, before I put on my makeup...'

And he likes this. It's like a modern gospel song, sung by a woman with a big, expansive Church voice. God would like this music, he thinks. And it's followed by another He might approve of.

'The only one who could ever reach me...'

Maybe he'd been wrong all along. Maybe God hadn't forsaken him. Maybe His word was spreading and reaching people in different ways. Through the music of popular radio. Of the dancehalls. Maybe Mima MacDonald's soul would be saved by such glorious, joyous gospel music.

The sketches lie before him. It has only been a few hours, but he doesn't remember the process of creating them. He is naked. And masturbating. He doesn't recall preparing for that happening either. Singers on the popular music for popular people programme, such as Glen Campbell and Hank Williams, have opened his eyes and his mind to a different God. One that Pastor McTavish has never previously introduced him to.

'Then Jesus came like a stranger in the night
Praise the Lord, I saw the light.'

And, filled with this renewed Holy Spirit, Doodle has once again drawn the woman who has occupied so much of his time ever since he saw her enter the courtroom a pace or so behind Jamesie Campbell. She is a woman he feels he's known all his life. Or at least since she suddenly appeared out of the acrid smoke and the burning rubble of the Clydebank Blitz.

Laughter in the street interrupts him. He glances at the clock on the mantelpiece. He squints then rubs his eyes. It's well past midnight. Almost one in the morning. *Sunday* morning. The Lord's day.

The laughing woman is Mima MacDonald. She's with a man. A tall man. A familiar-looking man. A man with ginger hair, although that might just be the sodium streetlight. He hasn't thought about Malcolm too much lately. They are standing in the doorway of a derelict tenement. And then they go inside. The building could collapse around them at any minute. But they are going in there anyway. Driven by their lust, their desire. This man wouldn't have been Doodle. Doodle would ensure she got home safely, and before midnight.

Malcolm, you selfish bastard!

+

18th August

Mid-Monday morning. He is staying at home. A heavy cold with periodic migraines weighed his Sunday down. It has built over a few days. The cocktail of medicines he's taken to combat the blinding attacks has made him continuously drowsy. He missed church yesterday. Questions might be asked. He has been drifting in and out of awareness. His errant brother Malcolm appearing in several obscure day – and night-time – apparitions since he saw him outside with his neighbour.

Doodle hears the screaming. The high pitch of it wakes him.

'Aw naw ... *naw*! Aw my God, Mima. No' Mima,' he hears.

The howls don't seem human. High pitch descends to low, slow growling. Shock turning to abject despair.

'Ma sister's been murdered. Ma sister's deid.' The words painfully drawn out.

Doodle slowly peeks out of his window. Only Margaret is in view. She is on her knees, in the middle of the street, hands over her face. And then her torso tips forward. She thumps the road's wet surface with first her right, and then her left fist. All the time wailing 'she's deid' repeatedly.

Doodle watches this until other women hove into view. Five of them, in similar dress, reach Margaret simultaneously. They encompass her before lifting her off the road. Doodle notices the ripped stockings and the blood from Margaret's skinned knees. He grabs a jacket and heads out to the street; something he realises he should have done immediately. He is on the close steps as the five carry her, wailing and sobbing, into her house.

'I'm sorry,' says Doodle. But none of them register it. None of them acknowledge him.

Poor Margaret. She is the one who found the body. Saw first-hand what he had done to her. Witnessed the reality of her unheeded warnings that 'someb'dy'll do you in, one day' come to pass.

There may be opportunities to console her.

Then: maybe a long spell in prison would be good for his brother. With God's help, the enforced discipline would turn Malky back into Malcolm again. Doodle's prayers would be answered.

It's early evening now. The building across the street is cordoned off. Suited men in hats have patrolled the street since just before lunchtime. Taking control. Ordering the uniforms about.

He knows they are in the close. Senses the heavy shoes, *tack-tacking* up and down the stairs. The dull, unambiguous *polis* knock on the door is predictable. Door-to-door inquiries have begun.

Did anybody see anything? Did anyone hear anything?

Doodle knows enough about the first forty-eight hours of a murder's aftermath to have anticipated the visit. If anything, it's happening later than he expected. But she lay there dead, in a back room of the condemned building, for all of Sunday. The Lord's day. Even so, in the Serious Crime department things still take time to gear up.

'Hello,' he says.

'Can ye open the door, sir?' the voice commands. 'It's the police.'

They hear the locks unlocking. Bolts being released from their catches. Finally, a latch turning.

'Christ, son, ye keepin' somethin' valuable in this dump?'

'Eh?'

'Ne'er mind,' says the first suit. 'Can we come in?'

'Em. Yeh.' Doodle opens the door wide. Soft hats stay on hard heads. Names are not exchanged.

'Dae ah know you?' asks the second suit. And before Doodle can answer: 'Aye. Ah *dae*. Ah know this fella,' he tells the first detective. 'Ye're in the station now an' again, so ye are? You're the Doodler, aren't ye?' he says.

'"The Doodler"?' asks the first detective.

'Aye, that's it, int'it?'

'Yeh. I'm a court sketch artist,' says Doodle. The cold adding an extra nasal, exaggerated monotone layer. His comfort blanket. It prompts the usual response.

'Ah knew ah'd seen you somewhere.' Slow. Loud. Speaking at him like he's not the full shilling.

'It's okay,' says Doodle. 'I lip-read.'

The first detective scans the spartan flat. 'No' got much, have ye? Whit's wi' the Fort Knox situation?'

'I'm sorry?'

The first detective turns his mouth to where Doodle can see it, unaware that Doodle heard him. He just didn't understand the reference.

'Aw the locks on yer front door? Whit the fuck ye hidin', son?' The first detective leans in. Serious accusatory face.

'Ach, lay off him, Davie. He's one ae us, eh Doodle?'

Doodle doesn't answer.

'So, ye'll know a wummin's been murdered, then? Across the road there. She lived in this block. A Jemima MacDonald. Ye'll have seen her aboot then, aye?'

'Yeh. She lived downstairs.'

'Know her well, did ye?' asks Detective Davie.

'No. No' really,' says Doodle.

'Ye must've spoke tae her though?'

'Only if she passed on the stairs,' says Doodle.

'Where were ye oan Saturday night?' asks Detective Davie. The tone changes. He continues to investigate the flat. Looks at the drawing on the table. Sniffs the tea-cup contents. Draws a finger along the mantelpiece.

'Em. I was here. In the house.'

'Dain' whit?' Davie the detective examines a nude drawing like a jeweller would a rare diamond.

'Sketching,' says Doodle. 'Reading.'

'Who's this? Yer fancy wummin?'

'I don't know what that means.'

'Looks a wee bit like Mima MacDonald, no' think so, Jim?'

'Naw ... nuthin' like her, Davie,' says Detective Jim. 'He's pullin' yer leg, pal.'

'Anybody vouch for ye bein' here. In the house. Drawin' pictures ae young women in the scud?' Detective Davie stares out the window into the street.

'Davie, gie it up, eh?' Detective Jim laughs. 'Listen, Doodle, if ye hear anybody talkin' aboot Mima or who she wis seein', ye'll let us know, right?'

They turn to leave.

'I did see Miss MacDonald early on Sunday mornin'. She was across the street. With a man.'

The CID men stop in their tracks. They turn simultaneously.

The panda car blares its siren and flashes its rotating blue lights for the entire journey. In the back, Doodle feels like a suspect. He had to get in the vehicle right outside the murder location. The occupants of flats not yet boarded up watching like gossipy hawks.

It takes less than fifteen minutes for them to reach Turnbull Street. Two coppers lead Doodle in as if he's a criminal. Davie and Jim have followed in their own car. When they arrive, Doodle is taken to an interview room. He holds his portfolio as if it contains official secrets. A cup of tea is brought for him. He didn't ask for it and doesn't drink it. Half an hour later, the door opens.

'Son, ah'm Detective Chief Superintendent Goodall.' A hand extended.

Doodle shakes it.

Immediately, five CID men file in behind. Detectives Davie, Jim and three others, only one of whom gets a name – 'Binnie, the man in charge', according to Goodall, even though it's he alone who speaks. They have an aura, the CID men. The size of the interview room seems to shrink as they fill it.

'They tell me ye don't hear, is that correct?'

'Yes, sir,' says Doodle. 'I read lips.'

'Everythin' that happens in this room – in this *station* – is totally confidential. Ye understand that, right?'

Doodle nods nervously.

'An' if there's anythin' ye want tae get off yer chest, anythin' ye want tae tell me, that ye don't feel comfortable sayin' tae the boys here, then ye know where ah am, okay son?' Goodall is keeping all options open.

'Yeh,' says Doodle.

'Good. We aw know where we stand then,' says Tom Goodall. 'So, ye saw somethin' outside yer flat. In the street. MacKeith Street. Early Sunday mornin'. Ye saw the deceased, Miss Jemima MacDonald. Ye saw her talkin' tae a man. Can ye describe this man?'

'Yeh. I can,' says Doodle.

'An' the boys here tell me ye could also draw a likeness ae this man.'

'Yeh.'

'Good lad.'

Goodall is salivating. Finding it hard to contain his desire to punch the air. The unsolved murder of another young women may be linked to this new one. It has been less than twenty-four hours since the latest discovery, but the strangulation, the battered bodies being arranged face down with the clothes lifted high around the torso, and the victims' handbags missing are shared features. That both women were menstruating at the time may just be an odd coincidence. But Goodall doesn't believe in coincidence. He believes in instinct. And his instinct tells him that Doodle is telling the truth.

'Son, can you wait in the station a while for us?'

'I've got nowhere else to be, sir.'

Overnight, Goodall makes the unprecedented decision to apply to the Crown Office for an identikit portrait of the suspect to be published. It would be the first time such a portrait will have been used in the hunt for a Scottish murderer. Doodle has provided various rough pencil sketches, but Goodall appreciates the benefit of involving artistic heavyweights in such a public situation. He makes some calls.

Doodle has been in the station for twenty hours. An open-door cell was offered. He accepted, but declined the pillow. He rarely sleeps these days anyway. Instead, he sits. He stands. He paces. Watching. Listening to conversations people assume he cannot hear. Sketching. A likeness of Mima. Waving. On her way to the dancing. Her last night alive.

'Doodle,' says Detective Jim. 'Here's a sandwich for ye. An' some milk. DCS Goodall says tae make sure yer looked after aw'right.'

'Thanks,' says Doodle.

Jim leaves, and minutes later Denny Dryburgh sticks his head around the cell's door.

'Jeez, you still in here oan Goodall's orders?'

'Yeh,' says Doodle.

'That's positive.'

'How?'

'We're gonnae need somebody high up tae go tae wi' aw the Sovereign Grace stuff when the picture's clearer. An' there's nane higher than him,' says Denny. 'He's a decent man, tae. Everybody says it.'

Doodle nods.

'Can we catch up later – once ye're done?'

'Okay.'

'Haw, Dry-*bugger*!' A loud, angry voice from down the corridor. 'Get yer bloody arse ootae there an' leave Helen Keller alone, right?'

Two hours after the sandwiches and milk, Doodle is taken back to the original interview room. Four men occupy it this time. As well as Goodall and Paterson, there's Binnie, and a new CID man. Four identical raincoats and brimmed hats hang from hooks on the far wall. All smoke except Goodall, who puffs on a pipe. It side-lips his mouth like he's Popeye.

'Son, this is Mr Lennox Paterson, the deputy head of the Glasgow School of Art. Mr Paterson is a very accomplished artist,' says Goodall, between puffs.

Paterson is the only man seated. He gets up uneasily. His posture stooped and awkward – maybe the consequence of a life-time sat in front of an easel.

'Hullo, young man,' says the artist. He offers a hand.

Doodle notices long fingernails spotted with paint. Dirt underneath them. Charcoal on the fingertips. The frayed ends of a shirt cuff that used to be white.

'Mr Paterson has very kindly consented to produce a drawing – a proper portrait – to help us trace this person you saw, d'you understand?'

'Yeh,' says Doodle.

'So, we're goin' to leave you with Mr Paterson, okay, son?'

'Yeh,' says Doodle.

'Describe the man you saw around midnight on Saturday to Mr Paterson here, an' between you, we'll get a better idea of who we're lookin' for.'

'Ah've made some sketches of my own,' says Doodle.

'All the better, son,' says Goodall. He pats Doodle on the shoulder. 'Ah'll be seein' ye.'

The contented chief smacks his lips on the pipe's stem and says, 'Let's go, fellas.'

He has lost all concept of time. Picks up a newspaper on the way home. It orientates him. Thursday.

'Midnight Stroll to Murder'. A headline at odds with Glasgow's East End. It's too glamourous. He imagines it fitting better in the fevered Hollywood Hills. In the shady canyons around Sharon Tate's house. Not amongst the dirt and the squalor and the grime and the rubble of MacKeith Street.

He reads his own words, reproduced verbatim: 'a tall, slim man with reddish-blond hair, wearing a good, well-cut brown suit.' Malcolm must have been doing well these past few years. Although theft and battery are not beyond him.

When he reaches MacKeith Street, normality has returned. The cordons have gone. Children run wild. The smaller boys playing football in the street. The girls pushing little prams with buckled wheels, bending over to fawn as they have seen the grown-ups do. Near the entry where Malcolm took Mima to her death, there is a set of mattresses piled four high. Bigger boys jump from first – and second – floor openings onto them. The activity seems to freeze when they catch sight of Doodle. But no-one shouts. No-one yells or throws something at him. They just stare.

In the close, Doodle encounters Mima's sister. She is standing at her front door. Holding a cake and talking to another woman. Doodle assumes it's a gift, and he wonders whether he should've got Margaret something similar.

Is that what you do in such circumstances?

'Hello,' he says in passing.

'Hullo,' says the other woman.

'How are you today?' he asks Margaret.

'The polis said ye saw him – the bastart that done her in,' says Margaret.

'Em, yeh,' says Doodle.

'Gaun up that manky close in the dead ae night,' she says.

He sees the anger rising. He won't be telling her that it was Malcolm, his brother. He won't be telling anyone that. He simply nods.

'So why, in the name ae God, did ye no' go doon there, eh? Whit did ye think wis happenin'?' she yells.

'Mibbe ah should go, Magret,' says the other woman.

'Did ye keep watchin'? Did ye, eh? Did ye see him come oot the close withoot her?' This was a question he had expected to be asked by the police. But they didn't ask it.

'Well?'

'No, I'm sorry,' he says.

'Sorry? Whit good is that tae her noo? She mighta still been alive if ye'd went doon there efter he came oot hisself!'

That hadn't occurred to him until now. His focus had been on Malcolm for most of the Sunday.

'Fucken useless, you are!' she shouts. 'USELESS!' She leans in. Making sure he can read the lips *and* feel the fury.

'It's not my business,' he whimpers.

'No' your business? Yer up there oglin' the both of us day an' night, an' the one time it woulda benefitted her, ye dae nothin'?'

Margaret drops the cake. The plate smashes. The icing splatters on the other woman's shoes. A hand slaps Doodle. Hard. The sound of the slap reverberates around the close.

'Gaun, fuck off, ya useless arsehole,' she screams. She isn't crying. He now cannot imagine her crying. Only furious. Permanently angry. All those pictures he's drawn of her over the years. The thoughts. The dreams. The private longings he's had for her. All for nothing. He backs away. Climbs the steps. Her voice chasing after him.

'Three wee weans, she's left. Taken awa' intae bloody care before she's even cauld? No' your business? Ya useless fucken arsehole, ye.'

He closes the door. Locks it. Sweating. Breathless. Panicked.

Malky, you fucking cunt!

+

September

Donald Malpas lives a life governed by routine. Work, read, worship, rest. Vary the ingredients slightly on the weekend. And then repeat. Spontaneity only increases his anxiety. However, after his visit to the police station he spends almost a month away from the courthouse, the newspaper offices and the Sovereign Grace Mission library – the pillars of his world. His mood changes. He adjusts the hands of his internal body clock. Day becomes night, and vice versa. Going out when it's dark means he has a better chance of avoiding Magaret MacDonald. He invents things to do. He reorganises the flat. Repositions the sketches and drawings of dead women and murder scenes that line his walk-in cupboard. He stores long-life food and drink like a man preparing for hibernation.

He plans, organising his time around the now regular evening meetings with Lennox Paterson at Glasgow School of Art. The deputy head of the institute has asked Doodle to imagine the nature of the person he created rough sketches of. These drafts, along with Doodle's detailed descriptions, should help flush Malcolm out.

Lennox Paterson continues to probe him about the man's expressions. About his movements. About the details that might help the CID men identify their suspect. Doodle knows how much details matter. He restricts himself to the outward appearance but there is so much more about this man. About Malcolm. And in considering Paterson's questions, Doodle is forced to confront buried feelings.

Malcolm is younger than Donald. But not by much. From birth, Malcolm was louder, more demanding than his brother. Soaked up far more of their mother's time and attention. Their father was always ambivalent about both boys. Despite this, Malcolm was a good child for the time they lived in Clydebank.

Several times during their sessions together, Doodle is on the verge of telling Lennox Paterson this. Of explaining how the signs were always there. Of divulging Malcolm's name and identity, and describing those characteristics that demonstrate how capable he is of this atrocious act. Of how surprised Doodle was to see him that night, across the street, with a nice young woman like Mima. But something stops him. And eventually he acknowledges that this is a two-way street. Salvation for Malcolm equals forgiveness for Doodle. He needs that before he can rest easily.

As they work on bringing Malcolm back to life, Lennox Paterson comes to recognise Doodle's artistic talent. Persuades him that studying fine art is something a creative man with a penchant for the solitary existence might find rewarding.

Thus, over the course of this unusual month, Doodle has helped put in motion a nationwide search for his missing brother. Has adjusted the rigid structure of his life to include nude life-drawing classes – which, of course, necessitates the mortification of the flesh, but that is a price worth paying – and has temporarily released himself from the binds of the Sovereign Grace Mission and his gnawing suspicions of its leader – that misanthropy may be at the heart of the pastor's piety.

Which is why he panics when he sees Pastor McTavish strolling up MacKeith Street, plastic grocery bag in one hand, big black Bible in the other. The pastor reaches Doodle's number. Looks up at the windows. Turns and walks towards the close.

Doodle stands by his closed front door. It feels as if his breaths have gone from nought to sixty in less than five seconds.

A note slides under the door:

> *Doodle, son, it's Pastor McTavish. The fellowship are worried about you. You've not been at worship for three straight Sundays. That's not like you, Donald. If you see this note, let me in please. Let me know you're alright.*

A pencil slips from Doodle's grasp, and the game is up.

The pastor thumps on the door, even though he believes Doodle won't hear him…

'Is that you, Donald? Ah can hear ye in there. Open the door an' let the Lord in, son.'

Doodle unlocks the door. Slides the bolts back. Opens it and stands facing his pastor. Shamefaced.

'Ye gonnae invite me in then, at least?'

'Yeh.'

'Ah got yer address fae Bobby McCracken, through his aul' man at the station. Says ye've been spending time wi' the murder squad. Witnessed the suspect fae this very window, he tells me.'

'Yeh.'

'Must be excitin', tryin' tae crack a big criminal case.'

Doodle shrugs.

'Ah hope they get the bastart,' the pastor says, and it jolts Doodle to hear him swear. 'Should bring back hangin' for the likes ae that yin.'

'Is it right for Christians to support the death penalty, Pastor?'

'Well, of course it is,' he says. 'After aw, Easter widnae exist without it, an' then where would we be, eh?'

Doodle considers this. And eventually nods in agreement.

'Got any tea?' asks Pastor McTavish, parking himself in the chair at the table near the window.

'No. Sorry,' says Doodle.

'Aw. That's a shame, well.'

'Why are you here?' asks Doodle.

'That poor woman – the MacDonald yin. Ah thought ah'd come an' offer succour tae her sister. Bestow the Lord's blessing oan her family.'

'They're Catholics,' says Doodle.

'We're aw God's children, when all's said an' done, Donald.'

Doodle considers the gradual erosion of his faith in the man sitting at his table. His questionable, performative demeanour.

'Pastor McTavish?'

'Yes, my son.'

'Why is Biruta Kruze living at the mission?' Monotonal. Slow. There's safety in the tried and tested 'village idiot' persona.

'Well, Donald, Biruta's a young lassie wi' a thirst for knowledge. When ah visited her in Kaunas last year, she expressed a desire tae travel an' tae study the Lord's work here wi' us in Glasgow,' he says. 'Why ye askin' aboot her?'

'She said she was only sixteen,' says Doodle.

'An' whit business is that ae yours, son? The Denton-Hall Foundation is her legal guardian.'

'She seems a bit ... lost,' says Doodle.

'We're aw lost, son. Aw desperately tryin' tae find oor way back tae God.'

'I'm worried about her,' says Doodle.

'Worried?' asks the pastor, surprised. 'Worried how?'

'What happened to those other girls from Lithuania might happen to her too,' says Doodle. 'You know, Emilija and Janina?'

The pastor is visibly rocked. As if he's been deceived. Taken for a fool. Like the village idiot has been revealed to be a Nobel Prize-winning scientist. He takes a few moments to compose himself.

'Donald, you're treadin' in tae dangerous territory,' he says. 'Those poor, unfortunate lassies were murdered by vicious, violent men. It's just a tragic coincidence that they were both studyin' here at the time.'

'And they went to weekend parties held at Raskine House.'

Pastor McTavish feels like he has been shot. That sudden shocking dread that he hasn't experienced since Italy in 1944. That moment after being hit and before feeling the pain from the bullet entry, still not knowing how serious the damage might be.

'Ah ... genuinely d-dinnae know wh-whit y-ye're ... talkin' aboot, son,' he stutters. Denial, he's been taught. That is always the holding position. To provide time. To let the big guns get in and stem the flow. Limit the damage. Dispose of the evidence.

Suddenly, the pastor feels the need to be somewhere else. He stands. Stumbles. Knocks over the chair. Heads to the front door like a drunk on a listing ship.

'Sunday, Mr Malpas,' he mumbles on the way out. 'We'll expect ye for worship oan Sunday.'

And Doodle watches his pastor head down MacKeith Street, as briskly as his limp permits. Support from his cane doesn't prevent the pastor from turning an ankle on a kerb halfway and then hobbling for the remainder.

+

19th September

He only opens the door once he's seen Margaret leaving. Her three children are dressed differently today. Formally. Like they are attending a Children's Court hearing.

He watches their car turn left at the end of the street. And then picks up his bag and heads out.

When he reaches London Road, he spots Denny across the street. He's sitting at a corner table in the Parkhead café.

'Christ, where've ye been?' asks Denny.

'In the house,' Doodle replies.

'For four weeks?'

'Yeh.'

'Ah've been tryin' tae get a hold ae ye,' Denny stresses. 'Ye need tae get the phone put in.'

'Can't afford that,' says Doodle.

'Ye want a tea?'

'Yeh.'

'A roll an' sausage tae, ah suppose?'

'Yeh.'

Doodle hasn't eaten much during his self-imposed house arrest. The last of the milk went off two days ago. Only the white pan loaf and some cheese remained viable this last week.

Denny orders. Waits at the counter, and then brings the tray back with a double helping.

Doodle unpacks his bag. Lays out his notebook. Opens it at the first page. Places a pencil, two blue biros and a small eraser next to it. Arranges them at perfect angles to the table's edge. Denny says nothing until the minor adjustments come to an end.

'Pastor McTavish wis askin' a barrowload ae questions on Sunday,' says Denny. 'Aboot you.'

'Uh-huh,' says Doodle.

'"Where's Doodle?" he asks. "Been helpin' the polis wi' their inquiries," ah told him. "Oan Sundays – the Lord's Day?" he says. Ah didnae know whit tae say tae that.'

'Police business doesn't stop for the Sabbath,' says Doodle.

'Aye, Christ, ah know that. He wants tae know who ye're talkin' tae. Whit ye're sayin'.'

'What did you tell him?'

'That ah wis way below the bottom rung.' Denny sneers. 'Ah see, hear an' speak nae evil.'

'There's a lot going on,' says Doodle.

'So ... whit've ye found out?'

'The girls are from Lithuania ... a Christian Mission in Kaunas.'

'Where's Lithuania?'

'It's in the U.S.S.R. North of Poland,' says Doodle.

'Russia? Jesus. How dae they get here?'

'Transported to Hamburg, then sail across the North Sea.'

'An' this is aw legit?'

'Don't know. Jamesie Campbell set up the mission in Kaunas in the 1950s, in the name of his wife's family.'

'Ah knew it! Ah knew they bloody Denton-Halls were involved.'

'The girls work here. Domestic service, mostly. They get board and lodging at the Sovereign Grace.'

'Is that it?'

Doodle turns a page.

'Some attend weekend parties at Raskine House. Jamesie Campbell and his wife own Raskine House,' says Doodle.

'Ah, the Weekenders,' says Denny. He nods slowly. It means something to him. But not to Doodle. Denny notes his blank look.

'Ah've heard the boys at the station talkin' aboot these parties. "The Weekenders", they ca' them. Celebrities, an' film stars, an' politicians, an' senior polis ... an' hookers. Drugs an' booze an' aw kindsa wild sex shit goes oan there, so they say.'

Doodle closes his notebook.

'An' ah'll bet that's why these young lassies are gettin' brought ower fae that place in Europe, just like factory chickens reared for the slaughter,' says Denny.

'Slaughter?'

'Well, ye know what ah mean,' says Denny. 'Tae get fucked instead ae plucked.'

'A new one. Biruta. She arrived a week ago.'

'Somethin' different aboot this yin, is there?'

'She's sixteen,' says Doodle.

'Well, that is interestin',' Denny says.

They both slurp. Two amateur sleuths, unsure of what to do next.

'We need tae find oot when the next party's planned for,' says Denny.

'I'll try,' says Doodle. 'I'll look for you next time I'm at the station.'

'Eh, naw ... naw, dinnae dae that. See, ah'll probably no' be there. Shift pattern's changin', an' besides, ah've got some leave comin' up. Naw, listen ah'll contact you, right?'

Doodle nods. It's enough for one day.

+

22nd September

Doodle heads towards the Sovereign Grace. There is a notable chill in the air. And not just because the late-autumn weather has taken a downward turn. A palpable anxiety clings to the streets like a thickening smog. Fewer single women out. Men eyeing up other men. Fists balled. Provocation far closer to the surface than normal. The gripping paranoia that a murderer of defenceless women is among the population once again.

After Peter Manuel was hanged, the East End took years to feel normal again. His crimes set the place on edge. Murderers still walked the streets, drank in the pubs, sang on the terracing. But their killings were of other men. Gangland rivals. Scores settled. Territories taken. Empires expanded. Legitimate beefs. Sectarianism and revenge. This is different. Agitated by sensation-seeking newspapers like the *Daily Star*, fearful suspicion is rising to the surface once again.

When Doodle arrives at the mission, the pastor is entertaining Big Jamesie Campbell once again. This time, though, the atmosphere is more congenial. Doodle knocks before entering the office.

'Ye aw'right there, son,' says the politician. He looks Doodle straight in the eye.

'Yeh,' says Doodle.

'This him?' Jamesie asks the pastor.

'Aye, it is,' replies Pastor McTavish. 'Hullo, son,' he adds.

'Is Biruta still here?' Doodle asks.

The two look at each other, and then back at Doodle.

'Ah told ye before, ye dinnae need tae concern yourself wi' her, son,' says the pastor.

'I have something for her,' Doodle says.

'An' whit would that be then?'

'A book ... to help her,' says Doodle.

'Help her wi' whit exactly?'

'Her studies,' says Doodle. 'Her Christian studies.'

'Whit's the book?' asks Big Jamesie Campbell.

'*The Divine Comedy*,' says Doodle. 'It's by Dante.'

'*Billy* Dainty?' asks Big Jamesie. 'The music-hall comedian? Ah've met him afore. Royal Variety Performance. That bugger's a scream. Never knew he'd wrote a book.'

'Ah'll see she gets it,' says the pastor, hand out.

Doodle reaches into his bag. Pulls out the book and gives it to the pastor.

McTavish opens it. Flicks through. Sees pages folded back. Numerous passages underlined in blue biro.

'That it?'

'Yeh,' says Doodle. He turns to leave.

A hand prevents him.

'Oh, by the way, we want you an' your wee pal Dennis back oot preachin' the gospel an' raisin' funds oan Saturday. Outreach ... in the suburbs. Understand?'

'Yeh.'

+

27th September

'You don't want to come too?' asks Doodle.

'To Easterhoose?' says Denny. He puffs out his cheeks. 'Nae chance, pal. Ah'm no' that desperate for salvation.'

'Okay,' says Doodle.

'Ah'm goin' tae take a drive ower the moors. Go an' get another look at Raskine House.'

'Okay,' says Doodle.

He lifts his donations box, his wooden 'Jesus Saves' placard and his Sovereign Grace Mission leaflets out of Benny's boot.

'Doodle, this is mental. It's like facin' the lions in the Colosseum wi' nae armour or weapons.'

'Pastor McTavish says that pain and suffering are like the kiss of Jesus.'

'Aye, ah'll bet he does,' says Denny. 'When was the last time he wis oot exposed in the schemes?'

'It has to be done.'

Denny sighs. 'Does it? Look, ye need tae be careful ae the pastor, Doodle. There's somethin' no' right about him – ye know that yerself now.'

'God's will can't be ignored cos of the temptations of men.'

It's a different Doodle that Denny is presented with today. Denny's noticed the different personality shifts that drive him on the weekends.

'Just watch yersel, aw'right? Folk are bloody mental round there.'

'Ther's fuck aw in his box, boys!'

A thick roundhouse fist ratchets Doodle's jaw.

'Stone the cunt, Chrissy Boy!'

'Crucify 'um, fucken dippit Jesus freak, *ha ha*! Cannae even fucken speak right, the daft bastart.'

Something sharp cuts into the skin. A knuckle-duster. Or a thick, ridged, heavyweight ring. He's seen some of the young men in the city centre favouring them, although not as much in the East End, it must be said. He briefly wonders if its imprint will show on his flesh, but a boot connects with his groin and the pain takes over. He tries to continue...

'God has forgiven you your sin,' he whimpers.

But another fist, gloved this time, bursts his nose and makes blood run into his mouth. Four more hefty kicks with unforgiving steel cappings take him down and he realises that, unlike previous attacks, this one involves multiple assailants.

'The law of the jungle', he had been warned. A stray gazelle, taken to ground by a single lion, and before the victim knows what is happening, numerous lions have emerged from the shadows to feast on the warm carcass.

Welcome to Easterhouse. Home of the Blessed John Ogilvie and his amazing cancer-curing powers. Of the Drummie, Pak, Rebel and Toi gangs and their legendary fondness for the razor and the machete and the dagger and the hatchet. And of Frankie Vaughan's lauded community-wide weapons amnesty, in which the famous crooner persuaded the community's angry young men to discard their knives and razors.

Blows rain down on Doodle. But no blades, thanks to Frankie. Spatial awareness is seeping out of his wounds and into the gutter, and streaming down the stank. Rivals appear to have settled their scores and unified under an anti-Sovereign Grace banner, so many and frequent are the limbs that strike him.

Doodle's temperamental hearing diminishes, and the distant in-struction from an elder for him to 'Stay doon, son. Stay doon!' is

258 DAVID F. ROSS

the last thing he hears before it goes altogether. After that, he curls, foetus-shaped until unconsciousness removes him from the scene and Frankie's mellifluous voice transports him to another place.

'When you walk in the garden, in the garden of Eden,
With a beautiful woman...'

+

10th October

And when he manages to force an eyelid open, she's there. At his bedside. A beautiful woman. Brown skin, deep and rich and comforting like chocolate. An angel, in a man's sharply tailored suit. And there are those words, lip-read by necessity:

'Little creature, formed of joy and mirth,
Go love without the help of any thing on earth.'

Her words comfort him. He seems locked in a space where no movement is possible. And without her there to reassure him, he would panic. But with her there, by his side, he begins to breathe a little easier. Becomes aware of some feeling returning. Of inhabiting more volume. A faint blow of hot air on his body. His eyelids fluttering like the wings of a butterfly emerging from the chrysalis.

And then his angel is gone. And he is being rolled gently onto his side. Hot, warm wetness dampens his face. His chest. His belly. It spreads to his back before he is returned to his original position by hands that are not his. He is sure his eyes are still open, but he sees nothing other than uniformly bright light. He hears nothing. Genuinely nothing. Not pretend nothing.

Is this Heaven?

His genitals feel warm. His leg is moved to the side, and the hands that are not his touch the folds of his groin, rubbing gently with a piece of warm cloth. Someone is touching his penis and it's not him.

This can't be Heaven!

'Sister?'

But I don't have a sister.

'What is it, girl?'

'Look.'

'For God's sake, have ye never seen an erect penis, before? Give me that cloth. Go an' get Dr Mackie. Let him know Mr Malpas is comin' round.'

'Yes, sister.'

'An' how are we now, Mr Malpas?'

'Where...' He coughs. Croaks. Tries to swallow. He sips the water the sister gives him.

'You're in hospital, Mr Malpas. You're goin' to be fine. You had a lucky escape though,' says the nurse, blurred but gradually coming into his focus.

She helps him to sit up slightly, to allow him to drink more easily. And in that process, he registers the various pain receptors sending urgent messages to his brain that his body is fucked.

'Aargh...'

'Yes, it's goin' to hurt for quite a while, but the medication should be helpin'.'

'Ah, Mr Malpas,' says the smiling doctor. His enunciation is good. Clear and unambiguous. 'You gave us quite a fright,' he says, smiling broadly as he says it. 'Thought we'd lost you at one point.'

'How ... *cough, cough* ... how long ... I ... here?' says Doodle. Will talking properly be part of the list of functions he'll have to relearn?

The doctor consults a clipboard that hangs from the end of the bedframe. 'Thirteen days,' he says.

'Oh,' says Doodle, the shock not permitting any further response.

'Do you remember anything about the attack?' asks the doctor. He holds back an eyelid and uses a tiny black telescope to look into Doodle's eye. Then repeats that for the other one.

'Frankie Vaughan was there,' says Doodle.

'The morphine,' says the doctor to the ward sister. 'Let's start reducing the dose.'

'You're going to be fine,' echoes the doctor. 'We'll have you out of here and home recuperating in no time.' He strolls away, the ward sister following him.

Doodle's awareness slowly returns. There are at least twenty other people in this room. In beds, or sitting around them, or standing beside them.

'Ye had a visitor, Mr Malpas,' says the nurse. His hearing has returned to its pre-beating partially defective level. She takes his tray from him and places it on the trolley. 'A few days ago. Ah almost forgot.'

'Yeh?'

'A lovely girl, she was. A relation, mibbe? Your daughter?'

'I don't have any.'

'Well, she sat here for the whole hour. Just holdin' yer hand,' the nurse tells him. 'Ah think she might've left ye a note. Will I look for ye?'

'Yeh,' he says.

The nurse looks inside the bedside table. She brings out an envelope.

'Aye. Here it is,' she says. 'Would ye like me tae read it to ye?' she offers.

'No,' says Doodle.

'Oh,' she says, surprised and a little disappointed.

He waits until she has gone. Then opens the envelope:

Dear Donald,

I am very sorry this has happened to you. Everyone at the mission was shocked when the pastor told us about it. I am not supposed to leave without permission, but I managed to find out where you were. I just wanted to come and say thank you for helping me and for the gift of the book. It is very dark

*and I'm not sure I understand its message, but I'm certain I
will someday.*

*I also wanted to let you know that I am expecting to be
leaving Glasgow soon. The pastor has arranged for me to accompany him to a party at Mr Campbell's Raskine House
residence at the end of this month. I am to meet a famous
television star and if things work out, I'll be going to work in
his household.*

*I hope you recover soon and get back to your library, and
to worshipping the Lord as strongly as you do.*

Goodbye.

Biruta.

+

14th October

'Holy shit,' says Denny. 'Well ye cannae say ah didnae warn ye,
Doodle.'

Denny Dryburgh sits. Opens the Lucozade and pours himself
a cupful.

He passes Doodle the newspaper. A crude black-and-white
likeness of Malcolm, similar to Doodle's sketches and descriptions,
stares out. 'Do You Know This Man?' the headline asks.

'They've done reconstructions, Doodle,' says Denny. 'It's aw in
there, look. Women officers aw goin' tae the Barrowlands over-
twenty-fives nights an' tryin tae flush this yin oot. CID plain
clothes in there tae. Attendances are right doon. Naebody's goin'
oot anymore.'

Doodle looks inside the *Star* for any other information on the
investigation but finds little. The media focus has shifted to the
latest mineworkers strike and growing public anger over the decision to replace the ten-shilling note with a seven-sided coin. He
gets drawn into an article about the upcoming Glasgow Gorbals

by-election. Big Jamesie Campbell is endorsing the Labour candidate, Frank McElhone. He is guaranteeing that the full weight of his own Shettleston campaign team – as well as several London-based celebrity chums – will be on the Gorbals doorsteps in the run-up to the vote on the thirtieth. Campbell, however, will be in England with his heiress wife Maude as guests of Prime Minister Harold Wilson at Chequers for a weekend of Labour Party general-election strategising.

Doodle becomes so engrossed in the article that he misses Denny Dryburgh opening Biruta's envelope and reading her letter.

'So,' says Denny. 'Now we know, eh?'

'Know what?' asks Doodle. 'Hey! That's private.'

'Aye, sorry ... ah know, but never mind that. This is just what we've been waitin' for. The Weekenders ... back oan at Raskine House. End ae the month,' he says, excitedly. 'We've got them, Doodle. We've fucken got them!'

'You shouldn't have read that.'

'Aye, but—'

'I want you to go.'

'Aye, ah'm gonnae go. Ah've been up an' sussed the place out. An' ah've got a plan tae. Once ye get out ae here, we can—'

'No. I want you to leave,' says Doodle. 'Here. Now.'

'Jeez. Aw'right, pal.'

'I'm not your pal.'

Denny stands. He is bemused. 'Look, Doodle, ah dinnae expect ye tae understand everythin'. This is important tae me. Tae ma family. Ah need tae dae somethin'. For ma da.'

Doodle looks away. The conversation's over as far as he is concerned.

'Ah'm gonnae fix this, Doodle. Ah promise ye,' says Denny Dryburgh before leaving Doodle's bedside.

It is half an hour before Doodle realises the envelope on his bedside table is now empty.

THE WEEKENDERS (1969)

Doodle discovers the truth about Denny – Denny is on the hunt for revenge – Doodle takes a trip into the heart of darkness.

19th October

'Who's this?' asks Elphinstone Dalglish.

'Ach, he's harmless,' says Inspector McCracken.

'Didnae ask what he is, ah asked *who* he is?'

'That's just Doodle. He's round the station here now an' again. Works at the High Court. Sketch artist. Sometimes helps us out wi' witness statements.'

'Jesus, you fucken uniforms. Gie him the fare an' get him oan the next bus tae fuck. We're runnin' a murder enquiry here. You clowns have got civilians roamin' free like it was a bloody DSS office.'

Dalglish is raging. The stress of the last three months is showing. Especially now that he is in charge. The body of his boss, Detective Chief Superintendent Tom Goodall, isn't even in the ground yet and everybody wants to know their orders. As if Dalglish has acquired some miraculous insight that he's been keeping to himself all this time. And everyone is commiserating with him about the chief super.

'He was a great man.'

'He was a brilliant detective.'

'Everybody loved the DCS.'

Tom Goodall was the head of Glasgow CID. And he was all the things everyone is saying he was. But he's dead now. His collapse and sudden death have left the department reeling. And on top of Dalglish's own workload, there's still a killer out there murdering young women. Dalglish is feeling the pressure. Everyone is looking to him for answers. And he currently has none. Turnbull Street is claustrophobic. It's closing in on him.

'Cannae fucken move for interlopers in here,' he shouts. A door slams. Thin partitions wobble like a typhoon is blowing through. A framed picture of the queen falls and the glass cracks.

Inspector McCracken snaps his fingers. Points. And then turns a thumb outward. No words are necessary.

'C'mon, Doodle, son,' says the desk sergeant. 'Mibbe lie low for a wee while. In any case, ye'd be better off at hame lettin' aw they bruises heal. Dinnae want folk thinkin' we've shoved ye doon the stairs, eh?' He laughs at his own joke.

Doodle doesn't. 'Is Denny Dryburgh on duty today, sir?'

'Dryburgh?' The desk sergeant wears a puzzled look. Like a toddler faced with assembling an Airfix model of a Lancaster bomber.

'*PC* Dennis Dryburgh,' says Doodle.

'Dennis Dryburgh disnae work here anymore, son. Dismissed without notice about a month ago, he was.'

'Dismissed?'

'Aye, son. Messy business.'

'What happened?'

The desk sergeant leans in. Puts a hand to his mouth. 'No' meant tae say.'

'I need to speak to him,' says Doodle. 'He took something from me.'

The desk sergeant looks left and right. 'He got caught. Trespassin'. Big Jamesie Campbell's place. Of aw the places tae get caught snoopin' about in, eh? Whit a stupid wee bastard.'

+

30th October

A week observing his movements leads to this. Doodle in the back of a hired black Hackney, following Denny Dryburgh's little car as it heads south-west out of the city and onto the black moors.

'This is as far as ah go, laddie,' says the driver of the cab. The red lights of the car being pursued have disappeared into the darkness.

'Okay,' says Doodle.

'That's five poun', ten shillings, bud.'

He hands over all his saved wages without counting. The driver is pleased with the tip.

'Watch yersel' oot here, eh?'

'Yeh,' says Doodle.

The car reverses, splutters like a geriatric smoker and pulls away.

Doodle turns and starts the long ascent up the gravelly incline.

It takes twenty minutes before he catches sight of Denny's car. Abandoned in a clearing. The form and shape of the imposing Raskine House is beyond, on the horizon. Light emanates from every available window.

Doodle sees the light. He follows the light.

He spots the silhouette of Denny Dryburgh. On the edge of the driveway. Over to the left of the house's frontage. Denny is on his knees. Waiting. Maybe praying. It is hard to tell. But despite reaching this place well ahead of his pursuer, he has done nothing with the time advantage.

Another fifteen minutes pass before Denny moves. He vaults the stone wall like a cat. And then sprints over to the side of the house. He waits at the base of a window. Even though his head is a good three feet below the sill, the light from inside illuminates him. He has something around his neck. It looks like a box camera.

Denny moves away from the window and disappears round the side of the house. Doodle follows. Keeping to the shadows. Glancing up to see the figures moving inside. Sensing the loud, bass-heavy vibrations without being able to ascertain if the music is popular music for popular people. Or some other flavour.

The path at the side of the house leads to the rear walled courtyard and several agricultural outbuildings. The corrugated door of one is slightly open. The flickering flame from a Zippo lighter betrays its occupant's location. Through a narrow fissure, Doodle sees Denny wrestling with a tall ladder.

Doodle searches the cobbles. Finds a discarded wooden block and wedges it into the metal door gear so the door can't be opened from the inside. The Zippo flame extinguishes. Doodle strains to hear something. Anything. When he's satisfied the low grumble was an 'aw, fuck' from Denny, he leaves.

He retraces his steps. Reaches the front of the house. Turns the corner and first a torchlight, and then a fist lands heavily on his face.

It's the smell that rouses him. Always the first of the senses to get up. Always awake before the others. The relay team's star performer. Its anchor. Reacting. Assessing.

Something pungent. Reminiscent of vinegar. Right there in his educated nostrils.

Voices. Distant at first.

'Christ Almighty, ah know him.' Doodle recognises this first voice.

'Aye, me tae.' And the second one.

'How the fuck did he get here?'

'How should ah know, Boaby?'

'We need tae deal wi' this, Tav. Big Jamesie'll blow a fucken gasket if he knows this yin's been here.'

'Ah know.'

'Jesus, *you're* no' even supposed tae be here, never mind him.'

'Ye dinnae think ah don't know that.'

'That wis his clear instructions. "Nane ae they wee Mission lassies this time," he said.'

'Ah bloody hear ye, right!'

'Ye still fucken brought wan ae them though.'

'Stop panickin', for God's sake.'

'So, whit are ye gonnae dae about this, then? 'Cos lemme tell ye, ah'm no' takin' heat aff the big man for this fuck-up.'

'Can you understand me, Donald?' the pastor asks him.

Doodle nods. Pain from his nose makes him lift a hand. He sees the blood and it shocks him.

'Sorry about that,' the pastor says slowly as Doodle stares at his lips. 'We didnae know it was you, obviously, but what are ye doin' here anyways ... so far away fae the East End?'

Doodle shrugs. 'Looking for my brother,' he mumbles.

'Aw for fuck's sake,' says Bobby McCracken. 'That mean there's another yin ae them oot there?'

'Naw, it disnae,' says the pastor. 'He husnae got a brother. Ah don't know whit he's talkin' aboot.' He turns to Doodle again. 'Look son, it's a wee party up here, that's aw. Nothin' bad's happenin', ye understand?' Doodle nods. 'We'll get ye cleaned up, an' then ye can come in. Say hello tae everybody, an' then we'll get ye hame, right?'

'Whit?' says Bobby McCracken. He covers his mouth to prevent Doodle reading his words. 'Are you fucken mental?'

The pastor turns away from Doodle. 'Let's have a wee bit ae fun, here, eh? D'ye know whit, get Nurse Mary – gie him a tab or two. Sling him intae the action, and see whit happens.'

'Fuck that. We're no' wastin' the acid on this weedy wee prick. Just get the cunt ootae here. Clatter him an' dump him in the woods.'

'Naw. A wee Lucy in the sky. He'll never remember anythin', an' if he does, whit's he gonnae say, eh? Who's gonnae believe him?'

'Right, fuck it ... But you're takin' the responsibility if this aw goes tits up.'

'Aye, aye. We'll stick him a cube or two. Let him wander aboot in the scud for a laugh, then put him in a cupboard, oot the road. We can dump him ower the wa' in the mornin'. Big Jamesie'll be nane the wiser.'

'Pastor McTavish?' says Doodle. 'Mr McCracken?'

Bobby McCracken smashes the trespasser in the face again.

'For God's sake, wis that really necessary?'

'He identified me.'

Pastor McTavish and Bobby McCracken strip the babbling Doodle. They move him into a large room where other naked people are. Music plays. Lights flash in a psychedelic sequence.

Doodle sits on a chair in the middle of the room, eyes streaming, no feeling in his legs, suspecting a broken nose is the latest damage. He cannot see his watch face. Has no idea of the time that passes before a woman approaches him. She strokes his thighs as others behind her laugh.

'Mr Malpas, you simply must try this,' she says. 'I insist,' she adds, holding the cube of sugar between her fingers. 'I'm Nurse Mary. I look after everyone who comes here,' she says. Doodle studies her face. The wrinkles around the eyes. She is older than him, although not old enough to be his mother, he thinks. Her voice is soft, kind and trustworthy. But still her other hand wanders.

Doodle ponders this nervously. The pain is intense. This can't be a dream. She reaches out to him. Her voice is so mellow. So calming. He wants to trust her. And she's wearing a nurse's uniform. He responds with an open palm.

'No, Mr Malpas,' she says. 'On your tongue.' And she opens her mouth wide to place the sugar cube that is in her left hand on her own tongue, as she prepares to put the one held between the thumb and forefinger of her right hand on his. 'It'll make you feel better, I promise,' she says. 'It'll take all your pain away.'

Her voice is hypnotic. The periphery blurs, and all he can focus on is her. This connection. Doodle and an older woman known to all as Nurse Mary. But as she lowers her shoulder, moves her right hand closer to his face, he senses the interested gazes of the pastor, Bobby McCracken and McCracken's cousin, the famous footballer. Doodle knows him from fundraising days at the mission.

'Hurry up, Mary, Christ's sake,' says one.

'It's only sugar,' the nurse purrs. And he feels his knees wilting at this strange power she possesses. His penis hardening as she fingers it.

He closes his eyes. He opens his mouth. The sugar rests on his tongue. Starts dissolving. And before his mouth closes, she lobs the other one in and..........

and

instantly, he feels it melting ...

```
                    melt  ing
                     m e l
                          t
                           ing
                              m
                               e
                                l
                                t
                                i
                                n
                                g
                                .
                                a
                                n
                                d
                                 .
                                  y
                                   o
                                    u
                                     see
```

Malcolm ...

reflected in a mirror where the gilded curlicues of the frame are morphing into fat golden fingers that grasp for his face and pull on his wispy, gingery beard, yanking his mouth open until it forms a yawning chasm into which you fear you'll fall, yet still he stares back at you, red-eyed with a burning anger that you haven't witnessed in such a long time, and he screams at you, pulling mephitic gas from his diaphragm, shout-ing, Donald, ya cunt, what've ye done? *and you open your mouth to tell him that you did it for him, to save him from himself, but no words come and you're left frustrated, staring at your bare feet and when you lift your head again, a Purple Haze runs through your brain and he's gone from the mirror's frame and it's only you there staring back, and deep deep deep down locked away in those con-demned rooms of your hippocampus you know that wee Malcolm's dead, and that you saw his wee body blasted apart by a German bomb and his wee head rolling down a Clydebank street with his wispy gingery hair on fire, and you know that because you were sup-posed to be holding his hand at the time but the wee bugger pulled away from you, it wasn't your fault even though they all said it was, apart from Auntie Carol who wasn't your real auntie, just a woman across the landing that took you in when your ma and da were screaming blue murder at each other and fed you a jammy piece, and she told you wee Malcolm was away with the angels, but everybody else said he was lost and surely it stands to reason that if he's lost he can be found cos the Bible tells you so, and anyway, you've since seen him loads of times, doing bad things in the street, or falling out of a pub drunk, or attacking that woman, or taking Mima MacDonald up a close to kill her, so it's no surprise that you glimpse him here, over your reflected shoulder, still in the fine tailored suit from the night he was with Mima, heading away amidst the loud abandon of the weekenders, looking for new sins to invent, and on he goes through an oddly angled doorway that seals itself and vanishes the moment he passes through it, you begin to ask questions of those that are there, engaged and engorged with each other, questions like* do you know my brother? *and* do you know where he would've gone? *but no-one even registers that you are here, so preoccupied are they in their disgusting orgiastic activities, these people, the men, the ones that you know from the pages of newspapers, where they're lauded for their cultural achievements or sporting prowess or law-making or administering those laws or, in one apparent ménage à trois over in the far corner, a celebrated lower-ranking royal whose shanks are the hind legs of a rutting stag, and it suddenly occurs to you that, even though you can hear their guttural moaning they appear deaf to your pleadings and none of them will stop their fucking and fornicating and fellating to help you in your quest, and, as you realise you will have to continue this journey alone, a horrendous squealing noise that curdles the blood draws your gaze upward to witness the sudden anthropomorphism of ugly, devilish gargoyle caricatures screaming as they stretch and strain muscle and sinew from their petrified place in the cartouche mouldings to grasp at the ornate plaster cornice and corbelling and slowly pull the ceiling down on top of everyone, but so myopically depraved is the thrusting of the men that you must leave these satyrs to their certain doom and identify a route out of this condemned den of promiscuity, which comes in the most unlikely form of a tiny fireplace that is located in the exact place where Malcolm escaped from the room, and which you hadn't noticed when he did so, and you squeeze your slender frame into the darkness of the fireplace's throat, feel around and find thick metal cleats embedded securely in the masonry, allowing you to ascend the flue, as you assume Malcolm did earlier, and so absorbed in the climb do you become that you don't notice that you are outside, in a dense forest, and that the shaft you have emerged from is a well, but no sooner has this realisation landed than the forest dissolves into a clearing and you are faced with a new vertiginous terror, looking upward at a bell-tower and knowing that, to find Malcolm, you will have to climb the old, rotting rungs of a wooden ladder leading to the tower's apex, and you have little option but to get on with the job, which is made a bit less fraught by a colourful bird, soaring from the depths of the dark woods to circle you and converse with you as you climb, a welcome relief, all the more so because the bird has human features, eyes, a nose, a mouth and rosy cheeks with which you are familiar, even though it's been many years since you last saw them, and then they were lying broken and in pain and watching you moments before a wet tarpaulin sheet covered her and her little face was lost to you, but here she is, Rose, or Rita, maybe, but no matter since you're sure it begins with an 'R', and she's speaking to you, telling you that Malcolm is lost but that it isn't your fault, and you know she's right because it's Malcolm you need to save, and it's his forgiveness you need, so you climb again, left foot first, and the beautiful coloured bird called Rose, or Rita, or something beginning with 'R', directs your gaze towards the various open windows that you pass, at a dirty room in which stained, bloody clothes hang from a ceiling pulley amidst the rising smoke from a hundred cigarettes, and the smog clears to reveal a heavy-set man sitting in a worn armchair, listening to a radio and alternately laughing and crying as a woman stands behind him, repeatedly bringing a heavy metal skillet down on the back of his head, and your heart suddenly pains for him, for the eternal suffering that he must endure and you ask your little winged companion why the man doesn't simply get up; why does he sit there, knowing the swing of the heavy pan is coming and doing nothing to prevent it, and the little bird is angry with you for your misplaced sorrow, saying this to you in response,* Be as a tower that, firmly set, shakes not its top for any blast that blows, *and resigned, you continue to climb, until another window hoves into view and you observe a preacher, a man of God, once again someone familiar to you but whose exact provenance you can't place as his face is half turned away, though you can hear him clearly and that astounds you because, as everyone knows, you've been plagued by poor hearing most of your life, since the bombs dropped right on top of your community when you were very young and Malcolm went missing for the first time, and the preacher is delivering a sermon, which, strange though its content is, still strikes a chord, especially when he says,* People tell you who they are, but for the most part we ignore it, because we only want them to be who we want them to be, and we're all flawed because we can never settle for what God gave us, we always crave more, and then find ways to justify that we deserve them, that God provided us with material things, or carnal desires because we are righteous but, you see, my child, the antinomian Weekenders believe in sexual freedom and that doing what they want is the true path to spirituality, after all, the Holy Spirit is as free as a bird –*and on he goes with a voice that's as soft and comforting as a silk blanket, hypnotising you like a siren, and you're so enraptured that you almost let go of the ladder and fall backward, and you let out a whimper, which the man of God hears, and he turns to you, revealing himself to be Pastor McTavish, whom you now witness to be naked from the waist down, his large penis being forced in and out of the mouth of a slight young woman with short blonde hair who you know to be only sixteen years old and to have just arrived in our country from the U.S.S.R, and this image shocks you but not as much as when the girl, on seeing you outside the window, high up on the ladder, hands bleeding from the splinters, calls your name and asks you for help, yelling,* it's me, it's Biruta, can't you hear me? Why won't you help me? Doodle, *Doodle, Doodle-doo, tears filling your eyes as you watch your pastor, a man you've come to regard as family, your* only *family, take his walking stick and plunge it into the poor girl's backside, and she screams like she is undergoing a secular exorcism,* Doodle, Doodle, *the little bird calls you and grabs your collar in its tiny claws and with a strength you could never have believed it possessed lifts you off the ladder and transports you upward, all the while telling you not to concern yourself, chastising you with the comment,* if thine eyes offend thee, pluck them out, *and you're aggrieved at this because it isn't clear why your tearful concern for the girl's wellbeing should draw such censure, until you're high high higher, much higher, and the top of the bell tower is in sight and you can hear its bells ringing dolefully, and the little bird says,* rid yourself of sin and proceed, *but your journey is halted by the sudden sonic boom of an explosion, close by and dead ahead, and inside this particular room you see yourself, it is undoubtedly you, albeit a much younger version, dirtier and holding a box that has lost its carry-strap, and voices beckon the younger you from the corners of the room to follow them, to forget the box and to run away from the explosions, but the younger you can't see them through the acrid smoke, the younger you can only hear them and is confused and he doesn't know which voice to follow so he does nothing, just stands in the middle of this room high up in the building where Pastor McTavish was doing a bad thing to the young girl called Biruta, and you still can't get that picture out of your head despite everything the little bird is saying to you, and the younger you's legs are suddenly hot and wet and he's pee'd himself, and then there's only black, and no sound, and if people are still calling the younger you from the periphery of this large ostentatious room then the younger you won't know about that because the younger you can't hear anything, so with your eyes tightly closed you say* The Lord's our Father, I'll not want, *but then you hear her, faintly at first but then much louder, much closer, that familiar voice shouting at the younger you:* Where's Malcolm, Donald, you had a hold of him but you've let him go, where is he? where the fuck is my wee boy? *and you remember now, that was the first time Malcolm got lost, and it was a long time before you saw him again, and it was your fault, they all said, why you had to move away from Clydebank, away from your school, and eastward to Glasgow, where your da could get work, but he couldn't get work, because nobody could get work and you had to live with your granny, who was an old whore, according to your ma, and they would always be fighting until either the drink or the dalliances with dirty men, or a combination of both, killed her and there was a little bit of temporary peace but still your ma blamed you for everything, and especially for Malcolm getting left behind in Clydebank and with no way of knowing our new address or with any means to find you, but you shake off this guilt and refocus, knowing that you saw him earlier and he must be just a little ahead, so you redouble your efforts and the little bird drops you on the dark plateau at the top of the ladder before flying away and leaving you alone again, facing ground that rises very steeply and there are what appears to be small, round boulders protruding from the surface, which at least should make clambering up more manageable, but as you draw closer, you see these boulders are heads, with any remaining hair on fire, burning their scalps and that terrible, terrible stench of burnt toast making you retch, but you know you have to press on, that you can't go back because the ladder has been pushed away and there's no other way down beyond jumping to your certain death, so, apologising, you put your left boot on the first face, and then your right on a flaming skull, and then you use your bleeding hands to pull yourself up using nostrils for grip, and you can only hope, as your heels, knuckles and fingernails knead the cooling flesh, as your touch lapidifies the screaming heads, that they are no longer in pain, no longer suffering in this infernal damnation.*

ABANDON ALL HOPE – NO TRESPASSING – BY ENFORCED ORDER

The sign hovers above you as if suspended on wires, but there are no wires, and cogitating on this momentarily robs you of your purpose; to find Malcolm and save him from whatever is on the other side of the lochan that lies before you, and it's only the persistence of a voice singing over some distant music, popular music for popular people, that brings you back to the situation in hand, and the voice gets louder and more insistent, singing, Please allow me to introduce myself, I'm a man of wealth and taste, *and even though you call out,* hello and my name is Donald Malpas, but you can call me Doodle, everyone does, *the voice doesn't respond, just keeps repeating this phrase over and over and over, until a beautiful gospel choir joins in, and when you look into the lake, from where the sound emanates, you see half-naked, demented people, the same gallimaufry of deviants that you've left behind fucking and fornicating and fellating each other in the house's grand reception room; they're here now, crawling amongst the reedbeds, dragging piss bags, howling this celestial noise and trying to escape the leg-irons that keep them sub-*

*merged in this bubbling water, and suddenly your fevered brain
clears sufficiently for you to see the fine brown suit on the far edge of
the lochan and the figure is no longer running, but waiting, and you
just have to construct a route across the water with large wooden
railway sleepers that will take your weight and block the deviants
from getting out of the lake and grabbing your ankles to pull you
down under the surface, where you'll surely drown since you've never
learned to swim, and the water's temperature is rapidly rising and
just as you approach the far bank of the lochan, a bony hand reaches
out and grips your trouser leg and you look down and see the furious
face of Pastor McTavish a few inches from the surface, bubbles indi-
cating that he is trying to say something although you can't hear him,
but you can lip-read, and he's pleading, exhorting you to answer his
question,* My God in Heaven, what have you done? Donald, what
have you done? *and you begin to cry because despite everything, he
took you in when you were at your lowest ebb, and he became your
new family, your* only *family and what is it to be Christian if not to
forgive those who trespass against us, and you're about to reach down
into the hot water, and regardless of the pain you know it will bring
forth, pull your pastor out of his purgatorial state, when a voice
beckons you; an angelic voice that you recognise, that you've heard
before in fearful moments of anxiety or stress or dependency, and you
turn, disregarding your pastor's plight, turning your back on your
family, your* only *family, and you listen captivated as the beautiful
woman with dark hair and brown skin, deep, rich and comforting,
just like chocolate, says,* My name is Birgitte. I told you I'd see you
again, *and she takes your trembling hand as the railway sleepers
ignite, and you hesitate and you're scared because the sleepers will
disintegrate and drop you straight down into this fiery cauldron
along with all these male sinners, the celebrities, the film stars, the
sportsmen, the politicians, the magistrates, the policemen, so you
hurry, because the elegant woman called Birgitte tells you it will be
okay, and that she will be beside you as you pass through this wall of
flames and she convinces you to remain brave because when you pass*

through the fire to the other side you'll finally see Malcolm, and he'll forgive you for forsaking him all those years ago, for letting go of his hand, and this makes you feel happy and relieved, but despite this the exertion of passing through the flames has left you exhausted and you fall asleep, on a cold, wet, wintery hillside, and when you awake there's a great brightness in the sky, like the most beautiful sunset you've ever seen, and the light covers you, and the heat from it warms you and the brightness permits you to see God and the Holy Trinity and you ask God, where is Malcolm? *and a hand touches your sleeve and you turn around to see little Biruta standing beside you, crying, eyes streaming, face blackened, clothes torn and partially naked, and then Birgitte de Maupassant is there and she says to you,* Donald Malpas, this is your home.

Sooner Or Later, God'll Cut You Down (1970)

'Nothing would be what it is because everything would be what it isn't. And contrariwise, what it is, it wouldn't be, and what it wouldn't be, it would. You see?'
  —Lewis Carroll, *Alice's Adventures in Wonderland*

'Ten minutes, that's aw ye've got?' says the guard as he stands back against the wall. 'An' ah'm here, watchin' every move, right.'

The two men sit. Opposite ends of a rectangular table. There are no external windows in this bare, square container. Just two doors. On opposing walls. One leading back to the cells. The other leading through a sequence of strict security checks to freedom. Beside this door is an internal window. Three men sit on the other side of the screen, observing the visit. Security cameras fixed high in each corner record every move. There's palpable tension here, as if these are the final manoeuvres in the World Chess Championship between Petrosian and Spassky.

'Well, this is a turn-up.'

'How have you been?'

'How have ah been?' The prisoner sniggers. 'Are you some kinda comedian?'

'Are they treating you okay?'

'Jesus Christ ... you really here tae ask me shite like this?'

'I wanted to make sure you were alright...'

'Well, whit dae *you* think?'

'That you might've opened your heart to God's love.'

The prisoner appeals to the guard: 'For fuck's sake, dae ah have tae listen tae this?'

The guard remains impassive.

The prisoner laughs. Sardonic. He shakes his head. He wags a finger at his visitor. 'Ye know somethin'. Ah've been locked up in here for months noo. Twenty-three hours a day in solitary, wi' nothin' tae dae but think about you an' this bumbling moron act that slides below everybody's radar, cos everybody thinks you're a fucken retard. But that's no' true, is it?'

The visitor shrugs.

The prisoner leans forward.

The guard tenses.

'So, tell me. There's just us here. And he's no' gonnae rock the establishment boat. No' now that they've got their man, eh?' The prisoner winks at the guard.

'You set that fucken fire, didn't ye? Just tell me, eh? It wis you that locked me in yon shed.'

The visitor says nothing. Gives nothing away. Makes no eye contact.

'Whit's up, mate? Ye suddenly been struck dumb as well as deaf?'

'I need your forgiveness,' says the visitor.

'Forgiveness? Ya fucken weasel,' barks the prisoner.

'I did it for you,' says the visitor.

'You torched the place, eh? You murdered aw they people, didn't ye, eh? An' then colluded wi' these pigs tae frame me for it.'

'You need to accept Jesus...'

'McTavish, the McCrackens, aw they yins that were becomin' a political embarrassment tae Big Jamesie Campbell...'

'...into your heart. Confess your sins...'

'...an' whit a bloody convenience, eh? The *Bible John* man killin' another woman oan the same night. Ye couldnae have scripted it better. A brilliant opportunity for a whole load ae awkward skeletons tae get buried aw at once, eh? Campbell's lot must've fucken lapped you up, son.'

'...and purge yourself, Malcolm.'

'Malcolm? Who the fuck's Malcolm?'

'...and your soul will be saved.'

'You're fucken cracked, ye know that?'

'...and you'll be with God in Paradise one day.'

'An' you end up a hero in aw the Denton-Hall papers for savin' they young lassies, an' draggin' them oot ae a burnin' buildin' ... oot fae a fucken blaze *you* started!' The prisoner starts a slow hand-clap. 'Aye. Hats off tae ye then. Ah mean it. Really. A criminal fucken mastermind, that's whit ye are.'

'...A place free from sin, experiencing eternal life and eternal joy and eternal peace in Jesus Christ,' says the visitor.

'An' what about the wee sixteen-year-old, eh? The evidence. Where's she noo?' asks the prisoner.

The visitor looks up. Their eyes lock for the first time.

'She'll stay with me. Until the baby's born. Or until I get moved out of MacKeith Street.'

The prisoner jumps up. A fire ignites inside him. He attempts to reach over the table. His cuff chain holds him back. The guard springs into action. A swinging baton rattles the prisoner's free upper arm.

'Sit down Dry-*bugger*, ya wee poof.'

'Aargh,' he moans. 'That wis fucken sore. Je-*sus*!'

'"Refrain from anger and forsake wrath! Fret not yourself, it tends only to evil",' says the visitor.

The prisoner looks at the guard.

'Aye, what *he* just said,' says the guard.

'For fuck sake, man. That wisnae needed.' The prisoner rotates the arm as if trying to re-pop a dislocated shoulder back into its socket. 'Look, just admit it, eh?' he says to the visitor. 'Tell me ye did it. He's no' gonnae say anything, is he? They're aw in oan it.'

The guard smirks.

The prisoner sighs.

'Two minutes,' says the guard.

'Ah knew whit went oan wi the Weekenders, up at Raskine House,' says the prisoner. He lowers his head to his hands. 'Ma da used tae go tae they Jamesie Campbell parties. Until he had a stroke shaggin' some prostitute. Some bad drugs. No' his fault, wis it? But after that, they shunned him. Silenced him. Caw'd him a grass. Kicked him oot the force. Pension revoked. A word oot ae place about anythin' an' they'd plant a story in the *Star* about him takin' kickbacks. Bribes. Drug stories. The works. They'd send incriminatin' photies tae ma maw. The cunts. Ah just wanted tae make somebody pay for it. Blackmail, though, that wis ma only intention. A wee bit ae righteous payback. No' murder. No' that. Ah'm no' capable ae that.'

The prisoner suddenly begins to cry.

'Aw, *boo-hoo*, wee man,' says the guard.

'Ye know what it's like for an ex-copper in here, eh? Can ye even imagine what goes in yer food? In yer drinks? Up yer arsehole?'

'Yeh,' says the visitor.

'So please, ye have tae tell me. Please. Gie me that at least.'

'I have something for you,' says the visitor.

He looks at the guard. The guard nods his approval. The visitor passes a package across the table. The prisoner pulls back the brown paper.

'*The Divine Comedy*?' he says. 'What fresh fucken hell is this?'

'This is your salvation, Malcolm. You're home now. This is your home.'

'Doodle!' the prisoner shouts. 'Tell me.'

The visitor gets up. The door that leads through security and on to freedom opens.

'Doodle!'

The visitor walks through the door.

'Doodle!'

The door closes behind him.

'Doodle!'

But he doesn't hear this one.

Genuinely doesn't hear it.

As opposed to pretend doesn't hear it.

Because the door is made of inch-thick steel.

Raskine House, 1947

Adult Fun (1975)

The ground floor of the main building measures fifty-foot square and is comprised of nine principal rooms – including the reception hall, expensively tiled with white Carrara marble from Italy (blood-stained grouting still evident if you inspect closely). Three of the chambers have narrow staircases concealed within the interior sand-wich construction. One stair leads to a hidden basement. The subterranean space was only discovered following a fire in 1938.

The main kitchen is a cold, high-ceilinged space of minimal dec-oration. Metal surfaces and metal cabinets lend the room a clinical air. At one end, large metal hooks hang from a circular steel beam bolted to the solid concrete surface above it. A recessed floor drain at least three feet in diameter lies below. Beyond, the kitchen stores lead to a rear courtyard enclosed by a high wall. The stables and a livestock enclosure are here, built in timber – lean-to structures that buttress the wall.

Overlooking the tennis court, on the highest part of the land, there is the well. Drilled into the peat before any other construction began, it was the source of water for Raskine House until large storage supply tanks were installed against the outhouse block walls in the mid-1950s.

In 1963, the Daily Telegraph *ran an exclusive story about the youngest daughter of Tsar Nicholas II, Grand Duchess Anastasia Romanov. It suggests she miraculously survived the 1918 massacre of her family. After fleeing Russia, assisted by a Bolshevik soldier, Anastasia made a new life in Great Britain. She lived anonymously for almost fifty years, before her existence was suspected by a visitor to Raskine House Mental Hospital. In the same week, Burke's Peerage, a publisher of books on the British aristocracy, investigated a claim that one of the queen's cousins, who had been placed in a mental institution some years earlier, had been reported dead. Both royal women were the same age. Before anyone could interview the patient residing at Raskine House, she mysteriously fell into the estate's forty-foot-deep well. She died instantly.*

'Lovely handwriting,' says Zak Needles. 'Is it yours?'

'Naw. Some aul' journalist fae the *Star* that wrote the history ae the place,' says Big Jamesie Campbell. 'We had it printed as part ae the sale documents.'

'Holy fuck, Jamesie. Is that all true?'

'Every word,' he says. 'An' that's no' even the half ae it, son.'

Rumour or legend? What difference does it make to the gullible.

'Why you selling, then? You're mad leaving something like this.'

'It's time, Zak. It's just time for me an' Maude tae move on. Back intae the city. This is a young man's place.'

'Bet some fun's been had in here, eh? Some fucking serious shenanigans.'

'Aye,' says Jamesie, before winking. 'Adult fun, pal.'

The rock star snorts. Giggles. Holds his crotch. Like a child about to piss himself.

'You got a smoke on you?' asks Zak.

Big Jamesie Campbell glances at his wristwatch. The rock star has no concept of time. Outside of night and day, the darkness and the light. Insulated from the harsher realities of life. Another rich, spoilt little cunt playing the rebel. The old Jamesie Campbell would've battered this privileged prick senseless. But unfortunately for the current Jamesie Campbell, he represents something very important: access. Zak Needles is a favoured nephew of Robert Maxwell. Jamesie was impressed by him during their few meetings in Westminster. And dismayed when Maxwell lost his seat in 1970.

'Keep a good eye on that one. Socialism's just an invisibility cloak for Bob Maxwell. He's going places,' Lord Finlay had re-marked, as early as 1967.

'Here.' Big Jamesie hands the younger man a silver cigarette case. He opens it. There's only one fag inside. 'You have it. Keep the case,' says Big Jamesie. 'Ah'm tryin' tae chuck them anyway.'

'Ye sure? Cheers.' Zak examines the case. 'Who's Stevie and Denice?'

'Fuck knows,' says Jamesie. He stretches his neck. He swallows. He sniffs through flared nostrils.

They have been wandering the expansive grounds and the inner recesses of the Raskine House estate for nearly two hours.

'My uncle told me you had a bomb shelter built here,' says Zak.

'Yeh, I did,' says Jamesie. He is becoming impatient. 'Had it put in, in late sixty-two – right after the Cuban Missile Crisis.'

'Woah ... what a great name for the new album!'

Jamesie takes the fob from his waistcoat pocket. Looks long and hard at it. Urging the message to land. It doesn't.

'Can I see it – the bomb shelter?'

'D'ye know, son, I once had a journalist locked in that shelter for a week. Nae daylight. Nae communication fae the outside world. Nothing. Total fucken sensory deprivation. Just some food an' water dropped down the vent pipe once a day.'

'Jesus Christ, what had he done?'

'He wasted ma fucken time,' says Jamesie. Quietly. Calmly. 'So ... we got a deal or no'?'

Zak Needles scratches his beard. Twists the pleats of it. Big Jamesie sees himself doing serious damage to this dopey cunt's stupid face. Taking two stubby fingers to the rock star's coke-per-forated nostrils and ripping the nose right off the fucker's face. Tipping tons of the white powder straight into the bastard's gaping facial cavity while...

'Too right we do, Jamesie. When can I move in?'

Handshakes.

A reluctant hug.

A signature.

Big Jamesie Campbell is free. Liberated from the curse of Raskine House.

It is someone else's problem now.

+

'We are each our own devil, and we make this world our hell.'
—Oscar Wilde

In the early autumn of 1975, the newly rebuilt Raskine House is owned by the controversial rock star, Zak Needles. The previous year, Needles left his rock group The Wyfebeeterz to pursue a solo career. In interviews at the time, he claims the devil made him do this. And that the devil called him to Raskine House to write and record a debut solo album, *Satan 666 – 0 God*.

The rock star's record company hires staff to run the house. Needles interviews for a personal assistant. He hires an exotic black woman with Caribbean heritage named Birgitte de Maupassant. Birgitte runs the house, organises diaries, fends off the record company's calls, and deals with press and media enquiries. She takes to the tasks like a duck to water.

Needles spends millions converting the basement, where members of a religious cult once died, into a top-of-the-range recording studio. While jamming, a once-famous bass player injects an empty syringe, thinking it's heroin. He dies of an air embolism. Session musicians brought over the Atlantic from the Muscle Shoals studio will not play in the place, citing the intense heat, the darkness, and the 'negative vibe'. Needles imports hundreds of carved wooden Madonnas, as if idolatry will sanctify the space. It doesn't. Needles then spends considerably more money hiring a mobile recording studio and parking it outside in the driveway.

Following months of writer's block caused by non-stop, drug-fuelled hedonism, Zak Needles flips out. In an otherworldly temper, the guitarist lifts the marble-topped card table and manages to hurl it through the window of the first-floor salon. It lands on a rare, black landrace goat. The goat dies instantly, its body sliced in half.

The following morning, Zak Needles departs Raskine House for the last time. De Maupassant offers to drive, but despite his inexperience behind the wheel, Needles snatches the keys from her. Gravel spits up as they accelerate out of the forecourt.

As the car speeds away from the house, Needles swerves to avoid two women who appear suddenly from behind a tree.

'They see you,' whispers Birgitte.

'What did you say?' gasps Zak Needles.

'They see *all* of you!'

His Jaguar XK120 open-topped sports car takes that final sharp corner of the snaking decline too fast. The car hits a pillar. Zak Needles hits the gatehouse wall. Head on. Face first. The rock star dies instantly, his left eye moved to the centre of his forehead by the force of the impact, so that he resembles a cyclops. His female passenger, Birgitte de Maupassant, strolls away from the vehicle unharmed.

She walks back towards the tree, where she is joined by the two young women. One has an unusual hair colouring; a deep reddish-brown, like the leaves that drop in late October. The other, curly blonde hair tied up with a ribbon and a beaming smile like Shirley Temple. They disappear into the descending mist.

The Devil's Jukebox

God's Gonna Cut You Down, by Odetta
(Traditional)
Available on Tradition Records, 1956

Long Agos and Worlds Apart, by The Small Faces
(Written by Ian McLagan)
Available on Immediate Records, 1968

Nowhere Man, by The Beatles
(Written by Lennon & McCartney)
Available on Parlophone Records, 1965

Dedicated Follower of Fashion, by The Kinks
(Written by Ray Davies)
Available on Pye Records, 1966

Sunny, by Bobby Hebb
(Written by Bobby Hebb)
Available on Philips Records, 1966

Tomorrow Never Knows, by The Beatles
(Written by Lennon & McCartney)
Available on Parlophone Records, 1966

Season of the Witch, by Donovan
(Written by Donovan and Shawn Phillips)
Available on Epic Records, 1966

She's Not There, by The Zombies
(Written by Rod Argent)
Available on Decca Records, 1964

How Can We Hang on to a Dream, by Tim Hardin
(Written by Tim Hardin)
Available on Verve Folkways Records, 1966

**Nimrod (Adagio) from Variations on
an Original Theme, Op.36 'Enigma'**
(By Edward Elgar)
Performed by BBC Concert Orchestra
and conducted by Barry Wordsworth

Strangers In the Night, by Frank Sinatra
(Written by Kaempfert, Singleton, Snyder)
Available on Reprise Records, 1966

April Come She Will, by Simon & Garfunkel
(Written by Paul Simon)
Available on Columbia Records, 1966

Summer In the City, by The Lovin' Spoonful
(Written by Sebastian, Boone, Sebastian)
Available on Kama Sutra Records, 1966

I Fought the Law, by The Bobby Fuller Four
(Written by Sonny Curtis)
Available on Coral Records, 1960

The Old Galway Bay, by Dolores Keane & John Faulkner
(Written by Frank A. Fahy)
Available on Gael Linn Records, 1983

Messiah, HWV 56: IV and the Glory of the Lord (Chorus)
(By George Frideric Handel)
Performed by the New York Philharmonic
and conducted by Leonard Bernstein

Don't Fence Me In, by Bing Crosby & The Andrews Sisters
(Written by Cole Porter and Robert Fletcher)
Available on RevOla Records, 1944

Coronation Rag, by Winifred Atwell
(Written by Winifred Atwell)
Available on Decca Records, 1953

A Man of Constant Sorrow, by Bob Dylan
(Traditional)
Available on Columbia Records, 1962

Oh Happy Day, by The Edwin Hawkins Singers
(Written by P. Doddridge, Arranged by Edwin Hawkins)
Available on Pavilion Records, 1968

Baby Let Me Follow You Down, by Bob Dylan
(Traditional)
Available on Columbia Records, 1962

Alone, by Lee Hazlewood & Suzi Jane Hokom
(Written by Marks & Marks)
Available on LHI Records, 1969

I Say a Little Prayer, by Aretha Franklin
(Written by Bacharach & David)
Available on Scepter Records, 1967

The Son of a Preacher Man, by Dusty Springfield
(Written by Wilkins and Hurley)
Available on Philips Records, 1968

Gotta Have Tenderness, by Glen Campbell
(Written by Ramona Red & Mitch Torok)
Available on Capitol Records, 1969

I Saw the Light, by Hank Williams
(Written by Hank Williams)
Available on MGM Records, 1948

The Garden of Eden, by Frankie Vaughan
(Written by Dennise Haas Norwood)
Available on Philips Records, 1957

Purple Haze, by Jimi Hendrix
(Written by Jimi Hendrix)
Available on Track Records, 1967

Sympathy For the Devil, by The Rolling Stones
(Written by Jagger / Richards)
Available on Decca Records, 1968

Elijah, by Donald Byrd
(Written by Donald Byrd)
Available on Blue Note Records, 1964

The Sound of Silence, by Chromatics
(Written by Paul Simon)
Available on Italians Do It Better Records, 2019

Acknowledgments

I'm indebted to Audrey Gillan for help and advice. Her podcast, 'Bible John: Creation of a Serial Killer', was logged in my mind as I was writing this book. It's a very moving, affecting piece of work and I'm grateful to Audrey for sharing some insights into the times and locations *The Weekenders* shares.

Thanks also to Douglas Skelton for offering direction where I needed it most.

Thanks to my family: Elaine, Nathan, Nadia, Lewis and Chloe for their love, support and encouragement. And to my *second* family, the Orenda Books Dream Factory: Karen Sullivan, West Camel, Anne Cater, Cole Sullivan and Danielle Price.

The magnificent seventh ... who'd have thought that possible, eh?